STEEL

(Book 3 of the Kalima Chronicles)

By Aiki Flinthart

2019

Thank you to the readers who have enjoyed my other books enough to leave nice reviews and to let me know. Because of you, I keep writing.

And...as always...thanks to my husband for his patience and encouragement. Seriously. Patient. Unbelievably patient.

A Cataloging-in-Publications entry for this title is available from the National Library of Australia.

ISBN-13: 978-0-3482878-0-4 (Trade Paperback)
ISBN-13: 978-0-6482878-9-6 (e-book)
Computing Advantages & Training P/L
PO Box 3388, Darra
QLD 4076, Australia

Discover other titles by Aiki Flinthart
at: **www.aikiflinthart.com**
Including:

The Ruadhan Sidhe Novels (YA Urban Fantasy)
Shadows Wake (#1)
Shadows Bane (#2)
Shadows Fate (#3)

The 80AD series (YA Adventure/Fantasy)
80AD Book 1: *The Jewel of Asgard*
80AD Book 2: *The Hammer of Thor*
80AD Book 3: *The Tekhen of Anuket*
80AD Book 4: *The Sudarshana*
80AD Book 5: *The Yu Dragon*

The Kalima Chronicles (YA Adventure/Fantasy)
IRON (#1)
FIRE (#2)
STEEL (#3)

Sold! (Contemporary Romance/Adventure)

Short Story Anthologies
Return
Like a Woman
Elemental

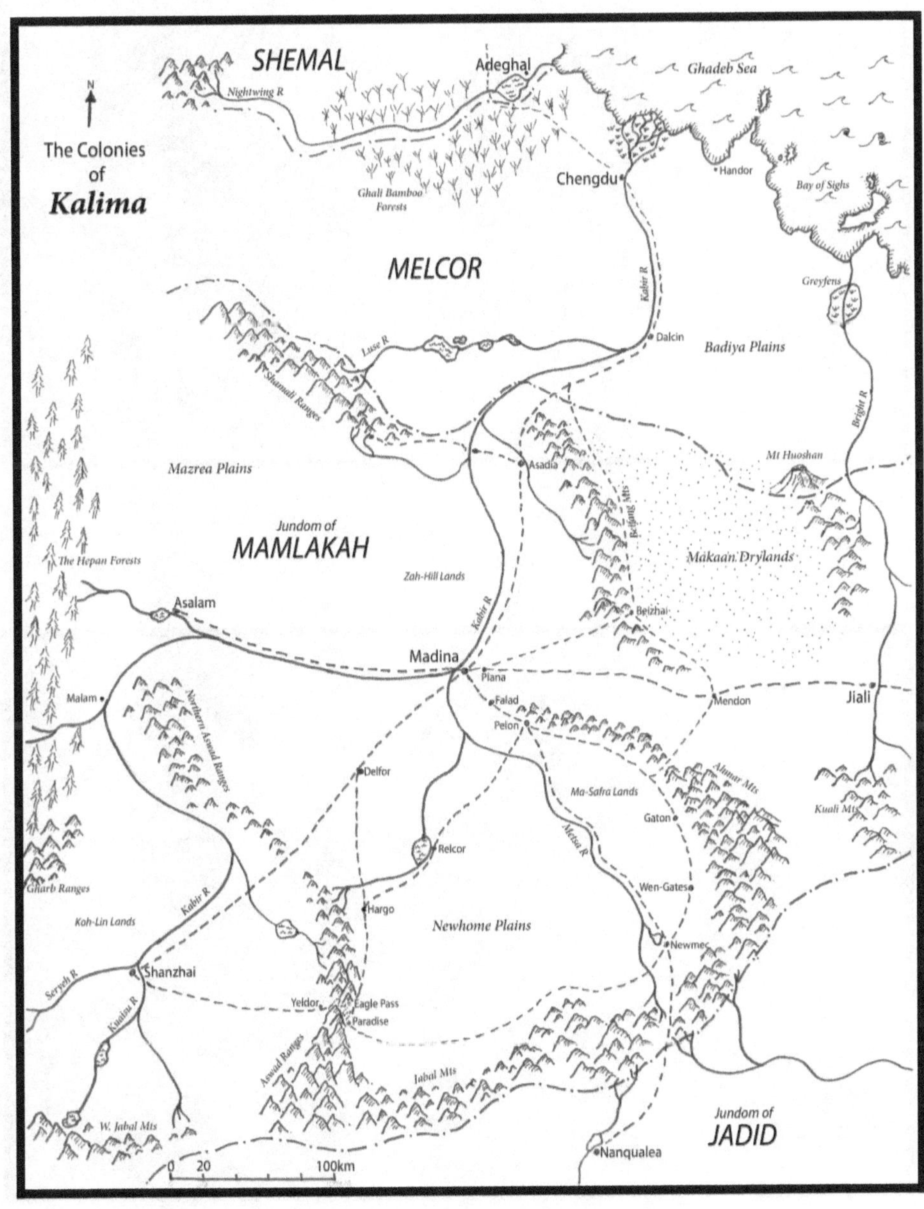

N
The Colonies of Kalima
SHEMAL
Nightwing R
Adeghal
Ghadeb Sea
Ghali Bamboo Forests
Chengdu
Handor
Bay of Sighs
MELCOR
Kabir R
Greyfens
Luse R
Dalcin
Badiya Plains
Shamali Ranges
Bright R
Mazrea Plains
Asadia
Beijing Mts
Mt Huoshan
Jundom of MAMLAKAH
Makaan Drylands
The Hepan Forests
Zah-Hill Lands
Asalam
Kabir R
Belzhai
Madina
Piana
Malam
Falad
Mendon
Jiali
Northern Aswad Ranges
Pelon
Delfor
Ma-Safra Lands
Alnmar Mts
Kuali Mts
Gaton
Metsa R
Gharb Ranges
Relcor
Wen-Gates
Koh-Lin Lands
Kabir R
Hargo
Newhome Plains
Newmes
Seryeh R
Shanzhai
Kuaini R
Yeldor
Eagle Pass
Paradise
Aswad Ranges
Jabal Mts
W. Jabal Mts
Jundom of JADID
Nanqualea
0   20   100km

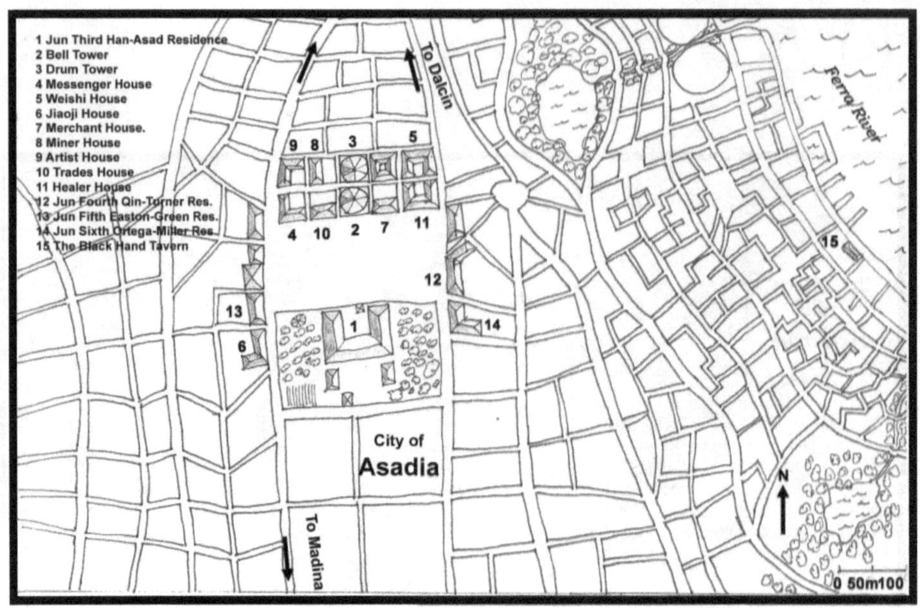

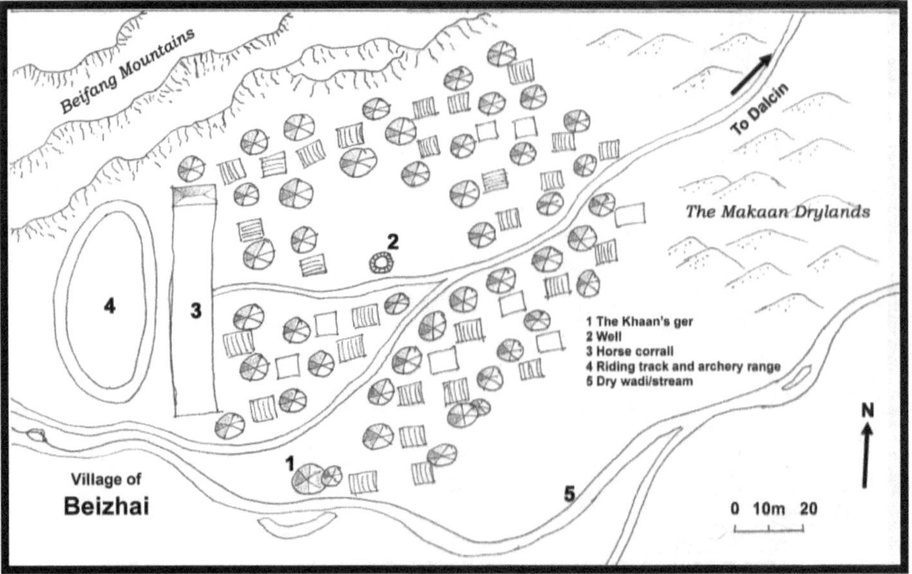

p8   *Aiki Flinthart*

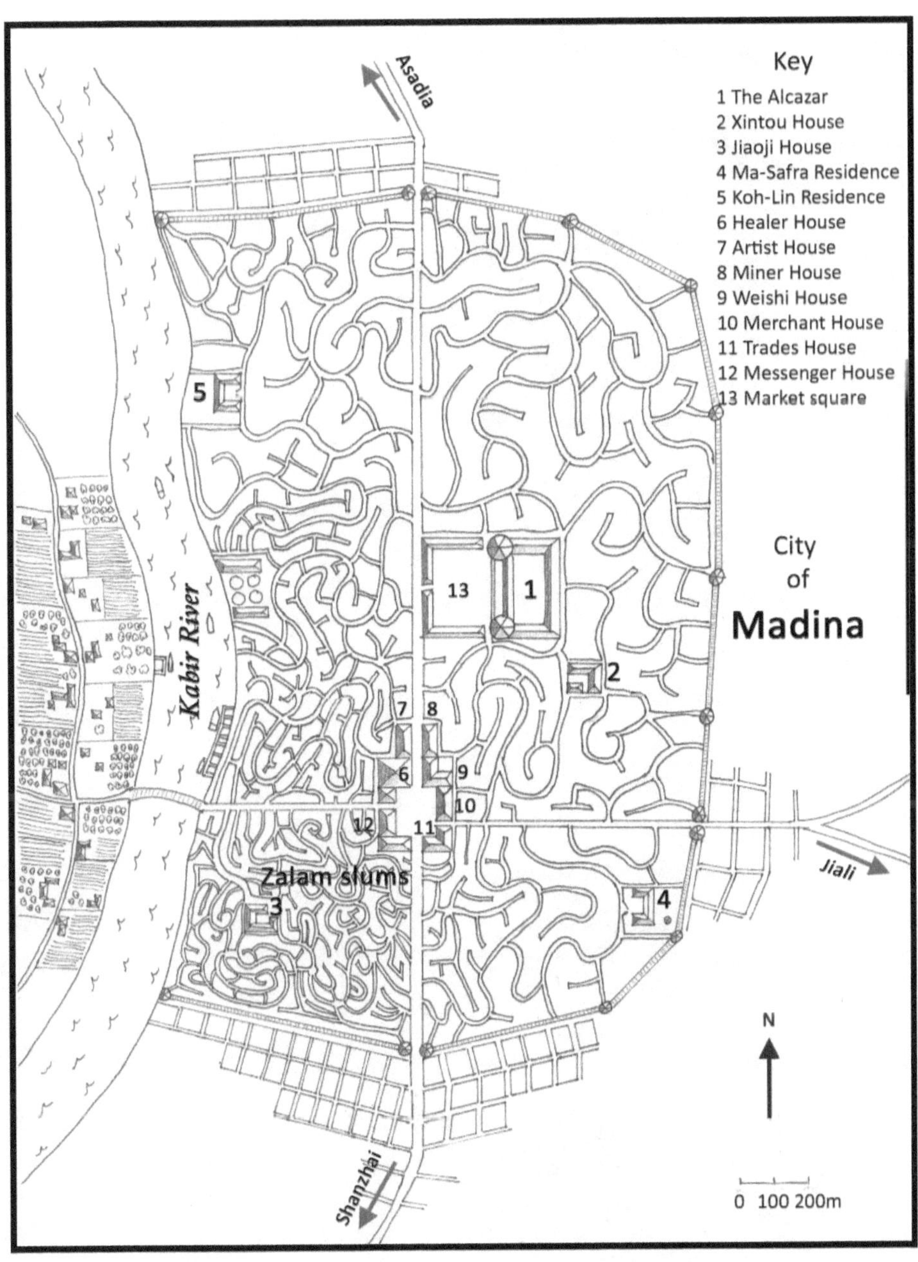

Asadia
Key
1 The Alcazar
2 Xintou House
3 Jiaoji House
4 Ma-Safra Residence
5 Koh-Lin Residence
6 Healer House
7 Artist House
8 Miner House
9 Weishi House
10 Merchant House
11 Trades House
12 Messenger House
13 Market square
City
of
Madina
Kabir River
Jiali
Zalam slums
Shanzhai
N
0 100 200m

STEEL

Aiki Flinthart 2019

NOTE:
This book is written with AUSTRALIAN
SPELLING/ENGLISH,
not USA spelling/English.
Don't panic.

PART I – Chengdu / Dalcin

CHAPTER ONE

ALERE

If change was inevitable and freedom so desirable, why did people resist both?

Alere emerged from the huoche and hesitated, shading her eyes against the aching vermillion glitter of sun on water. Between her and the dock's edge stood a shifting, surly tide of refugee ex-slaves and frightened citizens. Hundreds of people pushed and shoved, desperate to secure places aboard vessels leaving Chengdu city.

Behind her, smoke from burnt mansions still smeared the heavens with the ash remnants of the Slavemasters' filthy power. Out on the Kabir River, chuans rocked, their pencil-narrow masts writing the refugees' futures on the clear, teal-green sky.

Three days had passed since she and Mina had liberated the slaves of Melcor. Today was Ahad, First of Yiuye. First day of the new year. First day of a new life for these people. Yet, freedom seemed to mean nothing. The crowd still divided itself into two groups: former slaves, and Melcori citizens. They eyed each other with growing hostility.

The shimmering orange winter sun rose, heating the waters of discontent in the melting pot of Chengdu's mixed cultures. Nothing had yet happened, but that was probably due to a fear of retribution amongst those long habituated to punishment.

Alere sighed. Change in mindset took a lot longer than overturning mere laws on paper.

She covered her nose against the stench of close-packed, unwashed humanity, the sharpness of urine and fear, the gagging sweetness of rotting food. Babies squalled, and children cried their lack of understanding as parents hushed them, argued with each other, and yelled abuse at the chuans waiting, unreachable, offshore. The crowd's noisy uncertainty pressed against her ears and mind, almost overwhelming both.

The ex-slaves' desire to escape the city and return to their families was understandable, but why did free citizens of Melcor abandon their lives? Alere edged closer to a knot of men and women, who huddled together and regarded their ex-slaves with a strange mixture of fear and pitying superiority.

Understanding came from a few snippets of their conversation and a slight brush against their chaotic, unwarded minds. They were afraid to lose the luxurious lifestyle supported by slave labour.

Afraid of being murdered in their beds by angry, freed slaves. Afraid they might have to work and do the menial jobs formerly assigned to slaves.

Should she pity them, laugh at them, or slap sense into them? She'd fought for their freedom from Hallon's despotic rule. Lost a valued friend. Now she'd left behind people she loved in order to keep fighting for them. And what were they worried about? Their fat, lazy backsides and already-bulging purses.

They didn't understand the value of freedom, and their ex slaves were afraid of it. How ironic.

Had all her pain and loss even been worth it?

Alere turned her back on them. The huoche driver passed down her bag, Jarran's, and Mina's. Settling her bow across her back and weapons on her hips, she hefted all three bags and hunted for a path to the water's edge so she could signal Dalor Khan to bring his lifechuan closer.

Jarran emerged from the huoche, grunting as he repositioned Mina's limp body in his arms. Mina's long, white hair trailed in the dust on the cobbles, the pale ends darkening until they matched the regrowth near her scalp. They needed to find some white-weed and re-colour her hair.

Alere tugged at her own shoulder-length, dark hair, tied into a man's mawei at the nape of her neck. What a ridiculous thing to be thinking. Colouring her twin sister's hair hardly ranked as important. Getting out of Chengdu. Getting Jarran to Madina and onto the Jun First throne. They were important. Carting Mina's unconscious body around classed as sheer ziftishness.

'We can still send her back to the palace.' She made one last attempt to convince Jarran. 'Kett and Corin will be with her. We've got less than a week to get you back to Madina before Jun Fourth

Hassan Wen-Gates overruns the city and takes your throne. She can't handle a trip like this, Jarran. You know that, don't you?'

He gave her a contemptuous stare down the length of his aquiline nose. 'I know you think she can't, but you're underestimating her.'

'But she—'

The Jun-Heir glared, his gold-brown eyes glittering like the river. 'She's coming, and that's final. I promised her I wouldn't let you leave her behind. If you want to drug your friends unconscious and abandon them, that's up to you. I won't leave Mina.'

Alere glowered. 'Do you *really* think I wanted to leave Kett behind? He's been my best friend and weishi-bodyguard for a decade. Now he's more than that. Do you have any idea how hard it is doing this without him?' Her throat closed, and she ground her teeth to stop tears blurring her vision.

Jarran gave her a puzzled look. 'So—'

She turned away, unwilling to get into an argument she couldn't win. Jarran Zah-Hill promised to be a difficult travelling companion. He seemed to feel obliged to disagree with almost everything she proposed.

He'd refused to leave the Shah of Melcor's palace without Mina. Alere had barely had time to transfer the precious Lei Koh-Lin journal and explanatory note to Corin's slack hands and kiss Kett's sleeping face before Jarran had disappeared down the corridor with Mina in his arms.

And he was right about the insanity of leaving Kett and Corin behind, but she couldn't put them in danger. Gavon had died because of her mistake. She wouldn't lose Kett and Corin. Not if she could help it.

She cleared her throat and refocussed on the task at hand: getting Mina safely onto Dalor's chuan, the *Kuailong,* which rocked gently on the Kabir River's muddy waters. Dalor had probably anchored so far offshore to stop boarders from swamping his vessel. At least he hadn't taken the ready money on offer. He could have filled the *Kuailong* with people, and left Alere and her party behind.

Now she just needed to get his attention and get her sister, and Jarran, aboard.

Reviewing the amorphous, edgy crowd, Alere decided on a direct course of action. First step was to contact Dalor. She focussed her thoughts on the iron-yanstone necklace and bracelets – fastened around her hips and wrists. The silver-gilt warmth of their power oozed through her body, tingling beneath her skin. The faint taste of iron and smoke teased her tongue. Gilded strength expunged doubt, worry, and the raw grief still eating at her heart, lifting and empowering, both heady and frightening.

Alere sought Dalor's Outers and found him on the *Kuailong*. His mind was as disciplined and organised as his vessel. It was simple to insert a thought into his surface Outers without calling attention to her intrusion. Dalor believed the idea to be his own. Not exactly in line with the Xintou House ethics on which she'd been raised, but she was in a hurry.

A creaking and clacking signalled the lowering of a lifechuan onto the turbid waters. The crowd on the waterfront stirred in response. Alere grimaced. This could get messy.

She made for the ragged demarcation between the two groups. Using a combination of polite requests and pointed glares, she managed to open a path to the wharf's edge. The ex-slaves shuffled aside with apprehensive, resentful glances. The free citizens stood their ground and muttered rude comments about upstart peasants.

Alere didn't enlighten them. What good would come from saying she was heir to the second largest Jundom in Mamlakah and Jarran was the new Jun to the First? After all, they were in Melcor, not Mamlakah, and she was responsible for the predicament in which these people found themselves. The last thing she wanted was to call attention to her identity.

All the titles in the world wouldn't protect her from their wrath.

'Gangzhi!' A youth amongst the free citizens cried, pointing at Alere.

She groaned. Of all the people to encounter. She'd swapped her silk robe for his rough shirt only three days before, at the Wushi Games.

'Shunu!' He pushed through the crowd, hesitated, and dropped to one knee. From a sheath at his hip, he drew a bronze kris dagger and held it ceremoniously in outstretched hands. 'My blade is yours, shunu. You are gangzhi.'

Gangzhi. The word rustled through both groups of onlookers, uttered in tones of excitement, anger, and frustration. The boiling emotions found a release.

'You!' An overweight, florid man wearing brilliant blue silks and a pompous expression pushed forward. He thrust the boy to one side.

A thin woman, bearing the two blue marriage-mark dots on her forehead, tugged at his robe and begged him to come away. Her quick breaths fluttered the pink veil covering her nose and mouth. She whispered something and pointed at the rows of slaves, who pushed closer.

The man jabbed a thick finger at Alere, his wine-scented breath tainting the air. 'This is *your* fault!' He swept an arm around the dock, managing to imply the ex-slaves were less than human and the free citizens above reproach. His bulbous lips twisted into a sneer. 'You destroyed our society. You wrecked my business. I'm now forced to live as a peasant, with nothing but the clothes on my back.' He plucked at the silk. 'Me! Ballan Hagan. It's outrageous.'

Beside his bejewelled wife and three daughters, stood nine heavily-armed mharebi and five servants lugging heavy sacks, chests, and a pair of golden jin-birds fluttering and squawking in a cage. Alere said nothing. Angry mutterings swelled all around.

'No.' The youth from the Wushi Games leapt to her defence. 'She freed us from the oppression of Slavemaster Hallon Nasim and his kind. She's opened our eyes to how wrong it is to enslave others and gave us the chance to be better than we were. You weren't there. You didn't feel it. Here.' He thumped his chest. 'When Gavon Abdul-kin died in the arena.'

A stab of pain stole Alere's breath. She drew on the yanstones to calm her guilt.

'Shut up.' Ballan pushed the boy away. 'Filthy little Selb. Slave-lover. If you love them so much, why don't you stay here and mix with them. Pretend they're equals.'

He gestured, and two mharebi flanked him, hands on their kusarigama or sword.

Alere peered over the dock's edge. Dalor's lifechuan floated just below. She dropped the luggage and her bow and quiver down to the waiting crew.

She spoke to Jarran. 'Take Mina and get into the lifechuan. Stay there. I'll be along in a moment.'

He sent her an ironic look.

'Stop being so gaisi noble, Jarran,' she growled. 'On this trip, I'm weishi to you. My job is to protect you and get you back to Madina safely. I've trained half my life at this. You're a baker. I *don't* need your help. Get in the chuan.'

Ballan nodded to his men. 'Secure that lifechuan. It will take me, not this chouhuo.' Two of the mharebi shuffled to the edge of the wharf and peered over.

Jarran waved the boat offshore. The crewman rowed a few boatlengths away and stayed, watching. Jarran laid Mina carefully down behind a pile of crates lining the wharf's edge. He returned to stand at Alere's side. Unarmed, but broad-shouldered and tall, his imposing presence was enough to make the mharebi facing him draw a sword.

'Fine. But stay close to Mina,' Alere muttered. 'This could go suilie very fast.'

'Time to practice your Jun Second diplomacy skills?' Jarran murmured.

'They're a bit rusty.'

'Oh, I don't know,' he said, nodding at the steel sword sheathed at her hip. 'They look pretty sharp to me.'

'Young woman…' Ballan trundled forward again, invading her personal space. 'Order that chuan to return immediately. You've obviously no idea what you've done. Clearly, you don't understand our ways.' He sniffed. 'It's not decent to be walking around in men's clothing and without a veil or marriage marks. Given you aren't from here, I'm sure you didn't understand when you freed the slaves.' He waved dismissively. 'In fact, I'm sure the Shah has come to his senses by now. Those ridiculous laws will be revoked, and all you slaves will be back in your rightful places. Come, come.' He sneered. 'We—'

'Do you have a deathwish?' Alere found her voice.

Behind him, the crowd's temper shifted toward ugly as the arrogant words passed from person to person.

'My dear girl.' He puffed out his stomach.

'I'm not your dear anything, you zift,' she snarled. 'Nor am I stupid, as you apparently are.' She pointed to the former slaves, poised like a pride of hungry xiao-cats waiting for the command to kill. 'These people are *free*. Melcor is free. There will be no revoking the law. And, for all you're a complete hmar and don't deserve it, *you* are free as well – which you wouldn't be if Hallon Nasim had taken over. Trust me. I know what he planned for the city. Unless you've always wanted to join an army as a junren, you would *not* have liked it. Now, I suggest you use that freedom and get out of here before these people take whatever you have left as compensation for two hundred years of abuse.'

He drew himself up, his face suffusing dark red. 'How dare you speak to me that way. Our slaves were *happy*. They didn't want your freedom. Do you even know who I *am?*'

His ridiculous posturing disarmed anger, and Alere relaxed. She surveyed the crowd's scowling, vitriolic expressions. The situation needed to be diffused. She was wrong to let it get even this far. Kett would be disappointed she'd forgotten her training. She raised her hands, palms out.

'Look, shenshi, I apologise.' She moderated her tone, trying to drop the level of antagonism. 'You're right. I don't belong here, and I don't want to get into anything unpleasant. I'm just going to get into this chuan and go.'

Ballan lifted his flabby chin. 'No! I've been waiting almost five hours. You have no right to get passage before me. I am third cousin to the Shah. He relies on me, and he'll hear of this, I assure you.'

Uncertain, derisive laughter rippled. It might have all settled and dissipated into nothing, but some shazi in the crowd called a jeering insult at Ballan.

Ballan threw out his chest. 'Get her out of my way,' he snapped at his mharebi. Then he stepped back, smiling smugly as his men advanced and drew weapons.

CHAPTER TWO

ALERE

Alere sighed and slid her sword and knife free of their sheaths. All she wanted was to get on a jiche chuan. Now this.

An awed murmur billowed through both halves of the crowd. The word 'steel' hissed and washed through the onlookers like wind through everblue trees. Hardly surprising. With little minable iron available on the whole colony-planet of Kalima, they probably represented more steel than most ever saw in their lives. The metal of the blades, alone, was a fortune enough to last a family three or four years. The yanstones embedded into the pommels made it more like double that.

What mattered right now, was that her weapons were far better suited to their task than the bronze ones carried by the mharebi. Seeing the steel, the other mharebi hastened to join their brethren, forming a nine-person human wall of muscle, armour and aggression.

The freed slaves shuffled back. They muttered in angry undertones but did not leap to her defence. Fearful anticipation and hope blazed in their gaunt faces. Somehow, this one incident was now the next symbol of their clash with the free citizens of Melcor. And she was once again the champion of their cause.

'Nice diplomacy,' Jarran muttered, shifting his feet.

'Oh, shut up. Stay out of my way, protect Mina, and try not to get killed.' She studied the mharebi. Most of them were pale, their hands trembling, sweat dripping off their faces. Green kids. Used to schooling slaves into obedience, not facing warriors in actual battle.

There wasn't a lot of space to manoeuvre between the dock's edge and the eager crowd. Nine against one was not great odds, either. She couldn't count on Jarran. Perhaps she could still resolve this without bloodshed. She'd had more than her fair share in the last few days and Jarran was too vulnerable and too valuable to risk for such a stupid matter.

'Look,' she said, 'we don't need to do—'

Jarran leapt forward. His right hand swept a swift arc at the closest mhareb's throat. He moved on to the second man. The first swayed and collapsed where he stood, blood pouring from a gaping slice across his jugular. Jarran used his arm's return motion to cut backhand, appearing to punch the next man's throat. That mhareb staggered back, fingers pressed to neck. Blood spurted through. He gave a gargling cough and fell into the crowd. Shrieks of horror arose and the Melcori citizens scrambled to get out of the way.

'Any time now!' Jarran yelled. The rest of the mharebi finally reacted and came at him with weapons swinging.

Alere swore. So much for not shedding blood. She ran to his aid. What on Kalima was he using? She raised her sword and clashed with one of the mharebi. Jarran sliced across a forearm and his opponent dropped his weapon. He followed with a short, sharp jab under the uplifted arm. Blood spilled down the mhareb's side from a severed artery under his armpit.

The two men in front of Alere claimed her attention. One jabbed at her tentatively. It took little skill to flick his blade aside and drive her dagger through his leather armour. She aimed for his stomach. Non-lethal if he could get to a skilled healer. He made a small sound of surprise then dropped to his knees, clutching at the blade. It tore from her grip. The second man launched himself at her.

She sidestepped and cut at his bronze sword. It cleaved in two under the steel. He staggered past and she elbowed him in the kidneys, thrusting him to the dock's edge. He plunged over the side, into the Kabir's murky water.

A third mhareb edged toward Mina but watched Alere. Fear lurked in his eyes as he twirled the spiked weight on his kusarigama. She grimaced and hesitated. Her foot still ached from her last encounter with a kusarigama. But she couldn't let him near Mina.

Movement in her peripheral vision. A bronze sword descended at her. She avoided, deflected, and used the momentum to drive her pommel into his skull. The mhareb fell without a sound. Hopefully just unconscious.

The third man released the kusarigama weight.

'No!' Alere flung herself between the weapon and Mina's helpless body. The spiked weight slammed into Alere's left shoulder, digging into muscle and bone. She landed hard on her right shoulder, barely keeping a grip on her sword. The dock's wooden planks rattled under the impact.

The mhareb yanked on the chain, tearing the weight free. Alere screamed. Pain blotted out the world. She lay on the deck, gasping. Warmth trickled down her chest. Two pairs of booted feet swaggered closer. Fear swelled, blanking her mind. What could she do? She was losing blood fast and there was no way she could protect Mina and Jarran.

Zift! The word seemed almost to come from elsewhere. Of course she could. The yanstones. Drawing a sobbing breath, she steadied her racing heart and sank into the yanstones' welcoming golden warmth. Fear vanished. Pain eased. She felt Mina's mind, deep in lethargy but still close, and drew strength from her twin.

Alere rose. The mharebi took a backward step. They glanced at Ballan, who frowned and gestured them forward. She tightened her grip on the sword and raised it. She pulled a throwing knife out of her belt with her left hand, grinning fiercely when the mharebi's mouths fell open. Pain meant nothing. Mina had to be protected.

Jarran appeared by her side. Two against three and the mharebi looked much less certain.

'You alright?' he asked, panting. Blood streaked his cheek but he bore no visible injuries.

'I'll be fine,' she grated. 'Get Mina out of here. Let me deal with this.'

'You sure?'

'Go, Jarran,' Alere said quietly. 'Get her on the chuan.'

He glanced at her face, hesitated, then gathered Mina in his arms. With one last look at Alere, he jumped backward into the Kabir, landing with a massive splash. Alere kept her attention on her three opponents. Splashing and calls from the crew said Jarran and Mina were safe.

The mhareb with the kusarigama twirled and released the chain again. She closed on him, sidestepping. The spiked bronze ball brushed her thigh. It caught in the thick material of her trous and scratched the skin beneath. Not enough to worry about. She crowded close. Her blade sliced across his wrist. He yelped and dropped his weapon. She shifted so he stood between her and the other two men. A sword point pushed through his body from behind. One of his partners mistimed a thrust meant for her and killed his own man.

She shoved both men backward. They fell in a heap, blood soaking into the silvered dock timbers. The last man approached her slowly. His feet dragged and his fingers clenched spasmodically on his sword-grip.

'Look,' she tried again, as they circled each other, 'we don't need to do this.'

'What are you waiting for?' Ballan sputtered. 'Kill her!'

The mhareb's face reflected indecision then firmed into intent. Fine. Alere flicked a pair of throwing knives in rapid succession. The first flew true and buried the blade's length into his thigh. The second embedded into Ballan's silk-clad chest.

For a moment the merchant simply stared at the black handle protruding from the shining cloth. Then he gaped at her in wordless outrage and sank heavily to his knees. His wife shrieked and fainted into her maidservant's arms. Her daughters scurried around like flutterbugs, waving their bright, silken skirts in her face.

'You…you've killed me,' Ballan murmured, collapsing sideways.

Alere, her sword now at the mhareb's throat, smiled grimly. 'No, I haven't. You're too fat. The blade isn't long enough to reach your heart.' She lowered her steel and eyed the mhareb levelly.

He yanked the knife from his leg, wiped it on his trous and returned it with a respectful bow. He sat, hands pressed against the bleeding wound, sword abandoned.

His master was less courteous. He swore and cursed her, calling for a healer, the Shah's mharebi to take her away, his private xiongshou to assassinate her, *someone* to bring justice on this upstart of a woman.

Alere stalked across and bent over him.

'Oh, shut up, you pompous hmar.' She yanked out the knife and cleaned it on his robe, ignoring his squawk. She pointed the tip at one of his servants. 'You. Find an inn nearby and send for a healer for these mharebi. Make sure they're seen to first.'

The man jerked a shallow bow, failing to hide a grin as he dropped the large sack he carried and hurried away.

Satisfied it was over, Alere signalled to Dalor's men to bring the chuan in closer again. She withdrew her steel dagger from its gory sheath and cleaned it. The mhareb lived. She pressed his hands against the wound and told him to hold hard. At least three of the mhareb were dead. Too many, even if they were by Jarran's blade, not hers.

She quashed nausea and regret and headed for the water's edge again. The rush of adrenalin faded, leaving her limbs heavy and trembling.

Motion in the ex-slaves caught her eye. Their expressions awestruck, the ragged mob fell to their knees and bowed, foreheads pressed to the ground. Some free citizens did the same and the word 'gangzhi' drifted like bitter smoke through the cool morning air. Someone started a chantsong, slow and sonorous, the words in blurred old Mandrin. Almost as though they'd rehearsed, the harmonies split into eerie dissonances then cascaded back into something more comfortable to the ear. The words *steel* and *erheyi* recurred and Alere frowned. The song died away with a final ululating cry that sent a shiver glissading across Alere's skin.

The youth who'd begun the whole scene scrambled forward and knelt at her feet. Catching her hand, he kissed it reverently.

'Shunu. You are gangzhi.' He pointed to the crowd. 'We are your humble servants.'

'Oh, stop it.' She snatched her hand free and raised her voice. 'You're no-one's servants any longer. Go home. That's all I'm trying to do, too. I'm not your leader. Choose your own paths. You're free.'

'But, shunu…' The boy stood, spreading his arms. 'You *are* our leader. The time of erheyi is upon us. As foretold, the slaves have been freed by a xintou and her champion…you. We've heard of the unrest in Mamlakah. We know you're going there and we want to help. We are Selb.' From beneath his shirt he produced a small, pewter axe on a leather thong. Fervent expectation lit his eyes.

When she said nothing, he gave a disappointed little shrug. 'It's what we have trained for. Well, not the slaves, of course. But we've all waited these five hundred years. You carry steel. You are ganzhi. We're yours to command, shunu. Yours and your sister's. You are erheyi.'

'My sister?' She glanced over her shoulder, at Mina's unconscious form in the lifechuan. What did she have to do with it? 'We're not this erheyi thing, whatever that is. Leave us alone.'

The boy undid the cloth belt around his hips. 'At least let me bind your wound, shunu.'

'No, it's—'

He pulled back the torn cloth of her shirt and gasped. 'It's healed!' He raised his voice and threw his arms wide. 'Her injury is healed! She is gangzhi!'

Gangzhi! Made of steel. The word echoed through the ranks of slaves, repeated more loudly until it was a roar of adulation. The slaves again fell to their knees – followed by a third of the free citizens.

Silenced, Alere recoiled from the hope-filled faces. Why did they resist freedom and choose to be ordered around by someone again? Was it, as Gavon once said, that in times of difficulty people looked outside themselves for guidance? What did they expect of her? She owed them nothing. She was only twenty. Who was she to lead them? And to what end?

Yet, they were far from home, without food, money or protection. Her weishi training niggled at her. She was at fault for their plight. She'd toppled the Slavemasters and freed the slaves. She couldn't just abandon them now. Their fate was her responsibility.

So, as the devout expectations of hundreds of Selb pressed against her thoughts, their hope became her enslavement and her own freedom slipped, once more, from her grasp.

How was she supposed to get away from them?

CHAPTER THREE

ALERE

Alere waited on the dock for Liu Gray, tapping one foot. Offshore, the *Kuailong* waited for her. Hundreds of gongli south, upriver, Madina and the Jun First's throne waited for Jarran.

And every passing minute increased the chances Kett and Corin would awaken from their drugged sleep in the Shah's palace. It had been two hours and she'd given them enough for at least four, but she wasn't keen to be within reach when they woke. If they overcame her hypnotic suggestions, both men would be angry. Justifiably.

Only after Alere agreed to let them follow her to Madina, were the free and ex-slave Selbs content to let her leave. To prove her goodwill, she had been obliged to send to the shah's palace for Liu Gray, leader of what had formerly been an underground resistance movement in Chengdu.

Liu Gray arrived, his sharp gaze taking in Alere's bloodied shirt, the slaves, and the lifechuan containing Jarran and Mina. He said nothing, but bowed, elegant in severe black robes that disguised his gangly limbs and wiry frame. His lips curved into amused irony.

'Shunu,' he said. 'Your humble servant. How can I assist?'

'Oh, stop it,' she growled, pointing at the slaves. 'Talk to these people. I have to get Jarran back to Madina and they want me to stay and lead some sort of secret army. I don't have time.' She gestured to the boy, whose name was Dorran. 'Dorran, this is Liu Gray. He's Shah Jahil's…liaison to the slaves and refugees. You'll be under his command from now on. Understand?'

Dorran nodded so hard she worried he might hurt his neck. He bowed. 'Travel well, shunu. We'll meet with you at Madina to fight for the new Jun. Molian, shunu.'

'Er…good. Thank you.' She waved Dalor's lifechuan closer and clambered down into it. Shivering with a vague sense of apprehension, she turned away from the shore.

Dalor Khan's brow was creased with a deep scowl as he helped her over the gunwale and onto the *Kuailong*'s deck. Beneath her feet, the timbers creaked and the choppy river water, whipped into whitecaps by an ocean breeze, splashed against the silvery-grey magnal-coated hull.

'You alright, shunu?' he grunted, eyeing her torn, stained shirt.

She nodded. 'Dalor, this is Jarran. And my sister, Mina.'

'Where're Corin and the others?' Dalor's perusal of Jarran was disinterested. He probably knew who Jarran was – Jun First, Jarran Zah-Hill, new ruler of Mamlakah. His name had been bandied about often enough on the trip to Melcor. But Dalor wasn't easily impressed.

'They're staying in Chengdu for awhile to help with the mess,' she said, flushing. 'Thank you for waiting. You must have doubted we'd come back.'

'Yes. Especially when I heard you'd been taken to the Games.' He flicked his long, braided mawei back over his shoulder. 'You survived. Seems I underestimated you.'

She shrugged and changed the subject, unwilling to relive it to satisfy his curiosity. 'And these people? Can you do anything for them?'

Dalor curled a lip at the unruly mob. Someone fell into the river, struggling in the cold water until his flailing hand grabbed a timber ladder and he managed to climb back onto the dock. Luckily the giant golden salamanders in the river didn't put in an appearance.

'They've no money to pay passage and this chuan was already bespoken by yourselves. What should I have done, let them have your berths?' Something in his tone said it was more than just a superficial question. He tested her to find out what sort of person his new Jun Second would be when she eventually took over from her father, Rafi.

The problem was, she was no longer certain.

Part of her had compassion for these people. Most were former slaves, desperate to get back to loved ones far away. She had already accepted her responsibility for them. However, the cool detachment imposed by the yanstones would have her leave them to their fate.

'How many can you safely take aboard?' she said tersely.

'Maybe thirty.'

'Do it. Ex-slaves only. Single mothers and children first, then families. But make it quick. We need to leave within the hour.' She dropped five steel tiebi into his palm, recklessly depleting the small purse she'd taken from Corin. 'Will that cover their passage to Dalcin? Have you enough supplies on board for the trip?'

'Yes. It's only a day and a half.' He hefted the coins in his palm then tipped them back into her purse. 'Rafi's already more than paid me for this trip, shunu. Keep this. You'll need it to get home.'

She thanked him.

Jarran carried the still-sleeping Mina downstairs, into the cabins. He placed Mina onto a bunk in the same cabin Alere had occupied on her trip downriver. Together, they stripped off her wet grey healer's robe and wrapped her in a blanket. Alere stood beside him, staring at Mina's beautiful, relaxed countenance. With her night-black eyes closed and her mouth soft in sleep, the resemblance to Alere's own face lessened. She looked sweet and far too young. She was a healer, not a warrior. Would she be able to make the gruelling ride to Madina?

Jarran, still soaked from his dunking, shivered and stirred. His shoulderlength dark hair slipped free of its tie and his sturdy, brown bamboo-cloth shirt clung damply to broad shoulders and muscular arms. A frown furrowed his high forehead, emphasising angular, aquiline features.

'You should change.' Alere touched his arm. 'Thanks for your help on the dock. I wish you hadn't killed them, though.'

'Me too. But my mother always said surprise was the best attack.' He grimaced, the action crinkling the corners of his gold-brown eyes and making him seem older than his twenty-four years. 'Is that why you didn't use your sword and dagger to draw down lightning? Because you didn't want to kill them?'

Alere swallowed and looked away. With the yanstones set in the steel sword and dagger she could draw electricity to earth – channel lightning. But it cost her dearly, leaving her exhausted and nauseated; barely able to stand, let alone fight. A weapon of last resort.

And the memory of using the lightning to destroy the Slavemasters houses was still too fresh. The horrors hidden in the slave quarters too clear in her mind.

'There's been enough death for now,' she said, staring at Mina's sleeping face.

'Well,' Jarran said, 'not sure you needed help, even without that, but you're welcome. I'm a little out of practice, though.' He rotated his right shoulder and winced. 'They almost cornered me.'

'What weapon were you using?' Curiosity got the better of her.

He delved into a pocket and produced a small, claw-shaped bronze knife. Alere hefted the weight and admired how nicely the handle fitted her palm. The short, curved blade was designed to extend out the back of her fist, making it almost invisible until used at close quarters. The double edge meant it could be used fore or backhand. It was a beautiful, discreet, nasty little weapon.

'It's a karambit.' Jarran accepted it back, swinging his arm in a smooth arc at throat height. 'My mother was from Adeghal. It's the close-fighting weapon of choice there. She was mhareb to the King.' His mouth thinned. 'That's how she met Jun First Radan Zah-Hill – when he was visiting. King Yu fired her when he found out she was pregnant. She had no family so she went to Madina to get help from Radan.' He curled a lip. 'He kept her for awhile. Secretly, outside the Alcazar. But the kin-child laws started four years after my birth, so she sought sanctuary in Shanzhai.' He turned the knife over. 'She taught me how to use it. Liu got me this one yesterday.'

Alere frowned at him. 'I never thought to ask who your mother was. Is she still alive?'

Loss clouded his expression. 'She died a few weeks after my first daughter was born, six years ago. Without the Weishi House tattoo and training she couldn't get work in Madina. She took a job as mhareb to the Miner House Master in Jiali city in the Ma-Safra Jundom. The Master took a team to assess an actual iron deposit in the Ahmar Ranges, southeast of Madina. Raiders killed every single one in the party. Including my mother.'

'Iron!' Alere sank onto the end of Mina's bed. Raiders in the Ahmar Ranges could only be those led by Jada Marin-kin, Rohne's father. But, according to Mina, Jada's people had become peaceful traders and trappers over a decade before. And what iron could there possibly be….?

Glittering crystals flashed in her memory. The hidden valleys Mina led them to when Alere and Kett fled Madina so many weeks before. The walls in those valleys were exactly like those surrounding the meteoric iron underneath Shanzhai castle. There had been signs of digging in that first site, where they'd hidden after escaping the Alcazar weishi in Pelon.

Could it be? Could there be more iron? If so, how much? Enough to change the whole Jundom's economy and technology? Maybe not. Those valleys were small. Perhaps enough to change the fortunes of Jada and his mountain people. But she'd seen no evidence of wealth in her brief visit there.

Although…Jada had prevented her and Kett from entering his main settlement, hidden deep in the mountains. Supposedly to protect the settlement from the Madina Alcazar weishi, chasing Alere. But what if there was another reason?

'You alright?' Jarran asked.

'Yes,' she lied. 'Yes, I'm fine. It's just been...' She drew a long breath and slowed her heart. 'A long few days. I'm...sorry about your mother.'

She stood up, needing some space. 'We'd best let Mina sleep. You get changed or you'll freeze. I'll meet you on deck. I'd like to see how that karambit of yours works.' Alere swung her cloak over her shoulders and gestured him out. They left Mina and locked the room for her safety, since Dalor was in the process of filling the chuan with people.

Alere retreated to the back of the upper deck and watched the shore, drumming her fingers on the gunwale. She tucked a wayward dark curl behind her ear as the ocean breeze curled up the river and brought the scent of salt, fish and seaweed. The wind blew away the faint pall of smoke yet lingering over Chengdu. Evidence of the destruction of the Slavemasters' houses and fabric of Melcori society. Overhead, Luna Er was a faint, thin crescent high in the clear green sky, chasing the orange sun.

The distant eastern riverbank was just a dark line of low purple-black foliage, barely visible on the horizon. Dalcin lay upriver. Once there they would need to make good use of the horses bespoken by Corin for the return journey. But what if they couldn't get to Madina before Hassan Wen-Gates arrived at the gates with his army to usurp the Jun First Throne?

Would the city mount a defence? Would her father, Rafi Koh-Lin, be able to consolidate the other Jun families behind his leadership in Jarran's absence? Few Juns loyal to the ruling Zah-Hill family, would trust the Jun Second. Especially since the last Jun First, Ven Zah-Hill, had died at Koh-Lin hands.

Her hands.

She considered them. Calloused from years of weapons training, they had killed Ven, and so many others now. Easily. Too easily, perhaps. She'd left Madina more than two months before, frightened by her change of fortunes and sickened by her obligation to kill to save herself. Now, each death was simpler than the last, each face sooner forgotten, each memory compartmentalised with greater ease.

The yanstones helped. With them she felt capable of almost anything. Her mastery of the xintou skills they gave her improved each day. Telepathy and Reading others was almost second-nature now.

With the yanstone-given abilities came other benefits: all emotion vanished before their clean, cold logic. She wanted to give in and let their fire harden her against the grief. If she let them, would the stones temper her into the perfect soldier: detached and capable, but without compassion or hesitation?

Perhaps she needed to speak with Mina about it. As a healer, surely she would have some idea of what was happening; some idea of how to control it.

Jarran reappeared in dry clothing and she shelved the thought for later.

'So.' She cleared her throat. 'We should get to know each other a little better, since you'll be my Jun First and I your Jun Second.'

Jarran grinned. 'Oh, you'd be surprised what I already know about you.'

She groaned. 'Fine, you'd better tell me what Mina's said. It will save me repeating anything and I might be able to straighten out a few misconceptions.'

He propped a hip on the railing, fingers tucked under his arms, legs crossed at the ankles, facing her. 'I'm not sure Mina is capable of telling a lie. She's the most honest, most straightforward person I've ever met.' A gentle smile tugged at his mouth.

'I've known her to tell two, at least. One of which put you on the throne.'

'Ah.' His tone became thoughtful. 'Yes. Her part in your deception to expose Ven Zah-Hill's madness and corruption. That eats at her, you know. She has nightmares about his death.'

Alere gave a harsh laugh. 'That makes two of us, then. Go on: tell me what else she said.'

He tipped his head to one side. 'She told me about your parents and how Hanna Zah-Hill's kin-child laws made your existence illegal and forced your mother, Sura, to leave Shanzhai. And about how the two of you were separated at birth. She said you were raised first in the Jun Second Ma-Safra's house, then in Xintou House, thinking you were Elmira Connor's gene-daughter. You had cross-training as weishi and as jiaoji. She told me about meeting you. Your trip to Shanzhai to meet with your father, Jun Second Rafi Koh-Lin.

And your agreement to pretend to be his heir, your half-sister, Lianna.'

Alere scowled. That was all meant to be a secret. Why had Mina told all that to a man she'd only just met a couple of weeks before? She said nothing, waiting to hear what else he knew before she decided on a course of action.

'She also told me about Lianna's poisoning by Hanna Zah-Hill.' His expression became pensive. 'And about Radan Zah-Hill's death by poison. How could his own wife do that? What made Hanna hate her husband so?'

Alere hesitated. So, Mina either didn't know, or hadn't shared, that Alere had given Radan mercy in the last, painful moments of his life. It had been the right thing to do, but was not something Alere wished known to Radan's son. Either of his sons. She hadn't yet told Kett. The words wouldn't come.

As for Hanna, what could be said? Did Jarran know Hanna hated her husband not only for his weakness as a ruler, but also for his appetite for other women? After all, Hanna created the kin-child laws because Kett stood between her son, Ven, and the Jun First Throne. Those same laws resulted in wholesale slaughter of kin-children and forced Jarran's mother into hiding.

Did Jarran know Kett was his older half-brother? Did he know Kett had abdicated the Jun First throne in his favour?

'I think,' she replied cautiously, 'that Hanna may have inherited her father's insanity, as well as passing it on to Ven. I'm not sure either of them were fully in control of their… passions.'

Jarran gave a bitter chuckle. 'Diplomatic way of saying they were both power-crazed maniacs out to take Shanzhai by force, no matter what the cost. I know about the yanstone bracelets and the iron deposit under Shanzhai, too. I know you endured a great deal to stop Ven and Hanna from taking the city and using the iron to make guns.' He laid a gentle hand on her shoulder.

'Jiangui! Was there *anything* Mina didn't tell you?' Alere shifted away.

'Yes. Two things, in fact.'

'Oh? That many?' She folded her arms. 'I'm stunned. What?'

He scraped his dark hair back and, with a scrap of leather from his pocket, tied it at the nape of his neck before replying.

'First: why did Rohne Marin-Kin let Slavemaster Hallon keep us prisoner, and why did he then escape and leave Chengdu without us? I thought he was Mina's friend. They grew up together. Why would he leave her behind? Why is he so desperate to get to Madina?'

Alere lifted one shoulder. 'All excellent questions. Short answer: I don't know. Rohne is… complicated. I assume you're aware his mother, Nasra, was a Xintou Bonded to the Jun Second Ma-Safra family?' She waited for his nod. 'She went into hiding when she became pregnant with Rohne. He's a male xintou and we all know they're forbidden by Xintou House. We just don't know why. Our best guess about Rohne is that he's out to prove to everyone that he is… acceptable.'

'Well, I'm not sure he's chosen the right way of going about it.'

'Me neither. What's your second thing?' She put her back to the railing, flipping up the hood on her cloak as the ocean breeze cooled.

Jarran straightened and folded his arms, mirroring her, serious. 'Why are *you* doing all this? What's in it for you?'

She opened her hands wide. 'I fell into this when Radan Zah-Hill tasked me to warn my father about Hanna and Ven's plan to make steel weapons from the Shanzhai iron deposit. Now…getting you back to Madina so you can stabilise the Jundom…' She watched the last load of refugees clamber aboard the chuan. 'It's the right thing to do.'

She sighed. 'I've had duty and honour and responsibility so drilled into me by Weishi House and Xintou house, I feel uncomfortable *not* doing what I'm supposed to. Which really annoys me. Kett's convinced that's why I so often run counter to authority.' She gave a half-shrug. 'It's a bit pathetic when I say it out loud.'

Jarran looked at her quizzically. 'Not really. Shows you're self-aware.' He hesitated. 'But, as a businessman, I can tell you that doing the right thing – or even deliberately going against the rules just because you don't like them – isn't enough to drive most people. And it's certainly not enough to carry you through the really tough times. You'll have to do better to take on what's ahead of us in Madina.'

Bridling, Alere glared. She'd got through so far without his help and advice. Who was he to say she wasn't good enough? Unwilling to speak when she was likely to say something hot and regrettable, she stared over his shoulder, upstream, at the distant, smudged-purple horizon.

'I'm sorry.' Jarran cleared his throat. 'I didn't mean to anger you. I know you've done a lot for Mamlakah. I'm just concerned. Let me say it a different way.' He scratched at the back of his scalp. 'When you fought in the Wushi Games, was that because freeing the slaves was the right thing to do, or was there something else? Something so important it drove you to the point where you were willing to sacrifice your own life.'

She said nothing. He touched on subjects she didn't want to share with him. She didn't know him well enough and she missed Kett's steady strength so much it physically hurt. Right now, the rawness of his absence, and of Gavon's death, scraped too close to the surface.

Jarran turned around, his elbows on the rails and hands dangling out over the muddy water. 'For me it's my daughters. When their mother died, I swore I'd protect them no matter what. When Rafi came to me with the proposal to take the First Throne I refused.' He snorted. 'I didn't want to leave my businesses or uproot the girls. And, after all, what do I know about running a Jundom? Then Rafi pointed out that, if not me, the Jundom would end up in the control of either my half-brother, Dirat…' he screwed up his nose '…who is a spoilt brat and a hmar. He would finish Hanna's job of destroying the economy to satisfy his own stupid whims. Or my uncle, Hassan Wen-Gates, who by all accounts is a paranoid power-monger.

'So.' A hint of bitterness coloured his tone. 'As much as I'd like to emulate Kett and abdicate, I don't seem to have that luxury. If I do, I'm forsworn for there is no doubt that my daughters' lives would be short under either Dirat or Hassan.'

'Kett!' She gaped. 'You know? How? Mina wasn't in Shanzhai when he told us he was Radan Zah-Hill's firstborn.'

'He told me, himself, yesterday.' Jarran's mouth twisted. 'He even said he was sorry to give such a burden to me. Clearly not sorry enough to take it back, though.'

'Enough!' Alere slapped both palms onto the wood rail, rage boiling low in her stomach.

He stood up, towering over her, sardonic. One hand slid into the pocket where he kept his karambit.

CHAPTER FOUR

ALERE

'Kett does *not* deserve your contempt.' Alere gripped her weapons. 'You have *no* idea what he's been through and no idea what he's given up. I will not stand here and listen to such disrespect for a man worth twice what you are.'

There followed a thick silence wherein she glared at him and he returned it with cool hauteur. Then his expression softened and he pointed at her.

'And *that* is almost the passion that saved Kett in the Games three days ago. Now you just need to find something about *this* task to inspire that same fire.'

'You…you manipulated me!'

Jarran chuckled. 'I prefer to call it managing. I do have two small daughters and forty staff, after all. Understanding what motivates people and how to reward them is a valuable skill to learn.'

'I'm not doing this for a reward.'

'No.' He sent her a shrewd, sidelong look. 'I'd guess you show love for people in what you do for them. In the sacrifices you make. And you judge their affection by what they do in return.'

'Oh, stop it,' she snapped. 'I've studied all this in Jiaoji House. Stop trying to second-guess what I'm thinking. It's just annoying and I don't need you to manage me. Keep your mouth shut and let me do my job of getting you to Madina.'

CORIN

Waking with the mother of all hangover headaches, when it's deserved, is one thing. Waking that way without remembering the pleasure of being drunk first is another. Corin blinked blearily at the shadowy figure bending over him and swatted aside the large hand shaking his shoulder.

'Go away, Kett,' he grumbled. 'I feel like the back end of a desert tuo.'

A deep chuckle sounded. 'You look like one, too. Get up. We have work to do.'

Squinting against the late-morning glare, Corin stretched and yawned. His neck spasmed. His mouth was as dry as a desert tuo's ass. And tasted as bad. What the diyu had he drunk?

Still fuzzy with sleep, he squinted at the low table next to the couch. Four empty glasses and a wine bottle with just dregs left in the bottom. Just one bottle? There ought to be at least a dozen by the pounding in his brain. Why couldn't he remember a party that put him out so thoroughly in what appeared to be the middle of the day? Who else had been here?

Kett's words registered.

'What work?' Corin clutched at the couch back and dragged himself into a sitting position.

The tall weishi reappeared from the bathroom, towelling his face dry and smoothing his dark hair back neatly into its mawei again. He flicked the towel onto a chair and settled his steel sword on his hip.

'We're staying Chengdu to help Liu Gray and the Shah of Melcor to stabilise the economy, remember...?' He grimaced and stared into middle distance, running his tongue over his teeth. He studied the empty glasses and the rumpled bed. Then he pressed the heel of one hand into his forehead and squeezed his eyes closed, muttering to himself.

Odd. Corin waited. Kett was given to long bouts of stoic silence and a tendency to be overly-thoughtful and cautious. He was not, however, in the habit of talking to himself. The weishi stared out the window, his expression haunted.

'She left,' Kett said, bitterness edging his words. 'She promised she wouldn't.' His jaw worked and his fingers curled into fists.

'Kett?' Corin stood. The room swayed around him. No, not the room. Gaisi! *He* swayed.

He staggered around the table. The tip of his sword-sheath caught on the edge. He grabbed at the hilt, accidentally pulling off the suede cover he kept over it to hide the valuable yanstone set into the iron pommel. His thumb brushed a stone and a low-key jolt of energy crackled through his body. It swept headache and blurriness away, leaving his mind sharp and clear.

And he remembered.

'That sneaky little…' Anger piled like thunderheads as memory of Alere's trick surged back. Corin picked up a glass and swirled the dark purple dregs of wine.

'She used istilqa on us,' Kett confirmed, digging both thumbs into his temples. 'And she left us with a hypnotic Suggestion to stay here in Chengdu while she takes Jarran back to Madina. That's what's causing the headache – your mind trying to reconcile conflicting desires. Gaisi! I *knew* she seemed too innocent when she handed me that glass. What a little shazi. She's trying to protect us.'

'What from?' Corin worked out what was missing from the room. 'And where's Mina? She drank the wine, too. I remember her falling asleep.'

'Gavon.' Kett said succinctly as he rotated and stretched his neck, his eyes still closed.

'Gav's…' Corin clenched his teeth and forced the word out, '…dead. What does leaving us behind have to do…oh.'

'Yes. She's afraid she'll lose us, too. She's hurt and making stupid decisions.' His grey eyes opened, iron hard. 'We have to catch her.'

'Absolutely,' Corin muttered. 'If for no other reason but to lodge a complaint over the misuse of the only decent wine I've had in a week.'

Kett said nothing. He sank onto the couch and rested his head on the heels of his hands.

'How did you overcome her Suggestion to stay?' Corin touched the yanstones again. What an interesting new facet to their usefulness. The minor xintou ability of telepathy was already helpful. Perhaps this was just another expression of the healing ability he'd seen Alere use with hers. Worth exploring. As Rafi Koh-Lin's spy, Corin couldn't begin to count the number of times he'd had to tip out a perfectly good glass of wine, spiked in an attempt to extract information from him.

Sucking a deep breath, Kett straightened. The stricken expression hadn't quite faded, but he answered calmly, 'Weishi training. As proof against jiaoji using istilqa on us.' He bared his teeth and sucked a hissing breath. 'It's not easy, though, and I still have a killer headache. You?'

Corin thrust the stones forward. 'The yanstones.'

'Interesting.' Kett scanned the room. 'But, right now we have to work out how far behind her we are and which way she went.'

Corin patted his jacket pockets, heart sinking. 'She's taken my list of contacts for the return trip, and one of my purses.'

'No, she's not stupid, is she? Jiangui. That means she'll have taken Dalor's chuan. Call a servant. Find out if the *Kuailong* has left. There's no point chasing her to the dock if it's already gone.' Kett wiped a hand over his head and glanced out the window. 'With all the refugees leaving the city, we'll have a problem getting a berth on any other. Perhaps Shah Jahil has a private chuan he'll lend us to get across the river.'

'Good thought. He does.' Corin pressed the buzzer bell near the door.

Jahil owned a useful and quick little chuan that Corin had borrowed – for nefarious purposes – last time he'd visited Chengdu. With any luck it was still in good condition and in the palace boathouse. At least it wasn't far away. The sun's orange light glittered off the river beyond the garden outside this room.

Corin scanned the couch where he'd slept, hoping to find the list and money fallen on the floor. No such luck. There was, however, a small book and a folded scrap of paper lying on the carpet.

He picked them up. Bound in faded, brittle gold silk, the book smelled musty. Markings inside the cover were in old Mandrin, a language he'd never bothered to learn. Every page was covered in tiny, delicate script. He handed it off to Kett and opened the note instead.

'This was intended for Mina.' He flattened it. 'Why did Alere leave it with me? Do you think she changed her mind and took Mina with her?'

Kett shrugged, intent on the book. 'The servants will be able to tell us how many left and when. What does her note say?'

'Reading between the lines, I'd say pretty much what you said about wanting to keep Mina and us safe.' He skimmed through it, paraphrasing. 'And she's asked you to translate the book. She thinks it might contain information about male xintou and something called the Teachings of Lei? Evidently, it's the journal of a Lei Koh-Lin, who founded—'

'The Xintou House in Madina – along with the Edwards sisters – five hundred years ago, yes.' Kett flipped a page and traced down the columns of fine script. 'She's right. It is. And, if these first couple of pages are any indication, it may be more than just a simple diary.'

'Oh?' Corin tucked Alere's note into his jacket and collected the bottle of wine, sniffing it. 'You may be interested to know she didn't put the istilqa in the bottle, like she did in Shanzhai. Must have been in the glasses. It explains why she picked a decent, full-flavoured wine. The taste of istilqa would cut through the pissweak, green Melcori wines. I can't believe we fell for it this time.'

'Yes, I certainly wasn't expecting her to try the same thing twice.' Kett's lips twitched. 'Which is exactly why it worked. As I said: she's not stupid.'

Corin put the bottle down and prowled around the room, waiting for the servant. Kett continued to read with a methodical concentration that grated against Corin's instinctive need for action. He half-heartedly rummaged through the room's storage cupboards, but found only Kett's clothing and bag. Alere's things were gone.

Faced with the rumpled bed, he had to walk to the window to overcome the swift, unexpected surge of loss and anger. Admittedly, he'd been aware Alere didn't know her own heart when they'd begun their liaison. He'd even suspected her regard for Kett to be stronger than even she realised. But it didn't prevent the low burn of resentment and hurt at losing her.

'Just out of curiosity,' he threw over his shoulder, 'when did you meet Alere?' It was like picking at a scab, but he couldn't help himself. He'd almost accepted losing her to Kett, but he just needed to be sure the man cared enough for her; that he was worthy.

Kett lowered the book and directed a long, thoughtful gaze at Corin. Then his mouth softened into wry reminiscence.

'I was hired as junior weishi to Xintou House a few weeks before she arrived from Jiali.' He marked his place in the journal and set it aside, shifting to stare out the window that overlooked the river. The sun sparkled off the Kabir's ochre waters and flickered over his face. His gaze followed the soaring path of a white sea roc-eagle as it swooped down to snatch a fish from the river, then surged skyward again with great, sweeping strokes of its massive, leathery wings.

'I saw her walk into the House. A ten-year-old child dressed in silk robes and jewels, with her hair and makeup done and a haughty expression. I thought she was just one more arrogant xintou I'd have to bow and scrape to. Then the rumours started and I found out she had no powers, and never would. It didn't take long to see how the other girls despised her.' He shrugged. 'One day I found her clawing like a wild xiao-cat at three girls two years her senior. They had her cornered, drilling at her wards, but she had them in tears. Alere cried too, but more in anger and frustration than in fear.'

Corin watched, fascinated by the unusual play of emotion on the weishi's face. His doubts about Kett's feelings vanished. 'What happened?'

'I broke it up and took her to Mistress Li.' Kett lifted a shoulder. 'Luckily, the Mistress agreed to let me train her. I'm not sure what would have happened if she hadn't. The other girls left her alone once she started training. She complained a lot, but she picked it up so fast it was scary. I've never seen anyone so driven.'

'So…' Corin tried to think of a tactful way of broaching the subject and decided it was pointless. Kett would see through any equivocation anyway. 'You've obviously loved her pretty much since you met. What on Kalima took you so long to tell her?'

With a rueful chuckle, Kett replied, 'Because she'd come from Jun Second Petar Ma-Safra's household and had no xintou powers, I suspected she might be Petar's kin-child and Jun-Heir. I assumed Xintou House was hiding her as Weishi House had hidden me. That would have made her my first cousin.'

'Ah.' Corin grimaced sympathetically. 'And after she found out who she was? Why did you still wait?'

'Things got complicated really quickly.' Kett eyed him. 'Then she met you.'

'You're a gouri shazi, you know that?' Corin paced the room. 'She came to my bed because she thought Mina filled yours.'

'Yes.' Kett ignored the insult. 'But I only realised that after you two were together. And, in all honesty, she seemed happy. She does love you, too, you know.'

Unable to sustain anger at someone so good at not reacting, Corin released it on a regretful laugh. 'Just not the way I'd hoped she would. Fine.' He held out a hand. 'I formally concede defeat.'

Kett looked at it and smiled. 'She's hardly property for us to do deals over. She has a decided mind of her own.'

'Oh, yes.' Corin let sarcasm hide the renewed pain at losing her. 'That I do know. Just make sure you take care of her.'

Kett stared down at his hands, his fingertips white where they pressed against his thighs. 'I try. But…'

'But?'

'She left me behind, Cor.' His grey eyes darkened. 'What does that say for how she feels about me? Wouldn't you want the person you love most to be with you at a time like this?'

'Me? Yes. But you said it yourself – she's trying to protect you. People make stupid decisions when they're grieving. Look at me.' He flung out his arms. 'When Shasa and my parents died, ten years ago, I walked away from everything and everyone, changed my name and started a new life. Biggest mistake I made in some ways. I should have gone after the junren who killed them. Then I would have found Shasa before she spent ten years as a slave.'

There was a long silence and Kett gazed into nothing, sighed and stretched his neck. 'You're right. But the truth is: Alli deserves someone much better than me.'

'Yes,' Corin said heartily, 'yes, she does. Better than either of us, in fact. But she loves you, so do stop making me want to smack you upside the head for being a shazi.'

The weishi's frown eased. 'I don't think anything will stop you wanting that.' He resumed reading the Koh-Lin journal.

Corin inspected him. Kett was irritatingly difficult to dislike. His twenty years of weishi training gave him quiet confidence, extraordinary martial skills, and what Corin considered to be his only real flaw: a severely overblown sense of duty and responsibility. The man just didn't see the fun in a little underhandedness now and then. He did it, but he didn't like it.

A knock sounded on the thick timber door. A white-liveried servant slipped inside when Corin called out.

'Yes, shenshi?' the boy panted.

'Two things.' Corin held up two fingers, then added two more. 'No, make that four. Find someone who can tell me where Al…Lianna Koh-Lin went and whether the *Kuailong* has already left with her on it. Ask the kitchen to send food for two. Send for Liu Gray. And find Saric Wuming. My kid. You know him?' Corin held out a palm at about waist height. 'Short, blond, with an attitude. Lethal with a shuriken. Got it?'

The thought of his ten-year-old son still made Corin's head reel. And losing Saric's mother, Shasa, again left a wound he wasn't yet prepared to deal with. All he knew was that he had a son for whom he was now responsible. Him! Responsible.

So where was the kid?

The serving boy nodded. 'I can tell you where the shunu went, shenshi. I ordered the huoche for her.'

Corin fished a silver coin from a pocket and held it up. 'Where? There's a yinbi in it if you can remember every detail of what she said, who was with her, where they went, and when they left.'

The boy's fingers made little pincer movements. 'Shunu Lia took the huoche to the docks four hours ago, shenshi. The chuan would have left by now. The tall man she called Jarran was with her. He carried the other lady – the blonde one who looks just like Shunu Lia, except she's…er...blonde, shenshi.'

Corin waited encouragingly.

Words ran together as the boy's tongue tripped in his eagerness. 'The blonde lady was asleep and Shunu Lia and Jarran argued about whether she should go with them or not. He was refusing to leave her behind. She said the sleeping lady would slow them down.'

'Who won?' Corin was easily able to picture the confident and determined Jarran standing against Alere's decisiveness.

'He did, shenshi.'

Corin gave a crack of laughter. 'Well,' he called over his shoulder, 'at least we know where Mina is, Kett. And Lia's right: having her along should slow them down. If we leave now we can probably catch them on the other side of the Kabir river.'

'Oh.' The boy tugged on his sleeve. 'I was about to come and tell you when you rang the bell. Liu Gray is waiting for you downstairs in the blue salon. If you please.' He held out a hand.

Corin dropped the coin into it. 'Find me food and Saric and there's another in it for you.'

'Bai, shenshi.' The boy dashed away, his light footfalls fading down the lengthy hall.

Corin called back to Kett. 'Coming?'

The weishi waved vaguely at him, absorbed in his reading. 'You don't need me. If her chuan's already left, then my time is better spent on this. I have a feeling Alere was right. This could be vital,

Cor.' His gaze was troubled. 'I'm not sure I'm translating it correctly. But if I am then we may have found answers to some long-standing questions in this journal. Give me time to finish it, then we'll go after Alere.'

'What?' Corin scowled. 'How can a five-hundred-year-old journal be important enough to delay giving her a large and possibly rude part of my mind over abandoning us? I'm looking forward to it!'

Kett's mouth twitched. 'As am I. Which should tell you how important I think this could be.'

'Why? What's in it?' Corin half-turned back into the room.

Kett waved him out. 'Go talk to Liu, find Saric, and get everything ready. I'll be done by the time you are. Then we can discuss its relevance.'

'You are really annoying sometimes, you know that?'

'Yes.'

ALERE

Alere turned her back on Jarran… and almost collided with a diffident young girl wearing the orange uniform of a runner.

'The chuanzhu said I'd find an Alek Marin-Kin here,' she said.

'Yes,' Alere said. 'That's me. You have messages?' Perhaps updates from her father, Rafi, in Madina. Good news would be welcome. She could use a few extra days of breathing space to get Jarran back to Madina.

'Your identity papers?' The girl withheld the three thin, tightly-rolled flitter-bird messages.

Alere fished a forged set of papers out of her pocket and waited while the girl inspected them. With a raised eyebrow and a shrug, she passed the messages over and vanished back down the ladder to the *Kuailong*'s lower deck.

Rolling the three papers, Alere read the sender marks. One from her aunt Yasmin, Rafi's wife, in Shanzhai. That bore a date of two days before. The second was from Rafi, in Madina, three days old. The final bore the seal of Xintou House in Madina, dated one day before. It was missing the sender-identity mark that would normally say who wrote it. They all must have half-killed a dozen expensive, high-speed, long-distance flitters to make it to Chengdu so fast.

Who, in Xintou House, knew where she was and by what name she travelled? Perhaps Mistress Li? Rafi had confided in her when he'd arrived in Madina. But the last news reported her unwell and bedridden. And the Shah's Xintou, Valera, said her correspondence with the House had recently all come from other senior xintou. Not the Mistress. Who, then? Someone acting under Mistress Li's direction, perhaps? That could explain the lack of identifier.

Alere slipped a thumb under the seal of Rafi's message and decoded it. After reading it again, more slowly, she stifled a groan.

'What is it?'

She jumped at the sound of Jarran's voice by her shoulder, halting the trained flinch-response that half-raised her elbow to strike a body-blow.

'Don't *do* that!'

He pointed at the letter. 'From Rafi?'

'Three days ago,' she replied. 'Hassan was closer than we knew. He was only two days away when Rafi sent this. He'll already be in Madina.' She raised her eyes to his. 'We're already too late to stop him going after the throne. Rafi was still trying to rally support from the other Jun families to mount a defence against Hassan. But it sounds like he was being stonewalled by a cadre of Juns who don't want someone on the First throne who owes any allegiance to Rafi. By which they mean you.' She pointed at him. 'They're waiting to see what happens when the dust settles. The Zah-Hill troops – that

Rafi *might* have been able to command – were still at least a few days upriver, returning from Shanzhai.'

Jarran raised a brow. 'Anything else?'

She stuffed the message into a pocket. 'Only that there are more riots over the reversal of the kin-child laws. Centred around Asadia – where Rafi sent Hanna Zah-Hill after she was defeated at Shanzhai. Sounds like she's still trying to stir up trouble for him. He's worried she might be forming another army, but I can't see how she would. Most of her men are still marching back from Shanzhai. I think she's the least of his worries.'

'I wish you hadn't stopped Kett from killing her in Shanzhai,' Jarran said bitterly. 'I'd sleep better knowing she was dead.'

She smiled bleakly. 'Kett said pretty much the same thing. It seemed like the right thing at the time – for Kett, anyway. He's carried the guilt of the kin-child deaths close to his heart since he was seven. He didn't need to add her death to his load.'

'But maybe he should have.' Jarran gazed back at Chengdu. 'Did you ever consider that it would have *helped* him find closure – for all of us?'

'No,' she said flatly. 'Revenge doesn't make you feel better. It doesn't bring back the people you loved.' Gavon's lifeless face appeared in her mind and she pushed it away.

'But…' She took in the refugees milling aimlessly around on the lower deck. She indicated the pall of smoke from fires still smouldering in the Slavemasters' obliterated mansions along the waterfront. 'What if all this was for nothing? We're too late to stop Hassan from taking the throne.'

Jarran gave an ironic smile. 'Since "this" involved freeing me, Mina, Kett, and Corin from slavery – along with thousands of others – I'm pretty sure it wasn't for nothing.'

Alere wrinkled her nose. 'You know what I mean: all the deaths...Gavon...' Unwanted tears pricked at her eyelids and her throat closed. 'Ah, jiche.'

'It is alright to grieve, you know,' he said.

'No! It's not. At least, not yet. I have to figure out what to do now. Rafi says we should still get there as fast as we can. Then you can be around as the better, saner choice once the other Juns realise what a madman Hassan is. But what if that's taking you straight into a trap?'

'What do your other messages say?' He touched the papers still fisted in her left hand. 'They are later-dated. Perhaps they'll shed some light.'

She opened Yasmin's and skimmed the contents, her heart stuttering as she read it again in disbelief.

'She's insane!'

CHAPTER FIVE

ALERE

'Who's insane, Yasmin?' Jarran craned his neck, trying to read over Alere's shoulder. 'I've always thought her quite reasonable. Calmer than Rafi. What's she done?'

'We've only been gone, what…' Alere did a quick count '…a bit over two weeks and she's had the Miner House mining beneath the castle and the Trades House churning out swords and pikes. She's arming Rafi's junren. Evidently her Jun Third, Dal Lee-Hay, has routed the raiders attacking the outer villages around Shanzhai. So she's put him in charge of the army and is leading them to Madina.'

'Why? They won't arrive in time to stop Hassan. What's the point?'

'I have no idea, she just says "it" is unacceptable and she won't allow it. She's clearly pretty angry about something. Hassan taking the throne maybe? Let me read the Xintou House note.' Alere broke the seal and pored over the contents.

It was written in an elegant, flowing script she found familiar, but couldn't place, and still contained no sender-identity mark. But it was signed. The signature and first few lines were enough to weaken Alere's knees and she grabbed at the railing for support.

'What is it?' Jarran's grip on her elbow made her jerk away reactively, and stiffened her knees.

She paced a few steps further along the rail, reading the rest in privacy. She pressed cold fingers to her heated cheek and stared at the curling writing in blank horror.

'I don't know whether to believe this.'

'Why not?'

She tapped the signature. 'It's signed by Tali Edwards. She's just a senior student. A year behind me.'

'So?' Jarran's brows pulled together.

'She's Celia Edwards's daughter. The Xintou Bonded to Radan Zah-Hill. The woman I killed at Shanzhai.'

'Ah.' Jarran's frown deepened. 'So you're not sure if she's reporting correctly?'

'No. But what she says ties in with Yasmin's message. And she did try to warn me about her mother before I left for the Alcazar.'

'So, what does it say?'

She swallowed. 'If this is true, then Hassan has taken the city. His coronation as First is slated for the Ninth of Yiyue. Eight days from now.'

Jarran stilled, his hands clenching. 'My daughters?'

'There's worse.' Alere's hand trembled. 'Nasra Connor has arrived with him. She's replaced Mistress Li as Xintou House Mistress. She's confined my House sisters to their rooms. Mistress Li has been put into the Alcazar cells. Along with Rafi, Petar Ma-Safra, his wife Leah, and your daughters. Your kin-brother, Dirat, has been beheaded in the market square before the Alcazar.' She re-read the paper, slowing at the most unbelievable part. 'And Nasra has executed Jilla, Hassan's Xintou. And ten senior xintou of the House, as well as some of the students who resisted her.'

Jarran swore, long and eloquently. He gripped the railing until his fingers whitened, and kicked savagely at the timber deck. 'I'll kill her, myself.'

'Get in line,' Alere said.

He smiled thinly. 'At lease we know why the message is from a student.'

'Maybe,' she said. 'It could still be a trap. But, until I get word otherwise, I assume it's true. We must get to Madina before the Ninth. No matter what the cost. Even if it means leaving Mina behind somewhere safe, along the way.'

'What? No! Why?'

She fought against the trembling in her knees, the tears constricting her throat, and the anger pounding in her blood. 'Nasra's called for us to give ourselves up. If we don't, she's going to execute all the prisoners, in front of a crowd of thousands, at the coronation. Including your daughters and my father.'

She looked at Jarran. He stared bleakly back, then nodded.

Alere called one of the crewmen herding refugees around the lower deck. 'Tell Dalor to cast off. Now.'

CORIN

Liu Gray, when Corin finally found him, lounged at his ease in the blue salon, with his feet on a low table and a glass of dark purple wine twirling in his long fingers. He raised it to Corin.

'I'll give him this: Shah Jahil does know his wines. Wouldn't you agree?' He sniffed and held the glass up. The reddish afternoon light streaming in through the window changed the wine to blood. 'Care for some?'

Corin swallowed, nauseated by the thought. 'No, thanks. What I would like is information.'

'Ah!' Liu dropped his feet to the floor and stood, his bony, awkward frame made less so by an elegant black silk robe. He smoothed back his short, greying hair and smiled slyly, deepening the age lines around his eyes and mouth. '*That*, my friend, can be far more expensive, in many ways. What do you need to know?'

'Where are Alere and Saric?' Corin sat and leaned forward, pinning Liu with a strait stare. Most of the fun in the spy industry was in outthinking other spies, but he wasn't in the mood for the dance right now. As the leader of an extensive spy network in Chengdu, Liu had spent the last forty years playing the game. Corin didn't trust the man. Admire, yes. Trust, no.

Liu spread his hands, his thin face showing nothing but entirely unbelievable innocence. 'Alere, as I'm sure you know by now, is on Dalor Khan's vessel. She's headed for the other side of the Kabir and doing what she does best – stirring trouble.' He shrugged. 'Saric? He's a free spirit. He and his young friend, Wei, go where they will. I haven't seen him since yesterday.'

Corin waited in silent ill-humour. He'd been in the deception business too long not to recognise when he was being strung along.

The assassin-spymaster downed the last of his wine. 'You're no fun today, are you? Very well. But, before I tell you of local events, let me tell you what's been happening in Madina in your absence. Oh.' He pointed to a pair of leather boots sitting on a low table nearby. 'And the boots you asked for have arrived. Anything else you need before you go?'

'No. Tell me the flitter news.' Corin collected the boots and examined them as he listened in growing dismay to Liu's account. When Liu finished, Corin sucked a long breath and rubbed at the back of his neck.

'Khara! We have to catch up with Alere. Don't suppose you have a flitter big enough to fly people?'

Liu smiled. 'I hear the tribesmen east of the river are trying to tame wyverns to ride on. There aren't too many successes, yet. Several deaths.'

Corin rolled his eyes. 'What was Alere thinking, telling the Selb to form an army?'

'She couldn't think of another way to stop them hounding her, apparently' Liu said dryly. He rose and bowed. 'Let me know if I can assist.'

Corin rose, paused, and added, 'Actually, yes, there is something else.' He pointed at the silver-metal double-bladed axe pendant Liu wore around his neck. 'That's a Selb thing, isn't it?'

Liu fingered it, one brow raised. 'Indeed. Honorary, in my case. Because I've helped many of their children escape slavery. Why?'

Corin leaned forward. 'If we're quick, we'll get to Madina ahead of Alere. And the Selb waiting for her will be more likely to trust someone wearing that.'

The spymaster chuckled and dragged the leather thong over his head. 'Let me fill you in on a few bits of Selb etiquette, then.'

'Kett!' Corin flung the door to Alere's room open and strode in. They needed to move. Now.

The weishi still sat on the couch, steadily reading the last few pages of the Koh-Lin journal. Tiny bits of gold silk dusted the floor around him like expensive dandruff. He dragged his attention from the page.

'Something happen?' His tone was mild.

'Yes.' Corin grabbed Kett's travel bag and randomly jammed Kett's personal items into it.

Kett rose from the couch, tucked the book into his shirt and calmly took the bag. 'What?' He began to pack his own things somewhat more methodically.

Corin sat, threw off the house slippers he'd been wearing since the Wushi Games and dragged on his new boots. 'Rafi's been imprisoned in the Alcazar. Hassan's taken Madina without a fight and declared himself Jun First with a coronation scheduled for Thalatha the Ninth.'

'We expected that might happen. Rafi is a fool for staying in the city when he couldn't raise any support. What else?'

'According to Liu...' Corin blew a thick breath '...Mistress Li, Petar and Leah Ma-Safra, along with Jarran's daughters, are also imprisoned. And Nasra Connor has taken over Xintou House! She's brought in new girls no one has ever seen, all with xintou powers. And she's executed all of the senior Xintou, including Hassan's.'

Kett absently stroked a folded bamboo-cloth shirt. Then he placed it into the bag and continued packing; until Corin was about ready to shake a response out of him. Finally, Kett slung his horsebow and quiver across his back, an expression on his face that spoke ill of anyone getting in his way.

Corin did it anyway. 'I recognise that look. What do you know?'

'Nothing for certain.' The weishi held up a hand. 'But Nasra must intend to Bond Rohne as Xintou to Hassan. Then she'll have the power to run both Xintou House and the Jundom. Rohne knows about the iron under Shanzhai. Which means Nasra will know as soon as he gets within thought-range of Madina. The first thing Nasra will do is hold Rafi hostage for Alere and Yasmin's compliance, and Jarran's daughters for his. The second thing she'll do, once she has contained Alere and Jarran, is declare war on Shanzhai.'

He stopped, gazing out the window. 'If Alere gets to Madina before we do — and doesn't know what's happened — she'll be taken captive the minute she walks through the gates. Then Rafi will be redundant. Nasra will kill him and hold Alere to ransom in exchange for me.'

'You?' Corin blurted. That leap of logic was too lateral to follow. 'Why would she care about you? When she met you none of your companions knew who you were. I assume you were warding so she couldn't have picked it from your mind. And Rohne left Shanzhai before you told any of us.'

'True,' Kett said. 'But I had a feeling she knew me. Just something in the way she looked at me. She would have seen me as a child, in the Alcazar, when she was Xintou to Ma-Safra. She obviously didn't see any benefit to revealing it when we met in Jada Marin-kin's nomad camp. Now, she has to eliminate all the possible challengers to Hassan's claim.'

He took a step toward the door, halting when Corin grabbed his arm.

'There's more.' Corin grimaced. 'Alere has made an alliance with the Selb leadership of Chengdu. Those that are left, anyway. Most have already gone. Apparently, the remaining ones are forming an army to march on Madina in her name. They've decided she and Mina are some sort of mystics predicted to free the slaves and lead the Selb to victory over the unrighteous. They're declaring it's something called the time of Erheyi. I have no idea what that means, but it sounds like something they're taking very seriously.'

Kett's hand moved to his shirt front. He aborted the motion and allowed his arm to fall back to his side, remaining impassive.

'All the more reason to get there fast.'

Losing patience, Corin tightened his grip on Kett's arm even when the muscles beneath his fingers bunched.

'You're hiding something.' Corin kept his tone reasonable, but anger stirred hot in his guts now. 'If we're to work together you can't keep important things from me.'

Kett searched his face for something. Apparently satisfied, he broke free of Corin's hold.

'Is there anything special about these new xintou Nasra brought with her?'

The question was so unexpected and so insightful that, for a moment, Coin could only gape.

'Yes, how did you know? They're all twins. Identical. Eleven sets aged between fifteen and nineteen. Why?'

The weishi stared steadily at him. 'Erheyi,' he said, 'I've heard that word a few times recently.' He touched the book's flat outline. 'It's mentioned in this journal but only glancingly. As a Seeing by Kya Edwards with no mention of when or what it means.'

'But if it's five hundred years old, then it can't be related, can it?'

'Perhaps not,' Kett replied. 'But remember, after that alley-fight against Hallon's mharebi, when we were taken to see Liu? Alere used the yanstones to Read Shasa and Liu. Just before she collapsed, she said *erheyi*.'

'And?' Corin prompted.

'In old Mandrin it means something like "two in one". Loosely,' Kett elaborated, 'it could be interpreted as meaning twins.'

'So? What does *that* signify? How do the Selb's "time of Erheyi", Nasra's twins, and Alere and Mina all tie together?'

'I'm not sure. I recall Mina mentioning Hassan Wen-Gates had several sets of twins on his estates, though. Clearly, he and Nasra have been working together a long time. Hiding them. Preparing for this day. I also think we need to move. Now.' He headed for the door.

'How?' When Kett didn't respond, Corin barred his path. 'We have no transport once we're on the other side of the river. With the refugees on the road to Madina, everything will be spoken for. So, how?'

'You go speak to Shah Jahil about borrowing his chuan. Find out how far it can take us upstream before the spring flood current's too strong. Leave the rest to me.'

He pushed past Corin who, with a growl of frustration, asked, 'Where are you going?'

Looking back over his shoulder, Kett said, 'I think it's time I called in some favours.'

He vanished, leaving Corin to vent his frustrations with a well-aimed wineglass against a wall.

ALERE

'Here, drink this.' Alere held out a willowbark infusion and guided it to Mina's mouth as her sister groaned and pushed onto her elbow. Hopefully Mina would understand why she'd been dosed with istilqa and wouldn't be too angry.

'My head!' Mina gagged but managed to swallow the bitter liquid. She squinted against the low mel-oil lamplight. 'Where are we? I'm supposed to be in the Shah's palace. I've got so much work to do. Healer House is swamped with all the wounded from the slave revolution riots.' She tried to sit up, only to sag back with a groan and a hand to her forehead.

'Why did you take my bracelet?' Mina squinted at her own wrist and at Alere's, on which an iron and yanstone bracelet glittered, gathering in the mel-oil lamp's warm golden light.

'Sorry.' Alere stripped off both bracelets and offered them to her sister.

With the necklace, linked to Rafi's bracelet, around her hips, she didn't need them. She'd taken them from Mina's wrists as she slept in the palace, thinking it would prevent Mina from tracking her when she left.

Mina accepted the bracelets, running her thumb over the stones. She gasped, sitting up so fast she cracked her head on the underside of the bunk above. Rubbing her skull, she grimaced and, with a shudder, dropped the jewels to the bed.

'You drugged me and told me to stay in Chengdu! How could you do that?'

'How…?' Alere stopped. The yanstones. They must have cleared Mina's istilqa headache. How interesting. It was the first indication that Mina might be able to use the stones' healing powers.

Mina still waited, expecting an answer, her mouth set.

'I'm sorry.' Alere fought the urge to defend herself. Her sister had every right to be annoyed. Gouri Jarran. This trip would be much simpler with just the two of them. 'I just thought—'

'I know exactly what you were thinking, Alli.' Mina folded her arms. She glanced at the bracelets. 'I'm beginning to hate those things. When I wear them, I can hear everything you're thinking. Plus, I feel like…' She frowned. 'Like someone else is in my mind with me, listening. Someone other than you, I mean.' She hugged herself. 'It reminds me of Rohne controlling me, like a puppet, in Hallon's house. It's horrible.'

Alere reviewed her own experiences. Using the stones did almost feel as though a third party observed her. And yet, not quite. Unable to pin the feeling down, she pushed it aside for later contemplation.

She tucked the bracelets into a pocket. 'I'll hang onto them, then. They're useful and easier to use all the time. Given you don't have any weapons-training, you should learn to use the xintou skills, Mina.'

Her sister pressed her lips together. 'I don't *want* any weapons skills or xintou abilities. I'm a small-town healer. I took an oath to save lives, not take them. You seem to forget that every time you drag me into something like this.' She jabbed a finger at the cabin floor.

'Hey, this is Jarran's doing, not mine. I wanted to leave you at the palace, with Corin and Kett. Jarran wouldn't let me.'

'I *knew* it!' Mina's delicate skin flushed. 'I told him you'd try and leave me behind.'

'Hang on.' Alere stood and paced the tiny room twice. 'You just said I dragged you into things. You can't jiche-well complain about that *and* about being left behind. I was trying to protect you. I know you don't want to be part of the bloodshed that seems to follow me around….' She paused as suppressed grief rose in her throat and threatened to strangle speech. 'Gaisi! *I* don't want to be part of it either…'

Unable to continue, she turned her back. Covering her mouth, she swallowed hard in an effort to hold herself together.

The bed creaked and Mina's gentle hands pushed against her shoulders. Alere turned, reluctantly. Tears shimmered in Mina's eyes and she stroked Alere's hair back with heartwrenching tenderness.

'I'm sorry, Alli. That was unfair of me. I know it's been far worse for you.' She caught Alere into a hug. 'I don't mean to be so hard on you.' She sniffed. 'I should be thanking you for saving me from slavery. I know what you…what all of you…went through to set us free.'

Alere averted her face. 'Yes, but if I hadn't pushed you away in Shanzhai, you wouldn't have even *been* on the same chuan as Jarran and wouldn't have been kidnapped in the first place.'

'Oh, Alli.' Mina pulled her down onto the bed again. 'You must stop blaming yourself for everything. I decided to leave Shanzhai. I'm a woman grown. Stop thinking you have control over me – or anyone, for that matter.' Pursing her lips, she added, 'Unless you're so insecure or so stupid that you believe you actually *should* control everyone?'

Stung, Alere held back a hot reply and ground her teeth.

Mina raised one brow. 'I know you're not stupid.'

'So, I'm insecure?'

Her sister gave a small shrug. 'We all are, to some degree. You've spent your whole life believing you should be a xintou. That you were born wrong. You've tried to make up for it by excelling in everything else. By pushing everyone away who would get close to you.' She touched Alere's arm. 'But control's impossible. As is perfection. And absolute freedom. We're humans. Imperfect, stupid, tied to the people we care about.'

'No!' Cut to the core, Alere stood again, needing to put some distance between them. She allowed the yanstones clasped around her hips to siphon the discomfort away. Easier than getting into an argument.

Cool again, she opened the door. 'Jarran's on deck if you want to see him. I've got to talk with Dalor about getting some messages away. I'll see you at dinner. Dalor has invited us to his table.'

'Alli, please…'

She ignored her sister and pushed through the crowded corridor outside, into the clearer air abovedecks.

Several hours later, driven abovestairs once again, Alere rested her elbows on the upper deck railing and stared south, into the future, across the moonlit river. The last carmine streaks of sunlight dusted the western sky, rapidly fading to purple. Below her feet, the regular slap-slap of small waves made a soothing rhythm against the hull. The breeze stroked her skin with cold fingers.

Luna-Yi, solitary and red, rode high in the darkening sky, its path across the water turning the river to blood. Overhead, leathery wings flapped and a shadow passed across the face of the moon. The wailing cry of a wyvern on its final hunt for the day, drifted down. Not a true dragon of lore, but the largest reptile-bird on Kalima.

Silver-furred and capable of taking down a xiang, the huge lizards Dalor Khan intended to hire to tow the *Kuailong* back up to Madina. The wyvern soared closer, its wingspan longer than the *Kuailong,* its wedge-shaped head bearing a jaw full of teeth as long as Alere's arm.

She froze, watching its shadowy silhouette blot out the early stars.

She'd left her sword and dagger, yanstones, and alzin armour in the cabin so as not to incite greed in the refugees aboard. Perhaps that had been a bad idea. But the creature gave one last, mournful cry and glided east and out of sight. Alere pulled her cloak close and shivered, more because of the images in her mind than the external temperature.

The decks of Dalor's chuan were empty, with only a night crewman strolling the aft deck. Shifting sandbanks in this part of the river meant Dalor had to anchor for the night and that meant a few hours of solitude as passengers and crew bedded down.

Alere had come to regret the decision to transport the refugees. She was used to sharing the *Kuailong* with only a few people: her friends and a small, unobtrusive, crew. The presence of thirty strangers, along with the twenty crew needed to row the vessel upstream against the current, made it a claustrophobic, uncomfortable trip.

Even her cabin was not the shelter and solitude it had been on the way to Melcor. Mina slept there now. Woken by Mina's nightmares and afraid of her own, Alere dared not sleep. So she'd come to the upper deck and tried not to think about sparring here with Gavon, Kett and Corin. Or about the insanity of what she was doing. Or about who was missing from her life.

But the sharp pain of absence wouldn't go. She missed all three men more than she believed possible. Kett's steady support. Corin's joyous spark of life. Gavon's gruff, demanding intensity. More than anything, she regretted leaving Kett behind. His strength, his patience, his unwavering love. Leaving him had been the act of a frightened child, not a grown woman.

Hopefully he would forgive her – if she survived this.

Now, for the first time, she was alone. With no-one to guide, mentor or protect her. Responsible for returning the most important man in the whole of Kalima to Madina and the Alcazar throne.

What made her think she could do it? After all, she would be taking him into a city overrun by an enemy army and controlled by two of the strongest xintou she'd ever encountered. Was she mad to think taking Jarran back to Madina was the right thing to do? He was, after all, a kin-child, not a full-blood of the previous Jun First. He'd never been trained as Jun-Heir. How could he possibly quell a rebellion and unite the Jundom?

And what of this despotic tyrant predicted by both Celia and Valera? Both Xintou women had foreseen the coming of someone powerful. Someone who could destroy all Alere cared for, including Xintou House. Was it Rohne? Or Nasra? It must be one of them.

Alere dropped her head into her hands. Who was supposed to deal with them? What could *she* do? How did she handle someone who was worse than Ven Zah-Hill – a sadistic madman – and worse than Hallon Nasim, a man with thirty years experience in enslaving his fellow humans?

Admittedly, she'd killed Ven and Hallon. But they were both contest of physical combat – her area of expertise. Against xintou, she had only trained in theory. What did she know about defeating them on a mental level? She had barely survived Celia Edwards' attack. And had killed the Xintou with a knife. Nasra and Rohne would never let her anywhere close with a weapon.

They also had command of Hassan's army.

The Selb, should they even live up to their promise to help Jarran, were a mere rabble of extremists following some half-baked religious ideal she didn't understand, let alone agree with. Religion had been left behind on Old Earth seven hundred years before when the colonists had settled on Kalima seeking a simpler, peaceful existence.

Yet somehow, she now led a mob of religious fanatics into her own capital city, on a campaign neither simple, nor peaceful. Enlisting the Selb seemed like madness in retrospect. But it was done and she needed to get on with things. After all, there was little danger until they neared Madina and encountered Hassan's junren. That gave her time to think of an alternative to war.

Perhaps she could contract Weishi House. Pay xiongshou-assassins to kill Hassan, Rohne and Nasra. Though, as head of Xintou House, Nasra now had to approve any high-level political assassinations. Alere smiled at the irony.

Footsteps sounded on the bamboo deck behind her. She stilled. Four people…no five; the fifth more light-footed than the others. Not xiongshou or she wouldn't have heard them at all. She reached for her weapons, but she'd left them and the yanstones tucked into the storage lockbox in her cabin. She wore only bamboo-cloth tunic and trous, and a cloak. Little enough protection against a blade. Stupid.

Forcing herself to relax, she turned. Perhaps her instincts lied, and they were also just insomniacs.

'Gentlemen,' she said quietly, assessing them. She unclipped her cloak and held it in her right hand.

Five men. One in front, the other four spread out to attack from four vectors. Dressed in worn clothing, but with sturdy boots, they wore bronze and leather vests beneath rough woollen jackets. Dalor had decreed no weapons on board with the refugees. It seemed his

searches missed some. Each man carried a small, bronze kris-dagger.
The sinuous blades gleamed in the bloody moonlight.

CHAPTER SIX

ALERE

Alere drew a deep breath and let go of her purely physical reactions: thudding heart, sick-twisting stomach, shaking hands. She needed to overcome the adrenalin in her blood to view the situation clearly. Five men, five weapons, and limited space to move about. The deck was bounded by water on three sides and made slippery by spray. What would Gavon's advice be?

It was not hard to guess. He would say: *This is not yer weishi dojo, boyo. Let all that honour and duty feihua go in a real fight or it'll get ye killed.*

The smallest man, the one in the lead and lightest on his feet, jerked his chin. 'You're her. The Jun-Heir who ended the Games.' His sharp features contorted into a sneer. 'You're nothing much, are you? How'd a pretty little thing like you beat someone like Hallon Nasim? Had some help, did you?'

He swaggered closer, throwing his shoulders back. His gaze slid over her again and he licked his lips. 'Maybe I should teach you a lesson about interfering where you're not wanted, girl.' He fumbled with his belt-buckle. 'I think I'd enjoy that.'

The other four muttered encouragement, egging him on in a classic display of group male bravado. Quashing anger, Alere weighed the possible responses, trying to judge what drove them. Were they paid mercenaries or just arrogant hundans? If she called it incorrectly the next few minutes could be...messy. The weishi code began with: *avoid the falling rock.* The best defence was to avoid fights, if possible.

She'd never been great at that. Gavon had sneered at it as unrealistic.

But now, unarmed and outnumbered, it seemed like a good idea.

Failing that, the second code was: *one cut, one life*. But, after the Wushi Games' bloodletting and this morning's fight, she found herself reluctant to kill.

Holding up her weaponless hands – the cloak still in one – she edged sideways, lining them up so all five couldn't attack at once. She focussed on the leader's hands and relaxed to catch peripheral actions.

'I can see you're trying to make me angry,' she said. 'Can I ask why? I don't want to fight you.'

His mouth fell open, but his confusion didn't last.

'C'mon boys.' He shifted his weight. 'Let's show the lady why we're here.'

His grip on the kris tightened. They all took a step toward her, knives glinting red.

Right.

Two knives arced at her. She flung her cloak over one man's head. The second knife arm she blocked with her forearm. Her right hand gripped the back of his elbow and yanked it forward. The arm levered and gave. The sickening snap of tendons and ligaments crackled loud in the still night air. An unholy shriek of pain burst from his lips. The knife dropped to clatter on the timber.

Alere let his arm fall and clinched his neck in a sleeper hold. With his body interposed between her and his friends, she dragged him to the gunwale. The others hesitated. Her attacker whimpered and coughed. He grabbed at his mangled arm and uttered little cries of pain each time she applied pressure to his neck.

'Tell them to put their weapons down or I will throw you over the side right now,' she said.

The four exchanged looks and shrugged, advancing. Alere swore and thrust her prisoner over the gunwale. He screamed and splashed into the river.

She moved across the deck, lining them up again. The first thrust his kris. Alere spun out of the way and lashed a kick at his knee. A splintering crack, and he collapsed, clutching the twisted leg. The other three spread out but their steps were slower now.

'I'll give you another chance,' she said. 'Weapons down.'

All three rushed. She waited until the last second then dodged aside, grabbed an outstretched arm and wrenched. The shoulder dislocated with a pop and he fell, sliding across the wet deck, whimpering.

The other two skidded to a halt. One threw his knife down and raised his hands. The other glanced first at her, then at the knife he held. He opened his mouth. Whatever he'd been about to say ended in a gasp. He sank to his knees and sagged onto his stomach. Blood speckled the timber dark as he coughed.

A black shuriken protruded from his neck and two knives from his back.

Alere gaped then snapped her mouth shut. She pointed at the unarmed man. 'You, over the side. If you're lucky you'll make it back to Chengdu by dawn, before the golden salamanders start hunting.'

When he protested, another shuriken thunked into the deck by his feet. He choked on a scream, dived for the gunwale and rolled over.

The lower deck guard swarmed up the ladder-stairs. After one look at the body on the deck, and the two injured men, he relaxed. He was one of the original crew from Shanzhai.

'Were they bothering you, shunu?' He peered over the side at the thrashing swimmers.

'A little,' she admitted. 'Let them swim home.' She pointed to the one with knives in his back. 'If he's still alive, take him to your healer, Lars. There might be another two along in a minute.'

'Yes, shunu.' The crewman yanked out the blades and hoisted the man over his shoulder, disappearing belowdecks.

'Now.' Alere crouched by the man with the dislocated knee. 'Perhaps you'd like to tell me who sent you. If you don't, I'll drop you overboard. If you do, I'll let the healer help you. Deal?'

Her attacker nodded, whimpering again. 'Three days ago. The xiongshou…of Chengdu Weishi House, got a contract for…you from someone in Madina.' The words came out in a rush, interspersed with gasps. 'The House refused, so it came to us, instead. We do the jobs they don't want. I don't know who's paying, I promise. We were just supposed to kill you if you came out of the Games alive.

'And?' she prompted. There had to be more.

'They really want you dead, shunu. The fee is two hundred tiebe.'

'Jiche!' Alere fought for control, reaching for the yanstones, but they were too far away. Panic threatened to overwhelm her. She fought to calm her heart and allow her mind to absorb the idea.

Two hundred iron coins was a fortune only a few could afford: either Hassan, or Nasra. Why, though? Nasra couldn't possibly be afraid. She couldn't yet know about Alere's xintou powers. Even if she did, hers far outweighed Alere's. Maybe Rohne? When Rohne got access to the Zah-Hill treasures – which were certain to contain yanstones – his powers might outstrip even his mother's.

No, the contract couldn't be from Rohne. Three days ago he'd only just left Chengdu and couldn't have sent a message from Madina.

Alere shook herself. It didn't matter who'd paid. If news of this contract spread to all the centres between Chengdu and Madina, every gouri hired killer would be on the lookout for her.

The deckhand reappeared. She didn't want yet another death on her conscience so she passed her would-be assassins over to him for Lars' care.

She waited until they were belowdecks then folded her arms and glared into the moon-shadowed corners of the upper deck. 'You can come out now, Saric.' A long silence followed. Alere tapped her foot. 'Now!'

Two small shadows detached themselves from beside a storage-box and emerged into the moonlight. The curling ends of Saric's untamed, white-blonde hair stuck out from beneath a dark scarf. His face was darkened with some sort of makeup until only his grey-green eyes and white teeth were visible. He wore the mottled black-grey clothing used by xiongshou to obscure their outline in the shadows. Similarly disguised, his best friend, Wei, shuffled her feet and gave Alere a sheepish little shrug. Saric collected his scattered weapons, wiping and stowing them away in his clothing.

'How did you two get on board?' Alere held up a hand as Saric opened his mouth. 'No, you know what, that's not important. You can't come with me. You'll have to catch the next chuan back to Chengdu. Saric, Corin will be worried sick about you. Did you even leave him a message?'

The boy curled a lip and lifted one shoulder. 'I doubt he'll notice I'm gone. He's too busy playing advisor to the Shah to even care where I've been the last couple of days.'

Quashing her first instinct to defend Corin, Alere paused. This was a moment to tread warily. Saric was just ten. Alere vividly remembered being alone and unwanted at that age. At ten she'd been thrust into Xintou House, the only student there without telepathic skills; a pariah amongst goddesses, frightened and angry at everyone.

For Saric it must be even worse. He'd just lost his mother; murdered in front of him. Yes, Shasa had left her son's upbringing to Liu's cadre of other slave-got child thieves and spies, but she was still Saric's mother. He was just transferring anger at her death onto the next nearest target: his long-absent father.

Alere collected her cloak, wrapped herself up and sank onto the deck. Sitting cross-legged on the cold, damp timbers gave her a little time to think. How did she handle this?

'He's been too busy for you and you're angry at him?' She reflected back Saric's words and emotion. A technique, taught in Jaioji House, to diffuse potential arguments between jiaoji and client. A longterm jiaoji-client relationship was little different from a marriage, except that a jiaoji undertook years of training and preparation.

Saric spat over the gunwale and folded his arms. 'He doesn't care about me. All he cares about are the slaves and the jiche economy of Melcor. I snuck into the palace and listened to some of the meetings.' He screwed up his nose. 'It's all money and trade and the slaves and infra..infrastructure.'

'You feel like he cares more about money and the slaves than he does about you. You're missing Shasa and Corin doesn't seem to even notice you.' Alere patted the timber beside her.

Wei sank onto the deck, her long, dark hair slipping forward to hide half her face. A few seconds later, Saric joined her, crosslegged, elbows resting on bony knees, fingers fiddling with a shuriken. When he spoke again, his tone carried less anger and more hurt.

'I mean, you'd think he'd at least *ask* after me, wouldn't you?' His tone lacked its usual cockiness.

'What would you like him to do?' Alere leaned forward, copying Saric's pose.

The boy tucked the shuriken away in the dark folds of his clothing. 'I don't know. Just thought he'd be a bit interested in me, too. Thought he'd be here, going back to Madina with you and he'd left me behind.'

'Ah!' Alere lifted a finger. 'That one I can answer. It's my fault he's not here. He's still at the palace. He wouldn't have just left without telling you.'

Saric's eyes narrowed. 'Why's he still there? I thought the whole point of you coming here was to free your sister and the Jun-Heir and get him back to Madina. That's more important than fixing stupid trade agreements, isn't it?'

So, Alere once again explained her reasoning for drugging her two best friends and leaving them behind. It sounded more ridiculous each time she said it. When she finished, Saric and Wei burst into delighted giggles, clutching at their sides and each other. Alere covered her eyes briefly, then waited for them to finish.

'Oh…oh!' Saric wiped tears away. 'I wish I'd been there to see his face when he went under. I'm never going to let him live this down.'

'Well.' Alere stood and brushed herself off. 'He won't remember. He'll just be fixated on my Suggestion. You two should get yourselves back there tomorrow or he'll fret for not knowing where you are.'

Saric and Wei jumped to their feet. Saric raised his sharp chin and beamed at her. 'Nope,' he said. 'I'll send him a message. Without Corin and Kett you're going to need some weishi. We're it. We were sick of Chengdu, anyway.' He threw an arm around Wei's shoulders. 'Besides, Wei's always wanted to train at Madina Weishi House.'

Wei nodded, her large eyes sparkling in the moonlight.

'You can't stay,' Alere stated. 'I don't have a lot of money and we'll be riding hard. And now I'll have xiongshou on my heels the whole way. It's not a place for two ten-year olds.'

''Sclear you haven't spent much time on the streets in Chengdu. That's a normal day for us.' He gave a smug sniff. 'Besides, short of throwing us overboard, you can't stop us.'

'Don't tempt me. Hey.' Alere frowned at Wei. 'You didn't bring that gouri sky monkey, did you?'

The girl giggled. 'He hates water.'

Alere sighed in relief. Maybe, in the morning, she could prevail on Dalor to lock them away, but he wasn't returning to Chengdu so he'd only be able to hold them for a day at the most. She wouldn't put it past them to steal horses and come after her, out of sheer stubbornness.

This was madness. She couldn't be responsible for two small children, no matter how skilled they were. Corin would never forgive her if something happened to Saric. She reached again for the yanstones' gilded serenity to calm herself. Their absence wrenched at her gut. Her hands shook.

'Alere?'

Wei's small, cold fingers tucked into hers. Alere focussed on settling her heart and tried to ignore the sick flutter in her stomach. The stones weren't far away. She would hold them again in just a few minutes.

'I'm fine.' She squeezed Wei's hand. 'You're freezing. Have you two got a cabin?' When they shrugged their indifference, she tugged them to the ladder. 'Thought not. C'mon, you can share ours. Just don't kick in your sleep or you'll end up on the floor.'

Beside her, Saric snorted. 'Could be worse. Once I slept on a roof because it was the only place the three saafil kalbi that Bahad

Sinclar set on me couldn't get to. It rained, too. I'm glad you killed him. Sorry about Gavon, though. I liked him.'

Gritting her teeth, Alere clambered belowdecks and opened the cabin door. They found Mina already awake and shivering in the aftermath of a nightmare. A jumbled description of a forest, bandits, brains on fire, and a dying boy fell incomprehensibly from her lips. The children's presence distracted her. Alere recovered the yanstone necklace and held it. The iron settings bit into her skin but she didn't care. She sank into the silver-gilt, letting its embrace obliterate all that threatened her peace of mind.

Normally, she took the chain off to sleep as it dug into her skin. Tonight she hooked it around her neck, hoping morning would bring light into darkness.

'No!' Alere slapped a palm down on the map, the sound loud in Dalor's small cabin. Dust danced in the orange fingers of early morning light slivering through the still-closed shutters.

The cabin's other occupants stopped their arguing and looked at her. Jarran folded his arms. Mina smoothed her grey and white healer's robe in an unconscious, defensive gesture. Wei shrank in on herself, her dark eyes apprehensive, half-hidden behind her hair. Saric glared back at Alere, jaw jutting and thin shoulders set for a fight.

Alere smoothed the map.

'Here's how this works.' She lowered her voice. 'This is not a democracy. I'm running this trip. It's my job to get Jarran safely to Madina and this pointless arguing is only going to make it harder. I need to know that, when things go suilie – as they will…' she directed that at Saric '…I won't have to get into a debate before you'll do what I say.'

'Why?' Saric's question cut through the silence. The chuan jerked and rocked beneath their feet. The regular thud-thud of the oarmaster's drum directed the pull-and-sweep of the rowers belowdecks as they dragged the laden vessel upriver. Saric swayed with the motion, fiddling with a shuriken tucked into his belt.

Alere returned him a level stare. 'You've led your team in Chengdu. You know there needs to be a clear chain of command for this to work. If you don't like it, you're welcome to go back to Chengdu.' She ignored his outraged muttering and pointed to the map. 'Dalor is docking in Dalcin in about an hour. We have horses and supplies pre-arranged to take us south along the main route to Madina.' She traced the road.

'As I said, the biggest problem I forsee is here.' She tapped the dot representing Asadia, a major centre about three days hard ride upriver, just inside the Mamlakahn border. 'This is the Han-Asad family's seat of power and their lands straddle our route. If we go through, there's no way of avoiding an encounter with their border patrol.'

'So what?' Saric shrugged. 'You've all got false papers Liu gave you a couple of days ago. Wei and I can get some in Dalcin.'

'Hanna,' Mina whispered. 'You said Rafi sent Hanna back to her brother's estates after the battle in Shanzhai. He's Jun Third Kennor Han-Asad. She went to Asadia.'

'Exactly,' Alere replied. 'If she caught us, she'd see that Rafi has deceived the Juns by presenting me as Lianna. She'd also have to be blind and stupid not to realise we'd used our being twins to trick her son, Ven, into madness. If that happens, she'll use the Han-Asad weishi – and whatever junren are left in Asadia – to side with Hassan just to spite Rafi.'

'But why does it matter if you're not Lianna Koh-Lin?' Saric asked. 'Who cares? You're still Rafi's daughter and heir. You were older than her anyway, weren't you?'

'Yes,' Jarran put in, scratching at his stubbled chin. 'But Lianna was Rafi's full-blood heir. She died half a year ago. Because of that, the world would think Rafi orchestrated Ven Zah-Hill's death – and the rescindment of the kin-child laws – just to make Alere his new Jun-Heir.' He gave Alere a significant look and pointed at the steel pommel of her dagger. 'After all, he can't tell them the real reason Ven was there. The majority of Juns would turn against Rafi and support Hassan. They're already afraid Rafi has too much power. Given the chance to leave him without an heir, they'd take it.'

'Right again.' Alere sighed. 'We have to avoid Hanna. Plus, she's already whipping up resentment about Rafi overturning the kin-child laws. The last message from Madina said riots are centred in Asadia and gathering momentum. So, we go around Asadia. Which leaves either across the river to the west, or southeast around the end of the Beifang Ranges. Either way adds at least two or three days to the trip and there are dangers in both directions.'

Jarran's large finger landed on the map's western portion. 'This way takes us through Zah-Hill controlled lands. The further we are from that family's estates the happier I would be. At least until I'm officially Jun First. It'll be the slower route, too. More refugees. We need to get to Madina fast. My daughters' lives are at stake and that's more important than anything else.'

'Agreed.' Alere tapped the paper again. 'Which leaves southeast around the Beifangs. We'll be going through the edge of the Makaan drylands. But, as long as we're well stocked with water and food, we should be alright. It just means we won't have a change of horses, which will slow us down.'

Overhead, Dalor's crew shouted to one another. The chuan's timbers creaked as the helmsman changed direction, angling across the current. Wei staggered. Saric caught her up, holding her against his side until the *Kuailong* steadied.

Stepping free of his hold, Wei stroked a grimy fingertip over a tiny village, marked as Beizhai, at the mountain range's southeastern foothills. Her hair's uneven ends trailed across the map.

'My mother was from there, before she was taken by the slavers.' She raised hopeful eyes. 'Maybe some people will still remember her.'

Mina put an arm around the girl and hugged her close. 'I'm sure they will, Wei.'

Saric scowled at his friend, but she didn't see. He folded his arms and wandered restlessly away from the table and back again. Alere gripped his shoulder. He jerked free. His unwarded Outer thoughts revealed much. He worried about losing Wei if she found her people. Hopefully Wei would never have to choose. Saric had few people left in the world he could depend on.

Alere allowed the yanstones to push aside the surge of pain that knifed through her throat at the thought of Gavon and Shasa's deaths. She needed to focus and blaming herself didn't help.

Getting Jarran to Madina depended entirely on her and, as she measured the distance between Dalcin and Madina, Alere's stomach sank. Getting there before the ninth might not be possible. But she had to try.

CHAPTER SEVEN

ALERE

Alere reviewed her inexperienced crew with misgivings. 'It'll be a tough ride. I've asked Dalor to give us any supplies he can spare. I doubt there'll be much left for sale in Dalcin. Saric, make sure you have a bedroll, two waterskins and spare clothes, but keep everything else to a minimum. Get what you need from Dalor's quartermaster. Meet on deck in an hour. Can you two ride?'

Saric lifted a shoulder. 'Depends on what you mean by ride. You don't get much chance to gallop in the city, but we've both been on the farms Liu runs. I prefer walking. Horses are too temperamental.'

Alere hid a smile. 'Right, well, if you double with us it will save the spare horses, anyway.'

They all headed for the door. At the last second, Alere called the two youngsters back and waved the others out, casually. When the door closed behind Mina, Alere waited until her footfalls died away.

'Just remember...' she murmured. Two serious young faces gave her their full attention and Alere swallowed against the next, portentous words. 'Once we're on land we're fair game for the xiongshou contractors. There could be contracts out on Jarran and Mina. I haven't told them. And I can't be everywhere at once. I will need your help. You've done xiongshou training with Liu. You know what you're looking for. We have to get Jarran to Madina. His two little girls are only a few years younger than you. They'll be executed if we can't release them before the coronation on the Ninth. Got it?'

Wei drew her self up straight and nodded vigorously. She produced a scrap of leather and tied back her long hair.

Determination hardened the angles of her pretty face. Saric eyed her thoughtfully for a few seconds, scrubbed at his scalp, then gave slow acquiescence. Wei dragged him out, whispering excitedly about acquiring more weapons.

Alere sank onto a chair. She had a sword, a bow and a couple of over-eager, reckless children to protect her sister and the most important man in Mamlakah from highly-trained assassins. She hadn't been able to keep Gavon – an experienced mharebi warrior – safe. How the diyu was she supposed to do this?

Gah! She buried her face in her hands. What was *wrong* with her? Why was she obsessing about Gavon? Yes, his death hurt, but surely he and Kett had taught her the transience of life? Weishi House had trained her in understanding of grief and survivor guilt and how to work through it. Why was releasing self-blame and letting him go so difficult?

Around her neck, the yanstones warmed, spreading syrupy heat beneath her skin and deep into muscles too long tensed with anxiety. Her shoulders relaxed. She sank into the stones' quietude and safety just for a little while. Uncertainty slid away, self-doubt vanished into the dark corners of her mind, banished by the gold-light of conviction and the guidance of truth. Her path was clear, she just needed the strength to stay on it.

CORIN

'You want us to go *where?*' Corin stared at Kett. 'You can't be serious.'

Cool ocean air drifted in through the open windows, fluttering the paper and bringing the scent of salt and rain. White clouds scudded low in the pale green sky, gathering on the horizon with a promise of storms to come. The cry of a sea-bird, faint and plaintive, echoed Corin's protest.

Kett smoothed the map spread on the table in the Shah's cabin, flattening out a wind-folded corner. 'You're the one who's always complaining I'm too serious. Now you're complaining I'm not. Make up your mind. It's the fastest route. You should know, you planned it. And we've lost half a day. We need the fastest option.'

Their preparations had taken longer than they'd hoped yesterday and the Shah's chuan, long in dry-dock, wasn't ready for the water until late in the evening. They'd shipped out at the first hint of dawn with the maximum number of rowers possible.

Now they made steady progress across the river and upstream, but it was slower than suited Corin. Sand and mudbanks made this part of the river treacherous and neither threats nor bribes to the chuanzhu produced any effect on the speed. The man simply ignored both.

'Yes.' Corin stabbed at the little red dot of Asadia. 'But there were supposed to be six of us. Two or three with xintou powers enough to prevent the border guard from recognising us.' He thrust his hands into his pockets and stalked around the luxurious cabin, kicking a green silk cushion to one side with unwonted vehemence. 'I'd also planned on going across country to avoid the border gate on the road, *and* going through the city at night without stopping except to change horses. What you're proposing is madness. If we go on the main road and stop in Asadia in broad daylight to change horses it's…insane.'

Kett straightened, ligaments crackling as he stretched. He scrubbed at his face and yawned. 'I agree, but I also can't see an alternative. Alere knows her limitations and those of her companions. Without us she doesn't have the manpower to fight her way out of a corner. She'll also be aware of the consequences of being captured and recognised. She won't risk riding straight through Hanna's territory. With Jarran to protect, she won't go west onto Zah-Hill land. That only leaves southeast. If we cut straight through Asadia, we can make up for lost time and get ahead of her.'

Corin laid a hand over the city. 'I get all that. I just think you're mad to risk being caught by Hanna's men.'

'No more than you are.'

'It's not my head she wants on a spike, my friend.' Corin clapped him on the shoulder. 'However, if you—'

A knock on the door cut him off and the chuan's cabin boy poked his head in.

'Sorry to interrupt, shenshi, but a flitter's come in from Chengdu.' He passed over a tight-rolled message. 'Marked urgent.'

Corin tilted the paper toward the window and read the tiny, cramped writing by the glittering morning light. After reading the message twice, Corin pinched the bridge of his nose. It had been a long night, half of which he'd spent with Liu's people, hunting for his wayward son. Around two am he'd given up, figuring that the kid didn't want to be found, and that Saric would be safe enough in Chengdu until the fuss in Madina was over.

He read the note again. He didn't need this – any of it.

'Bad news?' Kett asked.

'When is it good news these days?' Corin rubbed at the back of his neck. 'Hassan has declared martial law and shut Madina's gates to all leavers except local farmers. He's also preparing his army on the plains outside the southern gates. Which is where the Zah-Hill junren coming back from Shanzhai will have to arrive any day now.'

Kett nodded. 'He'll try to sway them to his side. But he has to be prepared, in case the junrens' leader, Jun Fourth Bren Gray-Saud, has violent objections to Hassan's crowning. After all, Bren has a semi-legitimate claim to the throne as well. But that can't be what made you groan. It wasn't unexpected.'

'No,' Corin agreed. 'My son has, apparently, stowed away on Dalor's chuan and was seen in Alere's company in Dalcin. I spent hours looking for him and he'd already left the city. Could've left a note!'

'Ah.' Kett smiled faintly. 'At least you know where he is. You're getting the hang of this parenting thing, by the way. You even sound like one.'

'Helpful. That's not the worst. Someone's taken out a large contract on Alere's life. Chengdu Weishi House turned it down, but others won't.'

Only Kett's utter stillness betrayed his strong reaction.

Corin gripped the man's shoulder. 'You know I'd ride a dozen horses to death if I thought we could catch her, Kett.' He pointed at the map. 'But with the lead she has, and with the roads clogged with refugees, and the fact that we'll be doing well to get a che-ma, let alone a decent riding horse, I think we have no chance of catching up. You're right. We'll go through Asadia.'

Kett's jaw worked and his hands curled into fists on the table. He nodded once but didn't reply.

'But there's one more thing you need to know,' Corin added. 'Hanna's been whipping up resentment against the reversal of the kin-child laws. The worst in Asadia. She's spreading dissent and my sources think she might be building an army to march on Madina.'

'She's going to make another bid for the throne – this time in her own right.' Kett thumped the table. 'I knew I should have killed her in Shanzhai. Jiangui! When I was seven I swore I'd protect kin-children and serve some kind of justice on everyone who carried out those gouri kin-child laws.'

'That's a long time to hold a grudge,' Corin said. 'And almost impossible, given that would mean killing Mistress Li, every Jun, every Bonded Xintou, and every Jun's Shangwei.'

Kett sent him a bleak smile. 'I never said it was a realistic goal, but it kept me going during the years when children were being murdered every day in my name. And you have no idea how many times I was tempted to kill Mistress Li when I lived in Xintou House.' He laughed bitterly. 'But I couldn't do it. Weishi ethics are about protecting people and she was an old woman.'

'I suspect you would have found it difficult, anyway,' Corin said. 'She's not exactly a defenceless old woman. Hanna, however… To be honest, I was surprised you let Alere talk you out of killing her when you had a sword at her throat.'

Kett smiled wryly. 'You, of all people, know how hard it is to ignore Alere when she looks at you like her whole world depends on your co-operation.'

'True. It would be like kicking a xiao-kitten.' Corin grinned. 'Unthinkable and possibly lethal. Look at it this way. With most of Hanna's trained junren still marching back from Shanzhai to Madina, what sort of army could she raise, really? Farmers and grandparents? Hardly a threat. And who would she name as Jun-Heir now that her son's dead?'

'Probably her niece, Farima.' Kett smoothed back his dark hair. 'Remember? Lianna Koh-Lin's friend? The one who sent her the poisoned sweets?'

'You think Farima might not be a dupe in this, after all?'

With a grimace, Kett scrubbed at his face. 'I don't know. There are too many factions and too many agendas. But…'

'But what?'

'No, never mind.' Kett straightened. 'I need to send some messages. I know someone in Asadia who might be…useful.'

'Me too.' Needing action to stave off his sense of helplessness, Corin sauntered to the door. 'I'm going to send Liu a reply now. Anything you want to add?'

'I'll come with you.' Kett stared again at the map on the table. 'Ask Liu to have someone watch for us in Asadia. We may need them. If there's a contract out on Alli then there may be one on you or me, and we won't be able to ask Weishi House in Asadia to help, as I'd hoped.'

They went, together, to the messenger-bird handler. The dark cabin was full of cages in all sizes and reeked sharply of bird-shit. The trained flitters squawked, their leathery wings rustling and claws scratching. The handler eyed Corin narrowly when he requested a short-flight animal trained for the Chengdu Shah's palace. He passed over a small, restless reptile with thin fur patterned in shades of green and black. It fixed a beady blue eye on Corin and shook its horn-crested head. Corin scrawled a note to Liu and slipped it into the tube on the beast's back. He left Kett to write his notes and went in search of lunch.

When he returned to their cabin, Corin found Kett once again engrossed in the Koh-Lin journal. Curled up on a padded window-seat, the man looked every inch the scholar. Had he even noticed Corin's entrance?

Before Corin even put a silent foot forward in his half-formed idea to test the weishi's awareness, Kett spoke without raising his head.

'The cabin boy brought lunch, if you want it.'

'Really? I'm sure he saw me eating in the galley.' He sniffed at the sweetened bellnutmeal. 'But those days in the slavepens made me value a meal.' He collected a spoon and pointed it at Kett. 'You are good, I'll give you that. How did you hear me?'

Kett glanced up. 'I spent the first eight years of my time in Weishi House training as xiongshou. Hearing someone sneak became second nature.'

'What made you switch to being weishi?'

'Partly a conflict of ethics.' He lowered the book. 'I didn't like the idea of killing people for money. I guess I wanted to protect people more than I wanted to serve justice on everyone who carried out the kin-child massacres.' He went back to reading and added, 'And partly because I grew too big to sneak effectively in small places.'

Corin laughed. 'Now *that* I believe.' He slouched into a chair nearby and lifted the spoon to his lips.

'Wait!' Kett leaned across and yanked the spoon from Corin's fingers.

'Hey!'

'You said the cabin boy saw you eat?' He dipped a fingertip into the nutmeal and touched it to his tongue, then spat. 'Something in it. Dusu, maybe. Hard to be sure with the sweet xun.'

Corin sniffed but could only smell sweet xun. 'You sure?'

'Absolutely.' He drew his sword and dagger. A floorboard creaked outside the cabin.

The door burst open and a masked, black-clad figure leapt in. Another dropped through the open window beside Corin and rolled into a crouch. Daggerblades flashed in each hand. Xiongshou. Gaisi! Corin threw the bowl of nutmeal at the woman's face. She ducked, giving him time to draw sword and dagger. Xiongshou relied on stealth and close weapons or blowdarts. They didn't carry swords. Could he use that?

She flipped a shuriken but he managed to duck. Her dagger thrust at his stomach. He parried and slid his blade up hers, toward her unprotected fingers. She snatched her hand away and lashed a kick at his knee. He leapt aside, grabbed a silk cushion and hurled it at her. He followed up with a cut to her neck. She batted the pillow aside and swayed away from the swordcut almost lazily.

She jumped at him, trying to get inside his guard. Corin sliced across her arm, leaving a scarlet line. She sucked a gasp, retreated and flipped a shuriken. Pain lanced through his arm. Gouri! She pulled out another of the throwing blades. Corin hooked a silk throw-rug on the tip of his sword and flicked it at her. It tangled the shuriken and her dagger. Before she could free herself, Corin drove his sword through the gleaming fabric and into her body.

He waited for the life to fade from her before he pulled it free. Only then did he look around. Kett was busily searching the body of the second xiongshou. Another woman. They always worked in pairs. Her neck was broken. Blood stained the left side of Kett's tunic.

Kett glanced up and nodded at the bloodied silk rug. 'A little flashy, but nicely done.'

'Find anything?' Corin plucked the shuriken from his arm and dropped it. He cleaned his steel blades and sheathed them, stepping over the body.

Kett fingered the braided black-and-gold ribbon tied around his victim's wrist. 'This indicates one of the *jijin* – elite xionshou. Yours doesn't have one, so mine was the senior partner. The gold means she's from the Asadia Weishi House.' He unfolded a sheet of bamboo paper. 'Jiangui. Kill order against me. From Madina House.'

'You? Madina, not Asadia? But you're a Madina weishi. Aren't there some sort of rules or codes about that?'

'It happens.' Kett frowned. 'But not often and not without very good cause. And I like to think Master Anh would give me the benefit of the doubt. Ah.' He flicked the paper with a finger. 'Signed by Master Zand – Anh's second in command. Unfortunate.'

'That's an understatement. How did they find us?'

He smiled wryly. 'It's what they're paid to be good at. Finding and killing. No indication of who paid for the contract.'

'Hanna?'

'Most likely. Zand was always her favourite xiongshou and he disliked me. This will make travel slightly trickier.' He caught sight of Corin's arm and swore. 'She tagged you. Sit.'

'I'm fine,' Corin said. 'Just a scratch. What about you?'

'The jijin often poison their blades. Mine wasn't.' He wrapped a cloth around the four-pointed blade Corin had dropped and held it up to the light. A faint sheen of something yellowish discoloured the tips. 'Now would be a good time to learn to heal yourself with your yanstones.'

'Gouri…'

'Not si-xing at least,' Kett said. 'That's blue and too expensive to use on shuriken. Watu by the smell. Which means you have a little time. The antidote is easy to make, too.' He placed the blade down. 'You try the yanstones and I'll get the cook to make it.' He headed for the door and paused. 'Just don't fall asleep. It works faster if you do.'

Corin swallowed, his skin clammy and heart racing. Kett left and Corin stared at his own trembling hands. Right. Yanstones. It was one thing for them to clear away the istilqa aftereffects. Another to clean a poison from his system.

Or was it? Well, there was only one way to find out. He pressed his palms against the stones and tried to remember what Alere said about merging with them. Nothing. But the room took on a hazy darkness and his eyelids sagged. He forced them open and concentrated on the stones. Nothing.

Kett returned and Corin started.

'No luck with the yanstones?'

Corin shook his head, regretting it when the room swayed. Kett pressed a mug into his hand but he couldn't hold it. Corin blinked, his head too heavy to hold up.

'Oh, no,' Kett said. 'You don't get to die on me, Cor.' He peeled back Corin's eyelids. 'One of the first symptoms is blood-shot eyes and yours are the colour of hot steel. Drink.' He touched the cup to Corin's mouth.

Corin sipped and gagged. 'You're trying to poison me, aren't you?'

'That would be redundant,' he returned, calmly. 'If you don't drink, you'll go blind in about ten minutes. Then you'll go into convulsions and start bleeding from every orifice. Your choice.'

Corin forced down a mouthful. 'Tastes like someone blended a horse-crap with fish guts and a hint of cinnamon. What's in it?'

'You don't want to know. Just drink it.' He tipped more into Corin's mouth, continuing until Corin swallowed the last of the vile concoction. Then he watched Corin and checked his eyes several times, shaking him when he slipped toward sleep.

At last Kett sat back.

Drowsiness overcame Corin and he slumped on the couch. 'Do say I can sleep now? I'd very much like to.'

Kett checked his eyes once more and smiled. 'Yes.' Then he picked up the Koh-Lin journal again and read a few pages. There was a long silence, broken only by the sound of pages turning.

The room faded. Hopefully not for the last time.

When Corin woke, the afternoon sun blazed through the window and the cabin had been cleared of dead bodies and blood.

Kett glanced up. 'Ah. Good. You're alive. Alere would be upset if I let you die after she left you behind in the hopes of protecting you.'

'For a given value of aliveness, I suppose. I do feel like I've been trampled by a herd of runiu.' Corin yawned. 'Everything hurts. Thank you, though.'

'You're welcome. It will take a day for the aches to wear off, but you should be fine. There's food.' Kett pointed at a tray of meats and cheeses. 'I checked. It's safe.'

Corin helped himself, surprisingly hungry. Kett continued to read.

'What *is* so fascinating about a five-hundred-year-old journal?' Corin's question came out muffled and he swallowed a draft of thin Melcori ale to wash down the food.

Leaning back in his seat, Kett flipped the gold-bound book over twice.

'Assuming my translation is correct...' he tapped the volume. '...This little book could hold the key to what lies ahead of us in Madina.'

'How so?'

Kett brushed a few flakes of gold silk off his leg and held the book between his fingertips like it was something both precious and somewhat distasteful at the same time. 'I think this might be the journal referenced in the Teachings of Lei.'

Corin stared blankly at him. 'You're going to have to give me a little more to go on.'

'Lei Koh-Lin was married to Kya Edwards. She was one of the first recorded xintou. Along with her sister, Bree. This is the journal Lei kept about his son, Col – who was a male xintou,' he said. 'In fact, if I'm reading this right, I'd say Col was *the* male xintou that founded the whole notion that they should be forbidden.'

'Really? What did he do that was so unforgivable?'

'When he reached puberty,' Kett said bleakly, 'and came into his powers, he went insane. Took every unwarded mind for two gongli around with him. Eight hundred and thirty minds were locked into Fusion with his madness. They all died. Including Col. Only Lei, Kya and Bree survived.'

'And? If you're thinking of Rohne, I'm pretty sure he's past puberty. Though I admit his thinking is a bit juvenile. How's the book supposed to help us?'

'Rohne's past puberty, but I'm not entirely sure he's sane.' He held up the book. 'We have to get this information to Alli. It refers to xintou concepts I only have a vague idea about. It sounds like the Edwards sisters were close to a cure for the boy when it all went wrong.

'What kind of cure?'

'I'm not sure. There's a line that talks about the boy's potential to change the world. To be humanity's guide. So, I suspect they were trying to stabilise his gifts.'

'Stabilise? Not destroy? Interesting. How?'

'They were using something called a *shenhilya*. Kya Edwards seemed to think it was the key to fixing him.'

Corin raised a brow, waiting.

Kett shrugged. '*Shen* is one of those old Mandrin words that could mean a few things. *Deity, soul,* or even *mysterious.* And *hilya* is old Rabic for *trinket, jewel,* or maybe *ornament.*'

'Well,' Corin said, scrubbing at the back of his neck. 'That's amazingly unhelpful.'

'I know.' Kett frowned at the book. 'I need to get hold of the old language dictionaries in Xintou House to translate it properly.'

Laughing, Corin leaned back and clasped his hands behind his head. 'No problems. We'll just stroll into Xintou House when we get to Madina and ask to borrow a book. I'm sure Nasra won't mind.'

Kett didn't dignify that with an answer. 'My point is, that the Edwards sisters thought they could use this *shenhilya* to fix the boy. And whatever they tried could help when Alere confronts Rohne and Nasra.'

'Does it say *how* they used the shen-thing?'

Kett's mouth thinned and he turned the book over again before answering. 'Kya Edwards wanted to Fuse with it – or with her sister. I'm not sure which.'

Corin straightened. 'What the diyu? Even I know that Fusing is the one thing xintou fear most of all.' He threw his arms wide. 'Two people's minds bonded so tightly that they're impossible to separate. Both bodies *always* die. Were they mad?'

'Desperate, I think,' Kett replied. 'They were trying to save Kya's only child, after all.'

'Well, I don't think you ought to tell any of that to Alere when we find her.' Corin grimaced. 'She's got enough martyr tendencies as it is, trying to prove she's good enough to you and Rafi and Mistress Li.'

There was a long, tense silence and Kett's fingertips whitened on the book.

Corin cleared his throat. 'If the boy killed people, then it sounds like the Edwards sisters couldn't make it work, anyway. So maybe it's moot. Does it say how they stopped him?'

Kett turned a bleak look on Corin. 'Someone killed him. Dagger to the heart.'

'And if we can't find Alere when we get to Madina?' Corin voiced the worry that had been nagging him since he'd cleared the istilqa headache yesterday.

'We have to get there first,' Kett said, grimly. 'We have to find her. She's our best hope of defeating Rohne.' He shoved the book into his pack. 'With or without this journal.'

CHAPTER EIGHT

ALERE

When Alere and her party arrived at the Dalcin stables, she ignored Xintou House ethics again and inserted a thought into the stable owner's Outers. He released the horses to her without argument. Mina sent her a level look. Alere headed for the looseboxes. She quashed a flicker of guilt. This wasn't the time to debate morality and they had no other options for transport. Those desperate Melcori citizens able to buy horses and supplies had all but stripped Dalcin of everything available.

'Oh, I do love you Corin!' Alere flipped open a saddlebag and rummaged through the contents. 'You are an absolute genius.'

Tugging clothing out, she threw an orange cloak over her shoulders and tucked her hair into an orange cap. Now she was a rider. There were enough Messenger House uniforms for at least Mina and Jarran. The bag even contained the small brass trumpet riders used to warn of their approach and open gates. That, along with the distinctive orange uniforms, should help to clear the refugee-clogged roads.

'Looks like we've got dry goods and dried meats,' Jarran said, holding up a leather pack, 'but nothing fresh. I'll go out and see what I can find while you saddle the horses.'

'And I need some supplies from Healer House,' Mina said, hurrying to his side.

Saric and Wei, lethal and innocent-looking, slipped out behind the two adults.

Half an hour later, Saric sidled in through the stable door.

'We're back. Jarran's got some supplies, but not a lot. What he did get cost about five times what it's normally worth.' He sniffed disparagingly. 'He wouldn't let me help. I was just going to have a chat with the merchant about his pricing.'

Alere smirked. 'I imagine this chat would have been rather...er...pointed.'

'Har har.' Saric flipped back his jacket and produced a small, one-shot crossbow. 'Mina and Wei are back, too. Mina looks pleased.'

'Where'd you get that?'

Saric returned a world-weary, amused expression. For a moment, he was the image of Corin.

'No, I don't want to know.' She held up a palm. 'Was there any word for me at Messenger House?'

'Nothing. I did send one to Liu, just to let him know where Wei and I are.' He shrugged. 'He worries like an old hen if we don't report in at least once every couple of days.'

Jarran, Mina and Wei entered, bringing a gust of warm, damp air with them. The weather had changed, hinting at storms from the ocean later in the day. They needed to get on the road quickly. That way they could either outrun the storm, or at least get a reasonable distance before it hit and the road became a morass of sticky mud. Whether they reached the next village or not would be a matter of luck.

It took little time to distribute the loads amongst the six horses. Jarran was anxious to be away. Fear for his daughters showed in the permanent frown clouding his brow, and the reduction of his conversation to terse, pointed sentences.

Alere cupped her hands, ready to throw Saric up behind her saddle. He paused, his head snapping toward the half-open stable door. He lowered his foot and glanced at Wei, who flicked a lightning-fast hand signal. Saric nodded. More incomprehensible signals flashed between them. Silent, they vanished into the shadows.

Jarran murmured something into Mina's ear. She paled and snatched at three sets of reins, hauling her horse, Jarran's and one of the spares into a large loosebox. Jarran sauntered over to where Alere stood pretending to tighten a girth-strap. Bronze glinted in his fist.

'Ah,' a light cheerful voice hailed them from the doorway. 'The stableowner said I might find you here. Eshia, they're in here.' Short and slim, the man spread his arms wide, echoing his friendly grin. Somewhere between twenty and forty, he was remarkable only for his absolute lack of anything noteworthy. Dressed in hardwearing brown bamboo-cloth, he carried just a small, bronze dagger on his hip. With straight brown hair tied in a shoulder-length mawei, and brown eyes, he was so ordinary as to be invisible in a crowd.

Alere touched his mind. Solid wards brought her up short. Possibly xiongshou. Hard to be sure, yet. He moved with the grace of a xiongshou. A young woman, around her own age, slipped into the stables. Equally as nondescript as her partner, she gave Alere and Jarran a vague, sweet smile. Her dark eyes darted around the shadowed corners.

'Will they sell the horses, Gen, darling?' she lilted, moving close to the loosebox where Mina hid.

Alere needed to stop this before it started. Hopefully a bluff would work. She flipped a throwing knife. It landed, vibrating, in the timber post less than a handspan from the woman's nose.

Alere kept her eyes on the woman, trusting Jarran to do the same with the man. 'We're not selling and you're not here to buy, anyway. Why don't you both just leave before things go suilie? Believe me, you will pay a far higher price than the one you're trying to earn.'

Eshia stopped, but didn't react with fear or surprise. Instead, she sent Alere a cool, almost contemptuous sneer and pulled the knife out. Around her wrist was a length of braided blue-and-silver ribbon. Gaisi. Not just xiongshou, but one of the *jijin* elite. From Adeghal's Weishi House to the northwest of Melcor. They were a long way from home.

Bluffing was a bad choice. But hand-to-hand combat with one of the elite xiongshou would be insane. Even Kett would hesitate for they were the best Weishi House could train. Lethal. Alere swallowed and hid the trembling of her hands by gripping her weapons.

Derisive, Gen replied. 'Oh, you think you're that good, do you?'

Jarran shrugged. 'Me, not particularly. Her, yes. I wouldn't risk it if I were you.'

'Well.' Eshia curled a lip. 'You're not us. Give us the blonde woman and this doesn't have to end badly. It's only a capture contract, so give her over and she won't be hurt. Nor will you.'

Alere tried to keep a calm expression. They were after Mina? A capture, not a kill. Why send xiongshou for that? She strolled closer to the woman, but still outside fighting distance, and drew dagger and sword. Eshia's eyes widened at the sight of the steel.

'There's no blonde woman here,' Alere said. 'Go now.'

The woman leapt. So quick! Her hand flashed out. Stiffened fingers struck Alere's solar plexus and she staggered back, gasping for breath that wouldn't come.

'You're lucky.' Eshia twisted Alere's arm into a lock, forcing her to release the sword. 'That could have been your throat, but I'm in a good mood.' She pushed Alere away and stroked the yanstones. Alere sucked a shuddering breath and cried out. The woman's touch was sharpened steel tearing strips across bare skin, but left no marks.

Alere pulled a throwing knife out. A flick sent it toward Eshia's throat. The woman caught it in midair and stowed it away with a smile.

'I'll take that steel dagger you're holding, too.' She jerked her head at Jarran. 'Or you can let your friend die.'

Alere risked a quick look. Gen had Jarran pinned against the stable wall at daggerpoint, his arm shortened for the thrust. Jarran's karambit lay in Gen's fist, pressed against the Jun's throat. Jiche! She should have killed the woman immediately. Capture contract or not, she knew better than to give xiongshou a chance. Arrogance. Kett would be ashamed of her.

She sank into connection with the yanstones and let them clear away the fear and self-recrimination. There was no point wasting more time. She had other options.

Saric?

Was wondering when you'd admit defeat.

Don't kill—

There were two soft *phuut*s in quick succession. Eshia gasped and snatched a small, black-feathered dart out of her neck. Glaring, she tossed it away with an angry snarl. Behind Alere, Gen swore, but she couldn't take her gaze off Eshia. Her caution was unnecessary. The woman collapsed, twitching, to the straw-strewn dirt floor. Bloody froth formed at her lips. Moments later a soft thud told the man's fate.

Saric emerged from the shadows, tucked two unused shuriken into his belt, and peered out the stable door.

'Left that a bit late, didn't you?' he said to Alere. 'Should've just let me dart them straight away.'

She shrugged. 'I didn't see the wristband. You shouldn't have used black, though. They were on a capture, not a kill.'

Saric ignored her. Wei appeared, sliding a blowpipe back into her shirt. Her pretty, elfin features showed nothing but professional interest as she toed the fallen man. She sniffed with unmistakable disdain.

Jarran's mouth pulled down at the corners. 'Huh. I'm beginning to think I should have sent my daughters to Weishi House.' He prised his karambit from the dead man's grip.

Alere retrieved her sword and throwing knives.

Mina rushed out from behind the horses, knelt beside the woman and pressed two fingers against her throat.

'She's dead! Why did you kill them? Who were they?'

Saric shrugged, checking again the world outside the stables. 'Xiongshou.' He gestured to Wei, who took his place as lookout. Saric felt the man's pulse and nodded in satisfaction. Seeing Mina still gaping, he spread his hands.

'What? They were going to kill Alere and take you prisoner. What were we supposed to do, wait and see how serious they were?'

'But you didn't have to kill them,' Mina protested. 'They're people, too. They have families.'

Saric snorted a laugh. 'No, they don't. Xiongshou are orphans and Weishi House doesn't let them have families. Makes them too vulnerable.'

Mina turned a wide, horrified look on Alere, who nodded. 'He's right. Their loyalty is to their partner, the contract and the House. In that order.'

'That's horrible,' Mina whispered.

Saric searched the body, starting with the hair. He extracted a pair of lockpicks and two slim needle-blades, which he tucked into a pouch hanging from his belt. Next, he unstrapped two matched pairs of throwing knives from under the sleeves. He transferred the sheaths to his own forearms, tightening them to fit. A thorough search of the dead man's clothing produced a blowpipe and a long belt holding a dozen or more darts with different coloured feathers, a bronze stiletto blade, another pair of throwing knives and, in one of his shoes, a blade designed to flick out from the toes. Saric compared his foot and put the shoes aside. The rest of the weapons vanished amongst his clothing.

Then he swapped again with Wei, who performed a similar search, with similar results, on the woman's body. The blade-boot Wei offered to Alere who, after a moment's hesitation, shrugged and accepted them. The boots fit. The mechanism for the blade in the right one was easy to activate, too. The blade was sheened faintly blue. Useful. Unusual. Not the normal equipment for weishi. Maybe more common amongst those from Adeghal? She checked the shuriken tattoo on the woman's wrist. A tiny letter A under the image indicated she was definitely from the Adeghal Weishi House. Long way to come for a contract. Perhaps they'd been in Chengdu on another contract, or for Mianshou.

Wei handed over a thick ring. 'Too big for me.'

Made of gold – so it wouldn't react with poisons – the ring fitted neatly onto Alere's middle finger, leaving two blade-edged spikes protruding inward, hidden from view.

'Nice,' she said. The spikes were also coated bluish. Another unusual weapon. She took it off and wrapped it in a scrap of cloth torn from the dead woman's shirt. She wasn't used to wearing one and didn't want to risk poisoning herself. It went into a pocket.

Mina shuddered. 'How did you all *know?* You might have killed normal people by accident. How could you be so sure?'

Alere studied the still forms, not sure how to put it into words that made sense. 'You're just going to have to trust us, Mina. There were half a dozen little tells. That ribbon on her wrist means she's *jijin* – the best of Weishi House xiongshou. I'm pretty good. She was better. They weren't certain we were their target, or how many of us were here, and it was a capture contract, or they'd have killed us before we even saw them. I didn't kill him the minute he walked in because I knew he'd have a partner. I wanted them both in the open.'

Mina sucked a sharp breath. 'You expected this! What aren't you telling me? Stop trying to protect me, Alli. We're in this together.'

Alere finished buckling the flaps on the saddlebags. 'There's a contract out on me, dead. Another for you, alive.' She pointed at the bodies. 'Get used to this. There will be more. We'll have to be careful.'

Mina choked back a cry. Alere looked to Jarran for help. He gave her a quizzical half-smile before putting an arm around Mina's shoulder and murmuring soft reassurances into her ear. Mina leaned her head on his shoulder.

Alere caught sight of Saric. The ten-year-old watched the couple with an amusing mix of scorn and envy. Personally, she was glad Mina had someone to talk to. Although, if Mina fell in love with Jarran, she would have to give up her dream of living as a small town healer in Gaton.

Right now, though, every minute spent consoling Mina's ethical qualms was a minute wasted. Alere interrupted the couple's sotto voce conversation by thrusting the orange cloaks and hats at them.

She squeezed Mina's shoulder. 'I'm sorry we frightened you, Mina, but you need to accept that it's probably going to get a lot worse before we get to Madina. Put these on and tie one of the spare horses to your saddle. We need to leave now if we're going to get out of town and past the worst foot traffic today.'

ROHNE

Rohne kicked his tired mount into a reluctant canter as he topped the last rise and the city walls appeared. Laid out ahead, Madina was everything he'd hoped for. Against a backdrop of uneven rooflines and a low haze of purplish smoke, the Alcazar's twin towers soared silvery into the soft, teal-green sky. The blood-orange afternoon sun glinted off their smooth, curved surfaces, searing into his brain, beckoning him closer.

He squinted against the glare and pressed a thumb to his temple to ease the pain. Perhaps Nasra could tell him what caused these headaches. They'd been worsening since, well, almost since he'd left Gaton.

The citys enormous timber gates were set into a buttressed wall of sulcrete and sandstone that curved away east toward farmland and west to the Kabir River. Huddled against the foot of the walls were dozens of tiny bamboo and thatch huts, lined up in neat rows. Like children clutching at the skirts of an indifferent parent, hoping for protection.

Rohne ignored the peasants who peered at him as he passed between the huts and approached the main gate. Reining in, he assessed the weishi on guard duty. They wore the Han-Asad family's gold and black uniform, along with an air of pompous self-importance. Several caustic remarks Kett had made about the city weishi came to mind. Well, that would have to change.

With minimal effort, he slid into the Outers of both weishi and walked them, puppet-like, to the gate. Such a useful skill he'd learned from Alere. It became easier and easier to push people's consciousness aside and control their bodies. Even a warded mind, as long as they had once opened their Outer wards to him. He'd learned young to establish a link with people foolish enough to open their Outers. It made piercing their wards simpler the next time.

The weishi opened the ponderous gate and he trotted through, only releasing them when he was out of sight. He revelled for a moment in their confusion and fear as they found themselves standing in front of an open gate, then disengaged, smirking.

Surveying the streetscape, his interest became disdain as he took in the attractions of the much-touted city. Where he'd been expecting affluence and beauty, he found the dirty and mangled remnants of both. Buildings once housing rich merchants or middle class were now decayed and sordid. Sulcrete mortar crumbled from between red clay bricks, bamboo strips covered what once must have been glass windows. Slate-tiled roofs showed gaps like those in the mouths of the beggars who worked the streets and held out filthy hands to him as he passed by.

Rubbish and debris lined the broken remains of gutters, and jammed tightly into storm drains, rendering the drainage system useless in bad weather. The sweet-sick smell of decay drifted up. Rohne pulled his scarf over his nose, but it did little to obscure the scent.

Bony fingers grasped at his ankle and a chorus of pleas rose. Disgusted, he kicked out, catching the emaciated man in the cheek and drawing blood. The beggar staggered and fell to the cobbles. A great wailing arose from others and they surged toward Rohne, made brave by numbers and desperation.

Curling a lip, Rohne gestured. Tattered scarves and clothes tightened around grimy necks while skeletal hands scrabbled at airways squeezed shut. Gasping and choking, twenty or more dull-minded, unworthy scum fell in despoiled heaps. Rohne touched his heels to the gelding's sides and let it pick its way through the ragged, lifeless piles.

Madina just needed someone with a firmer touch than the old Zah-Hill rulers.

Even allowing for two more, similarly-irritating incidents, it took only half an hour to make his way along the main street to the Alcazar. As he approached the great citadel, cleanliness and order returned to the streets. Here, hard by the Jun First's seat of power, the houses, streets, and denizens better-reflected the city as it should be.

Grand, two storey mansions of sandstone and timber lined wide, tree-shaded streets. Huge, glass windows gave glimpses of elegant interiors. The minds he touched inside the houses showed greater education and culture than those in the slums. Graceful girls in shimmering silk robes, some even wearing the gauzy veil of the highest Jun families and Houses, paraded their beauty and flirted prettily with well-dressed young men. Tidy children played and giggled on clean-swept cobbles.

Rohne inclined his head regally as he passed. These people would appreciate his skills and have use for his talents. They would value and admire him; see that he was destined to change the course of history and guide humanity into a better world.

In the massive square before the Alcazar, a bustling market filled the dull afternoon with life. Dozens of stalls, with brilliant silk pennants snapping in the cool spring breeze, offered every manner of stylish frippery and pleasing distraction. Musicians strolled amongst the crowd, strumming ouds and striking tambors. Modestly-dressed dancers twirled with delicate, sensuous skill before them. A lean merchant caressed a bolt of rich red silk, extolling its virtues in a loud voice to a tall woman in jiaoji red, as though volume alone would convince her.

Further along, a stall offering dumplings and noodles reminded Rohne he hadn't eaten for several hours. Enticing though the rich, salty smell was, he ignored it. He would get much better in the Alcazar.

At the great, black-and-bronze outer wall doors, Rohne paused. A pair of black-and-silver clad weishi stood to attention, halberds grasped firmly, alzin and leather armour gleaming and spotless. Much more impressive, but still useless.

He pierced their basic Outer wards and plucked the daily password from their unskilled minds. Then, holding them frozen, he inserted a memory of hearing the password into their Outers.

Within moments, the locks clanked and the enormous, studded doors swung outward, admitting him without question. These people had no idea how to protect against a xintou. Too trusting by far. He would need to improve on that if Alere kept up her determined approach. She may not be as skilled as he, but she could, undoubtedly, achieve the same result.

What a pity she hadn't suicided in Chengdu, as he'd hoped. He'd been almost out of range at the time; his influence over her small. It had been worth a try.

Ignoring the blankfaced weishi swinging the gate shut behind him, he trotted into the courtyard between the two steel towers. In deep shadow at this time of day, its cold austerity held little appeal, except as a kill-box. Rohne acknowledged its potential as a defensive zone, while disliking its unwelcoming feel. Whoever designed the Alcazar clearly had protection in mind, not just imposing dominance over the city outside.

He swung down from his horse and tossed the reins to a compliant serving boy. After stretching kinks from his spine and legs, Rohne straightened his clothing, re-tied his mawei, and strode unchallenged into the building. The weishi at the door stared straight ahead, unseeing.

Inside the great hall he stopped. Overhead, a massive chandelier of electric bulbs saturated the huge space with golden, eye-aching light. Underfoot, warm, polished sulcrete spoke of an age when building on this scale was possible and even easy. An age when the Old Earth ships came with regularity to supply goods now long-unattainable. All around, in fact, evidence of Old Earth made the room almost a shrine to the original colonists and their ideals.

Holding himself invisible to the minds of the stone-faced staff guarding and passing through the hall, Rohne surveyed his new home. A map was affixed to the smooth steel of one tower wall. The blue-green marble of Old Earth, in all its unspoiled glory. But when the last ships left that planet, wars over resources and religions had almost reduced it to desert. The map was a memory of something long-dead.

On the other wall, Kalima was similarly laid out, its four continents displayed in tantalising majesty. Rohne stroked the insignificant part of the world comprising Mamlakah and the other three Jundoms. So much more to achieve. Such beauty and freedom. No wonder the colonists came here.

A sound and an awareness caught his attention. Rohne opened his Outers, inviting the mental equivalent of an embrace.

Mother. So good to see you.

Nasra Connor glided down the great sandstone staircase, her robes shimmering in the chandelier's glow.

The Gold suits you. He indicated the room. *As do these surrounds.*

Elegant and beautiful in the heavy gold robes, she was the epitome of Xintou. Her salted auburn hair was coiled into an intricate knot and the translucent gold veil over her eyes lent a regal air. She lifted the veil, her expression cool and with the faintest hint of…fear? What was she afraid of?

Then she caught his hands and he wasn't sure he'd seen the look at all.

My dear boy, I hardly recognised you. She pressed her cheek against his. *You've grown, I'm sure. Are you well?*

Tired from all the travel. A few headaches. He shrugged. *And Alere is going to be difficult. But, otherwise, fine.*

Headaches? A frown twitched at her brows, but she wiped it away and kissed his cheek again. Welcoming as her expression was, she held her wards against him, allowing access only into the shallowest part of her Outers. Interesting. Before he left Gaton they were as close as unBonded xintou could be. Sharing a connection deeper and stronger than most parents and children, with few secrets between them.

Something had changed. But what? What did she hide?

Her arm slipped through his. Her lips curved into a meaningless smile and she guided him to the stairs.

Come. You must be hungry and tired. Let's go upstairs where we can be private. We have much work to do. You have arrived just in time. The Bonding will be set for tomorrow. First you must tell me everything *that has transpired in your travels.*

She touched a servant on the arm, transmitting an order directly to the girl, excluding Rohne from the communication.

Baffled by her coolness, Rohne caught again the edges of a quick, wary glance she sent him from beneath her lashes. Disengaging his arm, he waved her ahead. She hesitated, then gathered her skirts and mounted the stairs before him.

Rohne followed, disturbed for no reason he could pin down.

CHAPTER NINE

ALERE

Alere glanced over her shoulder at the lowering northern sky and swiped a hand over her grimy face. They had ridden all day, stopping only to change horses, managing to stay ahead of the storm. Now the sun half-hid behind the western horizon and washed the great Kabir river valley with a soft, burnt orange glow. The smell of rain dogged their steps and lightning flickered. They probably only had half an hour before the deluge broke.

A muffled sob drew Alere's attention to the tears tracking down Mina's dusty cheeks. Mina saw her watching, hastily wiped her face and straightened in the saddle. Saric's caustic commentary and Wei's lighthearted, distracting chatter had long since dried up. Wei rode curled in front of Jarran, held tightly in place by his arm, sagging onto his chest. Saric had tied a rope around himself and Alere, and rested heavily against her back. Even she felt the strain, her thighs aching and backside bruised.

According to the map, a village lay only a few gongli south, but it was too risky to go there for shelter. They were due to change horses there tomorrow and that would be dangerous enough. The chance of being ambushed by xiongshou was far less if they stayed away from populated areas.

'Jarran,' she called. Behind her, Saric jerked and swore.

The Jun glanced over, his face set and jaw hard.

'We need to stop.' She pointed north at the steel-grey tumble of stormclouds. 'That's about to break and we're all exhausted.'

He scowled and looked behind, then at the road ahead. She held her tongue, resisting the urge to remind him it was his own fault if the pace was too slow. Finally, after noticing Mina's miserable expression, he nodded.

'Looks like a farmhouse up ahead,' he said. Set back from the road, surrounded by mature fruit trees, and freshly-turned, earthy-smelling fields, it seemed safe enough.

Alere nudged her plodding mount into the rutted path to the house and the others followed. As they approached the small dwelling of black basalt and terracotta tile, Wei stretched and yawned like a cat. She studied the house with open curiosity.

'Looks kinda homey. Let me go ask,' she said, when Jarran drew his gelding to a halt. She slid down from the saddle and staggered.

'But shouldn't one of us do it?' Mina protested. 'She's just a little girl.'

Saric chuckled. 'Just watch. There's not many can resist Wei when she bats her eyelashes and looks all lost and hungry. Wei,' he called. 'Knife.'

She shifted her dagger out of view.

Alere untied Saric's rope and swung down, glad of a chance to stretch her legs. Saric half-fell into her arms, groaning.

'I've decided. I hate horses,' he muttered, walking stiffly in circles. The horse huffed and stamped one foot.

Wei knocked on the door, clasped her hands behind her back, and smiled winsomely. An older woman opened the door, her eyes darting between Wei, Alere, and her companions. A huge sahalia, with short fur the colour of green copper-sands and a head as big as Wei's, ambled out from behind the woman.

Wei gave a cry of delight and crouched to wrap her arms around the desert-lizard. Its blue, forked tongue flicked her ear and she giggled, scratching under its heavy jaw. Apparently, its finger-long fangs didn't bother her. Alere shuddered. Three small sahalia kits emerged and frolicked around Wei's legs.

Wei asked the woman a question and patted the sahalia again. The ensuing conversation wasn't audible, but the woman relaxed and smiled. She extended the smile to Alere and the others, then pointed at a collection of barns and sheds a few dozen paces from the house. Wei bowed then threw her arms around the woman's ample hips. The woman laughed and stroked Wei's dusty hair. Wei picked up one of the sahalia kits and cuddled it. She sent Alere a pleading look. Alere shook her head and Wei reluctantly put the ball of green fur and fang down.

She skipped back, beaming. 'Her name's Vara. And the sahalia's name is Lenko and the kits are *so* cute! Mother told me about them. They come from the Makaan desert, where we're going. They eat the sand-spiders and make really good guards. I said you're my family. Vara says we can sleep in the big barn. There's feed for the horses in there, but we're to pay her a tiebe.' She looked anxious. 'Do we have that much?'

Alere handed her a steel tiebe and a silver yinbi. 'Tell her we don't have a lot of supplies to cook with, so if she has anything hot we could eat, we'd be grateful.'

Wei jogged back, handed over the coin and patted the sahalia. Alere envied the girl's boundless energy.

Jarran woke Alere some time before midnight for her watch. She dragged herself reluctantly out of a bed of piled-up hay, wrapped herself in a cloak and took up a post outside the barn door. Her breath frosted in the sharp night air. The clouds had cleared, leaving only stars dusting the sky from horizon to horizon. Neither moon was up and the night was breathlessly still and silent. Here and there, luminescent insects soared and danced like stars cut loose from their place in the sky.

She shivered and hugged the cloak tight, wishing for the familiar, secure sounds of Jacksa's caravan.

Her watch passed uneventfully, leaving her far too much time to think and to miss Kett. She was in desperate need of his calm good sense and vision. His warmth. His subtle, dry humour. Her mind was in turmoil as she formed and discarded a dozen plans. There seemed to be no viable way to free Rafi, Jarran's daughters and Mistress Li, and to also prevent Nasra's takeover of Xintou House and the Jun First throne.

An egg-heavy nightwing buzzed her. She drew her hood tight and the insect vanished into the darkness. She let out a sigh of relief. A bird wailed twice, its mournful sound sending a shiver down her spine. Suspicious, she stretched out through the yanstones, scanning the area around the barn for unwanted intruders.

She touched the dreams of the farmer and his wife, envying their sheer ordinariness. She sensed the scattered, drowsy minds of the farm animals, and the guard xiao-cat's hot, hungry thoughts as it stalked the grounds. Otherwise, there was no-one around for many gongli. Even the nearby road to Asadia was empty, its traffic of traders and travellers bedded down in nearby villages.

A brief, unsuccessful attempt to communicate telepathically with the xiao-cat was little more than a temporary distraction. It merely stared at her unblinkingly as it paced back and forth outside the enclosure, its green eyes luminous in the feeble starlight. Its enormous, tufted ears twitched at every sound. A lip curled back to reveal fangs longer than her hand. She gave up and released her hold on its mind. Its mottled grey and black body faded into the night.

At one point she considered trying to reach Corin, and thence Kett, through the yanstones. Eventually, logic prevailed. Contact with Corin could disrupt the Suggestions she'd given him and break the hold keeping both men in Chengdu. Kett was now far behind, safe and well-away from the approaching chaos. At least he and Corin would be alright, even if she didn't make it through.

Finally, the rise of Luna-Yi signalled the end of her watch and she slipped back into the barn. She still had no clue how to defeat Nasra, or protect Rafi, the House, Jarran's daughters and the Jundom. There must be a way, though. She just hadn't found it yet.

'Mina.' Alere shook her sleeping sister and whispered again into her ear. 'Wake up. It's time for your watch.'

Mina gave a sleepy, grumbling groan. She yawned and scrambled from her furlined sleeping bag. Not far away, Saric and Wei lay, curled like xiao-kittens, close to the fire, hands lax on weapons, faces soft with sleep. Across from them, Jarran cracked an eyelid then closed it again, rolling over to put his back to the fire.

Alere laid more wood on the coals. Sparks rose toward the high, shadowed ceiling and she waited for Mina to return from relieving herself outside the barn. She drank and rubbed water over her face, wishing for a hot bath. The lack of bathing facilities was the biggest downside to being on the road again. That, and interrupted sleep.

A gust of cold air made the fire jump and skitter, sending sparks drifting high again. Mina appeared, shaking with cold. She snuggled into her sleeping bag. Alere moved closer to the fire, warming her hands. Mina lifted her furs, inviting her to share the warmth. After a moment's hesitation, Alere joined her, tucking the furs around her back and under her legs.

Mina leaned on Alere's shoulder and stared at the crackling flames. 'I had another nightmare.'

Alere rested her cheek on her sister's soft hair. 'Sorry.'

'No.' Mina's words were thoughtful, reminiscent rather than fearful. 'It wasn't about Ven or the Games. It was the one about the bandits and something to do with their brains being on fire. Then I was with Rohne and he was trying to kill you with your dagger.

Then suddenly I was with a young boy I don't know. He was deranged and sick, but for some reason it was vital that I…I had to kill him. It was awful.' She sighed. 'I don't know. It seemed so real and made sense at the time. Sounds silly now.'

'Better silly than paralysing,' Alere said.

A long silence lay between them, filled with the crackling of burning wood, the smell of smoke, hay and horses.

Mina stirred. 'Jarran told me you threw yourself in front of a kusarigama to save me back at the docks.'

'I'm weishi. It's my duty.'

Her sister stiffened. 'Really? Is that the only reason?' She sat up, staring morosely into the fire.

'I…' Alere rolled the next words around on her tongue, tasting her own fear and uncertainty in them. Last time she'd pushed Mina away, her sister had fled Shanzhai with Rohne.

Mistakes were made to be learned from.

She raised her chin and said bluntly. 'No. I did it because I care, Mina. You're my only sister. I…I need you. You're part of me, now.' She poked at the fire and frowned. 'You're…important.'

'You really do have trouble saying things like that, don't you?' Mina glanced sideways beneath her lashes and smiled. 'But I can tell you mean it. Thank you. I love you, too, you know.' She leaned across again and rested her head on Alere's shoulder.

A small knot of fear and tension unravelled in Alere's chest and warmth replaced it.

After a few minutes, Mina spoke again. 'I so want this to be over. All I ever wanted was to go home to Gaton after I finished my healer training. I thought I'd never have to leave again. How did I end up halfway across the world?'

'I—'

'No,' she said, laughing low in her throat. 'I know the answer, Alli. And it's not your fault.' She straightened. 'At least, not entirely.'

Alere froze, staring into the fire.

'That was a joke.' Mina frowned. 'You take everything so seriously. Why is the weight all on you? It's ok to let other people help, you know? To let them in.'

Alere prodded at the fire again. 'Kett's been the only one I could ever rely on. But, before this, he was weishi and I was xintou. Sort of. And I was his student. There was always a distance. I guess I've always been alone.'

'Is that why you left him behind?' Mina frowned. 'I can't understand that. Why did you? Don't you love him?'

Alere made a hasty gesture. 'Of course. And I miss him so much it's a lump in my chest the whole time.'

'Then why—'

'Just stop, alright! It was a stupid decision. I'm a zift. I get it. And he'll probably hate me for it.' Alere gritted her teeth. 'I thought it was the right thing. I thought it would keep him safe.'

Mina put an arm around her waist and pulled her close. 'Oh, Alli. He won't hate you. And you have to stop hating yourself. You've only ever done your best. We all know it.'

Alere's throat was too tight to reply. They sat that way for a while, just watching the flames dance and the sparks drift.

Then Mina spoke again, 'Do you think we'll make it in time?' She angled her head, studying her sister. 'I mean, to save Rhea and Ashi, Jarran's daughters? And Rafi, of course.'

'I think we'll get there in time,' Alere said, jabbing at the vivid coals. 'I just don't know what to do once we're there, though.'

'You'll think of something.' Mina peered at her. 'Wait. You're really worried about it, aren't you? I can feel it. I'm not even wearing the bracelets and I can still sense how you're feeling. It's not as clear, but they're definitely your thoughts, not mine. How is that possible?'

Running her thumbs over the yanstones in the bracelets, Alere allowed their silver-gilt brightness to settle her mind.

'I don't know but, ever since we first put the bracelets on, back in Shanzhai, I've felt a...' she sought for the right word '...thread tying us together. If I stop and think about it, I can always tell what you're feeling. It's been getting stronger over the last few days, too. If I close my eyes I can almost see it, shining silvery-gold. Pulling us closer every day.'

Mina shivered and put space between them. She cast Alere a worried look.

Covering a flash of hurt, Alere placed another small log on the fire. 'I know: it's ridiculous. I'm sure it's just my imagination.'

Mina didn't say anything. Curiosity overcame a fluttery anticipation of fear and Alere asked the question she'd been pondering since they'd first discovered the yanstones' properties.

'Now that you've used the stones yourself, how do you think they work – as a healer, I mean?'

'I'm not entirely sure. Tell me how you feel when you're using them?' Mina reached for the brilliant gold-fire of the bracelets on Alere's wrist, paused, then withdrew.

Alere hesitated. Sharing her feelings about the stones was akin to opening the deepest of her wards, allowing someone access to her most intimate thoughts. Her connection to the stones felt...personal. Something she wasn't sure she could survive without, now. Yet Mina was also a part of that, which made the question important to both of them.

Working against vague apprehension, Alere forced her tongue to form words.

'It's almost like I'm observing myself from outside. Nothing seems overwhelming or frightening. All the emotion is stripped away. I'm left with the part of me that makes quick, logical decisions. It's a relief, actually.'

Mina stroked Alere's back. 'I can see the appeal, especially given all you've been through lately.'

Alere drew up her knees and rested her chin.

When she didn't reply, Mina continued, 'The brain is extremely complex and we don't have the technical skills to scan its internal workings any longer. The ancient texts do describe various electrical and chemical reactions. Plus there are sections of the brain, like the amygdala, that control our most basic fears.' Her tone became professional. 'From a purely physiological viewpoint, it sounds like the stones suppress those parts of your brain that generate emotional responses to external stimuli.'

'So, they stop me being afraid. How?'

'Well.' Mina sat crosslegged. 'You said the stones somehow channelled lightning when you burned the houses in Chengdu. And that they work best when you're touching them?'

Alere agreed, caressing the stones with her thumbs.

'Then maybe they conduct electrical currents – which is common enough in some minerals.' Mina shrugged. 'Maybe the yanstones – especially with iron around them – draw electricity from the environment and concentrate it.'

'Like they do with light?'

'Right. And touching them transmits it to you. The current then interferes with the electrical processes and neurochemistry relating to emotion. That could also be why using them sometimes causes you to pass out. Electrical overload to your neural pathways.'

Alere caught the undercurrent of disapproval in the last couple of sentences. 'Apart from the overload thing, being unemotional has to be good, doesn't it? I mean, right now, we could use someone who can make logical decisions. Emotions just mess with your head and I… you end up making stupid decisions when you're afraid or hurt.'

'Everyone does, Alli. It's part of being human.' Mina touched Alere's arm again, briefly. 'You can't separate yourself from emotion and still *be* human. It might be tempting, but don't let the stones distance you. Humans have a long and messy history of trying to avoid suffering by using drugs that interfere with brain chemistry. It never ends well. Working through pain, and grief, and love makes you a better person in the end. After all, you're responsible for many lives now. Without experiencing those emotions, how can you understand what others are going through?'

Rising and flinging the furs off, Alere stalked to the closed barn door, longing for the cool freedom of the night again. Her sister's words were not what she wanted to hear.

'You go back to sleep. I'll keep watch. I don't think I could sleep now, anyway.'

'Alli…'

Alere pulled her cloak around her, pushed open the door and closed it behind. Leaning on it, she stared into the star-washed night sky, gulping at the air's crisp cleanliness. Her breath condensed into wispy clouds that hid the glittering stars.

Mina was right. To separate herself from her emotions was lunacy when judged from a human point of view. But, right now, the aching well of pain and doubt was too deep. If she gave in to it, she would drown.

She didn't have the luxury of wallowing. Not only were the four lives inside the barn under her care, but also those imprisoned in the Alcazar. And all of Mamlakah. With Nasra and Rohne in charge, there was no knowing what the Jundom would become. Nasra had already executed a dozen senior xintou who might have stood against her. What would she do once Rohne Bonded to Hassan and she controlled the whole Jundom?

And Madina was still several days away. Tomorrow would be a hard day's riding. They would turn southeast, late in the afternoon, and follow the York River along the Beifang Range's foothills. Crossing the edges of the desert would be difficult enough. Every step of the way they'd also need to be wary of mercenaries and xiongshou seeking to claim the reward on her.

No, sound though Mina's advice was, clear thinking was more important than emotional self-awareness.

She needed to use the yanstones.

But every time she did, they seemed to eat away at her humanity. How would it end if she gave herself to them, entirely?

CHAPTER TEN

CORIN

'Well.' Corin sank into a seat across from Kett and took a deep draught of the ale waiting for him. 'Alere's been here, but she left the morning of the Second. It's now the end of the Third so we're almost two days behind her. We need to find some horses and go.'

Kett raised his glass and sipped, his attention drifting across the tavern's varied clientele. Corin recognised the habit: assessing the threat-potential of other patrons. But *The Wyvern* inn tended to be patronised by wealthier travellers. Anyone else stood out amongst the silks, furs, well-kept hands and paunchy waistlines. It still smelled of stale beer and sweat, but it was expensive beer and refined sweat.

'Agreed,' Kett said. 'Just a couple of loose ends to tie up. There's one pair of xiongshou here. They don't seem to be interested in us, or in a hurry to leave. Any word on whether Alere encountered any?'

'Oh, very much so.' Corin ate his way through the bowl of thick stew in front of him. 'There are a couple more still…er…hanging around town.' He grinned to himself and waved away Kett's inquiring look. 'But the word on the street is that several more pairs quit and left for Chengdu yesterday morning. I'd say they were discouraged from chasing her by what happened to the first pair.'

Yawning, he squinted against the glare of late afternoon sun streaming in through the windows. In one corner of the tavern, an underfed musician half-heartedly plucked at his oud. The D string was out of tune enough to make Corin's fingers itch. He gritted his teeth together as the sour notes screwed into his ear like a nightwing's ovipositor.

'Oh?' Kett sipped at his ale.

Corin raised his glass in salute to Alere. 'They were found dangling from the stable's rafters. The place where I'd hired our horses.'

'Hanging around, huh?' Kett sent him a dry look. 'Dead or alive?'

Corin grinned and tossed back a mouthful of ale. 'The horses? Alive and gone. The xiongshou, not so much. Dead and with a note pinned to one of them. It said: *Keep coming. We love target practice.*'

'A little showier than I'd expect of her.' Kett's mouth twisted. 'How did they die?'

'That's what makes me think the message was probably my son's flair for the dramatic, rather than Alere's. They both died of a poison dart to the jugular. Not Alere's style, but definitely what I'd expect of Liu Gray's students.'

Scraping the last of the stew, Corin sat back with a sigh of satisfaction. He'd missed tavern food. The Shah's chef only produced delicate, rich cuisine that left a man hungry. He lifted his empty tankard to the waitress, who refilled both tankards.

Kett wiped foam from his lips. 'I guess if it convinced some of them to leave Alere alone, it's not altogether a bad thing. I predict you're going to have a challenging time raising that boy of yours, though. Assuming we can catch him.'

'True.' Corin laughed ruefully. 'There are two pieces of bad news.' He held up a finger. 'One: if I'm any judge of character, the stable owner is annoyed at the mess and has told every gouri xiongshou still interested that Alere's group is travelling disguised as riders from Messenger House.' He raised a second digit. 'Two: she took all six horses, which means there's none left – in the whole town – for us.'

'I did tell you I was calling in some favours, didn't I? C'mon.' Kett stood and headed for the door. 'Assuming Jahil did as he promised, we should have four horses waiting for us at the local sharif's home.'

Admiration warred with irritation as Corin followed the weishi to the entrance. 'You let me chase around town for the last hour looking for horses, while you ate dinner and had this already organised?'

Pushing the door open, Kett stepped out into the cool afternoon sunlight. 'You were going stir-crazy and needed to do something. Besides, we had to make sure Alere really did take all the gear you'd booked. I was also buying supplies and waiting for a message to come in.'

'From who?' Corin fended off a hopeful, unveiled jiaoji girl who brushed artfully against him. Checking his purse, his fingers touched a folded paper in his pocket. The girl winked at him when he glanced back at her in surprise. Second time that had happened. He must be getting lazy. Pulling it out, he saw the signature and swore aloud before running to catch up with Kett.

The weishi strode into the street, jumping over the filthy remnants of puddles from last night's storm and avoiding plodding che-ma and impatient huoche drivers carting loads of fish and produce to and from the nearby docks. He paused and let a house-sized xiang stomp by. It's thick, dirty-white legs and round feet left deep prints in the muddy road. Its long neck carried a small head high above buildings and trees, while the long tail presented a danger to anyone near the thin, whippy end.

A harness around its chest led to straps and a net coiled on its back. The animal must be heading to port. Dalcin traders had recently begun using single animals to tow chuans through the shallows of the Kabir, back upstream to Madina, rather than overland on carts. On the beast's curved back, a small boy sat on a leather saddle, his skinny legs sticking out sideways. One hand held a sharp bronze prod he used to direct the xiang. Dark red blood streaked the animal's sides and it gave an almost sub-sonic rumble that thrummed through Corin's chest..

Kett frowned.

Reaching him, Corin repeated the question. 'Who sent you a message?'

'Liu.' Kett passed him a thin, curled roll of paper and stared after the beast. 'There's one for you, too.'

Corin snatched it, broke the seal and skimmed the contents. Then he held up the folded paper dropped into his pocket by the jiaoji.

'Saric sent me one as well, through less public channels of communication.'

'The jiaoji? That's a smart kid you have.'

Corin read it more thoroughly, slowing as he tried to decipher his son's tiny, inelegant script.

'Jiche! Listen to this: *Corin,*' he read aloud, '*I'm with Alere. She says she drugged you, but I figure you've probably overcome that if you've got half the brain she says you have. You and Kett need to catch up with us. Alere's acting strange. I think it's something to do with those yanstones. She won't let them out of her sight and she's kind of scary when she wears them. We're going to go southeast around the mountains to avoid Asadia. Get here as soon as you can.*'

'Mmm.' Kett's noncommittal reply gave nothing of his thoughts away.

'What did your note say?' Corin re-read Liu's and tucked both papers into an inner pocket.

Kett entered a wide, quiet street and surveyed the impressive bamboo and sandstone houses along the northern side. Massive khial trees lined the streets. Their strangely-knotted, intertwined branches, stripped by winter's cooler weather, formed shapes that teased the brain with illusions of familiarity. A horse. A chuan. An oud.

Corin shook his head and caught up to Kett again.

'Liu passed on the latest news from Madina.' Kett examined a scrap of paper he held, then moved on before continuing. 'Two days ago, Nasra and Hassan called a Council of Juns and House Leaders. She brought four of her twins with her. Liu's spy couldn't hear what was said in the meeting, but six Juns and eight House Leaders went into the room. Only four Juns and six House Leaders came out alive. The others were just…dead, with no obvious injuries.'

'Khara!' Corin couldn't even begin to get his mind around the ramifications.

'Exactly. I'd say it was a clear demonstration of power and intent. Especially given all House Leaders and Juns are taught to ward. The new Juns and House Leaders who fill those empty seats will have a vested interest in staying on her good side. Ah, here we are. Sharif Mennar should be waiting.'

Corin grabbed his arm. 'There was one more thing. In Liu's note to me.'

'And?'

'He says the Selb are coming out of hiding in all the Jundoms from Shemal down to Jadid. Spreading the word that the time of Erheyi is now. Heading for Madina with Lianna's name on their lips. Several hundred have already gathered on the plains northeast of Madina and more are arriving every day. By the time she gets there, Alere will have a ready-made army waiting for her.'

Kett stopped and frowned. 'I truly hope you're right, Corin. We'll need all the help we can get.'

ROHNE

Rohne pressed at his temples to ease the pounding and paced restlessly around his new quarters in the Alcazar. Nasra stood just inside the door and watched him with hooded eyes.

The traditional rooms set aside for the Xintou Bonded to the Jun First family were large and set high in the southern tower. But the space was sparsely furnished with plain pieces of heavy, dark timber softened by gold silk cushions and a violently-patterned rug.

The previous occupant, Celia Edwards, had left little personality stamped on the room. Just a few clothes in the closet and a small, dull journal of small, dull thoughts. A few pages of her agonising over Ven's mental state; over disobeying Mistress Li; and over her fear that Hanna might use the Shanzhai iron for more than just discouraging Melcor's alleged army, made Rohne want to kill the woman, himself. The only things of interest were her notes on the Selb and her rather cryptic Seeings, several of which sounded like they involved Nasra. They could be useful.

He regarded his mother. Her regal bearing held a hint of tension as she stood near the door. He had not seen her since his arrival yesterday. Now it was Thalatha the third and her appearance at his door heralded his Bonding to Hassan Wen-Gates. But Rohne was increasingly uneasy with the situation. Something beyond the obvious was going on. Nasra was avoiding him and he needed to know why before the Bonding tied him irrevocably to her plans.

She raised her brows in silent question and stepped further into the room, trailing an elegant hand along the back of one couch.

'So,' he said, opening his arms to encompass the Alcazar, 'this is what you've worked toward all these years? Was it for me, or for you, I wonder? Are the twin-xintou girls living up to your expectations? They should. You've been hiding them on the Wen-Gates estate and training them for eighteen years.' He heard the bitterness in his voice and strengthened his wards.

It had always galled him, how much time she'd spent training the eleven sets of twins she'd engineered. He'd often suspected her ambitions to be large. But she'd always said she was merely working toward freeing people from the stagnation suffered under Mistress Li's rule.

Her Outers were there for him to Read. *I was never certain I could make it happen for you.* She returned his scepticism with smiling condescension. *Even with the girls trained and ready, I couldn't be sure if the right opportunity would arise. Then Mistress Li's manipulation of Alere and the Koh-Lin situation fell into my lap.*

Rohne lifted a sardonic brow. 'You had no idea – when Mina and Alere were born to Sura and you sent Alere to live with your daughter – that something like this might happen?'

Of course I hoped. But I couldn't be certain Mistress Li would do as I expected. Nasra smiled enigmatically. *I'd met Sura's twin sister – Rafi's wife, Yasmin, – unveiled in the women's quarters at court. So I knew who Sura must be. Yasmin was childless so I suspected Rafi was the father of Sura's girls. I told Elmira and I knew she would feel obliged to tell Li.*

She sniffed. *Elmira was such a disappointment. Completely indoctrinated to Mistress Li's way of thinking. I was surprised she didn't tell Li I was still alive. Anyway...* She dismissed her daughter. *As I hoped, Li couldn't resist meddling with the Koh-Lin inheritance. The old fool has a compulsive need to have her fingers in everything, and that has come back to bite her.*

'And I suppose it was just a coincidence that Mina and Alere are twins?' Rohne folded his arms.

Nasra looked speculatively at him. He deflected her attempt to slide past his wards and Read him more closely. What did she seek?

Actually... She gave him a genuine, rueful smile. *It was their potential that first gave me the idea of using my nai-xintou skills to create twins. The Koh-Lin girls were natural identical twins. I did a utero-scan on them and saw they both carried the xintou and control genes, but each lacked the trigger gene. I realised that, by creating twins, I could hide new xintou from Mistress Li. One girl has the control genes. One has the xintou genes. I can artificially trigger the gene easily enough. And teaching my girls to near-Fuse means that, together, they have the control and the same powers as a House-trained xintou.* She spread her hands in smug satisfaction. *And now we're here.*

'You could have told me, Mother. You could have included me in your sweeping plans for my future.' Rohne stared out the window at the golden walls and red-tiled roof of Xintou House, not far away. Her ruthless vision was as impressive as it was unsettling. 'Didn't you trust me?'

Of course I did, dearest. She smiled. *But you were so young. And then you were so desperately in love with Mina. And it's hard to keep secrets from the person you love.*

He didn't reply to that. He had yet to decide what to do with Mina, when she and Alere eventually reached Madina. But it would be his decision, not Nasra's.

'What I don't understand,' he said, 'is what you intend to do now. You have everything you wanted. But what's the point of it all?' He indicated the Alcazar and the House.

She'd hidden so much from him, over the years. What else did she conceal now? Trying to pierce her wards was pointless. She was too skilled and knew him too well. Her mind was the only one he'd never been able to establish a thread-link to. Never been able to manipulate.

Although, with yanstones he might be able to best her. Somehow, before the day was out, he needed to gain access to the Zah-Hill jewelry and see what iron-yanstone pieces existed.

He had intended to share knowledge of the stones, anticipating impressing her with their potential to amplify the twins' powers. Now he warded the knowledge well. He would need every advantage to stay ahead of her in the days to come.

Nasra raised her veil, dark blue eyes glittering with bitter triumph. *With your help – and that of the erheyi girls – we will bring this jundom forward to where it should be. The House has stifled all growth for the last five hundred years. Fearing the same rush to self-destruction that wrecked Old Earth. Li is wary of change, just as every House Mistress has since Kya Edwards sat in her place.*

Rohne simply looked at her, saying nothing, waiting. None of this was new.

Li feared me when my parents sold me to her and I came to the House. Nasra sneered down her nose at the House outside the Alcazar walls. *As the first new-line xintou in over two hundred years I came to represent all she was afraid of: different thoughts, vitality, change, improvement. I was stronger than her. She hated me.*

Rohne interrupted her tirade. 'That's what this is all about? Your parents sold you to the House sixty years ago. You made Mistress Li into the monster of your childish fears. So you've been – what – stewing over revenge your whole life?' He directed a piercing thought at her wards, trying to find the truth in her.

She deflected it.

'Is that what I am?' he growled. 'Just part of your revenge plan? You hid the fact that you're nai-xintou from Mistress Li. You could have used your micro-telekinesis to prevent pregnancy. Or to create a girl-child. Instead you allowed me: a male xintou; forbidden and feared. Why? Am I just one more weapon against Mistress Li? What do you want from me?'

Nasra glided closer, nothing but concern and love in her expression and her Outers. She stroked his cheek.

Of course you're not just part of a plan, dearest. You are the treasure of my life. I have done all this for you, not me. When you were born, I knew I had to protect you. Together, you and I will be the catalyst for change this jundom needs. You're unique. A symbol of the future. The world will see they have nothing to fear from either of us. They will see how backward Li has been in her thinking.

Come. She held out a hand. *It's time for the Bonding. Once you're linked to Hassan and the First Family, you will be unassailable. You'll be able to show your true worth. Then we can begin our work.*

Reluctantly, torn between the life-long desire to be recognised for who he was, and the fear of the same, Rohne followed her into his future.

CHAPTER ELEVEN

ALERE

The blade flashed silver as it pierced a bare throat. Blood gushed over Alere's hands, staining them brilliant red, glistening in the sun. The iron of life drained onto the sand at her feet. Someone screamed, shrill and piercing. A palm covered her mouth.

Alere woke, disorientated in the darkness. Another scream. A real hand pressing on her face. The acrid stink of blackweed. A real blade rose high, glinting red in the moonlight. A dark form crouched beside her, silhouetted against the starry sky. The arm swung toward her throat.

For a terrifying moment, the world stopped. Her heart stopped. Her breath stopped. The blade filled her vision. Nothingness roared in her ears. All she could think about was how angry Kett would be if she was stupid enough to be murdered in her sleep.

She had to *move.*

She forced herself to grab the hand on her face. The motion freed her mind and her body to act. She rolled, twisted, and small bones in his wrist snapped. He gave a strangled squeal. She kicked at a knee and took out his support. Momentum threw the man onto his side. His dagger jolted free and fell into the fire. Sparks fountained into the darkness. She knelt on his back and ground his face into the dirt. The smell of rancid sweat wafted from his filthy furs and leathers.

Alere pushed to her feet and kicked at his temple. He sagged into unconsciousness.

An arm looped around her chest from behind. A knifeblade pressed cold against her throat. Grabbing the blade-hand she turned it away from her throat. She dropped her weight and flung her attacker over a hip. He fell messily, clutching at her, dragging her to the ground.

She controlled her fall, rolled and swung a leg over his back. He was quick and tried to scramble to his hands and knees. Her feet hooked around his inner thighs. One arm wrapped under his armpit and across his neck, strangling. Stretching out broke his balance. He collapsed, half on his side, feet flailing and one arm scrabbling to reach her. She hung on, tightening the strangle.

He sagged into unconsciousness. Alere knelt on his knife arm and wedged it into a lock between her knees. She pulled the knife from his lax grip and laid it against the back of his neck, but hesitated. It went against the grain to kill an unarmed, unconscious man. Yet she couldn't just sit here. There would be more of them close by.

He stirred, growled something incomprehensible and thrashed, trying to get to his knees. In one determined movement, he dislocated his own shoulder. A hoarse scream tore from his throat. He thrust her off, onto the dirt, then scrambled to his feet. His breath hissed through bared teeth. His arm hung limp. He rounded on her, left hand reaching for another dagger at his hip.

Vulnerable, lying on her back on the ground, Alere lashed a heel at his knee. It connected with an audible crack and he clutched at his leg, gasping. She rolled to her feet over one shoulder and escaped from the circle firelight. A shout went up behind her.

Once in the surrounding trees, she stopped in the deepest shadow. A few slow, deep breaths calmed her heart and settled her mind. Her hands shook uncontrollably. She kept still and studied the clearing behind. These were not xiongshou or she'd be dead. Which meant there could be more than just a standard pair.

There. Shadows shifted where they shouldn't, obscuring the pink luminescent insects on the trunk of a spreading hucha tree. It was hard to be sure how many shadows, though. Five, possibly six. She squinted against the low firelight. Jarran and the others were nowhere to be seen. All their bedrolls were empty and messy, but with no signs of blood.

'Come out and we'll spare your friends' lives.' A harsh masculine voice floated out from the darkness. The accent was the liquid, singsong tones of a Shemali native.

Cold sucked heat from her sleep-warmed skin. The chill seeped in through her thin clothing and through the soles of her bare feet, numbing toes and fingers. She needed to move soon or lose dexterity. What were the options, though? She had no weapons, other than the single, badly-balanced blade she'd taken from her attacker. Her bow lay by her bedroll. Even the poison ring she'd taken from the dead xiongshou in Dalcin lay in her pack, out of reach.

She gazed into the dark forest, seeing only flickers of pink luminescence from flying insects, and hints of starlight through the trees. No help. No weapons.

'Come out, come out, wherever you are,' the leader taunted, emerging into the dying fire's dim, reddish light. 'I have someone I'm sure you want.'

Alere peered around the trunk again. Jiangui! He held Mina before his body like a shield, presenting no visible target for a knife, even if she had a good one to throw. Mina stood on tiptoes, with his arm around her waist and a bronze knife to her throat. Her lips parted in tiny, whimpering gasps. A trickle of blood stained her throat.

Déjà vu.

Leaning back against the trunk, Alere stared at the skeletal, dark treetops overhead. What could she do? Weaponless, she couldn't take on six by herself. Why had she been brash enough to think she could protect Mina and two children on her own?

A glutinous pulse of warmth spread across her chest and into her blood. She touched the yanstones around her neck. Of course. Thinking in terms of her physical abilities and weapons was thinking like a weishi. She was xintou now as well. Hadn't she decided she needed to use the stones?

But without the sword and dagger, she had no way to draw down the lightning.

Could she take the xintou mental gifts and use them in weapon-form? Perhaps project thoughts into their heads? It went against every teaching on ethics drilled into her by the House. Yet Weishi House taught the use of any and all resources to survive and protect. Time to put aside xintou morals and see what the stones could do.

She sank into connection with them. Mina's fear was a beacon that thickened the golden thread joining her mind to Alere's. Her uncontrolled terror surged and Alere had to draw on the stones just to think clearly. She checked on the others. They were all alive and awake. Saric and Wei were both bound, angry and scared. Jarran had been taught to ward. Strongly enough to stop her reaching his Outers directly to make any plans.

Their attackers' minds, however, were wide open and unwarded. Alere spent a moment Reading them. Just as she suspected: mere hired killers who'd heard of the reward. They had none of the sophistication or training of true xiongshou.

Enough. She opened herself wholly to the stones. Woodsmoke and iron in her mouth. Silver-gilt fire warmed her and wiped out all traces of fear. Calm and detached, Alere tucked the knife into the back of her trous and emerged from behind the tree. She strolled into the firelight with empty hands raised.

A small part of her mind hauled at the thickening connection to Mina, drawing her sister's mental presence near, calming her fear. Now they entwined so closely it became difficult to know where her mind stopped and Mina's started. Alere grimly held them separated to prevent Fusion.

Power from the stones flared higher, dissolving both of them into its gold-fire embrace, welcoming. Mina's fear mounted again. Alere sent the yanstones' soothing detachment along the bridge. Her sister's terror waned into dispassionate distance. Power surged through the connection, feeding back into Alere's mind. Glorious.

Filled with engulfing energy, Alere threw her arms wide and felt the raiders' startled bemusement.

'Why don't you gentlemen all come out where I can see you?' She inserted the compulsion to obey into their minds.

Five more men, large and leanly-muscled, shuffled into the light like recalcitrant children. Dressed in sturdy leathers and furs, they were not desperate villagers attacking to provide for themselves and their families. These were well-armed fighters hunting Alere's party for the reward money. They didn't need her sympathy.

The leader, a tall, big-bodied man with a full, dark beard and a scar across one cheek, shoved Mina forward. His lips curled into a sneer as he examined Alere.

'You're mighty smug for an unarmed little girl whose friends are dead meat.'

Alere gave back nothing but silence. He shifted restlessly, weapon still ready at Mina's throat.

The stones' power blossomed and filled Alere with silver-gilt fire until it burned beneath her skin and crackled through her hair. She hardened herself to what must come next. Mina Read Alere's intent and tried to withdraw. Alere suppressed her sister's reaction.

She held the link between them firm and let the flames grow into a conflagration.

She released that fire into the raiders' minds.

All at once.

Shrieks, torn from their throats, began shrill and high and descended into guttural groans. The men dropped to their knees and thrashed on the ground. Fingers tore at hair and skin as they tried to get to the source of pain. Legs kicked spasmodically, backs arched and skin blistered. Eyes opened, staring blindly into death and darkness.

They died, slumping into drooling, contorted slackness. Blood trickled from eyes, nose, and mouth.

Satisfied, Alere relaxed her hold on Mina and released the stone-connection. But, as the fire drained from her body, horrified anguish backlashed from Mina, exposing the sickening reality of Alere's actions. The taste of iron turned to rust; woodsmoke to ashes.

The world vanished to darkness.

When she woke again, it was to a strange rocking sensation, a view of spring-new pink leaves and glimpses of clear sky, half-obscured by horse-backs.

'She's awake.'

That was Jarran's voice, but it carried tense undercurrents sounding almost like fear. What was he afraid of? Where was she?

The weight of more than just exhaustion dragged at every muscle of her body, beckoning her back to sleep. No. She fought against it. There was something wrong. Some reason for Jarran's fear.

She tried to sit up, only to find herself strapped into a sling being carried between two horses.

'Stop. Let me out of this.'

The horses ceased their plodding walk and Jarran's stern visage appeared. His brows crowded tight over his aquiline nose, gold-brown eyes hard and wary. Without speaking, he undid the knots binding her to the contraption and helped her stand. Mina appeared and touched a wrist pulse-point. Alere flinched away, cut to the raw by the distaste arcing like static from her sister's fingers.

The men. Last night. The fire from the stones.

What had she done?

She thrust Mina aside and ran from memories of death, covering her mouth as her body tried to reject the knowledge. Pushing her way through straggly bushes lining the path, she ignored the voices calling her name and ran blindly into sparse, open timberland. A family of tunnel-pigs burst from some low scrub and scurried, squeaking, to their warrens. Their mottled black and brown bodies were barely visible amongst the dried leaves and their long claws scrabbled, throwing dirt into the air as they scrambled away.

Alere staggered on, stumbling over tree roots and slipping on dried leaves, until a stitch in her side forced her to stop. Gasping and clutching at the pain in her stomach, she braced herself on a tree trunk and vomited her self-hatred onto the hard, dry ground.

Finally, spent, she stumbled to another tree and sank onto the dirt beneath it. There, she pulled her knees up and buried her head in her arms.

Footfalls crunched through the dry leaves, approaching slowly, not trying to hide.

'How long was I out?' She didn't bother to look up. Couldn't face him.

Jarran replied, 'Only a few hours. It's the morning of the Fourth. We packed straight away last night.'

'Oh.' She thrust her fingers into her hair and rested her forehead in her palms. Jarran's booted feet were in her peripheral vision. 'And the men. Last night?'

Fire-blistered skin. Wide-stretched mouths. Eyes filled with agony staring at her in disbelieving horror.

'We couldn't do much,' he said. 'We had to leave them.'

A gentle breeze rustled through the branches overhead. Somewhere nearby a bird sang its spring mating call. Life went on; for some.

'I…froze.' She choked on the admission. 'Then I panicked because I had no weapons. So I killed them.' She examined her hands. 'Not honourably, in a fight, where skill would decide who lived. I killed them…' she grabbed the yanstone necklace and threw it into the dead leaves scattered at her feet '…just by *thinking* about it. I set their minds on fire. What kind of death is that? What kind of monster can do that? I…I…' She curled into a ball, willing it all to go away.

Jarran shifted, leaves rustling as he sat beside her. 'I won't tell you I understand how you're feeling, because I don't. I know it must be pretty scary, though, to be able to do that.'

Alere gave a weak laugh, edged with hysteria. 'That is an understatement. Try terrifying. I didn't even consider just knocking them out. I…murdered them. And it seemed so…logical.'

'Yes. But they would have killed us. And followed us if you'd just knocked them unconscious. Mina fell asleep on her watch and they took us all by surprise. If it weren't for your actions Mina would be a prisoner for Rohne's pleasure. We'd be dead, and there would be no-one to save my daughters from the same fate.'

Alere said nothing, the weight of his expectations pressing down on her.

'Now isn't the time to have doubts, Alere. I have two daughters sitting in prison in the Alcazar.' His jaw hardened. 'And your father is there. What's his life worth?'

'What do you mean?'

He pointed to the necklace. 'If I could trade places with you or my girls, I would. Their lives are worth more than mine. What're Rafi's. Petar's and Mistress Li's worth to you? Would you trade your own for theirs? Be honest.'

Alere hesitated. When Kett and Corin were in the Games, her answer had been an unequivocal *yes*. While she respected Rafi, Petar and Mistress Li, if she were brutally honest, she didn't care for them as she did for the others.

It would be so easy – even expected – to play the heroine by sacrificing herself for them. But she wasn't sure she wanted to go down that path again. Memories of the pain inflicted by first Ven, then Hallon, were too fresh in her mind.

'Exactly.' Jarran broke the silence. 'I would have doubted your sanity if you'd jumped in with a *yes* to that question. You've already had more than most people's lives worth of suffering for others.' He picked up the necklace. Alere shuddered as his fingers brushed the stones and scraped painfully under her skin. He held the yanstones up to a stray beam of light, watching them absorb and intensify it into eye-aching brilliance. 'But you're also our best hope against Rohne and Nasra. You're my best hope for freeing Rhea and Ashi.'

Still Alere said nothing. Her throat closed and she hunched her shoulders. When she didn't reply he leaned closer.

'The truth is, Alere, if that passionate purpose driving you isn't strong enough, then you may *need* something else.' He held out the necklace. 'If I had the powers you have, I wouldn't hesitate to use them to save my girls. I don't. You're the only one who does. You're the only one who can do this.'

'But what if I don't want to?' she said. 'Every time I use those I feel like I lose a bit of myself. After last night, even I'm afraid of what I'm becoming.'

His jaw firmed. 'You became what we need to win this war, Alere.'

'What?' She curled a lip. 'We need a monster? Celia and Valera both had Seeings that predicted Nasra or Rhone as the worst possible thing for the Jundom. Do I have to be like them to defeat them?'

'No. Because you were raised a weishi *and* a xintou. You will do the right thing when it's needed. They won't.' He dropped the necklace at her feet. His eyes hardened, glittering like the stones themselves, not buying into her self-pity. 'You became a weapon, not a monster. A weapon is what we need right now. Stop fighting it, Alere. Finish this and deal with the aftermath later. Now you need to be gangzhi, as the Selb say. You need to be steel, or we all lose and my daughters die.'

She made a defensive gesture. Another set of footsteps crackled through the dry leaves.

Jarran rose. 'Mina wanted to talk to you. I'll wait back at the horses.' He kissed Mina's forehead and gave her a warning look.

Alere said nothing, resting a cheek on her folded arms and staring past Mina, into the forest's shadowy, dappled reds.

Her sister hesitated, poised to flee, her face pale. She rubbed her hands down her thighs. 'I fell asleep during my watch. It's my fault they caught us.'

'But I'm the one who killed them, not you.' Alere glanced at the glittering yanstones. 'And now you're scared of me. Jiche! *I'm* scared of me. I just didn't have a choice. I had no other options.'

'There are always other options,' Mina said. 'There had to be. I told you not to use the stones. What they do. The way they work. It must affect your brain chemistry. It can't be good for you.'

'Then give me an alternative!' Alere rose and Mina shrank away. 'What other choices were there, Mina? I'd love to know. I had no decent weapons and he had a dagger to your throat. They weren't going to let us go after a bit of a friendly chat.'

'I…I don't know.' Mina lifted her chin. 'You're the weishi. Didn't you say the code was to avoid confrontation?'

'Oh!' Alere clenched her fists. 'Don't you *dare* quote weishi code to me when I'm the one having to live with these decisions.'

Mina stiffened. 'But you're not the only one, are you? What about my code? The Healer's code to take no life unwilling. To heal and nurture. When is that important in your grand plans? When is what *I* want important?' She pointed at Alere. 'You dragged me into it last night. Again. Pulled me into connection with those…those *things* and gave me no choice but to help. It wasn't just you that killed them, it was me, too. I was right there with you. I couldn't stop you.' Tears tracked down her cheeks. 'You *wanted* to kill them. Just like you did in Chengdu. What are those stones doing to you, Alere?'

'Like Jarran said, apparently they're making me into the weapon we need to be to win this war, Mina,' she replied through gritted teeth.

'You're becoming—'

'What? Becoming what?' Alere flung out an arm and paced a few steps away and back. 'Some sort of sadist, like Ven? I know! But what am I supposed to do? Everyone's relying on me. Didn't you hear Jarran? I have to rescue his daughters. And Rafi. And Mistress Li. And the whole gouri Jundom. Again.' She stripped off one of the bracelets and brandished it. 'And if you can tell me how I'm supposed to do that without using these, I'd be glad to hear it.'

Mina folded her arms. 'I don't know. But I do know that if you keep doing this to me I'll leave again. I tried to run last time when

Rafi and Corin were turning you into their pet warrior. I couldn't watch it. You came after me. You're not just a weapon. Those stones can be used for good, as well. Learn to heal others the way you healed yourself, and Kett, in Chengdu.' She swallowed and stood straight. 'I won't let you use me to kill people again. Not if I can help it.'

Alere curled a lip. 'Not even if it's the only way to save Rhea and Ashi? Or Jarran's life? Or mine?'

Mina paled.

PART II – Asadia / Beizhai

CHAPTER TWELVE

CORIN

Corin considered the drab, shifting crowds on the main road through Asadia and grasped his dagger-hilt. A shiver prickled the skin on his back.

The trip to Asadia had taken two days – longer than he'd hoped because there were so few horses available to exchange. Instead of bursts of speed, they'd had to ride slower, for longer. Now he was more than ready for a decent bath and bed.

It was the afternoon of the Fifth and they'd just passed through the high city walls after a cursory perusal of their false papers by two bored weishi. As the city gates closed behind them, he'd hoped his uneasiness about taking this path might be just paranoia.

Now… Corin surveyed the main thoroughfare into Asadia's centre and grimaced.

The further they progressed along the broad, brick-paved street, the more burly, armed men appeared and the more uneasy Corin became. Asadia, on this calm, sunny afternoon, shouldn't be bristling with muscular people bearing pointy things. It was a good three-day by huoche from Madina and no armies massed at its doors. Things should be relaxed.

But the city bore marks of civil unrest. Slogans painted on the walls read *Full-blood only,* and *No kin-child.* Not far from the gate a house stood gutted and burnt, still stinking of charred, wet timber; anti kin-child slogans scrawled on its stone walls. A symbol, too. Three overlapping circles set inside a triangle. The old symbol for a house holding a Jun's kin-child. It hadn't been seen much for the last fifteen or so years.

Corin swore. His stomach churned. The last time he'd seen it was on the remains of Shasa's house, ten years before. Kett followed his gaze and his face hardened.

'Why the diyu did I let you talk me into this?' Corin muttered. 'Alere'll kill me if I let you get captured.'

He caught a warning, sidelong glance from Kett just before the weishi raised his voice and replied loudly to what Corin had meant as a purely rhetorical question.

'Given you do most of the talking…' Kett curled a lip in an arrogant sneer '…I don't think you can accuse me of talking you into anything. In fact, I've quite had my fill of your insubordination.' He waved languidly. 'I hired you to protect me on the way to Asadia, not bore me with your chatter. I have no more need of your services, boy. Here.' Reaching into his shirt he produced a small leather purse and tossed it across. 'Take your pay and take your gear. I don't want to see your uncouth face or your unwashed clothing again.'

He tugged a small pack from amongst their gear and threw it at Corin.

Corin knew a cue when he saw one. What the diyu was Kett planning? Why this charade? Not much he could do but play along, so he scowled and swept Kett a shallow bow.

'Thank you, shenshi. It's been an honour to serve. I hope the rest of your journey is pleasant.'

Kett kicked his horse's flanks. 'Out of your snivelling company, I'm sure it will be. I have no doubt that, within the hour, you'll find your murderous friends in some black, waterfront tavern, and will drink yourself into oblivion. As you normally do.'

He rode away. A dozen or more pairs of eyes followed him. None watched Corin. Keeping up the performance, Corin flipped his retreating back an extended fist with down-pointing little finger. A rude parody of the gesture xintou used to invite open telepathic communication.

He left the main street and headed into a side alley that cut between a shoe shop and a butcher. Washing lines full of limply dangling clothes spanned the narrow space overhead. A zibal scavenger-lizard scurried for shelter under a stack of rubbish. Corin glanced back. No-one followed, nor even paid any attention to his exit.

What the gouri was Kett up to?

Corin rounded a corner and yanked open the small pack. It contained the Koh-Lin journal and Kett's real identity papers. Tucking it in amongst his own belongings, Corin kicked his heels into his gelding's sides. The animal leaped into a clattering canter with the spare horse close behind.

Riding roughly parallel to the main street, Corin peered down every cross-alley, trying to judge if he was ahead of Kett or behind. Finally the road he followed curved away to the west and he abandoned it in favour of a narrow alley that rejoined the main street.

When he reached the end, flanked by a fruit shop and a stableyard, he dismounted. He avoided a stinking-sweet pile of rotting fruit, and eased up to the corner of the stableyard. He peered around, into the main street.

To his right, the road ended in a large, open square just a few steps from where he stood. A market filled the square's northern side. But there were gaps in the stalls lined up offering wares – as though some stall owners had foregone the market this week. Unusual. But, with the unrest, perhaps not.

Half a dozen stately sandstone mansions fronted the square's eastern side, their wide glass windows blazing fire as the sun edged toward the horizon. Many of the mansions were marked with the kin-child symbol. Several had boards over their windows.

A sandstone wall, some four times his height and broken only by a bronze-studded, timber double gate, took up the square's entire southern side. Three red-tiled, peaked roofs poked their dragon-decorated ridges above the wall. The residence of Jun Third, Kennor Han-Asad.

Opposite, stood the two-storey bell tower with its massive bronze bell. And behind that the drum tower, both intended to call citizens to celebrations on feast days, or sound in times of emergency.

Upraised voices and the clatter of hooves to his left made Corin turn. He swore.

Walking, and protesting loudly, Kett was being manhandled toward the square. Two burly individuals held his arms. Others carried his weapons. Twenty weishi guarded him so there was no chance of a rescue. From the tone of Kett's ineffective protests, it sounded like he intended to keep up the rich, insulted travelling nobleman routine.

Corin rubbed at his neck. To have that many junren and weishi waiting, they must have known Kett was coming. But how? And why were all his escorts alive and with all their limbs?

Unless…Corin groaned. The utter shazi.

Kett had sent a message ahead. He *wanted* to be taken prisoner.

But how was warning of his own arrival and setting up his own capture useful? Could he possibly intend revenge on Hanna Zah-Hill for her treatment of him as a child? That made no sense. He'd had ample opportunity to kill her, back on the battlefield in Shanzhai. Or he could have used his weishi contacts to take out a xiongshou kill-contract on her. Why come here, now? Why risk the delay when they needed to catch Alere before she rode unawares into the broth of revolution brewing in Madina?

Corin leaned against a cool wall and stared at his feet. Undoubtedly Kett's last words to him were a form of instruction. He wanted Corin to go to a tavern and wait for him. A black, waterfront tavern. Which could only mean the Black Hand: an unpleasant dive in the area of town servicing the Ferra River port facilities. He'd also mentioned 'murderous friends'. Probably a reference to whomever Liu had sent.

Corin scratched the four-day growth on his chin and scowled after Kett's retreating figure. Did he follow instructions and wait for Kett to get himself out of this mess, or did he go with his gut and try to get into the walled residence to be nearby when things went suilie? Kett was good, but Hanna was extremely angry.

He scanned the streets, seeking inspiration as Kett's escort led him through the great timber gates. Ahh. A Messenger House runner station. He gave a soft chortle of anticipation. That would work. Hopefully.

At the stable next door, he paid an exorbitant sum for care of the horses for a day, and for a secure locker for his bags. Then he strode into the runner station across the road and sent a message. The bored, orange-clad clerk behind the counter barely lifted an eyebrow at the receiver's name.

'A yinbi,' he said.

'That's outrageous,' Corin replied, but his heart wasn't in it. 'The delivery address is barely a hundred paces away.'

The clerk shrugged. 'They make us wait to get through the gate. Time is money.'

Corin pressed two of the silver coins into the clerk's sweaty palm and leaned close. 'There's one more, so halve the time and get that message delivered by the time I get to the tea stand in the market square.'

The second coin vanished into the clerk's pocket and he jerked his chin at the door. 'Go, then.'

Corin eyed him narrowly and left. A second later an orange-clad runner dashed from the shop and sprinted across the market square. Corin smiled and returned to the stable for some props.

Out of his baggage he withdrew a shirt of green silk, to match his eyes. He yanked off the travel-stained, brown bamboo shirt, hauled the green on, tucked it into his trous and brushed them off as best he could. Next, he used a splash of water to tame his wayward hair back into its mawei and to wipe the dust from his face and hands. Not much he could do about the scruffy beard. Hopefully it made him look interestingly dangerous rather than unkempt.

Finally ready, he reversed his cloak to expose the rich, red xiao-bear fur inside, slipped a steel and jade signet ring over his little finger, and tugged the suede covers off his sword and dagger hilts. He threw back his shoulders, raised his chin, and stepped into the rich, bored tourist character.

His quarry appeared through a door inset in the Han-Asad residence gate. Standing on tiptoes, she peered over the crowd toward the tea stand. Elegant in dark violet silk, she was accompanied by a large, black-and-gold-clad weishi with shrewd dark eyes and one hand on his short sword. Three others trailed behind, scowling. The girl strode to a silk stand and fingered the cloth, but her attention darted to the tea stand. She purchased a bolt of burgundy silk.

Corin strolled into the market, ostensibly reviewing the various wares for sale. Each step took him closer to the tea stand. He paused by a small-animal pet seller and debated. But bright green baby sahalia lizards and mating pairs of jin-birds didn't seem appropriate.

A stand displaying musical instruments tempted him, but he had no idea if she played anything. Nearby, three men in long, dark robes and conical caps spun endlessly, in time to the thin wailing of a one-stringed instrument, and a deep-voiced drum. Their skirts flared and their eyes were glazed in some sort of meditative trance.

Corin shook his head and moved on. He stopped at the jeweller's booth next door, keeping his objective in sight. A copper and amethyst bracelet caught his attention. Perfect. A quick negotiation had it in his pocket in a moment. He turned to leave and collided with a soft, calla-flower-scented body.

With an angry cry, the girl overbalanced and dropped her linen-wrapped bundle. Corin grabbed her around the waist and held her to his chest. Her heart thumped against his. Her soft mahogany hands fluttered on his arms.

She raised her pretty, plump face. The confused anger in her rich brown eyes shifted to wide-eyed interest. Her lips parted. Judging the timing finely, he held her a moment longer in silence, keeping his gaze fixed on hers. He let a small, appreciative smile curve his lips and shifted his hand on her waist. Just to make her aware of its existence. She flushed and dropped her gaze away.

He released her, collected the parcel and presented it to her with a low bow.

'Shunu.' He caught her outstretched fingers and brought them to his lips. 'My humblest apologies. I am hopelessly clumsy. I'm just glad I was able to save you from the ignobility of a fall in such a public place. Do forgive me.'

He kept his head bowed and watched the restless shifting of her slipper-clad feet beneath the violet silk skirt. Heavy boots appeared to his right and a worried, masculine voice broke in.

'Shunu, are you alright?' The big weishi stepped close, his body half-interposed between Corin and the girl.

'Yes, yes. Perfectly. You may move back, Tren.' Her voice was soft, but low and firm, belying her childlike air. 'Please, rise.'

Corin straightened, pasting on his most charming smile. He skimmed the weishi. At least two more weapons, hidden. And…ah! Now that was interesting. A leather thong around his neck, holding a silver-metal double-bladed axe pendant. A Selb, then.

Corin greeted him. 'Molian.'

Tren sucked a quick breath. Corin touched the leather thong around his own neck. The one holding the miniature axe Liu Gray had given him. Tren nodded and moved back several paces.

The young woman regarded Corin, a frown marring her smooth forehead.

'I feel I know you. Do I?' She patted her tight-curled black hair in its intricate coil at the crown of her head. Her gaze slid to the tea stand again.

Corin chuckled. 'I'm not sure whether to be insulted or glad you feel that way. I confess I know you. But you may only know me by reputation, and I fear it may be undeserved. Or perhaps not?' He let his smile slide into wickedness.

'Oh?' She raised her brows and held her parcel protectively across her stomach. 'Who *are* you?' She seemed more puzzled than annoyed or offended.

Corin extended an elbow and smiled again, this time in genuine friendship, with just a hint of sensual awareness. Enough to get her heart racing, not enough to scare her off. There was a trick to blending trustworthiness with enough dark mystery to appeal to a sheltered eighteen-year-old.

'You got my note, didn't you? Do let's go to the tea stand and share a pot? I'll tell you my life story there. I've just arrived in the city and I'm astonishingly thirsty.'

Her eyes widened. 'You sent the note?'

'Indeed. Come, Shunu Farima Han-Asad, your weishi are just behind you and this is a very public place.' He leaned in closer, his breath fluttering the dark curls of hair over her ear. 'I'm hardly going to seduce you here, am I?'

The pink stain in her cheek deepened to red and she backed away.

'You *do* know me. But…' She took in his rich cloak and the yanstones glittering in his weapons. 'We've never met…have we?'

'I'm sorry. I shouldn't tease. It's only that I feel I know you so well. Perhaps Shunu Lianna Koh-Lin mentioned me, which might be why you felt you recognised me.'

Farima took a half-step toward him. 'Lia! You *are* a friend of hers? The note said she was sending someone I must speak to. Is she here? Oh, it's been an age since I've seen her. Is she well again? Are the rumours about her and Ven true?' She laid her fingers on his arm and waved her weishi away when he protested. 'Let's sit. Tell me all about her, please.'

Corin purchased what he knew from Lianna to be her favourite – lillaflower tea – and joined her at a table. He sipped his own brew and tried not to screw up his nose at the over-sweet, floral taste. He glanced around to see no-one was within easy earshot. Farima leaned forward, her lips parted and eyes sparkling.

'My name is Corin Lin, shunu,' he murmured. 'Lia is well, but I don't know what you've heard about her and Ven. I can only tell you the truth, for I saw what happened.'

'But—'

'You may have heard Lia call me Corin Mal-kin, my travelling name. I'm a distant cousin of the Koh-Lins and I work with Rafi—'

'As his spy!' she breathed. 'Lia used to tell me all your adventures. Oh, it was so exciting. Like the time you snuck into the Jadidan Prince's palace and seduced his beautiful daughter in order to gather information about his plans to expand north into Ma-Safra territory.' She gazed at him dreamily.

Corin repressed his automatic headshake. That one was a figment of Lia's imagination but it would be counterproductive to deny it and shatter Farima's romanticised image of him. Instead he placed two fingers on her lips and scanned the square.

'Please, shunu, not so loud. I'm here under cover and if that story ever got back to Prince Soran it could mean war with Jadid.' He brushed his fingertips across her cheek, cupping her jaw briefly in his palm.

Her pupils dilated and the flush extended to her décolletage.

Allowing her to see regret, he withdrew his hand and placed it over hers where it lay on the rough timber table. She took a sip of tea, appearing composed though her fingers trembled.

'And Ven's death? What's the truth of that? He was my cousin, you know.'

'I know, shunu, and none regretted his death more than Lia.' Corin sighed and let his shoulders fall. 'She did kill Ven, but only after he kidnapped and whipped her, then threatened her parents if she didn't marry him. He tried to kill her at her nameday ball. She defended herself. That's the truth.'

He let her see utter sincerity and, after considering him for several seconds, she seemed satisfied, though her springleaf-pink mouth drooped.

'I'd heard but I didn't believe it. Ven must have truly been insane to do such a thing to the Jun-Second's Heir.' She shivered. 'He always frightened me. I am glad Lia is well, though. But you're a long way from Shanzhai. Are you here on her behalf to see me, or Rafi's for something else?

Corin squeezed her fingers. 'I need your help. Your aunt Hanna has had a man taken into your house, just a few minutes ago. She will kill him. I need your help to free him.'

A frown flickered across her expressive face and her lips tightened. She looked quickly at the timber gates behind her, and at the weishi standing guard not far away.

'Why? Who is he? What's he done?' Her eyes narrowed and she withdrew her hand.

Corin made a quick judgement call. This girl was smart and part of a powerful Jun-family household fraught with intrigue and ambition. He would be stupid to underestimate her just because of her doll-like prettiness. Lianna always spoke highly of Farima's intelligence and loyalty. The girl was also Jun-Heir to Kennor Han-Asad, so she was xintou-trained to ward, and that made using the yanstones pointless.

She had, however, now suffered Hanna Zah-Hill as a house guest for at least a week or two. Given the woman's unsettled state of mind when she left Shanzhai, that would be no sinecure. The kin-child protests were evidence of that. Farima probably normally ran the Han-Asad household here in Asadia, since Kennor was a widower and spent most of his time in Madina badly managing the city guards.

Based on her reactions to Hanna's name, Farima had probably been rudely supplanted. Now, having met her, he also doubted she had been knowingly involved in poisoning the sweets sent to Lianna. Her questions about Lianna's health were honest and ingenuous. If he offered her a way to disrupt Hanna's control, he suspected the girl would take it.

Luckily, she was a romantic.

'The man Hanna has taken is named Kett.' He lowered his voice and she shifted closer.

Her eyes flew to his. 'Do you mean Tekettan Zah-Hill? Radan's kin-child? He's here? Is he *mad?* Hanna's been making herself sick over him: wandering the halls for days, screaming insults and threatening to kill him in the vilest ways imaginable. Blaming him for Ven's death.' Her jaw firmed. 'He's the reason she's been stirring up my people against kin-children again. And she's livid that Jarran Zah-Hill has been given the throne. All she talks about is him being a kin-child and how he shouldn't be the First.'

Now it was Corin's turn to blink. He hadn't anticipated Hanna's need for revenge would be quite so public or voiced so loudly. She was more the plot-in-silence type. Khara. Perhaps Ven's death had unhinged her. That complicated things. Grief-crazed people were much less predictable to deal with.

Thinking fast, he nodded. 'Yes, we know. I need to get Kett out before she kills him. He's too important.'

'But...' Farima nibbled at her lower lip. 'Why is Kett so important? I...' Apprehensively, she checked the house and her weishi again. 'I can't do much. She has me followed every minute. Half of my weishi are her men, now.' She leaned forward, shooting quick glances sideways. 'She's been recruiting new junren from all over our lands. I overheard her talking to her Shangwei.' She lowered her voice to a whisper. 'She's going to march on Madina!

She wants to overthrow Jarran and Rafi. That's what you need to stop, Corin. Kett doesn't matter. He's as good as dead. She hates him so much I'd be surprised if he's still alive now.'

Corin ground his teeth, trying to stay calm. 'You're right. We do need to stop her. But trust me, Kett's important.' He poured on the sincerity. 'He's Lia's betrothed. It's been kept secret while all this furor is going on. He renounced his claim to the Steel Throne of the Jun First so he could be with her.' An outright lie, but it sounded good. 'And he's on his way to Madina to help Jarran and Rafi. If you want to stop Hanna, then help me get him out.'

Farima's anger segued into starry-eyed delight. 'Lia's betrothed…' She stared off into middle distance. Joy shifted to envy, then to resolution.

Anticipating her next question, he added. 'Rafi sent us to Chengdu on a diplomatic mission, but we got the news that he and Petar Ma-Safra have been taken prisoner by Hassan. We're trying to get back to Madina as fast as we can. Hence…' He spread his hands.

'Jun-Seconds are imprisoned?' Her fists curled and her jaw clenched. 'Hanna must be intercepting my messages. This has to stop.' She lifted dark eyes to his. They sparkled with new excitement and her next words revealed her youth. 'Freeing Kett will very much annoy Hanna, won't it?'

'Yes. But it comes with risks, too. If you think she's domineering now just wait until you've crossed her in this. You could be taking a huge chance, shunu, even if you are Jun-Heir.'

At this, deliberate, reminder of her status, Farima pulled her plump shoulders back. She rose gracefully from the seat.

'I am quite aware of that.' She lifted her chin, every inch the shunu. 'However *I,* and not Hanna, am mistress of this house and this city.'

Not far away, a thin man with a fanatical glitter in his eye leapt onto an upturned crate and launched into a speech about kin-children. A small crowd gathered, some nodding as he gesticulated and listed the ways in which kin-children destroyed the lives of full-blooded children. He appealed to the crowd, asking if they wanted their homes confiscated, their property taken away by a kin-child they never knew existed. He held up a flag bearing the triangle-three-circles symbol then exhorted them to march on Madina and demand the repeal of the new laws legalising kin-children. The crowd swelled, angry voices muttering.

Farima's cheeks paled. She turned her back on the speaker and smoothed the front of her robe with nervous hands. 'These riots she's stirring up. The army she's building. It's wrong. She needs to be stopped and I can't do it on my own. So if you'll promise to help me stop her, I'll help you get Kett out. If he's alive.'

Corin scrubbed at the back of his neck. Quelling riots and disbanding an army took time and they had none. But what choice did he have? 'Khara! Alright. I'll do whatever I can to help you get Hanna under control.'

She kissed his cheek, whispering, 'Come to the western side gate in an hour. If Hanna knows you then wear a disguise. Don't bring your weapons.'

Bowing, Corin allowed her to see his profound gratitude before he strode away.

How in diyu was he supposed to stop an entire army on his own?

CHAPTER THIRTEEN

ALERE

Every gongli took them further into the wastelands that hugged the eastern side of the Beifang Ranges. Dry-lipped and drooping in the saddle, Alere already regretted the decision to travel this way. Two days of travel and they were almost out of food and water, and at least a day more lay ahead – after they rounded the end of the mountains and left the desert behind.

Memories of the Kabir River's icy clarity intruded. She pushed them aside, resisted the urge to drink from their scant water supplies, and surveyed the landscape again instead. Gone were the river valley's lush forests and fertile fields. As the land slowly rose and dried, first the trees vanished, then the thorny scrubland. Now the horses plodded through rolling green-sand dunes that were broken by the occasional hardy tuft of purple grass or rocky outcrop. The only sounds were the hiss of wind across sand and the earth-rumbles underfoot as the distant peak of Mount Huoshan spat plumes of smoke and ash into the air. Winds carried the debris north, toward the ocean, and painted the sky a bitter grey-green.

'Is it much further to the village, Jarran?' Mina's faint question broke the hot silence.

Alere said nothing. Mina had barely spoken to her since their conversation about the bandits and yanstones, the day before. Alere, for her part, was too uneasy and ashamed to instigate a conversation she had no idea how to handle. She had taken off the yanstones, resisting their seductive pull, aching for their calming affect on her emotions. But, if Mina had noticed, she'd made no comment.

'The map shows the village should be at the foot of the Beifangs, that way.' Jarran pointed southeast at the nearest, dust-hazed foothills. 'We should be there in an hour or so at the most. Sunset will be in about two hours, so we've plenty of time.'

'Well, I'm excited.' Wei peered around Jarran's arm to where Saric sagged against Mina's back. 'This is where my mother came from. I'm sure she must have family here. They live in tents, you know, but they call them *ger* and they eat desert tuo, and they drink horse-milk, and they're really good at horseback archery. I want to learn that. Do you think they'll teach me?'

Saric grunted and turned away. His skin was flushed, his eyes half-closed. He wore a white shirt draped over his head. Wei sighed, her mouth drooping.

The wind picked up, scouring Alere's face with tiny sand particles. She pulled a cloth up over her nose and squinted. An eerie whistling sound – almost musical – drifted across the dunes. Alternating between three minor notes. Uneasy. She rose in the saddle, trying to pinpoint the source.

'It's just the singing stones,' Wei said cheerfully. 'My mother said they're all around here.' She pointed at a nearby outcrop of rocks, tall and slender with holes at irregular intervals up their length. 'The wind blows across them and makes the music.' Wei cocked an ear. 'I like it, but Ma said the villagers tell stories about spirits of the dead singing to people.'

Saric sniffed. 'Spirits. No-one believes in that feihua.'

She shrugged. 'Oh.' She pointed east to where a series of funnel-shaped depressions pockmarked the green sands. 'And stay away from those. I remember Ma telling me about the big sand-trap spiders.'

'Uh,' Saric said, 'how big, exactly?'

Wei held her hands as far apart as they would go, her expression solemn.

Saric glared. 'Are you telling the truth? You know I hate spiders.'

She grinned. 'True, I swear.'

He cast the funnel-pits a dubious look, then shrugged and faced the other way again. Wei's shoulders slumped.

They rode in silence a while longer, the heat slowly easing as the sun blazed muddy orange through the dust-haze. In the distance, a small herd of desert tuo strolled in a line along the dune ridges, their distinctive two-humped shape silhouetted against the sunset. Long legs with knobbly knees and a long neck made them look awkward and ungainly. Something startled them. They took off at a lolloping gallop and vanished behind a ridge.

Saric sat up, his gaze sharpening to somewhere beyond Alere. She checked and saw only another swirling mini-tornado of green copper-oxide dust so common in these parts. The column rose high into the air, deepening the green tint of the sky. She raised a brow at him. He nodded slowly. Alere unsheathed her bow and nocked an arrow. She held the bow in her left hand, out of sight. Saric nudged Mina and said something, simultaneously flicking a handsign at Wei.

Sand fountained at their feet. Alere's mare reared, whinnying in terror. Hooves flailed at the mounds of cascading sand emerging from the ground. Stumbling and rearing, the mare fell onto her side. Alere leapt free, curling in the air to land in a dive-roll on the hot greensand. Her arrows slid out of their quiver and sprayed across the ground with a hollow clatter of timber. She came to her feet, but her ankle twisted in the soft sand. Her back ached where she'd rolled on the quiver and throwing knives.

Momentum carried her forward, so she kept running. Sand grated in her eyes. She wiped them and continued, half-blinded. She needed to get far enough away to get perspective and to find an effective target for the single arrow still held on the string. Were they facing sand-spiders or something else?

A horse whinneyed. The dull thud of hooves on sand faded as the animal bolted. Voices, yelling incomprehensibly, echoed around the small dune-valley. More green sand erupted. Human shapes emerged, sand cascading off their shoulders like water. Wei's shrill voice screamed words that made no sense and made no difference to the chaos.

Glancing back, Alerc saw Saric duck behind one of the horses, blowpipe to his lips. Mina sat astride her panicked animal, struggling to control it. A man grabbed her leg and she lashed out with a kick. The horse reared and Mina fell to the sand, still clutching the reins. Wei slid off the back of Jarran's horse. She ran for the nearest assailant, waving her arms and shrieking gibberish. Jarran jumped down and ran after her, karambit flashing in his fingers.

Now clear of the melee, Alere drew the bowstring, searching for the leader. Too many to be xiongshou: at least six. All were dressed in mottled dust-green clothing, with cloth wrapped around their heads. Each wielded a wicked, curved bronze blade about arms-length. Except one. Short and stocky, he bore two blades and shouted incomprehensible orders at the others. They leapt to obey.

There was her target. Jarran ran straight at him, following Wei.

The leader raised his weapons to strike at them.

One green-clad man fell with a cry. He plucked a blue-feathered dart from his neck and Saric grinned. But a fresh attacker appeared on a dune-ridge behind the boy. The arrow in his curved horsebow was nocked and aimed at Mina where she lay, exposed and unarmed, on the ground. At the same time, three men spotted Alere and ran at her. They shouted to each other in an unintelligible dialect.

The leader's blade swept toward Jarran's neck. An arrow arced against the sky, aimed at Mina. Saric cried out as arms pinned him. He kicked backward and jabbed a green-feathered dart into the arm.

Alere drew back the string, her arrow aimed at the threat to Jarran. But Mina… She wavered.

Wei leapt in front of Jarran's attacker, yelling.

Alere hesitated, swore and adjusted her aim. She loosed the arrow and dropped her bow. No time to see if her shot deflected the shaft aimed for Mina. Instead, she snatched out her blades. The first man came within reach. His ferocious overhead strike clashed against her upraised dagger. She spun aside, letting his momentum carry him past. A pommel-strike to the back of his skull laid him out on the sand, unconscious. He slid into the bottom of a funnel-pit. The second man leapt at her. She swept his ankle with her foot as he landed. He fell awkwardly in a tangle of arms and blade, yelling and slicing his leg with his own weapon.

As he lay on the ground, clutching at the bloody gash, Alere backed away. The last of Alere's attackers skidded to a halt and approached with more caution.

In the distance, Wei spoke earnestly to the leader, who lowered his sword and yanked down the cloth over his face. Mina was alive, but with a sword to her throat. Jarran stood next to Wei, empty-handed. Saric toed a limp body at his feet and stiffened as a sword appeared at his neck. He scowled, but slid his blowpipe into its sheath on his back and raised his hands.

Alere lifted both her blades, holding them with her thumbs, palms out and fingers splayed, trying to show she didn't want to use them. She couldn't risk anyone killing Mina or Jarran in revenge.

She pointed over her opponent's shoulder at his leader, deep in conversation with Wei. He kept his attention fixed on Alere and continued to advance, slowly. Then his focus slid past her and his eyes widened. He shouted in genuine terror.

Alere spun and struck, hacking off the huge, scaled leg that reached for her. The leg twitched and a now-nine-legged monster scrabbled at the sand near her feet. Its dust-green, flat body was still half-buried in the bottom of a funnel-pit. One hooked leg curled around the man she'd knocked unconscious and dragged him close to the sand-spider's gaping maw.

With three quick flicks, Alere threw knives at the creature's three blood-red eyes. A squeal so high-pitched it was almost inaudible echoed across the dunes. The animal burrowed its way back beneath the sands, leaving the fallen man behind.

Swearing at the loss of three knives, Alere scrambled down. She sheathed her sword and dagger and latched onto the unconscious man's leg. His companion joined her and together they hauled the man to safety. When they reached high ground he swung on her, sword at her throat.

Raising her hands, she walked back to join her companions. A sack dropped over her head and rough hands tied rope around her wrists. Her sword and dagger were removed, along with her remaining throwing knives. Someone prodded her in the back and she stumbled forward.

Hopefully she'd made the right choices.

CORIN

Precisely an hour later found Corin outside the small western gate, dressed as a purple-hat musician again, with his oud across his back, his hair temporarily blackened, and a convincing pencil moustache and goatee stuck to his lip and chin. He'd shaved at the public baths and darkened his skin with black-nut juice purchased from a healer's market stall. He carried only a small, bronze Melcori kris. His too-distinctive sword and knife were locked away with his other gear. It wasn't the first time he'd gone under cover almost unarmed, but it always made him uneasy.

Resisting the urge to check the two other items tucked into the soles of his purpose-made boots, he knocked gently on the timber and stood back. The door creaked open. Farima gestured him inside, inspecting him critically.

'I barely recognised you,' she whispered. 'Perfect choice. Come with me.' She locked the gate, snatched at his wrist and dragged him along a picturesque stone path overarched with newly-budding calla-flower vines.

It would be a romantic walk in a few weeks when the flowers bloomed but, right now, with the sun hidden behind the high wall and the garden cast into gloom, it was just cold, damp and dark.

Corin grinned. Intrigue. This was more like it.

They reached the house proper. Each of the three wings was an unimaginative block, leavened only by ceramic dragons hunched on the roof. Farima knocked elaborately on a black-painted door. It opened and a blushing maidservant let them in.

'Just upstairs to the right, shunu,' she whispered. 'Perfect place. You won't be missed.'

'Thank you, Lissa.' Farima touched the girl on the shoulder. 'Go wait in my room.'

The maid scurried away down a half-lit hallway.

Suspecting Farima was deep in the throes of some impossibly-romantic and impractical escape plan, Corin stood his ground when she tugged at him again.

'You need to tell me what you're planning,' he said. 'I'm almost unarmed and I'd rather not be caught, skulking around your house, by Hanna.'

Farima threw him a dimpled, cheeky smile and tugged harder. 'You'll see in a minute. Getting caught is the whole point. I found out that Kett is alive. He's in the basement cells.'

A knot of tension unwound in Corin's gut. Annoying though the weishi was, he'd come to value the man's solid friendship.

'The trick is,' Farima whispered, 'getting *you* put into the cells, not killed on the spot. C'mon. It'll be fine, I promise.'

Corin grimaced. 'Oh, I see where you're going alright. But every gaisi time I hear those words something goes horribly wrong. Wait.' He produced a small, silk-wrapped parcel from his pocket. 'Here. Open it later. Two things in there. One is a thank you. The second is something you might find handy, if you've the stomach for it. If not, just hang onto it for me.'

She tucked the little parcel into a pocket secreted in her robe. Then she ran up a short flight of narrow stairs and onto a wide balcony. Corin followed.

The balcony overlooked an enormous hall below – clearly the main entrance to the house and the last place he wanted to be. Servants crisscrossed the dark-timbered floor without glancing up, intent on their destinations. Somewhere nearby a female voice rose in anger, the words indistinguishable. In a room below, someone practiced the lap harp. Badly. Smells of roasting meat wafted enticingly from an open door on the lower level.

Stopping near the top of a sweeping staircase, Farima glanced quickly around and nodded in satisfaction.

'Look,' Corin started, 'I—'

She pushed him over to a wall, pressed herself against him and planted a kiss on his mouth. He tried to grasp her shoulders and shove her away. She grabbed his arms and placed them on her waist, speaking against his lips.

'Don't be a shazi. This is the fastest, safest way to get to Kett. Trust me.' She huffed as he fended her off. 'Just kiss me.'

Light, swift footfalls sounded on the timber. A quick check told him everything she intended and none of it was good. Too late to back out now. He'd best make it appear worthy of imprisonment. Cradling Farima's face he kissed her with all the intensity and passion he could. She should get some enjoyment out of the scene before things went suilie. She was a surprisingly good kisser.

'Farima Milla Han-Asad!' A shrill voice broke the spell.

Farima broke away with a half-guilty, half dazed expression, breathing hard. Recovering, she shrank in on herself and directed a frightened look at Hanna and her entourage of weishi and servants.

'Oh, Aunt Hanna! I'm…I'm sorry. Please.' She clutched at Hanna's thin, blue-veined hand and fell to her knees. 'It was just a kiss. It's nothing, really. Please don't put him in the cells.'

Corin held his tongue, torn between admiration of her performance and shock at Hanna's altered appearance. While Farima, the epitome of fresh, youthful health, begged for mercy on his behalf, Hanna stood over her, disdainful, withered and bitter. Gone was the elegant, assured woman who had graced the Alcazar's throne room for twenty-five years. In her place stood an aged crone, her face lined, her luxurious blonde curls thin and lank.

Only her blue eyes still lived, but the fire in them was no longer the spark of ambition and drive. Now it was the blaze of utter madness, reined in by the last vestiges of sanity clinging grimly to the edges.

Against his better judgment, Corin pitied her.

Hanna sent him a contemptuous glare. He held his breath. Would she recognise him from the battle in Shanzhai? She merely signalled her men. Two of them seized his arms and removed his kris. He didn't resist or protest. One of the serving women hauled Farima to her feet.

'You silly little girl.' Hanna sneered at Farima. 'This is how it all begins. Just a kiss, then more, then you have a kin-child as your heir. I've seen it all before. All the problems facing the Jundom come from *this* sort of behaviour.'

A crafty smile pulled at her lips and she gazed off into middle distance. Corin had no doubt who she was thinking about.

Shaking herself, she pointed at Corin. 'Take him to the cells. A few weeks there will cool his ardour. Farima, you go to your room. I will have words with your father when he returns. He has given you far too much leeway.' She drew herself up and tucked her claw-like hands into the sleeves of her robe. 'It's a good thing I've come, I think. The management of my family's estates should not be left to an irresponsible child.'

A quickly-hidden scowl from Farima relieved Corin of one of his minor concerns. If he was any judge of character, Hanna would not have control for long. He flashed Farima a quick grin and let the weishi drag him downstairs. After a perfunctory body-search, and a gratuitous fist to the stomach, the weishi slammed the heavy timber cell door and left Corin, gasping for breath, in the thick, cold darkness.

He leaned back against the cold stone wall and counted until he was reasonably sure half an hour had passed. Then he yanked his left boot off. Pressure against the back of the heel popped a tiny hidden drawer out. He withdrew the steel lockpicks with great care. Dropping them to a dark, filthy floor would not help.

Replacing his boot, he felt his way to the door and knelt. The stone's aching chill bit through his trous. The lock clicked open. He heaved a relieved sigh and cast silent thanks to Liu for his swift replacement of the equipment taken when Corin had been captured by Hallon Nasim and thrown into the Games.

The cell's ink-blackness gave way to the slightly less black of the corridor outside. Corin re-closed the door with extreme care. He felt his way along the narrow hallway, running his fingertips across the rough stone, testing the handles on every door he passed. Only the last one was locked.

The picks scraped in the lock, loud in the dark-silence. He held his breath, every second expecting the blaze of discovery. It didn't come. His hands shook with cold and he silently cursed the stubborn tumblers. The lock finally gave with a dull thunk. Turning the handle with excruciating slowness, he eased it open.

The door flew from his grip. An iron arm wrapped around his throat. He didn't waste time trying to yell or claw at the muscular forearm. Reversing the lockpicks he jammed them into a tricep. With a hiss of pain his attacker tightened the sleeper hold. The darkness danced with multi-coloured stars.

Then he was free and sucking in great lungsful of air through a bruised throat. His knees sagged.

'Corin. You should have knocked.' Kett's quiet, amused words filtered past the ringing in his ears. 'Lucky I recognised your incoherent gargling from our sparring sessions.'

Repressing a cough, Corin merely said, 'You're welcome. Sorry about the arm.'

'I'll live. How did you get in?'

It was eerie hearing only a disembodied voice. A thin, slow squeal must be the door opening further. Kett's bulk was just visible as a looming darkness against the grey of the corridor.

'Not really important,' Corin managed. 'The trick will be getting out again.'

'Actually, it is important. I've got time.'

Recognising implacability, Corin told him. At the end of the tale, Kett gave a faint sigh.

'Well, you've achieved one of my three main objectives. But I would have appreciated the backup and messages Liu sent, had you bothered to go to the Black Hand as I asked.'

'No time.' Corin rubbed his bruised throat. 'I must tell you, as plans go this one is pretty abysmal. What part of being taken prisoner by a psychopath who hates you is good?'

'The part where you come to get me out.'

Corin snorted. 'So, I've achieved that – almost – what were your other objectives?'

Kett pushed him gently through the open door. 'Getting out was further down the list. You've achieved the first one, which was to make sure Farima would be ready and willing to muster men to support Alere.'

'That's crazy,' Corin whispered. 'Most decent Han-Asad weishi or junren with any training are already with those who marched on Shanzhai. They must have arrived at Madina by now and will either be sworn to Hassan or dead.' He peered around the corner and crept up the corridor. 'And apparently Hanna's recruited most of the able-bodied who are left into an army ready to march on Madina *against* Jarran. Besides stirring up the populations against kin-children in general. They're getting so out of control that Farima made her help tonight conditional on us helping her stop Hanna.'

'Oh, that's not a problem,' Kett replied, grimly. 'But we don't want to stop Hanna's new army. We need to turn it into one that will help Alli and Jarran when the time comes.'

'I doubt a bunch of untrained farmers will be much use. Besides, aren't you forgetting the Selb army? That's what they're for.'

'Not forgetting them,' Kett replied. 'Like you, I just like to be prepared.'

'For what?'

'Anything.'

'Well,' Corin said acerbically, 'that's both ridiculous and impossible. And I hate it when you're all...' he waved his hands then stopped, the gesture and ironic facial expression being wasted in the dark, '...enigmatic.'

Kett's reply was a soft chuckle as he ghosted past Corin and vanished around the next corner. A few seconds later, Corin found him waiting beside a thick timber door. He was just visible in the glow filtering around the edges, his ear pressed to the keyhole. He grabbed Corin's shirtfront and hauled him close, putting his lips against Corin's ear.

'Two weishi.' His words were almost inaudible. 'One asleep on the other side of the room and one at the table, drinking jiu by the smell of it. Open the door. I'll take the drinker. You make sure the sleeper stays that way.'

Corin took his place and worked on the lock. When the last tumbler clicked, he hesitated, awaiting an outcry from the other side. Nothing but a few mumbled words from the awake weishi and a sonorous snore from the other. He peered through the keyhole. The drunk guard sat, sagging and muttering, with his back to the door.

Corin eased the door open. Halfway through its arc it creaked like an ancient rocking chair. The weishi at the table jerked upright, his head snapping around. He fumbled for a weapon.

With an oath, Kett pushed past and covered the distance in two long strides. Hauling the man out of his chair, Kett broke his neck before he made a sound.

Corin, close on his heels, ran for the cot. The sleeping man snapped awake and leapt to his feet. He jabbed a punch at Corin's face. Corin ducked, sidestepped and drove a fist into his liver. The weishi folded, gasping. Corin slammed an elbow into his temple and the man sagged to the ground, his eyes rolling back.

An impressive array of manacles and torture devices hung from the wall. Corin grabbed manacles and a gag. In a matter of moments, he had the weishi gagged, bound and locked into Kett's cell.

When he arrived back in the guardroom, the dead weishi was arranged at the table to appear as though he slept. Kett stood at the tiny sink tucked into one corner of the room. He'd piled the bottle of jiu and several strips of cloth on the small table. Corin waited while he washed his face and drank four glasses of water.

Kett finally turned around and Corin understood the need for the jiu and the bandages. Hanna had taken out her frustration on the man she saw as her worst enemy.

His clothes hung from him, shredded and bloodstained. The gaping rents revealed purpling bruises and a long, shallow cut across his ribs that stained his skin freshly red with every movement. One eye was blackened and swollen almost shut. He spat blood into the sink.

Corin sat at the table, doused the cleanest rag in jiu and gestured for Kett to sit. The weishi did so, pouring himself a small glass to drink as Corin went to work cleaning the worst of the visible cuts. Kett didn't normally drink jiu and nor did Corin. The stuff was a raw and lethal clear spirit designed to rip an unsuspecting throat and liver out before pickling them. Kett's injuries must hurt more than he let on.

Kett pointed at Corin's face. 'Nice disguise. Suits you.'

'What, the sleazy musician? Thanks.' Corin indicated Kett's face. 'Can't say the same. His handiwork?' He jerked a thumb at the body.

'A man who seemed to thoroughly enjoy his work.'

Corin made no further comment, for there was little he could say. He rinsed the cloth out and passed it to Kett. 'You'll need a healer to stitch the cheek and the ribs.'

Kett held the cold cloth to his eye. 'Later. Right now, I'd like to achieve my second objective.'

Corin waited.

Squeezing the bloody cloth, Kett studied the watered red liquid dripping onto the table. 'I wasn't going to kill her. I'd promised Alli. I just wanted to know what her plans were so I could stop her, somehow. I didn't want an enemy at Alli's back when she arrived at Madina.'

A faint sound outside brought Corin to his feet. Moving to the door, he opened it slightly and peered out. Nothing. He returned to the table.

'What changed your mind?'

Kett walked over to the cot and opened a footlocker tucked at the base of the bed. Rummaging through it, he found a clean shirt and trous of coarse, brown wool. Shucking his mangled clothes, he wound strips of cloth around the slice on his ribs, another on one thigh, and the two lockpick puncture wounds on his arm. Finally, he drew on the clothing, grimacing and prodding at the darkening bruises across his torso.

Only then did he reply. 'Hanna made a promise. One I believe she will keep.'

'Alere?' Corin guessed.

'To begin with. Hanna *is* the one who took a kill-contract out on her. And the one on me. Hanna must have paid them an absolute fortune. They don't normally take contracts on members. But, then again, Zand signed it and he doesn't like me.'

'A man of taste, then.'

Kett smiled faintly and winced. 'She's also – as you said – planning to march on Madina and take the throne back in her own name. It's astonishing how much people will tell you when they think they have you at their mercy.' He laid the cloth back to his eye and sat.

'Then she swore she would engage xiongshou to remove the entire Koh-Lin family, and the Ma-Safras.' He leaned both elbows on the table and covered his face. 'Including Petar Ma-Safra's only living child.'

'But Petar and Leah have been married and childless, for what, almost fifteen years… oh.'

Kett straightened and poured himself another small shot of jiu, screwing up his nose as he threw it back. 'Petar's Jun-Heir is a kin-child. He and Leah have been hiding the boy in Jiali for the last ten years. Liu told me in his last message. With Petar imprisoned, Liu probably thought someone with an interest ought to know. The boy's name is Kenji. He doesn't know he's Jun-Heir.'

'And somehow Hanna knows of him?'

'And where he is,' Kett said. 'She quite enjoyed telling me she would extinguish the Ma-Safra line once and for all. And she will.' He looked at the door, or even beyond it, perhaps. 'Regardless of what happens in Madina. Regardless of repealed kin-child laws. She'll find a way. I can't let her.'

A bitter laugh burst from his swollen lips. 'The boy is named after my mother, Ji, and me. Petar thinks we're long-dead and he named his son to honor us. I can't let the boy die because of Hanna's hatred for me.'

Corin patted his shoulder. 'You don't have to justify it to me, my friend. I was ready to cut out her heart the second I saw you. Before, even. I think Alli would back me on this one, too. If you won't do it, I will. Happily. And I'll sleep quite well afterward, I assure you.

Here.' He sat, removed his second boot, and withdrew an elegant little steel dagger from the heel. 'You might find this useful.'

Kett inspected the knife then gave it back. 'Nice blade, but I have my own to retrieve. Hanna took it and I'm not leaving without it.'

Even though the sword in question was steel, it was quite plain. Kett rarely let it out of his sight. When the sword had been returned to him after the Games in Chengdu, Kett had grasped it as a parent might take the hand of a beloved child, letting out a sigh of relief that intrigued Corin.

A soft, scraping sound outside the door killed the question on his lips. Corin shot to his feet, dagger at the ready. Kett snatched a ceramic sword off the wall and slid into the space behind where the door would open. Corin plastered himself to the wall on the other side.

CHAPTER FOURTEEN

ALERE

Someone cut the rope around Alere's wrists and shoved her through some sort of flap and into smoky warmth that smelled of animals and unwashed humans. She stripped off the bag and squinted in the gloom. She stood still a moment, assessing her surroundings and injuries. Her right ankle felt stiff and swollen, but not with the excruciating pain of a break. Her ribs twinged where she'd landed on her quiver, but nothing bad enough to need the yanstones' healing powers.

Using them was the last thing she wanted.

Rubbing sand from her eyes, she took in the sloping, skin walls, bamboo supports and peaked roof overhead. A khiba. No, what had Wei called them? *Ger*. That usually meant a nomadic people, like Jada Marin-kin's raiders further south. This space was more a functional sleeping tent, not a display of wealth, as Jada's had been.

Five piles of mottled grey-green desert tuo pelts scattered around the room made for inviting beds but Alere declined their lure. Jarran stumbled through the door behind her. He yanked off his blindfold and blinked. Alere moved past him and lifted the tent flap. A bronze sword tip appeared at her throat. She backed up and let the skin fall. That brief glimpse of the dusk-shrouded village showed Mina, Saric and Wei being led into another ger; one of about twenty clustered around a central well and hearth area.

With a weary sigh, Jarran helped himself to a drink of water from a jug in the middle of the floor. Alere did the same. The water was warm and slightly brackish, but she didn't care and welcomed a second cup when she'd gulped the first. Then she sank onto a pile of furs and lowered her aching head into her hands.

Jarran paced the open space in the middle, his hands clenching and unclenching as he cast frowning looks at the door-flap.

'Can't you do something?'

'What?' she asked, wearily. 'They have Mina.'

'Use the yanstones,' he snapped. 'Get us out of here. I don't have time to waste in this gouri place. My daughters are going to be executed.'

'They took my weapons.' Alere rose and folded her arms. 'And I'm not wearing the necklace or the bracelets. They're in my pack – which they also took.' Even from a distance, the yanstones pulled at her, urging her to wear them, to use her gifts to free herself and Mina. A nagging, soft almost-voice she couldn't ignore, whispering in the depths of her mind.

She shivered, though her skin felt hot and dry.

He paused and stared. 'Why the jahim would you do something so stupid? Why would you give up such a huge advantage?' He jabbed a finger at her. 'You have no right to endanger all of us. I'm relying on you. That fight today could have ended much worse. With the stones you could have stopped it before it started.'

'I know,' she said, low and hard. 'That's the problem, isn't it?' She pointed at the door. 'With those stones I could do almost anything. Kill these people in a second. Control almost anyone. You, included. Is that what you want?'

He blanched and took a step backward.

'Exactly,' she said bitterly. 'Where do I stop? Where's the line between *us* and *them?* I put the stones away because I was losing sight of everything I valued. Everything I learned from Weishi House and Xintou House that was good. I stopped caring. And I have to care or I'll kill the wrong people.'

Jarran frowned and scraped his hair back, his shoulders relaxing. 'But you can't avoid them forever. When you go up against Rohne and Nasra you'll be facing two very powerful xintou.'

'I'll have to find some other way,' she said, swallowing down fear. 'Mina's right. If I keep relying on them I'll drag her into it, too. Each time I use the yanstones, I get stronger. And less compassionate. And our twin-bond grows. But we also get closer to Fusing – and that will kill us both. There *has* to be an alternative.' She wrapped her arms around her waist, holding in another shiver that wracked her body. 'Because I want to use them. So much it hurts. Which scares me.'

He said nothing more, only continued to pace. Alere sat and raised her throbbing ankle, trying not to think.

About half an hour later, just as restlessness and anxiety for Mina became unbearable, Wei came rushing in. Saric sauntered in a moment later. Where Wei's eyes sparkled, Saric scowled, his hands deep in his pockets and his shoulders hunched forward. A half-grown sahalia trailed them, snuffling at Wei and nudging her until she petted it and giggled.

Wei dropped to her knees beside Alere, her face alight, golden skin flushed. 'Are you both alright? You *have* to meet everyone. I've found my aunt *and* my grandmother *and* two cousins! They're all so nice and they were so glad to see me. But they were upset about Ma. They never knew what happened to her.' She rattled on, waving her arms. 'My aunt, Qara, is a healer, but not trained in Madina or anything. She and Mina are busy talking healer-stuff. There's a boy – my cousin – who's really sick. Qara's hoping Mina can help, 'cause she's tried everything and nothing's working. Her husband, Yuwan, is the khaan – the leader – here and he's already said I can go on their next hunt if I use darts that don't leave toxins in the animals because that might harm anyone who eats the meat. And—'

'Wei,' Alere interrupted the chatter, clearing her throat when her voice broke. 'I'm glad you've found your family, but we're running out of time. Can we keep it to the basics? Why did the villagers ambush us?'

Saric shrugged. 'They were hunting tuo. If we'd gone around they would have left us alone. Lucky Wei jabbered at them.'

'Very lucky for us you were here.' Alere gave the girl as much of a smile as she could manage. 'Does anyone speak Common?'

'Qara does,' Wei said. 'She wants to meet you. Not you, Jarran. Just Alere for now.'

'Help me up?'

The two children hauled her up from the floor. Alere tested her ankle and found it stiff, several shades of purple and blue, but not unbearable. The sahalia gave a strange, chirruping growl and rubbed against her leg. Its greenish fur was stiff and course, its nose dry, and tiny amber eyes full of intelligence. She scratched its head then leaned on Wei's thin shoulder as they emerged into the dust-silvered afternoon light.

A swift review of the village showed it to be more like about fifty or sixty skin tents, nestled against a steep cliff of green sandstone, hazed in dust and lit softly by the last faint, pink-grey light of dusk. Next to each was a small garden plot with fresh pink leaves poking through dark, green-sand soil that reeked of horse manure.

In the centre of the village, children giggled and ran in circles around a stone well, playing some convoluted game involving tagging and pulling a sahalia's tail. Beyond the gers, dozens of stocky, muscular horses shifted restlessly about in a large timber-fenced corral. Beyond that, three people in desert-green clothing rode ponies at full gallop as they shot arrows at practice targets in the two-humped shape of desert tuo. Not one arrow missed.

As Alere and Wei approached the well, three women watched, buckets on hips, their chatter dying away. They wore brilliantly-patterned tunics and trous of all colours, and matching hair coverings draped over straight black hair, bound in braids that dangled past their hips. Both had several silver nose-rings. The elder also bore a silver chain from nose to ear. Perhaps as a symbol of status or binding in the hunli. Their narrow, dark eyes followed Alere as Wei led her to a large, white ger.

Wei called out a greeting and lifted the flap when a hail answered. Inside, Alere gripped the girl's shoulder to hold her still long enough to allow her vision to adjust. The smell of smoke and animal urine dominated the space.

This tent was a little larger, with three green-haired goat-like animals stabled in a separate lean-to at one end. The central room was divided in two by a heavy skin curtain. At a hearth in the centre, a woman crouched before a copper pot, stirring the contents. The smoke spiralled up to escape through the roof's peak. She waved Wei in and patted a fur-covered seat.

She was middle-aged, with a decisive air and deep frown-lines between her thin, dark brows. Her features were broad, her skin golden and her dark eyes narrow and wide-set. She, too, wore the silver nose-rings and chain. Her headdress, tunic, and trous were a more sedate geometric pattern of greys and blues. She rose and picked up a steel-grey silk scarf from a rack nearby. Bowing, she held it out with both hands toward Alere, then spoke. When Alere returned nothing but a blank stare, she switched to the Common tongue. Her expression held a hint of confusion.

'Welcome. I am Qara. You should sit and put your foot up.' Her Common was heavily accented and with odd inflexions, and it took Alere a second to decipher the meaning.

Wei leaned close and whispered, 'Take the *hada* with both hands and bow. It's polite. Then you can put it around your neck.'

Alere did so, thanking Qara. The woman smiled and nodded. Alere sat, lifting her foot onto a stool Wei dragged over. Wei then carefully carried a thick mug of milky lancha tea and gave it to Alere.

'Thank you, Wei.' Qara inclined her head. 'You may leave us. Your grandmother wished to speak with you and your young friend, if you would. Then come back and eat. Bring Mina and Jarran, too, please.'

Wei bounced up and dragged a reluctant Saric out the door.

Alere sipped tea in silence while Qara continued to stir the pot. At last, apparently satisfied with the contents, Qara ladled out a bowlful and handed it over, along with a wooden spoon. Alere accepted it with both hands and a respectful bow. Only after they finished eating and cleaned the bowls did Qara take a seat opposite Alere and look directly at her.

'Why don't you Read me and understand our language?' she asked. 'Wei tells me you are xintou. But her thoughts about you are uncertain.' She touched her own forehead. 'Your wards tell me you're trained yet you don't use your skills? Have you taken some sort of vow? Or are you afraid of something?'

Alere stiffened as Qara's meaning became clear. She tightened her Outer wards against intrusion and reached for a weapon she wasn't carrying.

Qara was an untrained xintou.

CORIN

The handle rattled and the panel creaked open a fraction. Corin tensed. A riot of dark curly hair and a snub little nose poked through the gap. Kett yanked the door open and Farima stumbled in with a squeak. Corin caught her around the waist before she fell, holding her tightly, a palm over her mouth as she struggled. He spun her around. Her eyes widened and she relaxed.

He released her. 'What the diyu are you doing here?'

'I wanted to help. And I wanted to meet this Kett of Lia's.'

Her weishi, Tren, pushed in behind her, glowering. Corin hastily released her.

Farima touched Tren's arm. 'It's alright. Wait outside for me. Watch the stair and keep everyone out. We'll be gone in a moment.'

He bowed, raked Kett with a narrow look, then left.

Corin introduced them.

She hesitantly touched Kett's bruised cheek. 'Oh, I'm so sorry she did this to you. She's a horrible woman.'

He caught her fingers, pressing a kiss to her knuckles. 'I bear greetings from…Lia.'

She gave him a nervous little smile. 'I was so glad to hear she's finally better. She was sick for so long. And now she's engaged.' Her soft mouth drooped. 'Of course, things are a bit unpleasant at the moment, but I'm sure it will all settle soon. I expect an invitation to the hunli ceremony!'

Kett bowed, casting Corin a fleeting, amused look. 'Of course. But we do have a few obstacles to overcome. The first of which is getting out of here. The second is making sure Hanna can't carry out her threat to send an army against Madina – or to have Lia, Jarran, and all of the Jun Second families murdered by xiongshou.' He said it in a light tone but something in his expression caused Farima to flinch.

'She didn't!'

He nodded.

Corin added, 'She's already paid Weishi House xiongshou for Lia and Kett. I hate to say it, but if you don't control her, Hanna will take over your Jundom.'

Farima smoothed down the front of her robe and glanced back and forth between the two of them several times.

'How do I know you're telling the truth and you are who you say you are?'

'Good point.' He mentally ran through the letters he'd read in Lianna's room in Shanzhai. 'How about something only Lianna would know? You sent her favourite sweets, sugarfires, for Landing Day. And your father dislikes your lover, although Lia wouldn't tell me his name.'

With a breathless trill of laughter, Farima pressed both hands to her cheeks, her eyes glittering. 'You're so right. And you must be close to her if you know that. So I'll let you in on two secrets.'

'Oh?'

She took a hand of each man and tugged them to the door. 'One I can tell you. I have to show you the other.' She peeked out and waved them on. 'But be quiet. I don't want to be caught sneaking around with two men.' She gave them a fluttering little smile and ran ahead along the dim-lit corridor.

Kett followed her, ceramic sword still in his fist. Corin hesitated, then hurried after them. The girl was sweet, but she seemed edgy now. An over-excited brittleness that hadn't been there earlier. Clearly something had happened. The only way to find out what was to go along for the ride.

Tren waited for them and Corin gestured him over, waving Kett and Farima on. When they were out of earshot, he turned to the weishi.

'Molian, friend,' he murmured, pulling the silver axe from beneath his shirt. 'I bring news from Chengdu. The time of erheyi is on us.'

Tren sucked a quick breath, his fingers whitening on his sword hilt.

Corin rushed on, 'The champion and the xintou have released the slaves. An army of Selb gather on the plains north of Madina to help them enthrone the legitimate Jun First.' Corin gripped the man's arm. 'Can we rely on you?'

Tren nodded vigorously.

'Excellent,' Corin murmured. 'We know Hanna's building an army of junren. We need you to lead them to Madina. But don't join the rest of the Selb, yet. Wait in the village of Plana, just east of Madina. I'll send word when we need you.'

Tren bowed, weishi-style, with the flat of his hands pressed to his chest. 'You may rely on me, shenshi. The army Hanna has gathered has a few Selb, but the rest are not of our faith. I'm sure I can sway them, though. We'll be there in a few days.'

Corin tucked the silver axe away again, and rejoined the others, smiling.

A few minutes later they stood outside an ornate zitan-wood door on the second level of the house's western wing. Corin grabbed Farima's shoulder.

'This looks like the family's sleeping wing. Why are we here?'

'Because…' She ran her palms down her front again. 'Remember that little package you gave me to look after? Well, I did have the stomach for it and I need your help. I don't know what to do next.'

'Khara!' Corin flung the door open and ushered her and Kett inside. Then he asked Tren to keep watch and closed and locked the door behind them.

Inside the room, a dull-yellow electric bedside lamp lit the space. White-painted walls reflected the soft golden glow and the light glinted off much-gilded, carved timber furniture. An enormous four-poster bed dominated the room. Off to one side stood a spindly zitan-wood desk. On its surface lay scattered pages of monogrammed paper, all scrawled over in a shaky, looping script. Thin blue lines of smoke spiralled up from burning incense sticks set near the bed. The sweet smell didn't quite mask the distinctive, pungent odour of illness.

Hanna Zah-Hill, dressed in an embroidered black and silver night robe, lay askew on the bed. Her breath rattled, wet in her throat. She stared at the gold silk canopy overhead. A bed curtain, partly torn from its fixtures, was fisted in one hand, half-covering her chest. Dark purple patches stained the floral-patterned gold and grey silk bed cover beneath her. A wine-glass, still loosely held in now-lax fingers, dripped its dregs over the edge, onto the matching floor rug.

At the sight of her aunt, Farima gave a tearful little gasp. She covered her mouth and buried her face in Corin's shoulder. Stunned, he patted her back in helpless, useless comfort. She'd done it. He'd doubted her courage and he'd been wrong.

Kett approached the bed, his face eerily cold and calm. He twitched back the bed-curtain and examined Hanna dispassionately for a long moment.

Her eyelids closed in a slow blink. Her washed-blue eyes jerked across in increments until they fixed on Kett. The fingers holding the glass convulsed and opened, releasing it to fall onto the rug. She weakly gestured Kett closer. After a moment's hesitation, he leaned in.

Hanna's lips moved and her wasted face screwed into the ghost of an arrogant sneer. She coughed and brushed him aside. Her hands scrabbled at the shining bedcover. Her chest rising and falling rapidly, she let out a broken moan and muttered something. The only distinguishable words were 'kin-child' and 'die'.

Kett picked up the wineglass and sniffed at it.

'Dusu.' He held the glass out to Farima. 'Do you have any more?'

'What?' Corin gaped at him. 'What for?'

Kett lowered his voice, his expression as icy as his tone. 'Because I won't give her the satisfaction of using her death to hurt anyone else.'

'Wh-what does that mean?' Farima directed a fear-filled gaze to her aunt.

His expression gentled into pity. 'Dusu is fatal and incurable in the right dose. But, with too little, she could either recover or at least live for several days. If she lingers she'll tell everyone you did it. If I give her mercy…' He held up the sword. 'With Corin escaped, you could be implicated. We'll be accused of murdering an unarmed, ill woman. Every sword would be against us.'

'Oh.' Farima withdrew a small, waterproofed leather sac from the pocket of her deep violet robe. 'I…I didn't mean to…I thought it would work quickly.'

Kett took the dusu from her. 'Getting the dose right can be tricky, especially on someone as stubborn as Hanna. Let me.'

He laid the sword aside and measured a full tablespoonworth of the pink liquid into the wineglass. Then he added a mouthful of wine from the bottle. Next, with careful, distant gentleness, he lifted Hanna and placed the cup against her lower lip. She turned her head like a petulant child, screwing up her mouth and uttering an oath that elicited a gasp from Farima.

'Come, Hanna.' Kett's tone was mild. 'Drink it and your dearest wish will come true. When your people find me here, they'll know I did this. I'll be executed for your murder. Surely that's worth it?'

Her curled fingers swept back and forth across the bedspread. Then she angled her head to peer up at him.

'I always hated you, you know,' she said conversationally. 'You were so gouri perfect. Radan loved you, and your unveiled jiaoji of a mother. More than he ever loved me and Ven. And…my little Ven…was so…broken…' A single tear seeped down her cheek.

She scowled at the deep purple liquid in the glass.

'Are you sure you'll die if I drink this?' An echo of her old, autocratic bearing coloured the question.

'I'm sure,' he said. 'And the Koh-Lins and Ma-Safras, too. Everyone you hate so much will. You win. Drink.'

Her thin lips stretched in a feral smile. 'I win. I always win. *I* should have been Jun-Heir instead of Kennor. Father loved me best and I was full-blood, not Kennor…' Her voice trailed off. 'He was kin-child! The Jun Third title should have been *mine.*'

'Yes,' Kett said.

'No.' She pouted. 'No, I don't believe you. I'm strong. I'll get better.' Her fingers plucked at the bedclothes. 'I have to run…the jundom. They need me. Ven needs me.'

Kett's jaw worked. He glanced across at Corin, who withheld judgement. It had to be Kett's call. Personally, Corin was happy to stab the chouhuo through the heart and be done with it, but Kett was right. Her death had to look natural.

'Drink, Hanna,' Kett said, his expression hardening.

She glared at him. 'If that's what you want, then I won't, you gouri hundan.' Her breath gurgled and she coughed. 'Let them find me here, with you…escaped. Then they'll know I was right all along.'

'Gaisi!' Kett laid her on the bed and stepped away.

She grinned, showing teeth stained purple by the wine.

Kett paced the length of the rug, twice.

Corin caught him by the arm. 'Why are you wasting time? Just finish her. You must want to?'

Kett wrenched his arm free and swiped a hand over his face. 'That's the problem. I *do* want to. More than anything.'

'So?' Corin gave a half-laugh. 'I find that reassuring. Makes you human and I was starting to think you were a machine. At the age of seven, you swore to kill Hanna and everyone who implemented the kin-child laws. Now you're afraid to do it? Why?'

There followed a long pause, broken only by the sound of Hanna's harsh coughing and Farima's soft sobs. Kett raised his eyes and they held such stark fear that Corin sucked a sharp breath.

'I'll enjoy it, Cor,' Kett said. He stared at the glass, and then at Hanna's pinched, bitter expression. 'And it will make me no better than her…and just like Ven. And she's not the only one who was responsible for those laws. I want the people who actually sanctioned the laws. Ordered the hands that drove the swords in and murdered innocent children. I'm looking forward to watching them die, too. But they're Juns, most of them. Or their Xintou. Untouchable. What does that make me?'

Corin gripped Kett's shoulder. 'Kett, would you *ever* do anything to hurt Lia, or anyone else undeserving?'

A frown pulled Kett's brows close. 'Of course not.' He brushed Corin's hand off. 'Don't patronise me, Cor. I know what you mean. I just…It's a slippery path once you start down it.' He studied Hanna again.

Corin waited.

Kett sighed. He straightened, his shoulders and jaw firming. He strode into the bathroom and emerged with a towel. Hanna's gaze followed him. He shoved the towel under her head and looked down at her.

'Last chance, Hanna. Drink.'

She said nothing, merely closed her mouth, stiff in bitter defiance.

'Chouhuo,' he said. He pinched her nose. Her eyes widened and she writhed weakly on the bed.

Farima whimpered and hid her face.

Kett held on grimly. Hanna's mouth opened. He tipped the wine in then clamped her jaw shut. She tried to turn away. Her fingers clawed weakly at his arm. She stared, stark, begging. He held on, relentless, his teeth bared and body tense.

At last, her throat worked. Kett released her. She coughed, gasping for air. Dribbles of purple wine slipped down her cheeks and stained the towel. Kett used it to wipe away the liquid, eased her back onto the pillow, and walked away from the bed.

His hands trembled and sweat beaded his forehead.

Passing the glass and towel to Farima he indicated the bathroom. 'Wash the towel. Rinse the glass out then add a little more wine and lay it on the carpet next to the spill. We'll make it seem like she fell asleep and died naturally. Dusu breaks down after five hours and leaves no blood residue. Your healer shouldn't suspect if he doesn't see her until morning.'

Farima took the glass in shaking fingers and walked unsteadily to the bathroom. A moment later, she could be heard throwing up.

Kett approached the desk and shuffled through the papers spread out there. He switched on the lamp, inspected one of the papers and swore.

'How are your forgery skills, Cor?' He held two sheets up. 'The original contract for me and the one for Alli. Hanna's signature on both.'

Corin joined him in examining the other papers. Most appeared to be letters and instructions to various people, including Jun families Hanna once commanded as First Shunu. Her writing was elegant enough, though shaky with illness. He read some of the orders. She was clearly delusional for they were issued with the Alcazar's full authority behind them.

He sat, dipped pen in ink, studied her writing and made a few practice passes. When he was happy with the result he held it up to Kett, who nodded and threw the other orders into the fire.

'Now cancel the xiongshou contracts on Alli and me. We'll drop it to Weishi House here in case Hassan has blocked Messenger House communication to Madina. Weishi House has its own methods of getting messages through. It'll take a few days to disseminate but, by the time Alli gets to Madina, it will be one less thing for her to worry about.'

'What if they end up in the wrong hands in Madina Weishi House?'

'A risk we'll have to take. We'll direct them to Master Anh, privately.' He returned to Hanna's bedside.

Corin finished the notes and added one publically apologising for inciting anger against the new kin-child laws. He signed them with Hanna's flourishing signature, and finished them with the Zah-Hill seal resting on the desk just as Farima came back from the bathroom. Her face was white and set, her eyes bloodshot. He tucked the letters into his shirt and plucked the clean wineglass from her, urging her to sit.

Pouring a small amount of wine into the glass, he swirled it around then positioned it on the rug, next to the stain. Next, he reattached the bed curtain and secreted away the small dusu sack.

A soft, coughing, gurgling sigh, followed by silence, drew everyone's attention back to the bed. It didn't need Farima's choked sob or Kett's muttered curse to tell Corin what had happened.

Kett touched the pulse-point on Hanna's neck for what seemed like a long time. Finally, he straightened and studied her again. His blank expression slowly shifted to disbelief. He stroked his fingers over her forehead, closing the pale, staring eyes in a moment of poignant finality.

He took Hanna's hand gently. His next words were so quiet Corin had to strain to hear them.

'I protected him for you and you hated me even more. I would have given up the throne if you'd asked.' Kett put his back against the post and slid down until he sat on the dias step. He rested his elbows on his knees, dropped his forehead onto his forearms and sucked deep, shuddering breaths. His shoulders heaved and his hands shook.

Finally, Corin broke the stasis. Someone had to. He finished the task of tidying the room: making sure the papers in the fire were burned; that the bathroom bore no trace of Farima's presence; that the suite would appear normal to Hanna's maid the next morning.

At last, Kett raised his head, his bruised face drawn and weary beyond mere tiredness. He dragged himself upright and regarded, one more time, the wasted form on the bed.

'Why?' He rounded on Farima, his tone harsh.

ALERE

Alere stirred uncomfortably, looking away from Qara, into the crackling hearthfire. If Qara was xintou, she was untrained and a danger to her whole village. She should have been given over to Xintou House at puberty, when her gifts began to show.

Yet…how true was that? That was the House's teaching. But it was clear, now, that Mistress Li didn't always teach the whole truth.

Alere hesitated. The House taught that a wild xintou would use her powers for personal gain. But Qara's home was ordinary, filled with plain timber and fur or cloth furnishings. She wore the same, desert-tuo-wool clothes as the other villagers. If she was a healer to the village, then that job was not an easy one. She was married to the village khaan, but everything so far pointed to a hardworking woman who put the interests of her people first.

'Why do you not use your gifts?' Qara repeated. Her expression was curious, not hostile.

'I came into my…powers… late,' Alere said, 'and prefer not to use them.'

'But why?' Qara tilted her head.

Alere shifted on the seat. 'It's a complicated story and not only mine to tell. I'd rather not talk about it right now.'

Qara added wood to the fire. She moved the pot off the flames and gave it another stir.

'Very well.' She dusted her hands off. 'But the other villagers are wary of you and your sister. Most have never seen twins and think them…*azgui baidal*.' She frowned. 'I mean, bad luck. It was only Wei's words and your skill with a bow and blade that saved your lives. The men are still speaking of how you hit that arrow aimed for Mina. And how you killed the *els aalz* – sand spider. For returning Wei to us – and for choosing not to shoot Yuwen – I owe you great thanks.'

Folding her arms, Alere replied shortly, 'You're welcome. But we didn't begin this journey with that intention. It was just luck that brought us here.'

Qara's lips stretched into a thin smile. 'I have no faith in luck. You are here for a…what is the word…a reason. Perhaps it was to bring Wei back. But I believe it is something else. Something important that can only happen here, and now.'

With a bitter laugh, Alere held up her hands, palms out. 'Please. I've had enough of important things. I'm not sure I can take much more.'

Qara's expression softened. 'Wish not for a lighter load, but a stronger back. Don't close your mind to knowledge, no matter how painful the lesson. You have a difficult path and you will need what you learn here, I think.'

'How would you know? There is no predetermined path. I could decide just to stay here and let Madina rot in its own madness. There's nothing I'm destined to do. All that sort of fatalistic thinking went out a thousand years ago when our ancestors set out to establish a colony that abolished it.'

With a stiff back and cool hauteur, Qara rose and strode to the door. She glanced back over her shoulder.

'If that is true, how do you explain Mina's dreams lately?' She awaited an answer and, when Alere found none, she softened and added, 'You are too full of *temul* – the look in the eye of a bolting horse going where it wants, not where its rider wants. You must accept who you are and who your sister is – good and bad – before you can find true freedom and make the most of your gifts. Fighting yourself and your sister is tiring. It helps no-one but your enemies. Go back to your ger. Sleep. Morning will bring light into darkness.' She held open the door flap.

'Why did you poison Hanna, Farima?' Kett repeated.

Farima focussed on her hands, twisting her silk belt. She looked like a child caught in some wrongdoing and afraid to admit to it.

'I gave Farima the dusu this afternoon.' Corin shrugged apologetically. 'I honestly didn't think she'd use it. I just wanted it in the house in case I had a chance to dose Hanna after we escaped.'

Kett ignored him and kept his attention on Farima, unyielding. 'Why?'

Tears pooled, spilling. When she finally spoke the words emerged quickly, tumbling over one another.

'She thought I didn't remember, but I did. She came to visit us when I was just a child and...' she gulped '...she found my father had a son by one of our jiaoji. Nattis was only six and I was four. He was Jun-Heir...and she...he was her *nephew* and she had her weishi murder him!'

Kett swore softly and covered his eyes for a moment. 'But why now?' He swept an arm around the room. 'You could have done something like this any time, if you'd really wanted to.'

She threw her shoulders back, clawing composure from guilt. 'Because things are different now. She's no longer First Shunu and I...' she gave a tiny, secretive smile '...I am with child. My lover knows we can't join in the hunli. I'm pledged to bind with Rhetton Gray-Saud, brother to Jun Third, Bren. Rhetton will think it's his, but I'll know.'

She focussed on the body on the bed, her sweet face hardening into determination. 'She's been stirring up the people against the change to the kin-child laws. Dozens of innocent children have died – just like twenty years ago. That awful symbol all over houses in Asadia. And when she caught Corin kissing me today, she ranted at me. I knew then she wouldn't let me keep the child if she found out, no matter what laws were retracted. But I'm Jun-Heir. She had no right. Then, when I opened your packet and saw the dusu… It was too good an opportunity.' She gave a helpless little gesture. 'But now I don't know what to do. What do I do?'

Her voice rose into hysteria and Corin stepped closer. She buried her face in his chest and he rubbed her back until her shudders softened again and she regained control.

'I'm sorry,' he murmured. 'I wouldn't have given it to you if I'd known. Putting you in this position is unforgivable.'

She sniffed defiantly. 'Well, I can't say it's something I'd like to go through again. But I do feel…lighter. I should thank you. There's something quite cathartic about ridding the world of someone like her.'

Corin forced a smile. 'Then you and Lia will have one more thing in common to talk about when you see each other next.' He handed over the letter he'd written in Hanna's name. 'Here. Distribute this to Messenger House and get them to cry the contents around the city. That should help quell the anti-kin-child riots.'

Farima read the letter and her mouth fell open. Her eyes filled with tears again and she threw her arms around Corin's neck. 'Thank you.'

'A good thought, Cor,' Kett said. 'Farima, Cor and I have to get out of here. Wait until morning and discover her.' He ran a hand over his head. 'Our disappearance may cause suspicion. You'll need to get rid of the guards' bodies and produce witnesses who will testify that you had us escorted off the grounds well before midnight. Can you do that? We can't afford to have her weishi on our tail now.'

Farima's jaw firmed. 'Yes. My weishi, Tren, will help. And I have people loyal to me who'll be glad to be rid of *her* staff.' She touched her belly protectively once more. 'Go. We'll be fine now.'

'There is one more thing,' Kett took her hands, exuding concern, his earnest focus on her. 'Two, really, and you'll need to keep both secret. Things in Madina are going to be unpredictable and unpleasant in the next few days. It's important you stay away from it. Don't come to the coronation. You'll endanger yourself and your child. Promise me?'

She nodded, seeming mesmerised by his intensity as he continued.

'Lia's going to help Jarran oppose Hassan's claim to the throne and we'll try to rescue Rafi, Petar and Mistress Li. Will you send men to help Lia? If you can get a message to Kennor as well, that would be perfect. If he knows Hanna is gone and you're safe, he may be willing to support Lia and Jarran.'

'Mistress Li, too?' Farima nodded again. 'Of course! But most of my men are already sworn to Hassan. A message just came in this afternoon. I'll send one back to my father straight away. He escaped and is hiding outside Madina with a few men. Not many, though.'

'And your Xintou?' Kett said.

Tears glistened in Farima's dark eyes. 'Didn't you hear? Dellia was with the army that marched on Shanzhai. All the Bonded Xintou travelling with the Juns were murdered. She's dead.' She stifled a sob.

'I'm sorry.' Kett stroked her arm. 'I'm sorry. We'll do our best to end this, Farima. I promise.'

'I'll send as many men as I can to join my father. Where to?'

'I know the perfect place for *us* to hide inside Madina.' Corin grinned in anticipation of seeing Kett's reaction. If that didn't shock the stoic weishi, nothing would. 'But it's not large enough for a small army.' He directed his next words to Farima. 'Send Kennor and your men around to the village of Plana, just east of the city. I have a friend there who will be a contact. He can show them a safe place to camp out on the river. I'll give you a password. I already spoke to Tren about this and he's happy to lead them.'

'Consider it done.' Farima kissed both of them on the cheek. 'Thank you.'

After a final review of the room's staging, they slipped out. Farima pocketed the key and promised she would be up in time to open it and be there when Hanna's maid discovered the body. She led them through the depths of the house, to a discreet exit through the servants' wing.

As they emerged into the cool night, Kett grasped her wrist. 'My sword and gear. Where would it be?'

'And my oud,' Corin added. When Kett sent him a weary look Corin shrugged. 'You have your tools, I have mine.'

'I know where Hanna would have put everything,' Farima said. 'Go out of this courtyard and to the left. You'll find your horses in the stables.' She stripped a delicate gold signet ring off her middle finger and dropped it into Kett's palm. 'Show this to Cho, the weishi in the guardhouse. Tell him the password: blackwing; and that I've given you leave to go. I'll send my maid out with your gear in a moment.' She hesitated. 'I'm glad Lia has you both. You'll look after her, won't you?'

'We try.' Kett's expression was haunted. 'Thank you for your help. Be safe.'

'And you.' She fled back inside, closing them into the night.

Jamming his hands into his pockets, Corin puffed a cloud into the cold air as they headed for the stables.

'We'll have to pick up my horses and gear as well. We should stay and rest, at least tonight.' He waited for the weishi to object. He'd never make the trip to Madina without time to recover.

Kett only gave a grunt of acknowledgment. Surprising.

Relieved to have avoided an argument, Corin didn't push the point. He glanced back at the house. 'Remarkable girl, Farima,' he commented. 'Not surprising Lianna liked her so much. She has a lot of strength under that softness. Smart, too.'

Kett said nothing, but pressed a palm to his side and grimaced. He wiped fresh blood off on his trous.

'Y'know,' Corin continued, 'every time I think I have you pegged you surprise me. *She* was what this was all about, wasn't it?'

The weishi still didn't reply, but merely swept the open courtyard with a wary gaze. Corin grabbed his arm and forced him to stop.

'The second and third objectives,' he persisted, searching Kett's face for confirmation. 'It wasn't killing Hanna. It was cancelling those contracts and making sure Farima didn't come to Madina. You wanted a friendly army *and* you wanted to make sure the girls don't meet. You think Farima will realise Alli isn't the girl she grew up with.'

'Your point?' Kett shook him off and made for the guardhouse, lit and occupied in the centre of the stableyard entrance.

'You intended this right from the start. Right from when we planned this trip on the chuan at Chengdu. You sent a message here, telling Hanna you'd be coming through.' Corin shook his head. 'I don't think I've ever met anyone who thinks so far ahead. Remind me never to play qi with you.'

'I did tell you I like to be prepared,' Kett's lips curved upwards. 'And I'd quite enjoy a game of qi with you. You have a suitably devious mind. You just prefer to make things up as you go more than I do.'

'Thanks, I think,' Corin chuckled. 'Did it ever occur to you that Hanna could have just killed you outright, before you'd achieved anything?'

'Of course.' With an indifferent shrug, the weishi added, 'But every qi game involves risks and has minor pieces that are sacrificed. It's part of the game.'

'You consider yourself a minor piece? Not sure Alli would agree with you.'

'Well,' Kett replied evenly, 'if we're extending the metaphor, you'd have to say Alli's the queen, Jarran's the king and I'm just a footsoldier so her agreement is moot.'

'Wait.' Corin grabbed his arm again. 'Do you honestly doubt you're worthy of her?'

Kett stilled, his face shadowed. 'As I said before: I think she deserves someone better.'

'You really are a shazi,' Corin retorted. 'You think just because someone like Hanna couldn't love you, that you're not worthy of Alere? Is that what this is about?'

'Shut up, Corin. We need to go.' He yanked his arm free, avoiding Corin's eyes.

Corin opened his mouth and shut it again. Probably best to let this slide. Kett wasn't ready to let go what Hanna had done to him, yet. Not with her death so fresh. Time to lighten the mood.

'Gaisi!' he muttered. 'If you think you're not good enough for Alere, all bets are off. I'll steal her right back.'

Kett's shoulders relaxed. He gave a genuine crack of laughter, then hissed and touched the bruises around his eye. 'Think you could?'

'Oh, I know it.' Corin grinned. 'I'm incredibly charming.'

'If you say so.' Kett eyed him with amusement. 'Farima did seem to think so.'

'That reminds me.' Corin changed the subject, hoping to divert Kett toward the future. 'Why *are* you so keen to have Farima send more men to help at Madina? Surely the Selb massing there, together with Yasmin's men from Shanzhai, will be an army enough to face whatever Hassan has?'

Kett fiddled with Farima's signet ring, seeming to stare through, rather than at it. Outside the high walls, a drift of music and the scent of sweet wine spoke of evening revels in a house nearby. The town lights all around dimmed the brilliant sweep of stars overhead. He gazed south for a long moment before replying.

'Have you ever wondered who the Selb's leader is?'

'Do they have one? I was under the impression they were a bit…ad hoc. Liu certainly never mentioned one. Nor did Gavon.'

'Possibly. It'll be interesting to see what their army looks like when we get to Madina.'

Corin frowned and glanced over his shoulder. 'Farima's weishi, Tren. He's Selb and I sent him on to meet up with Kennor at Prana, outside Madina. Do you think that was a mistake?'

'He's leading junren loyal to the Han-Asad name,' Kett replied, thoughtful, 'so probably not. And, as you said, the Selb are pledged to stand with Alere and Mina. I just wish I knew who was running their show.'

CHAPTER FIFTEEN

ALERE

Sleep eluded Alere. Alone in the ger, not even warmth and safety settled her skittish mind. Every time she slipped into sleep, the uncomfortable feeling of impending…something, woke her. For the first time in her life, Alere felt uneasy with her own company. If the rift between herself and Mina was healed, she could unburden her thoughts to someone. Were Kett here, his dry clarity would give her perspective. In his absence, her fears spiralled into nightmares that scattered sleep before them.

She must have drifted off, eventually. She woke in the grey light of dawn. Saric and Wei lay curled up asleep under furs nearby. Jarran snored softly on the opposite side of the ger. Mina slept by his side, one hand touching his.

Alere lay back on the furs, trying to forget the dreams of death, and fire, and darkness.

When the sun rose, Wei skipped out and returned with food. Two wary-eyed tribesmen dumped Alere's pack and the rest of their gear on the floor and left without speaking. Alere scrabbled through her things, her heart sinking.

Her weapons weren't there. And the yanstones were missing.

'They've taken the yanstones,' she said, dully. Their absence was an ache in her bones, a sickness in her gut that made her want to vomit. Her hands trembled and feverish shivers shook her body. But part of her was grateful. The decision to use them was out of her hands.

Mina sent Alere a sidelong look. She flipped back the collar of her shirt. The Koh-Lin necklace sparkled against her skin. 'I have them.'

Alere dug her nails into her palms, resisting the urge to snatch them, to cradle them, to submerge herself into their golden warmth.

Mina backed toward the door. 'I-I'm trying to use them to heal people.' She vanished outside, leaving Alere staring after her, stunned.

She swore and lay down again, bitter helplessness burning acid in her chest.

The day passed slowly. Alere couldn't even pace, her ankle too stiff and swollen. Mina returned briefly, bound it with a sweet-scented poultice and bamboo-cloth bandages, but said little. She left the ger shortly after and stayed away all day. Jarran went with her, a dark scowl of impatience knitting his brow. But every time Alere tried to leave, bronze swords halted her.

Saric came back at dusk bearing more stew and the news that Jarran and Mina had argued over when to leave the village.

'She wants to stay and help Qara cure that boy,' Saric said, shrugging. 'Jarran wants to get on the road again. Keeps going on about his daughters.'

'Why won't they let me out?' Alere asked bitterly.

He grimaced, spooning stew into his mouth like he hadn't eaten for a week. 'Fraid of you. Something about twins and steel. Wei was translating so it didn't make much sense.' His scowl darkened. 'Don't think she knows the lingo as well as she thinks she does.'

'Jiche!' Alere threw up her hands. 'Are there men posted around the whole ger? I can use the xiongshou flickknife in my boot to cut through the back.'

Saric raised a sardonic brow. 'How far would you get walking on a twisted ankle, with no water? They're guarding our horses, too.

Why do you think Mina hasn't let you use the stones to heal your ankle?'

Alere gasped. 'She's keeping me here? Why?'

'No idea,' Saric said. 'I hate the place. Stinks like animals. But Wei won't hear a word against it and Mina's obsessed with curing Wei's cousin, Batu. He's got some sort of fever.'

Alere ran her fingers through her dust-thickened hair. 'What is she *thinking?* We have to get out of here.' She gripped Saric's bony wrist. 'Tell her to come and see me. Now!'

His mouth thinned. 'I'll tell her, but I don't think she'll listen.' He slipped out.

Alere threw her bowl across the ger and swore long and fluently.

He didn't come back, and neither did Mina. Eventually, Alere slept, her dreams haunted by blood, fire and darkness again.

She woke, dagger-drawn, to find Qara standing over her, visible by the last glow of coals in the firepit. Wei and Saric slept on the furs nearby. Jarran and Mina were both missing.

'Come,' Qara whispered. 'Your sister needs you. She's been helping me with Batu.'

At last, a chance to talk some sense into Mina. Alere threw off the blankets and stuffed her feet into her boots, with a hiss of pain for the swollen ankle. She threw on her cloak and followed Qara into the cold, grey night. Overhead the sky sparkled with the diamond-crisp clarity of a moonless night. The air smelled dry, cold, and dusty. Qara spoke to a guard posted outside Alere's hut, who nodded and regarded Alere with suspicion.

'What was wrong with the boy?' Alere whispered, limping alongside the older woman. 'What does Mina need my help with? I have no healer skills.'

Qara pushed the white ger's door-flap open and gestured her inside. Mina rose from beside a bed and hurried over, her hands outstretched. She still wore the same clothing she'd had on when they were captured and the circles under her eyes were so dark as to be almost bruises.

'Mina!' Alere hesitated, shocked at the change in her sister, all her anger slipping away. She took Mina's hands, only to release them when the formless brunt of Mina's emotions washed through the contact. Alere gritted her teeth against the urge to snatch the yanstones from her sister's wrists. Wait, how could she feel Mina's emotions so clearly without wearing the necklace, herself?

'I'm sorry.' Mina groaned. 'I'm tired and I'm not warding well. I can't do this on my own. I need your help or we'll lose him.' She pointed at the bed. 'He's just a boy, Alli.'

Reluctantly, Alere approached. The boy was about thirteen, his skin pale, dark hair sweat-plastered against his scalp. His eyes were closed, but he shifted restlessly, moaning and crying in his sleep. His fists knotted in the bedclothes and his legs thrashed, despite being held by Jarran and Yuwen, Qara's husband.

'What's wrong with him?' Alere asked. 'Fever?'

'No.' Mina laid a gentle palm on the boy's forehead. The yanstone bracelet sparkled on her wrist. The action seemed to settle the boy for a moment. But as soon as she left his side his distressed mutterings began again.

Qara stroked the boy's hair. 'He's my son and he's xintou. We didn't know until just a few months ago. He started to Read people. In my arrogance, I trained him as I would have a daughter. Then he began to get headaches. I didn't realise...' She turned away, but not before Alere saw tears.

'I don't understand.' Alere looked askance at Mina. 'What's wrong with him?'

'Do you remember what we talked about in Shanzhai?' Mina wiped wearily at her forehead. 'About the genetics of male xintou?'

Alere tried to recall the details of the conversation. 'You said male xintou have the trigger gene but lacked the control gene.' She looked at Batu. 'What does that mean, exactly?'

Mina frowned. 'The missing control gene is responsible for production of vital proteins that stabilise brain chemistry. The reason there aren't any male xintou is partly because Xintou House won't allow them, and partly because the rare one that happens naturally, dies at puberty.' She swallowed. 'And I read one text that warned of danger to people near the dying child. Exactly what danger, it didn't say. But I know people have died – not just the xintou boy.'

'Oh.' Alere studied Batu once more. 'So how did Rohne survive, then?'

'I don't know.' Mina rubbed her hands down her thighs. 'Nasra must have done something to stabilise him. To save Batu, we need to work out what it is and replicate it.'

'This is why you've kept me prisoner for a day? We've lost precious time, so you could try to save a male xintou?' Backing away, Alere wrapped her arms around herself, quashing the burn of anger in her gut. 'Mina, if this is a lethal gene, then it's for a reason. If he survives he could pass this on and no-one would be here to help his sons.'

'That boy is dying.' Mina jabbed a finger at Batu. 'He needs our help. That's all there is to it.'

'But it's not, is it? I know you've taken a Healer's Oath and you're obliged to do everything in your power to save lives. But what if saving him will have ripple effects we can't even imagine?'

Mina folded her arms. 'And I suppose that's what you were thinking when you decided who to kill in the Games arena?'

'That's not fair and you know it.' Alere mirrored her pose, trying hard to maintain her calm before Mina's anger. It was unlike her sister to be this vehement. A disconcerting role-reversal.

'What's not fair…' Mina's voice rose '…is that everything you've asked of me, I've done.' She pointed south toward Mamlakah. 'I left my home and my mother to follow you to Shanzhai. I compromised my healer's ethics to help you discredit…' the words broke '…and kill Ven. And I did it again to help you free the slaves in Melcor and *murder* the slavemasters. You used me to achieve what you thought was right. You owe me, Alere!'

Tears glistened on her eyelashes. 'I haven't asked *anything* of you. I'm asking you now. Use the stones to heal instead of killing. Help me save this boy.'

Alere gritted her teeth to keep in hot, defensive words. Mina was right, but why was she so passionate about saving someone she'd just met and had no personal interest in?

Ah. Personal interest. That was it.

Alere gripped Mina's shoulders. 'This isn't about him, is it? This is about Rohne.' She eyed the writhing, groaning boy. 'You think this will happen to Rohne and you're hoping you can save him, too.'

Averting her face, Mina wiped away fresh tears. 'Partly. He started getting headaches after we left Gaton. But it's partly because… I'm scared, Alli.'

'Of what?' Alere stroked Mina's dusty hair back. When had she become so absorbed in her own fears and insecurities she'd neglected her sister?

With a heavy sigh, Mina looked down at her hands. 'Of my dreams. I saw those bandits you killed before it happened. And I saw Batu.' She glanced at the bed and shuddered. 'In my dream I killed him. I need to know that my dreams don't have to come true. I can't murder a helpless child.'

Alere released Mina and limped to the bed. She twisted a lock of her hair around one finger as she stared down at Batu and debated. So much could go wrong. She had no idea how to even begin to cure the boy. But Mina had sacrificed so much already. Surely Alere owed her sister the attempt to save a life, rather than take one. But what would happen when she put the necklace on, again? Could she control the power; the link between them?

Could she stop them from Fusing? They'd been very close to it when she killed the mercenaries.

Jarran was right, too. If she had to face Rohne and Nasra, she'd need to be able to control the stones and the gifts they brought. This was her chance to learn how.

'Alright.'

'Oh! Thank you.' Mina embraced her and clasped the yanstone necklace around Alere's throat. Alere shuddered as the metal settled, heavy and cool, against her skin. A flare of joyful recognition burrowed into her mind. The faint, ever-present, silver-gilt chorus sang. Iron and smoke, warm and bitter, on her tongue. The nausea and feverishness that had plagued her vanished, leaving a sense of wellbeing.

Mina hurried to the opposite side of the bed.

'Are you sure about this?' Alere wiped sweaty palms on her shirt. If she committed herself — to the stones and to Mina — as completely as this sort of work required, who would she become? Would she even care about the work, the boy or her sister? Or would the soulless soldier the stones produced simply kill everyone in the room?

Certainty gathered in Mina's expression. 'I'm sure. We have to try.'

The air in the ger reeked of sweat, fear, and woodsmoke. Seated on either side of the bed, Jarran and Yuwen held the boy's hands and legs. Qara held Batu's head still. Only the fire's crackling, and Batu's low, muttering moans, broke the silence. He yelled something incomprehensible, his fingers curling into claws, head thrashing in Qara's grip.

Expectation thickened around Alere as her sister and the others watched her with varying degrees of worry, hope, and speculation. But she hesitated, still reluctant. Something about the whole situation frightened her more than any imminent battle or potential enemy. Them she could see and fight. This was beyond her physical control.

And what if she couldn't do what was needed? Neither she nor Mina had any experience in this sort of xintou work. No xintou in living history had any medical experience beyond the basic DNA manipulation done by the nai-xintou. And that work was taught by rote, not by deep understanding of the genetics involved.

The whole situation was madness.

Batu moaned again. The pressure of his terror and pain pushed against her Outer wards. Mina winced and Jarran pressed at his temple. Outside, a child screamed, perhaps woken by a nightmare or perhaps affected by Batu's broadcasting. A murmur of adult voices, edged with panic, followed as people called out and questioned each other in the grey, pre-dawn light.

Alere shivered. Non-xintou weren't supposed to be able to sense the intrusion of a xintou's thoughts. Batu was untrained, uncontrolled, and in pain. If she and Mina couldn't rein him in, he could hurt every unwarded mind in the village by dragging them into his own agony.

She could no longer afford to hesitate.

With the yanstone necklace lying heavy against her chest and the bracelets glittering on Mina's wrists, Alere grasped her sister's hands across Batu's writhing body. All of Mina's fears slammed into Alere's Outers and Alere gasped.

Mina wasn't used to the strict emotional control required of xintou work. In a situation like this, with two minds linked and focussed on the task ahead, the slightest loss of command could result in Fusion and death.

Alere raised her wards in automatic, defensive reaction. But that hindered their blending and reduced the stones' power. Reluctantly, she lowered her Outer wards. Gritting her teeth against the emotional onslaught, she sent a sharp warning to her sister. Mina's response was, at first, startled resentment then she dampened her fear into something more manageable.

Blocking all the external distractions out, Alere opened more of her wards. At the same time, she opened herself to the stones' warmth and influence. They siphoned off fear, leaving her calm and distant from the mental turmoil all around. The comforting taste of smoke and steel seeped into her mouth.

Why had she feared them? This was exactly what she needed to keep Mina's emotions in check. Without the restraints of sentiment, she pulled Mina closer and thickened the connection between them once more. Then she removed Mina's worry about her own inadequacy, leaving her sister's mind as calm and icy as a lake in winter.

Now, with both their minds composed and close-bound, words became unnecessary. Alere passed as much information about nai-xintou work to Mina as she could remember. It would be difficult telekinesis, carried out on a microscopic scale throughout the boy's whole body. In a series of flickering images, plans were drawn up and discarded as fast. At last, in agreement, they surveyed Batu.

Using Mina's insight into how the yanstones might work, Alere focussed on them. Yes, she could sense it now; their ability to act as a conduit and a lens for electricity, or heat. Alere absorbed and passed the power to Mina as her sister delved into Batu's cells. Mina's brow furrowed and Alere saw what she attempted: splicing genes. She was trying to copy the trigger-gene from Batu's X chromosome, onto his Y to replace one of the inactive genes there. Then she could tweak it to replicate the control gene that produced the right proteins. And his body would have the ability to manage his brain chemistry.

The difficulty lay in the disparity between intention, knowledge, and ability. Mina had read of gene splicing, but not what it entailed on a molecular level. She worked from half-remembered, seven-hundred-year-old texts about terra-forming biospheres. Written in a language altered by time, containing words that no longer had meaning. It was like trying to build a puzzle, in the dark, with one hand tied; all guesswork and hope.

But if they got this puzzle wrong, it was a boy's life at stake. Possibly more.

CHAPTER SIXTEEN

ALERE

The room grew colder as Alere channelled more energy. Mina's concentration faltered. Exhaustion and fear crept back into her thoughts. Alere drained them again. Mina straightened, the strain around her eyes deepening as she plunged once more into the boy's body and mind. She worked so deeply and minutely Alere could no longer follow. Batu relaxed and ceased to moan or move. But how could they tell if it worked?

As if triggered by her doubt, a strange, detached sense of wrongness grew. She watched her own actions and disapproved of them. She struggled against the sensation, trying to re-establish the seemless, emotionless connection between herself and Mina. And failed. Distaste for what they attempted blossomed from somewhere; elsewhere. It frayed the silver-gilt thread binding them.

The artificial calm and distance shattered. Pain and fear lashed through Alere's body and mind. She dropped Mina's hands and clutched at her head.

Mina called Alere's name. On the bed, Batu panted, his face contorting in shrieking agony. Mastering the pain, Alere sought the yanstones, sinking herself wholly into them. She dragged Mina into their thrall. Re-establishing the bond, she extended it to include Batu. Now the three of them were engulfed in a silver-gilt other-world, separated from everything and everyone, their minds almost Fused.

The temptation to allow complete Fusion was seductive. The promise of total understanding, absolute control and harmony, difficult to resist. Surely there could be no harm in something that felt so complete and empowering?

No. Fusion meant death for all three of them. She knew that. Every Xintou House class drilled it into the students. Alere focussed on holding them apart. Her body shook with the effort.

At the same time, the sensation that something was wrong, grew until maintaining the connection became almost impossible. Her mind was being squeezed between two opposing forces and something had to give.

Hurry, Mina, she cast out to her sister, *if you can finish it, do it now. Something, or someone, is trying to stop us and I'm not sure how long I can hold this.*

I'm trying! You have to give me more.

I'm giving you all the power I can!

Not power, Mina replied, *more of you. We need to blend even closer. I've almost got it but you're holding back and I can feel—*

We can't. We'll Fuse. I'm barely holding us apart as it is. Work with what you've got.

There was a long pause and Mina's face flushed. Her hands trembled.

Finally, she released a shuddering breath. *I can't be sure I've done it right...but...there. It's done. I hope. Release us.*

Alere relaxed her mental hold on her sister and Batu. She allowed the energy and connection to dissipate. The external pressure vanished. On the table, Batu's head lolled to one side, his mouth open and eyes closed.

Qara tested the pulse in his throat and smiled up at Mina through tears.

'He's alive.' She kissed her son's forehead and stroked his damp hair.

Jarran rose from his kneeling position and put an arm around Mina's shoulders, kissing her and murmuring reassurances. Alere leaned on the table, sighing. Exhaustion sucked the stones' artificial strength from her limbs.

A faint groan from Batu brought them all crowding around, his parents anxious and hopeful. Then he opened his eyes. Alere flinched. Within lay, not the clarity of a mind free of pain, but the sharp, unrestrained wildness of a mind overwhelmed and broken.

His internal chaos exploded, catching them offguard and hauling all five into anarchy. Lost in the black vortex of his turbulent thoughts, Alere struggled to separate herself even as he clawed at the core of her Inner wards. The silver-gilt thread binding her to Mina began to unravel.

Batu extended further, capturing other minds and reeling them in. The darkness roared with the thousands of voices that chattered inside peoples' heads. Screams echoed. It was impossible to tell if they were inside or out in the real world. Alere's body and the ground underfoot vanished. Only dark-chaos existed, shattered by red explosions of pain and fear, peopled by dozens of other lost minds in conflict. Reality became a dream; the hope for a dream.

Seeking a path to freedom, Alere saw… no, that was the wrong word…sensed the tattered remnants of the golden thread linking her to her sister. She pulled on it. Struggling like a hooked fish, Mina's mind approached; all fear and incoherence. She settled as they touched. Recognition gave the illusion of security.

Yet it needed only that momentary solidity for Alere to orientate. She found the yanstones and buried herself and Mina in their protective warmth. Alere drew on the power thrumming through both of them. She pushed back the blackness and calmed the turmoil. The minds lost in it she released, one by one, back into their own bodies.

The last was Batu's; a feverish, roiling, bottomless pit that nothing could put right. All that had been Batu was gone, disintegrated into random disorder. Alere unpicked the last remnants of herself and Mina from the tangled web of his irrationality. By sheer force of will, she imposed a sphere of wards around what was left of Batu. Then she pushed Mina free with a final instruction. Alere remained, focussing all her strength on holding the snarling, writhing storm at bay.

Excruciating agony lanced through her chest. Once more aware of her own body, she heard a choked gasp emerge from her own mouth. She opened heavy eyelids, long enough to see Mina standing over Batu's body. Sobbing, Mina wrenched Alere's dagger free of the boy's thin chest. Blood dripped onto his clothes. His back arched then collapsed. He stared sightlessly at the ceiling.

The yanstone-powered wards holding Batu shattered into a thousand golden shards. The Batu-blackness within disintegrated. Only half-conscious, Alere dragged herself free as the boy's mind fell into final oblivion.

Qara screamed and clutched at her son. Jarran leapt, catching Mina as she sagged, cradling her close. The dagger fell from her fingers. She wept into his shoulder.

There were no safe arms for Alere, but the ground came up to meet her like an old friend.

ROHNE

Rohne sat up in bed, chest heaving, head throbbing, dagger ready and bed curtains slashed. He half-expected the ceramic blade in his fist to be steel. The frenetic, dark dream was so vivid it was hard to believe he lay in his room at the Alcazar, not in some stinking khiba in the desert.

Pinkish morning light edged the heavy gold curtains. The distant clash of weapons said the Alcazar weishi were awake and training in the courtyard. Rubbing sleep away, Rohne flung the dagger aside and slid from under the quilt's suffocating warmth. He stumbled to the deep-set window, dragged the curtain back, and squinted into the bloody morning light.

In the courtyard below his window, a dozen weishi practiced sword-drills, only their whitish ceramic blades visible in the gloom. Their rhythmic chanting and stomping was almost reassuring, for it meant continuity. Nothing had changed overnight. He was still Xintou to the First Jun of Mamlakah. He was not some pathetic boy-child, terrified and lost in the throes of agonising death.

He rubbed at his temples. The headache was worse.

Dragging a chair up to the window, he sat and stared pensively out across the rooftops. He shook himself free of the dream and studied the quiet city. The sun hovered just above the horizon. Cold, purplish shadows reluctantly gave way to the red light inching across the roofs. Beyond the courtyard wall sloped the red roof of Xintou House, with its bell-tower standing proud over the surrounding buildings. The bell remained silent. For the first time in five hundred years, no senior staff rang the girls to classes.

Were the girls – locked in their shielded rooms – trying to escape? Doubtful. These young women were soft. Too steeped in years of worshipful treatment to know what to do in a situation not of their making. Yesterday, Rohne had slipped into the House to peruse their library. He'd heard nothing but silence from behind each closed door in the regimented halls. The weishi on duty reported no trouble.

These xintou, as Nasra said, were nothing. Indoctrinated to obedience and duty by Mistress Li, they lacked the ability to think for themselves. Caught in stagnation of their own making. Ordered to stay in their rooms, they obeyed because it didn't occur to them to behave any other way.

Had she been there, Alere would have caused more trouble than his mother's men could cope with. For all her irritating dutybound outlook, Alere was worth more than all the weak little girls locked in the House. Why she thought herself less was hard to comprehend.

Frowning, he recalled his dream. If his Seeing was right then, somewhere to the north, Mina and Alere were either about to murder a young boy or had already done so. Impossible to tell which. But why? What would drive someone as gentle as Mina to break her healer oath to such a degree?

Rohne patted at his chest. The pain of the stab wound lingered. So real it was hard to believe he was uninjured. Just as real as the whirlpool of mental incoherency that had almost sucked the girls in. What was that? The dream-Seeing was too fragmented to understand, yet the image contained something important. Something he needed to understand and simply couldn't.

Something to do with Mina. And him.

A discreet knock on the door announced the arrival of breakfast. He shook himself free of megrims as best he could. This was no time to wallow in the stupidity of others. Mina had chosen her path and he needed to accept that. She'd never loved him the way he had her. He'd been naïve to think she ever would.

He'd hoped that, once she saw him in his rightful place as a Bonded Xintou, she would waken to what he offered her. Now, that would never happen. If the glimpses he'd Seen over the last few days were right, she had fallen out of love with Kett only to fall straight into Jarran's arms.

Was she just more mercenary than he'd ever realised? Had her time in Madina made her crave the soft life of a rich man's bed? Had all her protestations of wanting to return to Gaton fallen by the wayside when she saw an opportunity to be with the new Jun First?

Sneering, Rohne stood and shoved aside the remnants of his food. Well, she'd chosen poorly. With Hassan Bonded and under control, Jarran would never usurp the throne. Hassan's junren, combined with those sworn in from the old Zah-Hill ranks, made up the largest army ever seen on the planet. Nothing Alere drummed up stood a chance.

Not even Yasmin Koh-Lin's fifteen thousand, marching up from Shanzhai, had a hope. The stupid woman was so blinded by anger at her husband's capture she had simply formed her army and marched north with no consideration for strategy or tactics. What did she know of warfare? Yasmin's advisors were her Shangwei and her Jun Third, neither of whom understood the extent of Rohne's powers or those of the erheyi twins.

How could anyone understand? This was the first time in the colony's history such a coup had succeeded. Control of Mamlakah finally lay with Xintou. He, Nasra, and the erheyi girls would change the world.

Oh, Hassan was there as a front, but the man was lost in his fantasies. His time was taken up with dreams of a purified, ideal populace controlled by fear of superior weapons he planned to make. He already had his blacksmiths scrounging every scrap of iron to make weapons. If only he knew.

Rohne laughed, anticipating the next few days' revelations.

In the mean time, let Hassan enjoy his tyrannical little games. The executions were helpful, although the square in front of the Alcazar had taken on a rather morbid tone and the paving stones were permanently stained with the blood of those Hassan deemed unclean. Most were just thieves, beggars and the like. Law-abiding citizens had nothing to fear. A good cleansing was what the city needed.

Once Yasmin's pathetic rebellion was eradicated, and Jarran's spurious claim to the throne dealt with, Rohne would unite all three senior jundoms under Hassan. Mamlakah would step into a real future. This time there would be no Jun Councils, or Xintou House Mistress to hold back progress by whispering in the Jun's ear. Nasra had been right all along: the whole colony stagnated in the bronze age because Mistress Li and her ancestors – right back to the Edwards sisters – were afraid of change and afraid of male xintou.

It was time they had a taste of both.

Rohne dressed and slipped out of his room. Dismissing the single weishi who habitually followed him around, he headed for Hassan's bedroom. At this hour, the man would have breakfasted and be in the throne room, brooding on his captured seat of power. He liked to hold court in the mornings, having left his prisoners in the cells of the northern gate watchtower overnight. Suitably softened and persuaded by the cell guards, most confessed to whatever wrongdoing took Hassan's fancy when they were dragged before him.

Having little stomach for such timewasting, Rohne refused to attend after the first day's bloodshed. Hassan did not need his skills for such barbarity. The man's disorganised mind and rampant paranoia was distasteful. With the Bonding in place, Rohne needed only to be within range to know what Hassan was doing. Little skill was needed to redirect Hassan's thoughts when he got too out of control.

Normally, at this time, Rohne met with Nasra to plan the Jundom's future. Today, she was in a training session with the erheyi girls and unlikely to emerge from the North Tower until after lunch. It was also the first time she had left him without a close-guard of three weishi and two erheyi girls. She'd said it was for his protection. But the twins watched him as though he posed a threat, which was interesting on many levels. While he could have easily distracted the weishi, the erheyi twins were proving more difficult. Their minds were strong and well-warded.

So, this was his first opportunity to search for yanstones.

Hassan's room was locked, but unguarded. The hallway remained empty so Rohne opened the lock telekinetically and slipped inside. Flicking the soft overhead lights on, he surveyed the room. A massive, timber and iron bed dominated the space. Bookshelves, jammed with dusty, leatherbound tomes, lined two walls. Otherwise, only a few, scattered pieces of heavy timber furniture served to lessen the room's severity.

A quick perusal of two other doors revealed a bathroom, a dressing room and, beyond that, a servant's sleeping room. Rohne stood in the main area and turned a slow circle.

Where was the most likely place for a safe or hidden room?

The bookshelves. They appeared to be fixed to the walls. By some intuition he bypassed the first and stopped at the second. A thin layer of dust on the shelves and books indicated Hassan was not much of a reader, and the servants were slack in their duties. It did, however, make finding the latch a little easier. The only disturbed dust was at the end of the middle shelf. He found the small button beneath. Pressing popped a hidden catch and the bookshelf swung silently away from the wall.

Rohne felt around and flicked on the lightswitch. Perfect. The small room, revealed by the single overhead bulb, held three wall units, each with dozens of shallow drawers. He opened the nearest and gave a soft, triumphant cry. Yanstones, glittering in their gold settings, flared in the light.

He stroked them lovingly, expecting the intense depth and connection he'd felt with the Koh-Lin bracelets. Nothing. He examined them. They had to be real. No other gem caught, held and amplified light in such a way and no jeweller was yet able to create a fake that stood up to scrutiny.

Dropping the chain, he yanked open the next drawer. More yanstones, this time set in a silvery metal. Still nothing when he held them. How could that be? What was it about the Koh-Lin stones that made them special? Or had it simply been his imagination? Surely not. The connection, the expansion of his abilities, the sensation of almost unlimited power – those had been too real to be imaginary.

Opening another drawer revealed several more sets of stones, all exquisitely set in silver, gold, bronze and copper. All lifeless. One drawer yielded a delicately-beautiful pendant and matching earrings made in steel, with five tiny stones trembling in the filigree necklace and two in each of the earrings. Another held a wide-banded ring set with a single stone. The band's iron caught the light in fascinating, crystalline striations, reminiscent of the Koh-Lin settings.

Yet, even holding all of them, Rohne felt no surge of heady power. With a wordless growl, he flung the stones aside, slammed the drawer shut and left the secret room. There must be a reason. Something unique about the Koh-Lin stones that amplified his powers. If none of the Zah-Hill jewels worked then he would have to take the bracelets back from Alere when she arrived.

If she arrived.

Gaisi! He needed to change some of his plans – without letting Nasra know why. That would require some thought and skill. And a hefty fee to Weishi House.

CHAPTER SEVENTEEN

CORIN

Corin stretched and rose in the saddle, trying to ignore the ache in his lower back and legs. Just ahead, Kett rode as comfortably as ever, so Corin resisted the urge to groan and complain. Between them they'd ridden ten horses to exhaustion and slept a grand total of about two hours in the last twenty-four. The coronation was just days away and they had to find Alere before she walked into the city, unsuspecting.

Now they topped the last rise in the road and Madina's walls loomed in the distance. It was Ahad the seventh and just after dawn, but the overcast sky and snow-sharp southern wind made it seem earlier. To the west, the Kabir River wound past the city, carrying chuans under full sail north toward Chengdu. Wading upstream, close to the shore, one of the huge, grey-white xiangs towed a chuan into port. The animal raised its long neck and blunt head and trumpeted; a lonely, unearthly sound.

To the east lay rolling, grassy hills; pastures for the vast herds of runiu that supplied meat for the city. The sound of a distant drum rattled across the open spaces. Corin rose in the stirrups again to look. A tent-city emerged from behind the low hills, northeast of the city. Several large pavilions bore fluttering black pennants, but their symbols were too distant to be distinguished.

He nudged his gelding alongside Kett's mount and pointed.

The weishi nodded. 'Selb, I suspect.'

'Shouldn't we go wait for Alere and talk with them? Let them know Alere and Mina are on their way?' Corin fingered the axe pendant around his neck.

Kett cast a narrow glance at the tents. 'I'd rather find Alere, first. Our best option is to get into the city, meet your contacts and send out scouts familiar with the landscape to find her.'

'What if Alere's already there? With the Selb. We—'

Kett's jaw clenched and he directed a hard look at Corin. 'Don't you think I want to go find her, Cor? You've tried with the yanstones and can't reach her. Be realistic. We're exhausted and there's only two of us. Besides, from the way Liu told it,' he added, 'Alere was forced into leading the Selb. Gavon mistrusted them so she'll be wary. She'll try to sneak into Madina and rescue Rafi and the others, herself.'

Corin blinked at him. 'Don't get me wrong, I'm all for sneaking, but that's insane. If she's got a gouri army, she should use it. Yasmin's probably only a day or so away. If the two armies join forces they'd outnumber Hassan's men.'

Kett scrubbed a hand over his head. 'You're forgetting how Alere was raised. Clarity, responsibility and all that? She'll believe this is her fault and her responsibility. She won't want to lead an army into mass murder unless it becomes unavoidable. Remember how hard she argued against it in Shanzhai when we faced Hanna?'

'Then what's your excuse for not talking to the Selb on her behalf?'

'I don't know what their agenda is,' he said. 'When we're all together and we can meet their leader as equals – then we can see what they have to offer.'

'So,' Corin mused, 'what you really mean is that you'd rather be with Alere when she meets them?'

Kett's mouth twitched into a small smile. 'Something like that.'

'Anyone ever mention your control-issues?'

'Alere. Frequently.'

Throwing up his arms in defeat, Corin kicked his tired mount onward. 'How the diyu does she stand up under the weight of so many self-inflicted burdens? You two make a good pair of martyrs. No wonder she liked being on the road with me so much. She had nothing to do but shoot raiders, practice with Gavon and play the whistle at night.'

Kett only gestured him toward the city.

Corin laughed. 'Fine. But do let's hurry. I have a surprise for you.' He kneed his mount southeast. 'This way.'

'City gate is that way.' Kett pointed south.

'So it is,' Corin agreed. 'But it's the servants' entrance on the south side for the likes of us.'

'There you go,' Corin said, flinging out an arm. 'Our road into the heart of Madina.'

Before them loomed an arched, brick-lined tunnel, set into the riverbank. Sludgy water trickled into the river, bringing unpleasant lumps of stinking refuse and the occasional bloated, dead zibal lizard.

Kett dismounted and picked his way past a jumble of mud-covered stone blocks. 'Of course. The stormdrains. I should have known.'

'Was that an insult?' Corin grinned.

'Only to some.'

'Lucky I'm too tired to hit you,' Corin said. He squinted up at the late-morning sun, hazed by thin cloud and lavender smoke from the city's thousands of fireplaces burning seaweed. 'We'd best get a move on.'

Kett glanced at the collapsed remnants of the city's southern wall and scowled. 'I had no idea the wall along the river was in such bad repair.' Broken sandstone and chunks of sulcrete mortar littered the river's stinking, mud-slurried banks. Half a watch tower teetered, cracks gaping in the mortar.

'Good for us it is. The city guard are too scared to patrol this part of the wall. Otherwise we'd have had to wait 'til night to get in. Welcome to the under-roads. Frequented by thieves, scoundrels, and the occasional red salamander, so do keep your blade loose.'

Kett paused. 'Red salamanders? I thought they were a myth.'

Corin shrugged and pulled back one sleeve to reveal a perfectly circular bite-mark on one arm. 'They aren't big, but they are vicious little blood-sucking beasties. No venom, at least. Shall we?'

'If we must. But you're responsible for cleaning my boots.'

'Where the diyu are you taking me, Cor?' Kett's question drifted from the foul darkness behind and Corin laughed softly.

Fifteen minutes of splashing carefully through this rank underworld and they were near to their destination. Corin eagerly anticipated a bath and a decent bed. He was so tired he barely managed to lift his feet free from the muck dragging at his boots. He held up a lantern and surveyed the massive, bricklined tunnel ahead with satisfaction. It had been a year or so since he'd been this way, but he hadn't forgotten the route. Left at the next junction.

At his feet, a squeak and the scrabble of tiny claws on brick told him other denizens still inhabited these storm drains. Behind him, Kett uttered an oath as his horse gave a frightened whinny. Before Corin even snapped a warning, Kett had the beast's nose in a silencing grip and the animal settled. It had been difficult enough getting the skittish animals into the tunnels. If they bolted in fear the noise would warn people living overhead that more than just zibals occupied the drains beneath their houses and roads.

Kett's quiet voice echoed. 'Much further?'

'Just around this corner. There's a goods-loading dock built into the side of the tunnel. Assuming the guard is someone I know, we should be admitted with no problems.'

'Do I want to know what seedy dive you're taking me to?'

Corin tugged his mount onward. 'You malign me, and the inhabitants of said dive. I won't repeat your words as they would be mightily offended and that could end badly for you.'

'I'm terrified. We're running out of time, Cor,' Kett added, more seriously. 'Are you sure these friends of yours will be willing to help find Alere? Preferably before she arrives at the gate and is taken prisoner by Hassan's junren?'

'Ah.' Corin grinned as the loading dock came in sight. 'These particular friends have spies everywhere. They'll be able to get word to us the instant Alere comes within an arrowshot of the city walls.'

'And then?'

Corin led his horse up the ramp to the dry, open space beyond. 'And then we ask them politely to bring her here.' He thought about it a moment. 'Of course, we'll probably have to pay them. It's only fair. Loyalty to Jun and Jundom only goes so far and has no economic value.'

Kett joined him, inspecting the solid timber door at the end of the long, arched dock. 'Well, I guess you'd be the one to know about that, wouldn't you?'

'And again, you wound me,' Corin said, not particularly offended. He knocked on the door. The sound echoed in the space and startled the horses again into head-tossing, hoof-stamping nervousness. In the distraction of settling them, Corin and Kett were forced to put their backs to the door. The distinctive double-click of a two-bolt crossbow being cocked cut through the horses' heavy breaths.

Corin turned around… and let out a sigh of relief.

'Mattus, you scared me. Do put that thing away before you shoot me by accident.' He jerked a thumb at Kett. 'This is my friend, Kett. Take us upstairs and have someone see to the horses, would you?' He pointed to the ceiling, indicating a massive timber hatch. 'If the goods elevator's still working, they could probably use a decent washdown in the stable. And mine looks like it has a red attached to its fetlock.' He shuddered and indicated the engorged, burgundy-coloured salamander wriggling on his gelding's leg.

Mattus, a burly, swarthy individual, bearing a nose shaped by too many rowdy customers with swinging fists, studied him for long enough that Corin cast his mind back. Had he offended the establishment in his last visit? Surely not. At least, not much.

Finally, the man uncocked the crossbow. A young boy appeared from behind the door and took charge of the horses, assuring them the salamander would be removed, and their gear would be delivered upstairs as soon as the animals were unloaded.

Unspeaking, Mattus led the way inside, climbing the timber stairs with surprising speed and silence for someone of his size. Knowing him of old, Corin didn't bother to try and make small-talk.

The stairs climbed in a narrow corridor between timber walls, through which floated mingled voices, snippets of music and the clink of glasses. At regularly-spaced intervals, little covered eye-holes pierced the walls. Corin glanced over his shoulder to see what Kett made of it. The weishi remained unmoved, even faintly amused.

Mattus stopped before a section of wall that appeared no different from the rest. He pointed at it and vanished into the darkness. Corin depressed the hidden latch and pushed the panel open. Squinting in the blaze of light, he moved aside so Kett could enter. Overwhelming after the tunnel's miserable dankness, it took a moment to absorb the exotic elegance of their surrounds.

The suite comprised a large sitting room, leading into an opulent bedroom. The sitting room walls were painted the colour of fresh blood. Hung on them were several large paintings of beautiful women and men, all naked. Heavy gold curtains, closed across the large window, made it difficult to tell only a few hours had passed since dawn.

Corin walked further into the room and his footsteps became muffled. He swore, and stepped back onto the polished bamboo floor. Damp stains now marred the gold-and-grey silk rug underfoot.

Grouped about a crackling fireplace, stood five gold-brocade upholstered seats, plump and inviting. A low table held an empty glass of wine, a bowl of fruit and the remains of what smelled like roast pork. The delicious scent was somewhat overpowered by the heady aroma of sandalwood incense and a light, feminine perfume rich in nona-flower and red-root notes.

Cloth rustled from within the bedroom. Both men straightened as a woman appeared. She stood in the doorway, tying the belt of an ornate blue and silver robe. Somewhere in her mid forties, she was regal in her bearing and seemed unfazed by the appearance of two large and unkempt men in her suite. Her strong-boned face was elegantly made up and her long, white-weed-blonde hair was drawn back in a deliberately-messy plait that gave her a youthful, fresh appearance at odds with the years of cynicism in her wide, dark eyes.

She pushed a button near the door. A tinny, distant response sounded. She leaned closer to a grille set into the wall and spoke in a throaty, amused voice.

'Please ask Leeli to make up two rooms. Ready in fifteen minutes. With food.' She wrinkled her nose. 'And baths. Thank you.'

Releasing the button, she swayed closer, arms held out. 'Corin, lovely to see you again. It's been awhile.' She held up a scarlet-nailed finger when he would have replied. 'But I believe my ledger says you still owe me three tiebe.'

'Er...' Corin patted his flat purse. The last few horse exchanges had all but emptied it. 'I apologise. I was in a bit of a hurry to leave last time, what with Han-Asad's men beating on the door.'

'That's no excuse for leaving a bill unpaid,' she said with mock-sternness. 'And I should probably charge you for the bribe I had to pay Kennor to call his doqan tracker-dogs off your scent.'

'It's true, I owe you.' He bowed over her hand. 'And I'm afraid this latest emergency has taken the last of my travelling funds. I think I'll owe you some more, once you hear why we've arrived unannounced.'

'You will. But at least I know you're good for it. Usually.' She kissed his cheek, her stern expression softening. 'So, let me find someone nice. You shouldn't still be single.'

Corin shrugged. 'I do admit, the idea has merit. After the last couple of months, the privations of the road are palling, and the temptations of a soft, occupied bed grow.'

Her lips fell open in an O of surprise, for this was an old interplay between them but he usually deflected her offer with a jest. To prevent her digging into what was a somewhat painful subject, he transferred her attention to Kett.

'In the mean time, may I introduce—'

'Kett, my dear, dear boy.' She lit up with genuine delight. She kissed both the weishi's cheeks, regarding him like a mother whose favourite son has come home. 'I'm so glad you're alright. We were worried when you and Alli vanished and all those dreadful rumours started about her.'

Corin, slack-jawed, was left standing by the wall as they moved to the fire. Recovering, he joined them, sinking into a chair and catching Kett's gaze in question.

The weishi chuckled. 'Surely, you didn't think to shock me by bringing me to Jiaoji House, did you?'

Houlia, Mistress of Madina Jiaoji House patted Corin's wrist. 'My dear boy, I've known Kett since he was a blushing teenager, ordered to escort Alere here once a week for dance lessons. He used to wait outside. So formal and duty-bound.' She gave him an arch look. 'When she grew older and came for jiaoji lessons as well, naturally we couldn't let the poor boy wait for hours out in the weather. All my jiaoji adore him. And you, too, of course, dear. They'll be so glad you're both back.'

Chuckling, Corin relaxed in the chair and waved their amusement away. He was too tired to bother with a witty comeback. He should have known better.

Houlia turned serious as she examined Kett's still-bruised eye. 'What have you done to your face? And where's Alere? Please tell me you haven't brought her here. Hassan's men have orders to kill both of you – and Lia Koh-Lin and Jarran Zah-Hill – if any of you show in the city. They already raided the Koh-Lin residence three times, looking for Lia. And Ma-Safra House looking for you and Alere.'

Kett frowned. 'It's probably best you don't know all the details, Houlia. Were you at the meeting with Nasra?'

Houlia shuddered, her scarlet-tipped fingers whitening on the chair-arm. In the corner a caged pair of jin-birds chirruped into the thick silence.

'I was. I take your point.' Her eyes narrowed. 'We lost the Master of the Merchant House and the Mistress of the Miner House in that meeting. Plus Jun Fourth Qin-Turner and Jun Fourth Knight-Hun.'

'What happened?' Kett leaned forward, watching her closely.

She rubbed at gooseflesh on her arms and stared into the fire. 'They were stupid. Any shazi could see Nasra was not going to tolerate insubordination. She waited for someone to say something ziftish. Then she made examples of them.'

'But how, exactly?' Kett pressed. Corin sat up, fighting to stay awake.

Houlia shivered again. 'They just died. Those…awful twin girls simply looked at Master Quyi and the others and they just…died. Screaming.' She shrugged. 'The rest of the Houses and the Juns fell into line after that. Most of them have now snuck out of Madina.' Her red lips curled in a sneer.

'And you?' Kett's hand dropped to his knife. 'Where do you stand?'

Houlia's mouth softened into a wry smile. 'My dear boy. I'll always put my House first, you know that.' Her dark eyes glittered. 'And Hassan and Nasra are *very* bad for business. The curfews. The executions. Those that can afford our services easily have left town, and the rest are too afraid to go out after dark. I would be obliged if you removed her from the world. Permanently. And that abomination of a son she's installed as Xintou.'

Kett glanced at Corin. His gaze fell pointedly to Corin's blades. Then he leaned back in his chair and smiled at Houlia.

It took Corin's tired brain a second to interpret the silent request. He surreptitiously slid his thumbs under the suede covers and connected to the yanstones. Liquid warmth oozed into his veins and eased his exhaustion somewhat. Houlia's wards were likely to be strong and he was unskilled and tired. But Kett was right: they needed to know if she could be trusted.

CHAPTER EIGHTEEN

ALERE

'Alere, wake up!'

Someone shook her shoulder. She grabbed in automatic defence, but her arms wouldn't obey.

'Alere, it's Saric. C'mon.' The boy's voice wound into a higher pitch than normal. His fingers dug deep. 'You have to wake up, please?'

'Alright, alright.' The words came out slurred. Dirt grated beneath her fingers as she clutched at the ground and gathered the strength to push upright.

'My head hurts,' she croaked. No, it pounded, thick and stupid.

'Mine too. You look worse than I feel, though.' Saric studied her anxiously.

She peered blearily around the ger, shivering as cold crept in through her shirt. In the hearth, nothing but blackened coals remained of the large fire. Silver-white smoke coiled lazily up to the ceiling. The room was cold.

Wei crouched by Qara, tears streaming down her face as she stroked her aunt's slack face. Blood dripped from Batu's body, blackening the earth beneath the table. On the floor beyond, Jarran sat with his back against the central post, eyes closed, Mina held loosely in his arms. Her eyelids fluttered and she groaned. Jarran jerked awake, squinting, the karambit gleaming in his fist. Yuwen, lying near Qara's feet, twitched and shifted, scrabbling at the earth.

Alere grabbed at Saric and he hauled her upright. She held his shoulder as the room swayed alarmingly. Saric cocked his ear at the door-flap. By the sound of it, dozens of people gathered outside.

'What's happening?' she asked.

'I came here to find out from you.' He indicated the ger. 'I woke up feeling like my head had exploded. When I went outside, everyone was screaming and crying. All Wei could understand was that they're worried Qara and Yuwen aren't coming out. They think it's something to do with you and Mina.'

'What time is it?' How long had she been unconscious?

'Just after dawn. What happened?' Saric's gaze travelled to the table.

Batu was only a few years older than Saric yet his life was over, his dark eyes blank with the starkness of death. Blood stained his rough clothing and the sharp, metallic smell of it mingled with smoke in the chill air. Saric seemed unmoved. He picked Alere's dagger off the floor, wiped it clean and balanced it in his palms.

'You used the stones?' It was almost an accusation.

Alere brushed dirt off her clothing, plucked the knife from him and tucked it into her belt. The throbbing pain in her head eased and coherent thoughts returned. If it was just after dawn then only a few minutes had passed.

'I didn't want to. Mina insisted.' She swallowed against the memory. 'I shouldn't have done it. Every gouri time I use them someone dies and I—'

'Alere?' Mina's shaky question interrupted her.

Jarran rose, one arm around Mina's waist. Yuwen and Qara both staggered to their feet. Qara grasped at her husband. Her face contorted in grief and she buried it in his shoulder.

Wei, left standing on her own, stared forlornly at her cousin's lifeless form on the table, and at her aunt, sobbing in Yuwen's arms. Wei raised burning eyes to Alere. Taking three long strides she closed the gap between them. Her fist flashed out.

Still half-stupified, Alere managed to stumble backward. Wei's blade caught her shirt and left a line of fire across her stomach.

'Wei!' Saric grabbed Wei's knife-hand, twisting it up behind her in a painful lock. Wei snarled at him, tears streaking her face. She produced a black-feathered dart and held it ready to throw. Behind her, Saric scowled and pulled her arm harder.

'Drop it, Wei,' he ordered. 'Don't be a little zift.'

'She killed him! She killed my cousin.' She rounded fiercely on Alere. 'I *hate* you! I only just found my family and you've destroyed it. You destroy *everything*. First my family with Liu, then Shasa, and now this. I wish you'd never come!'

Alere sank onto a stool and pressed a palm against her belly, sickened by the kernel of truth in Wei's words. She shrank away as Wei's angry accusations continued unchecked. A sharp slap resounded. Saric shook his hand and Wei held her cheek, eyes wide.

Mina's muffled sob broke the silence.

Saric yanked the weapons from Wei and inspected the knife before tucking both it and the dart away.

'Get a grip, Wei,' he snarled, his expression a mix of scorn and hurt. 'Liu and Shasa would be ashamed of you, behaving like a stupid little girl. *I'm* ashamed of you.' He jerked his chin at Alere. 'Did she tag you? The knife's not poisoned at least.'

'I'm...I'll be alright,' Alere managed, her tongue stumbling under the weight of guilt. 'I'm sorry, Wei.'

Wei folded her arms and said nothing, glaring at Saric and Alere. Qara broke free of Yuwen and wrapped her arms around Wei's slight form.

'No, no, little one.' She caught Wei's jaw and forced the girl to meet her gaze. '*I* asked Alere and Mina to help. Alere didn't want to. She was afraid this would happen.' She cast Alere a look equally weighted in guilt, lingering horror, and grief. 'Alere tried her best to save Batu. They both did. They almost succeeded. But he was too damaged. If Mina and Alere hadn't acted, dozens would have died.' She held Wei's gaze a few moments longer, until the girl folded into misery and sobbed into her shoulder. Yuwen embraced his wife and niece.

The angry murmurings and questions outside grew; as though the sun's rising drove their fear with it. Voices shouted Yuwen and Qara's names, anxious. More voices joined in. Footsteps scuffed closer to the entrance. The occasional clink of weapons became audible.

Jarran, his arm still around Mina's waist, murmured.

'We should leave.' He cocked his ear at the door. 'Wei won't be the only one angry about this.'

Yuwen listened. He called out something to the crowd outside. His words caused a flurry of questioning responses. He cut them short with a barked command then spoke to Jarran.

'I've bought us a few minutes, but it won't be long before my warriors come in. They believe you're holding us. Cut a way out the back.' He pointed at the ger's back wall. 'Directly behind is a dry wadi. Climb down into it and head south. You'll be out of sight. When you reach a large, green boulder high in the western bank, you'll be well clear of the village. Wait there. I'll bring your horses, gear, and supplies to see you through to Madina. The horses are well-rested and fit. It's half a day's ride southwest of here if you know the right path and you don't spare them. I'll make sure you have nosebags and feed for the animals, and water.'

Jarran thanked him and used the karambit to slice an opening in the skin wall. Peering out, he gave the all-clear and vanished through it.

Mina spoke to Qara. 'I'm sorry. I'm so sorry.'

'It's not your fault, child. I should never have risked bringing a boy into the world.' She gazed bleakly at her son's body. 'I thought I knew better than Xintou House. Go, and be safe.'

Numb, Alere stumbled after Mina. Saric joined her, ducking under her arm when she tripped on a loose rug. At the opening he paused.

'Wei?'

The girl raised a tearstained face and took half a step toward him. Qara still held her by the wrist. Wei glanced back and forth between them with hope, doubt and longing. Then she looked at Alere and something like fear flickered over her face. She retreated into the protective curve of Qara's arm.

'I'll stay.'

Saric hesitated, then shrugged with apparent indifference. 'Whatever.' He showed his back.

'Saric?' She ran to him and kissed his cheek. 'Be safe and come back for me sometime, if you can.'

He snorted. 'This is *not* my kind of place. I'm not coming back. I'll be in Madina if you get bored.' He slipped out through the slit and vanished, leaving Wei looking lost and miserable.

Hoping to repair the damage she'd done, Alere said, 'I'll make sure Master Anh knows to keep a place in Weishi House if you do want to join.' She touched the girl's shoulder. Wei flinched and Alere repressed a surge of anger and hurt. 'I'm sorry, Wei. I really did try.'

Had she? If she'd given her all, as Mina had asked, would that have worked? Or would they have Fused and both died with Batu?

Qara came up behind Wei. 'I'll make sure she understands. This is the best place for her. I will train her to be my apprentice. When she comes into her powers she'll know what to do.'

'Powers?' 'No!' Alere and Wei spoke together.

Qara hesitated. 'Had you not seen it in her? She will be xintou when she comes of age in a few months.'

'Then she should come to Madi—' Alere stopped. 'No, you're right. She's safer here, especially now. You'll be alright with Qara, Wei.' She saw fright in the girl and knew a moment of sour realisation. 'Don't worry, you won't be like me, or Batu.' She turned away, not wanting to see the relief.

Qara touched her arm. 'Thank you for trying and I'm sorry Mina had to...' She wiped at fresh tears. 'Go. You have a difficult road ahead. This is not the last blood you will shed.'

'I never thought it would be,' Alere said bitterly. 'I'm getting good at forgetting the blood I've had to spill. Otherwise I can't sleep.'

Qara's dark eyes were serious. 'You must not forget this, Alere.' Her expression held not anger or grief but worry. 'There is a lesson here you needed to learn. If you run from it, many more will die. If you understand it, you may yet succeed.'

'What lesson? That every time I touch those gouri stones someone dies? I think I've learned that, thank you. Or is it the lesson that I'm better off on my own because people get hurt...want too much from me...but somehow I can never give enough?' She cleared her throat and looked away.

Qara's shoulders slumped. 'I don't know, but if you truly understand what happened here, some good will come of it. If you do not, then everything you love will be swept away and destroyed. Mamlakah will squirm beneath the iron grip of the worst tyrant this world has ever seen.'

Alere ground her teeth. 'So I've heard. Three times now. Everyone is great at predicting *what* I need to prevent, but not *how*. Or why it has to be me.'

Qara kissed both her cheeks and the centre of her forehead. 'I wish I had more to give you, but I can only See darkness and the same gold-fire we saw today. What comes out of that chaos is up to you.'

Alere slipped through the cut in the ger's back wall and half-slid down the sandy gully behind. She crouched low and ran along the dried creekbed until she was out of sight of the village. Behind her, a great keening and wailing arose. The rhythmic thudding of drums accompanied the cries of distress. Hundreds of voices took up a throat-sung, monotone version of the *Song of Passing* in the common tongue. A tinny bell rang four times, the sound echoing off the great sandstone wall. In the distance, the wind drew a mournful counter-tune from the mouths of the singing stones.

Rounding a corner, Alere found the others waiting by the boulder Yuwen had described. Mina paced back and forth, rubbing at her arms, her boots crunching in the dry green sand. She froze when she saw Alere. A heartbreaking sequence of expressions flickered across her features: relief, hurt, cold anger. Jarran leaned against the rock, arms folded. Saric watched both with wary tension, his hands not far from his dart-belt.

Alere paused a few steps away. 'Mina, I—'

'Don't.' Mina held up a finger. 'You don't get to apologise, Alli. Not this time.'

'I tried,' Alere shot back, her stomach roiling. 'You tried. There was nothing more we could have done. It wasn't your fault.'

'You don't get it, do you?' Mina moved closer, fists clenched. 'I know it wasn't my fault. It was yours.'

Alere stepped back, heart stuttering. 'He was too broken. I was barely able to save myself, in the end.'

'We failed because *you* are too broken, Alere. You do this every time someone tries to get close to you. You push people away.' She cast Alere a pitying look, unshed tears glistening. 'What made you so afraid of getting close to people that you'd let a little boy die rather than open up to me?'

'That's not true,' Alere whispered, but her throat tightened.

'Mina,' Jarran said. 'Ease up. That isn't fair.'

Mina whirled on him. 'Yes, it is. She pushed me away in Shanzhai. She left Kett behind, instead of letting him help. And now, when I needed her the most, she held back. If she had opened to me, we could have saved Batu.'

'No!' Alere said. 'If I'd opened to you, we would have Fused and died. You know that. This isn't about me. It's about how dangerous the yanstones are and how dangerous a male xintou is. How dangerous *I* am when I use the stones. You just don't want to face the truth – that we can't fix Rohne. You still care about him.'

'Of course I do! He's been my friend since I was born.'

'Don't you get what that meant back there?' Alere said, pointing up the dry stream bed. 'If Rohne is like Batu, then we have to kill him.'

'You're wrong. We can cure him if you just help me, properly. He needs me. Yes, he's made mistakes. But I don't discard my friends just because what they need from me is difficult.'

Saric interrupted with a snort. 'He left you behind to be a slave. Not what most friends would do.'

'Really?' Mina snapped. 'Your best friend just left you.'

Saric paled. 'I'll go wait for Yuwen.' He stalked back toward the village, his thin shoulders set.

'Mina!' Jarran gripped her shoulder. 'Enough. You're upset the boy died. But you did force Alere to help. You can't lay all the blame on her.'

Mina recoiled like he'd slapped her.

'I was trying to protect you,' Alere said, stiffly. 'Fusion is impossible to come back from.'

'I'm not talking about opening your mind!' Mina's face flushed. She laid a fist on her chest. 'I'm talking about your heart. You're surrounded by friends, but you're alone because you'll never let anyone in, Alere. You're always looking for how they're going to hurt you, or tie you down. And something tells me you'll never master the yanstones until you understand that about yourself.'

'Maybe not,' Alere said, low and hard, 'but it's better than being so afraid of being alone that you latch onto the nearest man who rescues you from your own stupid decisions!'

'Oh!' Mina covered her mouth, wiping at her face.

'Stop it!' Jarran stepped between them. 'You're both tired and overwrought. Behaving like children won't help.' He lowered his voice. 'You're both trying to do the right thing in a difficult time.'

'Maybe.' Alere sighed. 'But our idea of what's the right thing is so different I'm not sure…'

Mina's shoulders slumped. She flickered a glance at Alere then scrubbed her hands down her thighs. 'Imagine how much good we could do with those yanstones if we could truly work together. But all you can think about is how to use them as a weapon. How to *be* a weapon.'

'It's how I was raised.'

'But it's not how you have to *be,* Alere. You're free to choose your own path now, remember?'

Alere looked away, resisting the temptation to dive into the yanstones silver-gilt reassurance. 'I'm sorry, Mina. I'm trying. I'm sorry I couldn't save Batu.'

Mina gave a broken sob and walked away.

Yuwen appeared with Saric, leading their loaded horses and putting an end to the conversation. He handed over Alere's sword. Thanking him, Alere sheathed both weapons and mounted, letting Jarran discuss the route to Madina with Yuwen. She didn't argue when Jarran handed out the messenger orange uniforms and took the lead.

She couldn't deny the truth in Mina's words. They might spring from Mina's own pain and self-doubt, but they cut straight to the bone and laid Alere's heart open for inspection. And the result was awful to contemplate.

Mina was utterly right.

Alere wiped her face with a sand-gritty sleeve and stared blankly at the dry horizon. She'd been isolated her whole life. Even her childhood in the Ma-Safra household had been one of lonely privilege with no siblings or friends. Elmira had been distant and often absent, as Xintou to Petar Ma-Safra. Then, living in Xintou House had taught sharp lessons on how to keep her thoughts and feelings firmly under control; deeply hidden. To keep people at a distance. Safe.

If she had accepted Mina, her sister would never have left Shanzhai. And if she had truly let Kett into her heart, she would never have left him behind.

But to do what Mina wanted – to open heart and mind to her twin and the yanstones – that was to invite more than just Mina in. Ridiculous though it sounded, the stones wanted her to be the weapon that would destroy Rohne and Nasra. There was no way to give herself completely to the yanstones – to Mina – without losing her humanity.

No, she couldn't go down that path again.

She drew a slow, shuddering breath and straightened in the saddle. But she could at least help with her sister's pain. Through their connection, Mina's anger and self-blame smouldered and burned. Jarran was wrong. Mina wasn't to blame. Alere had chosen to help cure Batu. And she had chosen to withhold from Mina. It was only fair that she take away her sister's hurt.

Turning her gaze inward, she began siphoning off Mina's pain and burying it deep in her own mind.

CORIN

Corin slid his thoughts across Houlia's wards. She was well-trained, her wards smooth and hard. Nothing. Not a crack. It wasn't like they had a lot of choices, though. They needed somewhere to stay. Houlia was the least likely of the various House leaders to succumb to Nasra's threats.

But she was also a pragmatist. And she was still alive, which meant she hadn't stood against Nasra. He caught Kett's attention, grimaced and shrugged. The weishi pressed his lips together then continued to chat easily with Houlia. Corin listened, resting his head on the seat-back. Kett regaled Houlia with a much-expurgated version of the trip to Chengdu. Somewhere between Chengdu and Madina, sleep dragged Corin's eyelids closed.

A touch on his shoulder brought him to his feet, dagger-drawn.

'Relax, Cor.' Kett pushed the dagger aside. 'Houlia brought Kennor here to speak with us, and she's sent messages alerting her people to watch for Alere.'

'Messages,' Corin muttered sleepily. 'We need to let Yasmin know we're here.'

'All taken care of,' Kett assured him. 'Wake up now. We need to speak with Kennor. Tell him where to take his men.'

Corin scrubbed at his face, yawning. 'Right.' He slapped himself. 'I'm good.'

Houlia opened the door, gestured Kennor inside then left the men alone.

Kennor Han-Asad strode in and hesitated, frowning. His nose wrinkled as he looked them over haughtily. Thinner than when they'd last seen him in Shanzhai, his face was grey and tired.

Corin bowed. 'Shenshi. Thank you for meeting us. We bear word from your daughter.'

Han-Asad started. 'What word? What of her? If you've harmed her—'

'No, shenshi,' Kett cut in calmly. 'Quite the opposite. We met her in Asadia. Farima is quite well. But your sister is dead.'

'Hanna! How?' Han-Asad glared and looked Kett over. 'Who are you? How do you know?'

'She died of natural causes. She was unwell, as you probably know. We met Farima by chance and she asked us to pass on the news because she didn't want to entrust it to a flitter or runner. She also asked if you would help us.' He held out her signet ring.

The Jun Third stared at it then nodded slowly. 'Do what?'

'We need to rid the Jundom of Hassan, Nasra and Rohne.'

Kennor passed a trembling hand over his long, grey-streaked hair. 'I've been down this path once before and it didn't end well. Most of my men and my Jun Fifth and Sixth have sworn to Hassan to save their own necks. I chose the wrong side.'

'I know, shenshi.' Corin approached. 'Now you're choosing the right one. We speak for Rafi and his Jun-Heir, Lia. I'm Rafi's chief counsel.'

The older man made a dismissive noise. 'Rafi's imprisoned and Lia is somewhere in the north, busy freeing slaves, I hear. Jarran Zah-Hill has disappeared, too. Yasmin's army has no experienced leader and is outnumbered by Hassan's.' He raised bleak eyes to Kett. 'The only good news I've had is that Hanna is dead and my daughter is safe. I should never have supported Hanna. I was a zift to believe her lies. But I was so afraid I'd lose Farima, too.' He dropped his head into his hands. 'I can't see a clear path and I can't endanger Farima again.'

'If I gave you a chance at redemption,' Kett said quietly. 'A chance to help Lia and Rafi win this war and put Jarran safely on the throne. Would you take it? If they succeed, I can guarantee Jarran will pardon your mistake in backing Hanna. Farima will be safe. As will her child.'

'She told you?' A glimmer of hope sparked in Kennor's eyes. 'You can do that? How? Who are you?'

'Tekettan Zah-Hill. Jarran's brother.'

'Tekettan! I thought Hanna…' The Jun Third sucked a swift breath and straightened. He bowed. 'What do you need me to do?'

Corin stepped forward. 'I've spoken with Farima's weishi, Tren.'

'He's a good man.' Kennor nodded.

'He'll bring the new junren Hanna recruited and meet you in Prana, east of the city. Wait there until I send you a message. You'll most likely either join up with Yasmin's forces, or with the Selb army on the north side.'

'Very well.' Kennor tugged his shirt down and settled his weapons on his hips. 'Thank you. You've given me hope.'

Shortly after, Houlia returned and escorted Kennor out.

'Whatever you told him,' she said speculatively, 'that's the happiest I've seen him for several days. Years, in fact. He was a good man. Before Hanna became First Shunu, that is. Then he was just afraid.'

Kett bowed. 'There's still a lot to do. You don't have an Old Mandrin translation dictionary here, do you?'

With an astonished laugh, Houlia shook her head.

'Jiangui!' Kett swiped a hand over his mouth. 'I need to get into the Xintou House library, then.'

Corin groaned. 'It's the middle of the day, Kett. We can't go traipsing around the city now. Unless your death-wish is showing more than usual.'

'My dear boy,' Houlia said, 'you both need to rest awhile. You look like diyu.' She screwed up her nose. 'And bathe. You've ruined my rug.'

Kett laughed. 'Apologies. Add it to Corin's bill.'

'I will.' Houlia pressed a bell to summon a servant. 'And, when you've rested, there's someone else you should meet who might be able to help.'

Kett and Corin both kissed her cheek, followed a servant to their rooms and parted ways, arranging to meet again in four hours. Corin stripped and washed. Not even the food laid out on the table tempted him from the luxury of the first real mattress he'd seen in a week.

ALERE

'We go in through the southern gate.' Alere stared blankly down the slope at Madina. She and the others stood at the edge of a copse of trees to the northeast of the city. To the north lay a huge tent city with black pennants flapping in the sharp, southerly breeze. The clash of weapons and whinny of horses and che-ma rolled across the low hills. Behind her, a herd of runiu grazed, lowing occasionally and swishing their long tails.

Jarran pointed at the encampment and spoke in the patient tone of a parent dealing with a stubborn child. 'The Selb army is right there. You promised to lead them. They're your best chance of standing up to Hassan Wen-Gates' army.'

Alere dragged her gaze to his face, forcing herself to focus. She swayed in the saddle and blinked slowly, trying to think through the miasma of distress emanating from Mina's mind.

'No.' Each word was solid and heavy in her mouth; the wrong form of communication. 'South gate.'

'Oh, for…' Jarran flung up his hands. 'You're just going to walk right into enemy territory, in broad daylight? The city junren will arrest us on sight, you know that.'

She managed a bleak smile. 'They won't see us.'

His expression turned sceptical. Mina's lips pressed thin, but she said nothing.

Alere gave a short, bitter laugh. 'The gates are guarded by shazis these days. I can use the yanstones to make them ignore us – without killing any of them.' Alere kicked her mount into a walk and headed south.

Behind her, Saric murmured, 'You sure about this?'

'You, too? Yes, I'm sure.' She shifted in the saddle, easing sore muscles. 'If nothing else, a day of using the stones constantly to manage Mina's emotions has made me absolutely certain of some things.'

'Such as?'

She sucked a shuddering breath and forced down a wave of resentful despair from Mina, letting the yanstones silver-gilt strength wash it away. 'That I've been holding back a lot of myself in a lot of areas.'

'Why?' Saric leaned around and studied her face.

'Because I've been afraid to hurt people I care about.'

'Would you?'

'On my own? No. Under the stones' influence? I'm not sure.' She kicked the horse again and pushed into a canter, cutting off any further conversation.

When they reached the Pelon-to-Madina road, Alere stopped and removed the messenger orange cloak and hat. She shoved them deep into her pack and told Jarran and Mina to do the same.

Jarran, of course, questioned her.

'Because we've been seen wearing them by people in Dalcin and the villages we've passed through,' she explained.

He looked blankly at her.

'The xiongshou contracts, remember?' She rode a wave of fear from Mina and soothed it away. 'That stable owner in Dalcin was sure to tell everyone what we were wearing. The word would have spread. They'll be watching for us.' She drew out the little tub of sticky sap Mina had given her so long ago and used her knife to hack off a small handful of hair. With the sap, she made a moustache and pressed it to her lip. Her hair was long enough to stay tied in a mawei, now, so she looked older than she had when she first donned this disguise. Jarran had not shaved for several days and sported a short, dark-red beard that changed his face dramatically.

Wordless, she handed the sap to Jarran and pointed at Mina. He managed to coax her into changing into Alere's spare set of clothing. He then handed Mina's grey healer-robe and veil to Saric, who dragged it on over his clothing without protest. Alere helped him pin the veil in place over his eyes, ignoring his caustic comments about the stupidity of not being able to see clearly. She took off the journeyman's white apron. Now he was an apprentice Healer.

Three men and a young healer girl rode up to Madina's south gate. A thin disguise, but Alere was confident she could manage the junren at the gate, so it was just a show for any spies.

A pair of bored junren gave them a cursory glance and didn't even bother to ask for identity papers. Alere frowned. The messages she'd received all indicated Madina was in lockdown. Why weren't they checking papers? Then the junren held up a convoy of merchants leaving the city with huoches full of barrels of mel-oil and bales of silks. Papers were checked and an argument arose when the junren began methodically searching every bale and tapping every barrel.

Of course. They were only worried about people leaving the city. A sign of Hassan's need for control and Nasra's arrogance, perhaps. Or was Rohne so confident he wasn't worried about Alere and her companions sneaking in?

The main street led straight from the gate, north, toward the twin towers of the Alcazar, just visible above the surrounding tenements and buildings. On the western side, narrow streets curved back through the close-packed Zalam slums. Buildings climbed atop each other; crumbling brick and splintering bamboo. Wooden shutters rather than windows. To the east, the streets still twisted and turned, but the houses and buildings were slightly larger and better-built. Sandstone and violet bamboo. Glass windows and front gardens.

Alere frowned. The main north-south route usually teemed with people and huoches. Normally there were dozens of open storefronts, merchants loading and unloading wares, visitors buying silver-painted models of the Alcazar and gold-clad xintou dolls. Now it lay desolate and half-empty.

Huge thorn-tuft trees marched down either side of the empty street like weishi at attention. Their straight, black trunks – dotted with spring buds of brilliant white flowers – towered over the buildings. On the western side of the street, a near-finished three-storey building stood unattended, swathed in bamboo scaffolding. Piles of building materials – logs and stones – lay abandoned.

A few people scurried along the street, sticking close to buildings. With cloaks tight-wrapped against the bitter winter breeze, they kept their heads down and eyes averted. There were no runners crying news, no dancers or musicians, no hawkers selling unwary travellers badly made wares. Not even any beggars. Many of the shops were boarded shut, their bright displays of clothing, furniture, food, and home goods hidden away. Only a healer's herbal store and the weapons store flew the red flag to show they were open.

Opposite them, a small branch of Messenger House also flew the red, but no rider mounts stood ready outside and no flitters squawked in the cages awaiting messages for other cities.

Alere swung down from her horse. 'Jarran, you go to the Messenger House and check for the latest news of Hassan. We need to know what he's planning for the coronation. It's only two days away. Saric, you stay with Mina.'

Without awaiting an answer, she visited both the Healer and weapons shops. When she remounted, she passed a small phial and a linen sack to Saric. He unstoppered the phial and sniffed.

'Si-xing?' He whistled. 'That must have cost an arm.'

She nodded. 'I have a feeling you're going to need it soon. That's as much as I could afford. Had to replace my throwing knives. The sack is the makings for smoke bombs.'

'My favourite distractions,' Saric said, grinning. 'You do know the way to a boy's heart. Where are we going?' He tucked the phial away.

Alere pressed at her forehead, trying to think clearly. She couldn't go to Xintou House, or the Koh-Lin or Ma-Safra town houses. They would all be watched. And, as much as Houlia of Jiaoji House was wonderful, she was also a shrewd and practical businesswoman. She would play both sides of the war to make sure she came out with her House intact. It was possible Houlia would hand Alere straight over to the Alcazar.

'Weishi House,' she said at last. 'Weishi are neutral parties until they sign a contract. I have enough money left to contract Master

Anh to hide and protect us for two days. Maybe even enough to hire a couple of ronin weishi to help us rescue the prisoners in the Alcazar.'

Saric's brows shot up. 'There are contracts on you and Mina, and you're going to walk into Weishi House? Seems…insane.'

'Last place they'll look for us,' she replied. 'In plain sight. In their House.'

'Makes sense…I guess. Then what?'

'Then,' she said grimly, 'we find a way to release the prisoners.'

'Good.' Jarran remounted his horse. He held up a public news slip. 'The coronation is set for mid-morning on the ninth. In two days! That wisix hundan Hassan has a list of a hundred people to be executed during the ceremony. Like it's some sort of light entertainment for the crowd.' He crushed the paper in his fist, his face steely. 'My daughters are scheduled to be murdered *as* the gouri steel crown is being placed on his head.'

Alere swore. She kicked her tired horse into a walk and took the lead. A block and a half from the centre of the city, she headed down a narrow side-alley. The four main roads leading through Madina met at a large square, which was always full of people and market stalls. Too big a risk of being seen by spies. Now, her years of making Kett take the back alleys between Xintou and Jiaoji Houses paid off. She took a circuitous route through the city, checking frequently for followers.

Arriving at the back entrance to Weishi House, she dismounted and tied her horse to a hitching post. The others followed suit.

'Should we leave them out here like this?' Saric asked, studying the surrounding houses. 'They'll get stolen.'

Alere smiled faintly. 'No one steals from Weishi House in Madina. They're safe. Trust me.'

She knocked on the black wooden gate and a pair of dark eyes appeared at the eyeslit. 'We're here to see Master Anh. Tell him we have a message from Kett Peter-kin.'

The gate creaked open. A boy a little older than Saric waved them in and instructed them to wait in the training square. She didn't know him, which meant he wouldn't recognise her, either.

Alere paused in the middle of the open space and felt her shoulders relax. This was familiar territory. She'd spent so many days here, with Kett, training. The walls on two sides were sheer and twice head-height. One was of smooth-cut sandstone with no joins. The other was glassy-black basalt. Both were topped with broken glass and coils of barbed brass wire. The other two sides of the square were the L-shaped buildings of Weishi House. Two storeys and with odd construction. Four different types of roofs: terracotta tiles abutted slate tiles on one roof. And thatch rubbed shoulders with shingles on the other building. Unnecessary drainpipes and oddly-placed extra roof projections poked out of the building walls. Eight different kinds of railings fenced in verandahs and balconies.

Jarran raised his brows. 'Someone had an insane builder.'

'Training grounds,' Alere said. 'So the students can learn how to climb different walls and walk silently on different roofs.' She pointed to the sandstone wall. 'That one's the worst. Nothing to grip and suction cups won't work. I hated it. Broke my ankle falling off it.'

Mina shivered and glanced around the square, her arms wrapped tightly around her body.

'Wei will be sorry she missed this,' Saric said, sighing. Alere draped an arm across his shoulders.

'She'll be alright. Family's important. When she's a little older she'll come around, I'm sure.' She glanced at Mina, who looked gravely back.

Saric shrugged.

Alere frowned, listening. She peered into the darker space inside the left hand building. Maybe a dozen shadowy figures moved in utter silence, blocking out fighting kata in pairs.

Saric followed her gaze. 'What?'

'Xiongshou. Training.'

'Really?' He started toward the room but Alere held him back.

'Bad idea. And…'

'And what?' Jarran prompted.

'There are usually about forty xiongshou here, but I only count twelve. They can't all be out on assignment. Xintou House law mistresses have to approve high-level political assassinations. And the lower level ones don't usually take more than one or two xiongshou teams out of the House at once.' Alere laid hands on her sword and dagger, uneasiness knotting her gut again. 'Something's not right. We should leave.'

She turned and stopped. 'Jiche!'

The others spun. Mina gasped and edged closer to Jarran. Standing between them and the exit were ten black-clad weishi. Alere dropped into a fighting stance, hands on her weapons. None of the weishi bore House or Jun colour markings. But all wore alzin chest armour and the hooded half-mask of a one-contract, ronin weishi protecting their identity. Hired for one job.

None bore the *jijin* xiongshou ribbon. They were weishi and about her own skill level. So it was a capture contract, not a kill contract. Which gave Alere a slight advantage.

But who had paid them? She must know at least some of the weishi. She'd practically grown up in this compound, training daily with Kett and the weishi from Xintou House. Could she appeal to them? Sway them? Unlikely. The contract held highest priority.

'Saric,' she murmured, 'blue or green feathers only. No blacks. Got it?'

'Bai, shifu. Say the word.'

'Mina, get in the middle,' she said. Her sister hid behind Jarran.

Alere palmed five of her throwing knives, gripping the blade instead of the handle.

'Now, Saric.'

Saric leapt for the nearest climbing wall and scurried to the top like a sky-monkey. The weishi ignored him. Alere flicked the knives in rapid succession. Three weishi dodged or caught the blades. Two misjudged. The knife-handles cracked audibly against their skulls and both dropped, unconscious. Not lethal if they got to a healer. Alere swallowed. Did she know them? She refocussed. Now was not the time for sentiment.

Behind, two soft breaths from Saric were followed by cries of anger. Two weishi to her left collapsed. The rest edged closer, closing the circle, still not fighting back. Another two fell with green darts in their throats. Three split off and headed for the wall on which Saric sat. He stomped on grasping fingers then leapt to the tiled roof behind.

The closest to Alere came within ma'ai – fighting distance. Alere lashed a low kick. The woman shin-blocked. A hand struck at Alere's face. She slapped it aside and jabbed stiff fingers into an exposed throat. The woman choked and staggered back. Another took her place. Alere blocked a flurry of strikes. A blade-hand slipped through her guard and caught her on the jaw. Lights sparkled behind her eyes.

Six more weishi appeared. Jarran's deep voice cut through the eerie silence with a yell of pain.

The weishi fanned out, silent, surrounding Alere's group.

Alere swore again.

Too many. She slipped her fingers onto the yanstones and opened her mind to the stones around her neck. The full force of Mina's fear struck her like a blow and she quashed it ruthlessly. There was no time to baby her sister. Alere stretched through the silver-gilt rope connecting their minds.

We must work together, Mina. We can take all of them out at once, if you let me control the connection.

No! Behind Jarran, Mina cast Alere a stubborn glare. *Stop thinking everything can be solved by violence, Alli. Talk to them. You must know some of them?*

The contract overrules friendships. They won't care who I am. They're being paid a lot of money not to care. This is the only way. I'll just knock them unconscious.

But Mina withdrew, closing herself off with obstinate intensity. Her wards were strong enough that it would take too much concentration to break through and that would leave Alere vulnerable to physical attack.

Rage boiled in her stomach. She tried to access the yanstones' power anyway, but without Mina the xintou gifts were the ghost of a memory. If she drew the sword and dagger to pull down the lightning, that would force the weishi to up their attack to lethal levels.

Reluctantly, she straightened and took her hands off the weapons. The weishi halted their advance.

'Saric,' she called, 'stand down. But stay there.'

'Whose are they?' he yelled.

'I don't know,' she replied. 'But we can't take them.'

He growled, low in his throat. 'Speak for yourself.'

She addressed the nearest weishi. 'Who is your contractor? Who wants us?'

None of the weishi spoke, as she knew they wouldn't.

'My dear girl,' a throaty, feminine drawl drifted from a shadowed doorway, 'I never thought you'd make it so easy for me. I'm almost disappointed.' A woman emerged into the burnt-orange afternoon light. One hand on her well-curved hip, the other fiddled with a long braid of whiteweed blonde hair that slipped over her shoulder. She smiled and her eyelids drooped.

'Houlia?' Alere stiffened. 'What do you want?'

Houlia swayed closer, a sultry smile curving her lips. 'Why, you, of course.' She cast a quick glance over the others and pointed a red-nailed finger. 'All of you.'

Master Anh appeared by her side. 'Now, Houlia, don't drag this out. You don't have a lot of time.' Tall and skeletally-thin, his narrow fingers danced idly across a row of throwing knives around his hips. 'I haven't yet signed off on the second capture contract, so get her out of here before Zand sees them and insists on precedence.' He bowed. 'Alere. Good to see you again. Sorry to be so formal, but this is business.'

Alere shivered. Master Anh was protecting her from a contract Zand wanted to authorise? Zand was his second in command. A man with eyes of steel, a shaven head and a mouth like a blade. He was xiongshou and she had suffered more injuries training with him than anyone else in Weishi House. But who was behind Zand's contract? Whose side was Houlia on? There were too many players in this to see clearly.

Houlia sashayed over to Jarran.

'You must be Jarran Zah-Hill. Nice.' Her gaze passed over Saric without interest and settled on Mina. 'And you'll be Mina.' She returned to Alere. 'Interesting. You really are identical twins.'

'What do you want, Houlia?' Alere repeated. There was a time when she would have counted this woman very much a friend. But times had changed.

Houlia leaned closer, her perfume light and delicate. 'I have some people who want to see you. They're making it worth my while to bring you in.'

The weishi circle drew closer. Mina's fear broke through her wards and Alere fought to stay in control. It took all her concentration. She was drowning under the deluge of Mina's fear and guilt. Her worry that, by refusing to help Alere, she had condemned them all.

Houlia tapped Alere's cheek. 'Come along, then. Let's not keep the client waiting.'

PART III - Madina

CHAPTER NINETEEN

CORIN

A servant woke Corin far too soon.

'I'm up, I'm up!' Dismissing her, he stumbled to the bathroom to relieve himself and wash his face.

The image in the mirror confirmed that four hours was not enough. Two days probably not, either. Maybe a week would suffice.

Well, in a day or so he'd either sleep forever or get his wish.

Philosophically, he wiped his face and tied back his unruly hair. Fresh clothes hung over a chair and he pulled them on gratefully. Clean bamboo cloth and good quality linen again. One could only stand so much itching and dirt.

Food was next on the agenda and he was pleased to see hot, fresh dishes, redolent of the rich spices for which Houlia's chef was famed, on the table. Steadfastly ignoring the temptation to fall back into bed, Corin finished his meal and ventured out. Somewhere amongst Kett's conversation with Houlia, he vaguely remembered agreeing to meet the weishi in his room: number thirty. That was two doors away, so Corin sauntered along the corridor. The sound of muffled giggles from behind one across the hall made him feel at home.

Knocking on thirty, he heard the gurgle of running water. Kett must be in the bathroom and unable to hear the door. Corin picked the lock, slipped in and closed it softly. A quick check showed a typical room for Jiaoji House. Luxurious furnishings of silk and velvet. The bed rumpled. A blue robe hanging over a chair. Houlia must have lent it to Kett while her staff cleaned his clothes.

With a groan, Corin dropped into a seat near the fireplace and held his hands out to the flames. It was pleasant to sit in a chair again, and warm himself by a fire he didn't have to build or sit up half the night watching. He picked up a jilla-fruit from the bowl on the table. And food. Food he didn't have to hunt or cook was a bonus, too.

Maybe his words to Houlia were true. After ten years, he was just about done with life on the road. He'd originally taken that path as a way to search for Shasa, while he served Rafi and the Jundom. But, even long after he'd given up on finding her, he hadn't been able to settle.

Meeting Alere, loving her, changed all that. For the first time in a decade he'd entertained thoughts of a hunli partner and a family. He'd let her close. Even though it hadn't worked out as he'd hoped, she'd at least opened his heart to the possibility.

Right now was not the time to be looking for a life-companion, though. Diyu, he wasn't even sure he'd live through the next two days. No, he had to stay focussed on the task: getting Jarran into his rightful place on the throne. Women would just have to wait.

The door to the bathroom opened.

'Y'know, there is such a thing as being too clea—' Corin shot to his feet.

A young woman stood in the doorway, her mouth open. The front of her midnight blue robe fell open, giving tantalising glimpses of a slender, gold-skinned body beneath. Wherever Mistress Houlia discovered her, this girl must be the House's star attraction and destined for permanent contract to some lucky Jun any time now.

She flushed, and hastily tied her robe closed. The rush of pink to her cheeks served to emphasise her elegant cheekbones and jaw.

'Who are you? What are you doing in my room? I'm sure the door was locked. Please leave.' Defiance raised her chin and added luminosity to her eyes, so dark blue as to appear purple.

Corin scowled.

She backed away, with hands raised defensively. 'Listen, I'm not—'

'Oh, shut up,' he growled, 'and tell him all bets are off.' He looked her over. 'Although I can see the temptation, I'm pretty sure Alli won't be impressed when she hears of this.'

She flipped back a fall of waist-length, blue-black hair. 'I have no idea what you're talking about, but I think you've made a mistake. I'm not—'

'Not what?' Corin sneered. 'On duty? Well, you're not wearing the red, so I'd already guessed that. Just give him my message.'

'I'm no-one's runner.' She curled a lip. 'And, if you're going to sneer, you need to learn to do it better. Yours lacks conviction. You look like a hurt xiao-kitten.'

Corin opened his mouth to retort, then closed it again, not in the mood to get into an argument with Kett's jiaoji lover. Stalking to the door he yanked it open…and almost ploughed into the man himself.

Before Corin uttered the scathing words of accusation on his tongue, Kett looked into the room behind him and froze. Then he pushed Corin back inside, stepped in and closed the door.

'Would you like to explain?' Kett's low voice was harsh.

But what excuse did *he* have for being angry? Save that he'd been discovered betraying Alere.

'Kett?' The girl's voice behind Corin held more genuine surprise than seemed right. 'It *is* you!'

She ran forward, holding her hands out, the furrows in her brow clearing. At the last second she hesitated and tucked her hands into the sleeves of her robe.

Kett gave the girl a respectful bow. 'Shunu, I'm sorry to intrude. Your voices carried into the hall and I recognised Corin's. Do you know each other?'

She clutched her robe about her. 'He just appeared in my room and started carrying on about giving someone a message and about someone named Alli being annoyed. What's going on? What are you doing here?'

The thunder in Kett's expression eased into amusement directed at Corin. 'Now would you care to explain?'

Corin found his voice. 'I came to meet you. Found her here, half-naked, in your bathroom. Maybe you should be the one explaining.' Even as the words left his mouth, he tasted regret. He was about to look like a complete zift.

'Half-nak—' Kett gripped Corin's arm so tightly his fingers tingled. 'If you've touched her—'

'Kett!' The girl reached toward him, paused and pulled back. 'It's alright. He was only here for a minute before you came. Just calm down and tell me what's going on, please.'

'Corin Mal-kin.' Kett gestured. 'May I introduce shunu Tali Edwards, xintou and daughter to Celia Edwards, late Xintou of the Zah-Hill family.' He jerked his thumb at Corin. 'Shunu, although Corin is my friend, he's also an untrusting hundan who clearly mistook you for a lady of this House, rather than a guest. He also mistook your room, thirty, for mine, thir*teen*, thus jumping to the understandable conclusion we were...together.'

'Understandable!' Tali pressed slender fingers to her cheeks. She took a hasty turn around the room. 'I'm flattered at being mistaken for a jiaoji, but you deserve this—' she slapped Corin across the cheek, hard '—for doubting Kett. He's been in love with Alere Connor for the last ten years and no other girl ever stood a chance.'

Corin blinked, his cheek stinging. He didn't object, though. Nothing he could say would make his assumptions palatable.

'Shunu,' Kett protested, but his grey eyes danced.

She rounded on the weishi. 'Oh, stop it with the "shunu" and stop acting all surprised. The only person who didn't know was Alere. She so worshipped the ground you walked on she was blind to the way you looked at her. Oh!' She paced back and forth. 'You two used to annoy me, so much.'

'Shu—' Kett paused when she sent him another fulminating look. 'Tali, what are you talking about?'

'You and Alere.' She jabbed a finger at him. 'Why on Kalima didn't you just run away? Neither of you *had* to be in the House. I used to hope, every morning, that I'd wake up to find you both gone. Escaped to live a real life.' She threw out her arms. 'Instead, every gaisi morning I'd see you in the training dojo with her. Trapped by her stupid, desperate desire to be something she didn't have to be: a xintou.'

She sank on to the seat Corin had vacated and stared into the fire. 'I remember once, Alere put fanghu into the water at dinner. All the others were terrified when it blocked their telepathy. But I cried when it wore off. I would have given *anything* to be her. To have even the remotest possibility of being free of the House and the life I'd been designed for.'

Before either man responded, a soft knock fell on the door. Tali jumped to her feet, her eyes wide.

The knock repeated. 'Shunu? I'm looking for masters Kett and Corin. Mistress Houlia is asking for them. Their guests have arrived and are waiting in the Mistress's suite.'

Tali called back an acknowledgment and sent the servant away.

'Guests?' Arch humour coloured her question. 'Are you two working here now?'

Corin grimaced. 'I deserved that, I suppose. No, we're just meeting friends here.' He drew Kett aside. 'It has to be Alli. We can't leave this girl alone now. One word to the wrong person and this House becomes Hassan's next target.'

'Agreed.' Kett eyed her thoughtfully. 'I'd also like to know how she got out of Xintou House. We'll take her with us to Houlia's rooms.'

'To meet Alere?' Corin stared at him. 'You're going to take Tali *Edwards* to meet Alere? Well *this* I have to see.' He added, because it would annoy Kett, 'Maybe I should search her for weapons first?'

Kett lifted a brow. 'Only if you don't want your arms any more.' Without waiting for a reply, he addressed the xintou. 'If you will, shunu, we'd like you to come with us.'

Tali hung back. 'Why? The fewer people who see me the safer I am. And the Mistress, too. She's been kind enough to take me in. I can't repay that by endangering her.' She sighed. 'And please *stop* calling me "shunu". My blood is no more noble than yours, Kett.'

Corin laughed aloud and slapped Kett on the back. 'And Kett would be the first to agree he never wants to be ennobled.'

Now it was Kett's turn to stare icily at him.

Raising his hands, Corin headed for the door. 'Tali, you're going to want to meet these guests.' He thought a moment. 'Or maybe not. Either way, you may as well do it gracefully. Otherwise I'm quite certain Kett will overcome his ingrained respect for xintou and throw you over his shoulder.'

Tali studied both men, conflicting emotions flitting across her countenance. Finally, she snatched up a day-robe and stalked into the bathroom. Moments later she reappeared, elegantly robed in dark green silk and with her long hair held in a loose knot by a bejewelled hairpin. Even angry she moved with extraordinary grace.

The door to Houlia's suite opened and Corin prepared himself for a tongue-lashing from Alere. After all, she'd left them behind to keep them from danger. He'd worked out precisely what he would say to her, in return.

As soon as he caught sight of her, every harsh word slipped from his tongue. She, Mina, Jarran and Saric stood in a tense group by the brick fireplace. Although Alere's hands lay ready on her weapons and her body was in a fighting stance, her eyes held a blank, dull distance. This was not the strong, determined young woman they'd last seen in Chengdu. Her inner fire, undimmed by Ven's maltreatment or the bloodbath of the Games, was quenched.

Her expression didn't change when she saw Kett, either. She merely straightened and stared into the fire. Mina leaned into Jarran like her legs had given way. Both women were hollow-cheeked and thin, with dark circles beneath their eyes.

Corin's first instinct was to take Alere in his arms. He had to put a couch between them to stop himself. He waited for Kett to speak. Instead, Kett stilled, his expression haunted. He approached Jarran but continued to watch Alere.

Neither sister spoke in the subdued exchange of greetings. Mina stayed close to Jarran, clinging to his arm. Alere didn't react when Tali was introduced.

Corin frowned. He'd seen something like this before. Withdrawal was a basic survival technique; a response to trauma too horrifying to deal with. What could possibly do that to someone as resilient as Alere?

Saric came to greet Corin. 'Not dead, yet, then?'

'Or you, I see. This is Tali. Saric.'

Saric bowed with unexpected grace and a flourish worthy of court. He flickered her a saucy wink, and she returned a small bow, smiling indulgently.

'Tali, can you give us a moment?' Corin pulled Saric out of earshot and sat down on a gold-brocade couch. 'What's happened to Alli and Mina? Where's Wei?'

'Long story,' Saric said.

'I have time. And, by the way, don't pull a stunt like that again – leaving Chengdu without asking.'

'I haven't asked anyone's permission to do anything since I was five. Not about to start now. You wanna hear what happened, or are you going to spout some more fatherly feihua?'

Corin rubbed at the back of his neck. Clearly, he needed more sleep. 'Right. Sorry. Tell me.' He listened in growing dismay to Saric's account of their trip, even as he strained to hear the exchange between the others.

Kett approached Alere and touched her shoulder. She flinched, drawing her dagger and backing away in automatic response. She blinked several times, slowly focussing on him.

'Kett? No, you're not…you're not here. You're safe in Chengdu.' Her voice emerged hoarse. Recognition and a hint of fear replaced confusion. She touched his cheek. 'You're real?'

He laid his palms on her upper arms, sliding them down until he gripped her hands. He eased the dagger from her fingers and tucked it into his belt.

'I'm here, Alli. It's alright. Everything will be alright.' With infinite care, he held her to his broad chest, stroking her hair as he murmured reassurances.

She stood still in his arms for a moment then, with broken cry, threw her arms around him and buried her face in his neck.

'Kett,' her plea was muffled. 'I'm so sorry. Help me, please. I can't do this. I thought I could… I tried…I just can't.' She raised her face. 'You have to cut the Bond between Mina and I. Please? I can't take it any more.'

CHAPTER TWENTY

CORIN

Corin studied Alere in confusion. What the diyu was going on here? Kett carried her to a chair in a corner of the room, pressing his lips to her forehead. His worried gaze met Corin's. She curled into him and her eyelids drifted closed. In the warm, opulent room, only the crackle of wood in the fireplace broke the breathless silence. Then Mina gave a choked sob.

'She's been like this for days.' Saric looked pityingly at Alere. 'Both of them. But worse since what happened in the village.'

'What happened?'

With a shiver, Saric related the tale of her encounter with the raiders, then what he knew about the death of the boy, Batu. Since he hadn't been in the ger, his version was sketchy. Alere and Mina apparently wouldn't speak of it and Jarran had been preoccupied in getting all of them safely to Madina. It had fallen to Saric to care for Alere.

'She needs more than food and water.' The boy tapped his temple. 'She's gone somewhere. Inside her head. And Mina can't seem to get over that she had to kill Batu and she's blaming Alere. Something to do with Alere holding back and not giving everything when they tried to save the kid.'

'Doesn't sound like Alere.'

Saric shrugged his non-comprehension. 'Alere keeps saying that if she had, they would have Fused and would both be dead. But I think Alere's blaming herself as well. In the end, Mina stabbed him.' He curled a lip. 'I don't see the problem. The kid was burning up everyone's brains. What choice was there? Either he died or we all did.'

'I'll see if Kett can make any sense of it.' Corin grimaced. 'I'm sorry you had to leave Wei, but I appreciate your taking care of Alli. Saw your handiwork in Dalcin, too. Nice job. I'd still prefer you hadn't gone, though. Scared the diyu out of me.'

'What do you care?' Saric snapped.

Corin gripped his shoulders. 'Hey. You're my responsibility, now.'

'Is that what I am? Your responsibility?'

With a sigh, Corin rubbed at the back of his neck. 'Look, Saric. I'm trying, ok? This is new to me. You're my son and I have no gouri idea what to do. But it's just you and me, now. So do try not to hate me too much.'

'I don't…I just…' Saric's green-grey eyes held unexpected vulnerability, and echoes of the last two weeks' horrors. Corin caught the boy into a hard hug, warmed when Saric's wiry arms wrapped around his waist.

'I…miss her.' The broken words were muffled in Corin's shirt.

'Wei, Shasa, or Alere?'

'All of them.'

Corin stroked the boy's back. 'Me too, kid. You did everything you could. None of this is your fault.' He put a finger under Saric's chin and lifted. 'Got it? Not your fault.'

Saric swallowed hard. 'Will she be alright?' He peered beneath Corin's arm at Alere.

'I hope so, kid. If anyone can bring her out of it, Kett can.'

But Alere broke free of Kett's hold and rose. She stared intently at Tali. Puzzlement flickered in her shadowed eyes. Recognition surfaced.

Her voice came out flat. 'I know you. Tali Edwards. There was something…Oh. I remember now. I killed your mother.'

Tali gaped and sank onto a settee. She sought confirmation from Kett. He said nothing, merely reaching out to hold Alere in place when she took a step toward Tali. She shook him off and sat at the opposite end of the couch, studying Tali with detached disinterest, like a bug she considered squashing.

'But…' Tali found her voice first, shaky though it was. 'I was told Lianna Koh-Lin…'

'Yes.' Kett crouched between them, interposing his bulk. 'We should have warned you, I'm sorry. There's something you need to understand but, before I tell you, I need to know a few things.'

Wordless, Alere got up and stood by the fire, staring once more into its shifting, hypnotic depths. She seemed to dismiss Tali and Kett, sinking again into the depths from which Kett's presence had briefly roused her.

'Kett,' Jarran's soft call interrupted. 'I'm going to put Mina to bed. We haven't slept much these last couple of days and things aren't going to get any easier. She needs rest.'

The weishi eyed Mina's drawn face. 'Is she having nightmares?'
Jarran nodded.

Kett waved them to the door. 'Then you stay with her. You need rest as well and she'll sleep better with you there.'

'But…' Jarran's flush would have made Corin tease him under other circumstances. He squirmed like a teenager forced to admit his first crush to his parents. Or, in this case, his older brother.

Kett stood and aimed the Jun First at the door. 'Don't be a shazi, man. We have no idea how the next couple of days will play out. You're wasting what limited time you may have left with her. Believe me, I did that for far too long to stand by and watch anyone else make the same mistake.' He regarded Mina and Alere. 'Besides, there's something strange going on here. Somehow, I think healing her will go a long way to helping Alli as well. So…look after her.'

Jarran's flush deepened, but his grip around Mina's waist tightened and he led her out the door.

At that moment, Saric slumped under Corin's arm. The boy slept on his lap, his mouth open and pushed to one side. Sleep's softness wiped away the cynicism characterising his sharp face. Corin eased out from beneath him, gathered the slight figure into his arms and caught Kett's attention as he headed for the door.

'I'll be back.'

When he returned from putting Saric to bed, he found the three in an unchanged tableau: Alere staring into the fire, Kett and Tali facing each other on the settee. As Corin slipped in, Kett finished the tale of their travels and what he knew of Alere's.

Tali spoke, 'If everything you're saying is true, then I think I might be able to help her. I think I can cut their Bond.'

Corin dropped into a chair opposite. He might be overly-suspicious, but why would she make such an offer? After all, what did she have to gain by helping Alere? He leaned forward, resting elbows on knees, trying to assess her character.

'Why should you? Didn't you hear what she did to your mother?'

Tali regarded him coolly. 'Yes, and I also heard everything else Kett told me she did for the Jundom and for Mamlakah.'

'And you believe it?' Corin snorted. 'Diyu, *I* don't believe half of it and I was there. So, in spite of her murdering Celia, you'd have us trust you to heal her? Why should we?'

'Cor,' Kett cut in.

Corin waved him away. Alere and Kett had told him a little of how she'd been treated by the other girls in Xintou House. Why should this one be different? Especially one with the name of Edwards.

Instead of reacting angrily to his deliberate provocation, Tali sighed and tucked a loose hair behind her ear. 'Because I loathed my mother. I didn't ask to be xintou.' She gave Corin a direct, open look. 'I hate that I had no choice in my life. That Celia *created* me in some ideal image she fancied perfect. All that mattered was Bonding an Edwards to the Jun First family to continue the tradition. Bonding is something so intimate...' She shivered. 'And to have that sort of connection with a mind as warped as Ven Zah-Hill's. How could she do that to her own daughter?'

She glanced at Alere. 'I envied Alere. I wanted what she could have: freedom. But she never took it. I didn't believe she'd killed the Jun, or Mistress Renna. She was too stubbornly honourable for anything like that. And when you were gone, too...' She smiled at Kett. 'I knew she was alive and free.

'Now...' Standing, she paced the room twice. 'To find she was another victim of my mother's machinations... That she's endured so much and has been fighting so hard for not just her own freedom, but mine and everyone's....'

She shook her head. 'It makes me feel petty and silly. The day Nasra came to the House, I just ran. I didn't even take any of the younger girls with me. I feel like a coward.'

'No,' Kett said, gently. 'You aren't. Fearing Ven and running from Nasra were the marks of intelligence, not cowardice. You did the right thing.'

Tali shivered again, her gaze sliding uneasily from him back to Alere. 'No, I'm a coward. You have no idea how glad I was to hear of Ven's death. I'm just sorry it had to come at such a cost to Alere. I wish I could have been a friend to her, but she always kept everyone at a distance.'

'Then help her now. You said you could. How?'

She rubbed her slender hands together. 'In the library I once found an old book. It was jammed behind others and I don't think anyone had even read it for centuries. A journal by Kya Edwards' daughter, Yera. There's a lot about preparing for the advent of some great thing or person, but quite a few pages are torn out. So I don't know exactly what that means. My Mandrin is pretty good, but the journal is old and so many words have several meanings. There is mention of one thing: the bond between twins.'

Kett gestured Tali back onto the couch. 'What did it say?'

'It was talking about the Edwards sisters. They were twins, too.'

'Ah! Of course.' Kett straightened. 'I didn't know, but that makes sense. What else?'

Tali gazed off into middle distance. 'It describes a bond between the sisters, forged when they attempted some sort of dangerous nai-xintou work that went wrong. The bond deepened over time until it became an almost-Fusion that nearly killed them both.' She grimaced. 'The entries stop after that, so I don't know what happened. But other records show they both lived to well into their eighties. Could explain why xintou are forbidden to birth twins. They were afraid of that bond.'

'But you think it could be severed and their minds separated?' Kett pressed. 'Mina's never killed anyone before. She's a healer. She's sinking into an abyss of self-blame and taking Alere with her. I think that's why Alli's asked for the bond to be broken.'

Corin interrupted. 'But why can't Alli just use the yanstones to heal her mind, the way she did her body?'

'The yanstones are the problem. From what she's told me, each time she uses them, the bond strengthens and their two minds get closer.' Kett glanced over his shoulder at Alere. 'This… shuttered apathy is her attempt to stay sane. To prevent Fusion. If we had time,

I'd take them to Healer House and let them work through the psychology. We don't. Alli is the focal point for the Selb. She's the ransom for Rafi. And she's the only one who has even the vaguest hope of defeating Nasra and Rohne. We need her. Now. If that means cutting her connection to Mina, so be it.'

'What will that do to her, though?' Corin asked.

'I don't know. But you heard her. She wants it cut. And I agree.' When he caught Corin's frown Kett gave a harsh laugh. 'Believe me, this was not my first choice, Cor. If I could take her to the other side of the world and keep her safe, I'd do it. But Nasra and Rohne's poison will spread to every corner of the four Jundoms. There's nowhere we could go and be safe, being who we are.'

Turning to Tali, he gripped her wrist. She flinched and he released it with an oath. 'I'm sorry. Tali, if you honestly think you can help, do it.'

She stole a quick look at Alere, then at Corin.

He held up his hands. 'This is way out of my realm of expertise. She did ask, though. We do need her.'

'Very well,' Tali straightened, every inch the haughty xintou. 'But on one condition.'

'Name it,' Kett replied.

'Help me free my House sisters,' she said. 'I'm the most senior left. They're my responsibility and I left them behind. And…' her eyes slid back to Alere and she swallowed '…I might need one of the older girls' help with cutting the connection. Help me and I'll help you. Deal?'

Kett, after a fleeting check with Corin, agreed.

She brushed down the shining silk of her robe and gave a decisive little nod. 'Let's go.'

Corin gaped. 'Now? It's not like just the two of us can storm the place without something like an army to back us up.'

'I've been planning for days. We don't need an army. We have a secret tunnel that connects this House to Xintou House. That's how I got away.' She held up a finger. 'Before you tell me I can't come, you'll need someone the girls trust. They don't know you and the last they heard of Kett he'd betrayed the House to run with Alere. Now, put Alere to bed and let's go.'

'Did I tell you I think this is a bad idea?' Corin whispered into the darkness.

'Three times now,' Kett's even reply came back. 'And you do this every time we do anything you don't agree with. However, since you don't have a better idea, I wish you'd refrain.'

Corin gave an involuntary chortle then shut his mouth when Tali frowned over her shoulder. Dramatically side-lit by the little candle-lantern she carried, her exquisite face was all sharp shadows and golden highlights in the tunnel's blackness.

'Shut up,' she hissed. 'We're almost to the entrance. We're inside the wall between the great hall and the library and sounds carry.'

Corin repressed the urge to laugh. Unpleasant as the rigors of the road were, this was the one thing he would hate to give up: the blood-pounding adrenalin rush of spying, sneaking and generally behaving with ill-intent.

Tali stopped and pressed a tiny lever on one wall-stud. The panel swung open, revealing grey half-lit gloom beyond. She crept through. Corin and Kett followed, loosening weapons in scabbards.

They emerged into the hushed, oppressive silence of a massive library. Most of the windows were shuttered, closing out the dusk. In the dusty orange light, filtering through a few high windows, Corin made out row upon row of bookshelves, reaching almost to the vaulted ceiling. Four heavy yar-pine tables stood in a neat square before them. The smell of old paper and leather caught in his nose and he pinched it to prevent a sneeze. Not even a whisper of sound disturbed the heavy silence.

Tali's tiny light bobbed away as she strode off with the confidence of one who knows for sure there is nothing to trip over. Corin proceeded with a little more caution, Kett close behind. Tali paused by a bookshelf, selected a slim volume and tucked it into her shirt before continuing. She stopped at another shelf and swore.

'The Old Mandrin to Common translation dictionary isn't here. You'll need it. I have Yera Edwards's journal, but some of the words are obscure.'

Kett headed for the door. 'There's no time to hunt for it now. Keep going.'

At the main entrance, Tali tried the handle with quiet care. It stopped partway and she scowled, jerking when it didn't give. Corin tapped her on the arm and held up his lockpicks. Her mouth dropped into an O, but she moved aside. It was an old, precision-made lock that gave with well-oiled ease under his tools.

He leaned over and blew out Tali's candle, opened the door and examined the dim-lit corridor outside. Kett slipped past and took the lead. Corin waved Tali ahead. Although untrained, she did a reasonable job of sneaking through the hallway's mottled gloom. Clearly this was not the first time. What an interesting place Xintou House must have been with her and Alere both in it. Corin grinned to himself. Probably lucky for Kett the two girls hadn't formed a close friendship.

They made several turns and climbed a set of stairs, encountering only three weishi along the way. Kett dealt with the first two, breaking necks with dispassionate ease then lowering each to the ground, in a shadowed corner. The third appeared from a side corridor just as Corin passed. The man's mouth opened. Corin drove a fist into his solar plexus and the weishi collapsed, gasping. Corin grimly despatched him with a sleeper hold from which the man wouldn't wake. It went against the grain to kill unnecessarily, but these weishi had pledged loyalty to Hassan and Nasra. They couldn't be trusted.

Tali waited, white and wide-eyed as they hid the final body. She pressed trembling fingers to her cheeks. Corin waved her on. She hesitated, then led the way further into the building. Corin frowned. Three seemed like a small number of guards. Where were the rest? He couldn't ask without breaking silence, so he followed Tali, hoping nothing surprising would leap out at them.

At the top of the stairs, she gestured to Corin and Kett, raising her little finger and tapping her temple to indicate she wanted to speak telepathically. Corin shook his head, not prepared to trust her to that level. She pursed her lips but leaned close to whisper in their ears.

'These are the students' bedrooms. Only two weishi. One halfway along each corridor, right and left. Seated directly below a lamp. I can't use thoughts against them. Nasra picked men who can ward well.'

Corin unsheathed a blowpipe he'd borrowed from Saric's gear. He didn't particularly like using one. But sometimes results were more important than flair.

Kett produced a pair of black throwing knives. On Kett's soft word, Corin blew. The dart hit on target and the right-hand guard gave a choked cry. He staggered to his feet, the scrape of his chair too loud in the quiet of the House. A few seconds later, he crumpled to the ground, skull thumping loudly on the timber. To the left, Kett's man slumped in his chair, the knife handle just visible in his neck, blood staining his shirt.

'Fast.' Kett's focus was on the sprawled body in the corridor on Corin's side. 'What are you using?'

Tucking the unused second, black-feathered dart back into his belt, Corin replied succinctly: 'Si-xing.' A hint of surprise flickered across Kett's face and Corin shrugged. 'It's quick and the fewer of Nasra's men we have at our backs the better, if you ask me. Is there a problem?'

'No. Si-xing is expensive. In Weishi House it translates to "death penalty" – when used on a contract target. Or "to act recklessly" – when wasted on an unimportant target.'

'Are you trying to tell me I'm acting recklessly?' Corin raised his brows. 'Because I'll take that as a compliment.'

'I'm saying…' Kett gripped his shoulder. 'I agree with your choice. Anyone who supports Nasra in this endeavour is our enemy.'

'Y'know, you really need to work on being less obscure. It wouldn't kill you to speak like a normal human, sometimes.'

'Where's the fun in that?' Kett's lips curved. 'I saw a key on my man's belt. I'll use it on this side. Tali, you go with Corin. He'll open doors, you wake the girls, keep them quiet and gather them here.'

Tali, her horrified gaze fixed on the guard's corpse, merely nodded.

They ushered the twenty plus frightened girls into the hall. Tali peered anxiously at each face and counted each head. Then she checked them all again, her eyes haunted.

'Is that all of them?' Corin whispered. She hesitated, glanced back at the corridor of open doors, and nodded. Her shoulders slumped. Corin laid a hand on her back and she flinched.

'Don't beat yourself up, Tal,' he said. 'We knew Nasra had killed quite a few in order to control the younger ones. You would have been one of the dead ones if you stayed.'

She flushed deep crimson and chewed on her lip.

'Right,' he said. 'Let's get out of here. There are probably guards in other sections, so tell the girls to keep quiet.'

Tali took the lead with Corin behind and Kett bringing up the rear. They crept down the dark corridors, the only sounds the whisper of the girls' night robes and the occasional creak of a board.

As she rounded the last corner, Tali stopped short. Corin paused and glanced back. The young xintou girls all stared at Tali in fixed concentration. If he touched the yanstones now, would he hear the silent, fearful babble going on behind their eyes?

'What is it?' he whispered.

'There's a light in the library.' She pointed at the closed door. A pale-gold line of light seeped beneath the carved timber door. 'But you blew my lamp out.'

'Can you tell who it is?' He tapped his temple.

'No. Very strong wards. I don't recognise the mind and if I push too hard they'll feel me.'

Corin slipped his thumbs under his sword-cover and let the yanstones' warmth wash through his tired mind. He reached tentatively out...and recoiled.

'Get all the girls into hiding. There.' He pointed at a closed room nearby. 'Keep them absolutely quiet. Understand?'

Tali nodded, her eyes huge. She gave a silent order and the girls responded with almost military precision, vanishing into the room. With a backward look, she followed them.

Corin waited until the door clicked softly shut then whispered to Kett. 'It's Rohne.'

'How do you know if he's warded?' Kett frowned. 'You didn't get access to your yanstone-powers until after he'd left Shanzhai.'

'I'm sure of it. A xintou's wards feel different to a normal person's. And a woman's feel different to a man's. So…unless there's another male xintou out there you haven't mentioned?'

Kett took a step forward but halted when Corin gripped his arm. 'We can't. He has ten people with him. All warded. Could be weishi. We can't risk the girls.'

Swearing softly, Kett nodded. 'We wait. He has to leave sooner or later.' In the grey half-light his teeth gleamed. 'Got another si-xing dart? Maybe we'll get lucky.'

CHAPTER TWENTY-ONE

ROHNE

'There *has* to be something.' Rohne threw aside a battered text on the failed Jun rebellion of two hundred years before.

'What are we looking for, shenshi?' one of the weishi asked respectfully. He held a lantern up, his head tipped sideways to read the books lined up along the shelves.

'Anything about yanstones,' Rohne snapped. He would have preferred not to say, but there were more books here than he could possibly check in one evening. Once, the sight of so many would have delighted him. Now, it was just frustrating. Especially since there seemed to be no logic in their shelving. But there *must* be something in here, somewhere. Something that would tell him why some stones worked and how.

Hurried footsteps sounded outside the door and his weishi guards tensed, laying hands on weapons. The door burst open and one of the weishi set to guard Xintou House prisoners half fell into the room, panting and his face sheened with sweat.

'Shenshi, they're gone.' He gulped.

'Who?' Rohne picked up a treatise on economics and dropped it again.

'The xintou, shenshi. Their rooms are open. The guards are dead. One with si-xing, so someone's hired xiongshou. And the girls are all gone. I swear they haven't come out any of the exits, though.'

Rohne looked up, anger hardening into rage until his whole body trembled. 'Alere. It must be. I didn't think she was here, yet. Gouri little…' He ground his teeth. 'Find them. If they haven't left, then they're hiding somewhere in the complex. Make sure every exit has two men on it. Four of you stay here in case they try to attack me. The rest of you start up in the dormitory levels and spread out. Search every room.'

'Can't you…' The weishi tapped his temple. '…you know, *find* them, shenshi?'

Rohne drew himself up. 'I'm not here to pick up after you. It was your job to keep these girls under control.' He had no intention of telling anyone his ability to Read was limited to those he had met or at least seen. Or that people with strong wards were…slippery and difficult to pinpoint. 'Find them or you'll be the next person kneeling under Hassan's axe.'

The weishi paled, bowed, and hurried out, waving the others along with him.

Rohne did a swift search of the grounds and House, focussing on Alere's thought pattern. Nothing. She was somewhere in the city, he could sense that, now he was looking, but something masked her exact location. And Mina's. How? No one had the ability to hide that well. Did they? He eyed the myriad of books. Had Nasra taught him everything the House knew?

For the first time, doubt shook him. He'd trusted her. Believed in her implicitly. But she'd hidden other things from him. What if she'd hidden essential skills as well? Why would she hamstring his gifts, though?

Unless she feared him. Or wanted to keep control. Yes, that would be like her.

Jiche! He needed to get his hands on those yanstones.

And there was only one way to do that. If he couldn't find Alere, he needed to bring her into the open and take them from her.

Which meant he had to get back to the Alcazar and plan a way to draw her out.

Rohne picked up the economics book and hurled it at a wall. The pain in his head doubled, then trebled. He lifted his face to the dark ceiling, pressed his palms to his aching temples and screamed. Shelves trembled. Books shot out and smashed against the walls. Paper fluttered like leaves to the floor. With an almighty crash, one of the huge shelves tipped and fell, scattering books and broken timber.

Sucking a slow breath, Rohne lowered his hands and squinted against the lantern's sharp yellow light.

'Escort me back to the Alcazar,' he snapped. 'Then bring more men to search here. I want those girls found.'

'Bai, shenshi,' the weishi said breathlessly. He hurried to the door, crowding too close for comfort as they headed for the front exit. But Rohne was in too much pain to even berate the man.

Alere would pay for this.

CORIN

Corin and Kett waited for Rohne and his escort to pass. Unfortunately, they'd offered no clear shot for a dart. When their footsteps faded, Corin slipped back to the room where Tali and the others hid.

'All clear,' he whispered through the door. 'Get the girls into the secret passage now.'

The door swung open and Tali ushered her charges into the library. Kett and Corin joined them, stopping in astonishment. The girls huddled together. Corin turned to lock the library door, then thought better of it. That would only arouse suspicion.

'How did he do this?' Tali muttered, staring at the chaos of torn books and broken furniture.

'He's telekinetic,' Corin said. 'But I didn't know he was this strong.'

'Large-scale telekinesis!' Tali sucked a sharp breath. 'There's no record of any xintou *ever* having that sort of power.'

'Oh, good,' Corin replied. 'I needed to hear that right now.'

Kett opened the secret passage and waved the girls through.

'Get them back to the House and settled, Tali,' Kett murmured as Tali passed. 'Then meet me in Alere's room.'

Corin frowned at him. 'Do we really need to do this tonight? Alli's exhausted.'

'Yes, we do.' Kett surveyed the destruction. 'Rohne is far stronger than any of us suspected. We need Alere lucid.'

'Will they be alright?' Corin stood in the stormdrain loading dock under Jiaoji House with Houlia and watched the last of the xintou girls trudge into the stinking gloom, their lanterns swaying like marshlights. It was late evening now, and Mistress Houlia had uncomplainingly given the girls clothing, supplies and an armed escort to take them south to meet with the Koh-Lin army. Corin sent a message for Yasmin along with the eldest. With any luck they should only be on the road a day.

Houlia, dressed in utilitarian grey trous and shirt, with sturdy boots and her white hair tied into a mawei, patted his arm and smiled. 'They'll be fine. Mattus knows how to get them out of the city unseen. They'll join Yasmin tomorrow and she'll know what to do with them.'

'What, exactly?'

Houlia's smile faded. 'She'll need weapons against those twins of Nasra's. These girls you've released are Yasmin's best hope of that.'

With a shudder, Corin turned away. What right did they have to pit teenage girls against each other like this? Nasra must be mad.

'You'd best get back upstairs, Cor,' Houlia said. 'Kett didn't look in the mood to wait for anyone.' She tugged on her mawei. 'I hope Tali can fix Alere. I'd hate to see Kett lose her as well. He's been through so much, the poor boy.'

Corin blinked. 'You know who he is?'

'Of course.' Her brows rose. 'His mother, Ji Ma-Safra, and I were dear friends. She and I had a contract for five years. The last two were during the time Kett was born. When Ji died, I contracted to Radan for a year to keep watch over Kett. It broke my heart to see how Hanna treated him. Of course, I didn't know he'd survived Hanna's purge. Not until he showed up escorting Alere one day.' She shrugged. 'I never told him, for there was no advantage to it.'

Leaning in, Corin kissed her cheek. 'You never cease to amaze me. If I could find someone like you, I think I would settle down.'

'My dear boy,' she said, amiably, 'I'm far too easygoing. You need someone who won't put up with your wandering ways. Someone to keep you on the straight and narrow. Someone respectable.'

'Don't wish that on me.' He laughed. 'I'd better go.'

He hurried upstairs to Kett's room and found Kett, Jarran and Tali gathered around the bed. On the white and gold embroidered quilt, lay Alere and Mina, side by side, with their heads at the foot of the mattress. Kett sat by Alere, holding her hand, his face a mask of stone. Jarran, seated across from him, stroked Mina's long hair back.

The room seemed over-warm, a large fire crackling in the fireplace. Yar-pine by the smell. The heavy white and gold curtains had been drawn, hiding rain and sleet that lashed the windows. Thunder growled overhead. The mellow electric lights flickered, dimmed, and died. Not unusual. Jiaoji House's power came from ancient and unreliable solar cells on the roof. Kett lit three mel-oil lanterns and positioned them around the bed.

'Right.' Tali hugged herself, regarding the two women.

'Before you start,' Kett said. 'One question. While you were getting the xintou girls away, I read that journal by Kya Edwards's daughter, Yera.' He pulled the slim volume out of his pocket, along with the gold-silk-covered Koh-Lin journal. 'And this is the missing journal of Lei Koh-Lin. It could be relevant to what you're doing here.'

Tali gasped. 'The Teachings of Lei journal? Where did you get it?'

'Doesn't matter.' Kett flipped open both and pointed at the tiny, elegant writing. 'There's a few words in Lei's journal I couldn't interpret. It looked like he'd started to write something about the erheyi, then crossed it out. His words are repeated in Yera's notes, but there's more detail. Tell me how you interpret this?'

Tali leaned down and frowned over the Xintou House journal, her lips moving as she read the passage.

'Well,' she said, 'I think it basically reads: *when the two are one, the time is near. The strong men in service to nature must rise in defence of the erheyi to wash away ignorance once more. Then the true guide shall teach all her will and the path will be regained.*'

'That's a bit different to my reading,' Kett said. 'But you could be right. My Mandrin isn't the strongest and I'm interpreting it as a weishi would. I wish you'd found that dictionary.' He ran a hand over his dark hair. 'So you don't think the *two are one* refers to Alere and Mina by any chance?'

Tali studied the two women. 'It's a five-hundred-year-old journal. How could it possibly relate to them? No Xintou has ever Seen past a few days or weeks.'

'True.' Kett tucked the book away, frowning. He flipped a few pages in the Koh-Lin journal. 'What about this?'

She sucked a sharp breath. 'This says Kya Edward wanted the sisters to Fuse in order to fix Kya's son. Was he…?' She glanced at Kett, who nodded.

'Male xintou. But read the next bit.'

She worried at her lower lip and traced the columns. 'Fusing with the *shenhilya?* Spirit ornament? Strange.' Her frown deepened. 'That sounds familiar but I'm not sure where from. Something to do with Xintou House Mistresses, maybe?' She pushed the book back into Kett's hands. 'No. I don't know. But if they were planning to Fuse in an attempt to save the boy they really were insane. No-one can survive that.' She turned back to the bed. 'But Mina and Alere are very close to it, so you have to let me get started or we'll be too late.'

Corin grabbed Tali's wrist as she went to lay it on Mina's head. 'Hey, are you sure about this?'

The xintou snatched her hand away. 'A deal's a deal. You helped me, now I help you.'

'But can you actually do it?' Corin persisted. 'Khara! You don't even know what you're dealing with, do you?'

'I don't think it's much different from severing the Bond when a Xintou gives way her position with a Jun-family to her gene-daughter.'

Corin snorted his disbelief.

Unease flickered in her indigo eyes. 'Alright, I don't know that for sure. Twins are so rare and there's no records of xintou-twins, apart from the Edwards sisters. From what you say, the bond has been artificially enhanced by the yanstones – which I've never even heard of. Just…give me a chance to see what's going on.'

'Didn't you say you needed one of the older xintou girls to help? Can you do it on your own?'

She cast her eyes down. 'None of the older girls knows how to cut a Bond.'

Corin folded his arms. 'Fine, but—'

'I know, I know, there's a lot at stake.' She grimaced. 'All I can say is that I hope, one day, I can understand how Alere inspires people like you and Kett to love her so much. I'd give a lot to be loved like that.'

The honest yearning in her words startled Corin out of his angry fear for Alere's life. As Tali's fingers brushed across Alere's forehead, he regarded the xintou. He'd always believed xintou girls had the life of dreams. Pampered and feted since birth, their life-course laid out without doubt, hesitation or obstacles. Riches, skills and power beyond the hopes of most men or women. What more could anyone want?

Maybe he'd been a little hard on her. Crouching by her side, he touched her wrist. She pulled away.

'I wasn't going to hurt you,' he said gently.

'Sorry.' She rubbed at her skin. 'I'm just not used to being touched. They discourage it in the House. It's supposed to help us stay emotionally detached.'

He stilled. What an appalling upbringing both she and Alere had endured. Holding Tali's gaze, Corin reached slowly out. He slid his fingers into the hair at the nape of her neck and stroked his thumb across her smooth cheek. She stiffened. Her lips parted and her pupils expanded into darkness. But she didn't withdraw.

'Y'know, I remember Alli mentioning you.' He let his gaze travel across her features, let her see his admiration, saw the hopeful interest his words piqued in her. 'She said the senior staff said you were the brightest they'd ever taught.' He drew a long, slow breath and she unconsciously copied the action. 'You were the only one who never said an unkind word to her, or used your powers on her. You can do this, Tal. She trusts you.'

She started, her gaze falling from his.

Rising, he kissed her forehead and stood back. Tali hesitated, then laid her hands on the twins' foreheads and closed her eyes. After a long, heavy silence, she sat back.

'I can see it – like a thick sort of silvery-gold rope between them. And there are four more, much thinner ones. But there's something else...' She frowned.

'What?' Kett's low voice held a hint of unease.

'A sort of...I don't know how to describe it...a kind of glowing golden haze around the connections that's stopping me from even getting close. Hiding their minds. If Mina and Alere weren't right here in front of me, I don't know that I'd even be able to find them.'

'Wards?' Corin hazarded.

'No, Alere's wards feel different, more...black and smooth. Incredibly strong for a non-xintou. Or even for a xintou. She is warding, even in her sleep, but that wouldn't stop me cutting the connection. It's something else.'

Kett scanned Alere's slender body, outlined under the dark purple robe she wore. He met Corin's speculative look with one of his own and they spoke together.

'The yanstones.'

'Has to be.' Corin added. 'I've heard her describe them as sort of silver-gold. She must have them on. Try around her hips, that's where she usually wears the long chain. Mina's not wearing the bracelets, though.'

'Mina refused to wear them after the village,' Jarran put in. 'I have them in my pocket. I think Alere took to wearing hers around her neck.'

Kett opened her robe's lilac collar. The exposed yanstones flared into glittering life as they caught the gold of the overhead lamps and amplified it.

'Oh!' Tali reached out. 'They're beautiful. I've never *seen* so many!'

'No, don't touch them.' Kett lifted the chain over Alere's head. Alere moaned. Her fingers flexed into claws.

Tali continued to watch the stones. 'My mother took me into the Jun First's jewel-room once. Most of the yanstones in the Alcazar are set in gold or silver. Only one or two in steel. There used to be more, but they'd been stolen years before and Jun First Radan refused to replace them.'

'Interesting,' Kett said.

Corin understood. That meant Rohne might not have access to yanstones to amplify his powers. In a time when every other piece of information filtering out of the Alcazar was horrific, it was a small gleam of hope.

'Why can't I touch them?' Tali asked, just a hint of envy in her question.

'Watch.' Kett stroked the stones.

Alere shifted, arching her back, a small, sensuous smile curving her lips. Mina gave a little whimper.

Tali stared at them. 'But they're dosed with maqa. They shouldn't be able to even move.'

'It's only a light dose,' Kett said, 'but the point is that the stones are somehow tied to her. I noticed it first in Shanzhai when I touched the ones in her swords and she reacted.' He laid them across his lap. 'I don't know what would happen if someone she didn't know well – with the gene – touched them. I won't risk it. Try now.'

With a shiver, Tali laid her palms again on the girls' foreheads.

'Yes,' she said. 'I can do it now. But I honestly don't know how it will affect them. The bridge is very strong.'

'What about the other connections?' Kett stroked Alere's cheek. 'Can you start with them as a test?'

'I think,' Tali's gaze flickered to Corin, 'they're sort of mental symbols of emotional connections to people. One goes to you, Kett, one to Corin. Two go somewhere else, outside this building.'

'Rafi? Elmira?' Corin asked.

'Could be.' Kett bowed his head. 'I don't want to take them away from her. Cut—'

'Mine.' Corin gripped the weishi's shoulder. 'Cut mine, Tal. Time to cut the symbol as well as the actual.' He avoided Kett's gaze to hide the pain the words caused.

Tali closed her eyes. Corin laid his hands on his own yanstones, wanting, in a masochistic sort of way, to feel the moment. It was worse than he expected. Tali seemed to reach into his head and rip part of his mind out. For the briefest moment, steel knives lanced through his brain and his breath stopped. He dropped to his knees and choked back a cry. Tears gathered and fell onto the polished bamboo floor. Gasping, he sucked over-warm air into frozen lungs. There was a hole in his heart now. Something integral was missing, but he couldn't say exactly what.

'Cor?' Kett helped him to his feet.

Corin pushed him away with an oath. 'Is she alright?'

'She reacted and it obviously hurt, but she's fine. What about you?'

Dragging a chair closer, Corin sat and reviewed how he felt. He still loved her; still missed her laughter, and her hair tickling his chin as she curled against him in bed. Still wished he'd won her heart. So what was different?

'I'm not hearing her thoughts any more,' he finally admitted. 'Now it's gone, I realise it was like a low-key, soft sort of murmuring. Just at the edge of hearing. Only at close quarters, though. I used to think I'd heard her call my name, but she always denied it.'

Kett paused. 'Yes, I can hear it, now you've described it. Gaisi! She's in such pain!' He frowned. 'No wonder she's struggling. Mina's miserable and afraid and she's pouring all that into Alere's mind. And Alere's deliberately trying to take all the anguish she's caused Mina away. It's going to hurt them, but we have to cut the connection.'

'Wait.' Jarran put in as Tali tried to start again. 'What's so bad about taking away Mina's pain?'

Tali sent him a pitying look. 'Because Alere can't. This sort of mental anguish is self-created. Mina is *choosing* to think that way. She can keep it up forever. But Alere has tucked her self deep within her Inners to cope. Eventually, Mina's pain will drill right through and Alere will be exposed. They'll Fuse. Kett's right. We must sever it. I just don't know if they'll survive.'

'I don't think we have much choice,' Kett said. 'Do your best.'

'You'd better hold them down.' She drew a long breath and set her shoulders. 'Here goes.'

Mina screamed first and Jarran's deeper shout joined in as he fought to hold her thrashing limbs still.

Alere's back arched. Her mouth opened and the scream that emerged was knives down glass. Corin shivered. She fought Kett's hold, almost breaking free.

'Hold them *still!*' Tali snapped. She gripped their heads. Her brow furrowed in concentration.

Alere kicked, catching Kett in the stomach. He gasped and doubled over. Corin grabbed her arms. She struggled, wrenching at his grip, whimpering. Her back arched again. Her nails drew blood on Corin's arm. A knife-sharp blaze of white-gold light exploded from the yanstones lying on the floor next to Kett. The mirror over the fireplace shattered, glass cascading to the floor.

The screams stopped and Corin blinked, trying to focus past the purple-black dots before his eyes. Alere's head lolled and Mina relaxed. Tali released them and drew a sobbing breath. Corin let go of Alere's wrists. His fingers had left red marks on her skin.

'No!' Tali breathed. She hurried around to Mina's side and shoved Jarran out of the way.

'What?' he asked, peering over her shoulder. 'What?'

'Mina's heart has stopped.' Tali rested a hand on Mina's chest.

'Get out of the way.' Jarran pushed her roughly aside and placed both hands on Mina's ribcage.

Alere moaned, thrashing again in her sleep, crying Mina's name in heartwrenching, slurred pain. Kett clamped her legs and Corin held her arms. Tears tracked down her face.

Jarran pressed sharply down on Mina's chest. Something cracked and Alere screamed. He pressed again. And again, counting under his breath.

'You broke her rib, you shazi,' Kett said.

'I'm trying to restart her heart,' Jarran grated. 'My kin-sister is a Healer.'

'Stop it,' Tali scried. 'I can fix it. I can restart her heart.'

'No.' He kept pumping. 'You did this to her. I'm not letting you touch her again.' He kept counting. Then he paused, held Mina's nose and breathed into her mouth.

Corin looked on, helpless, holding Alere's twisting body, trying to block out her screams of agony.

Tali grabbed Jarran's shoulder. 'I'm nai-xintou, you zift! I can restart her heart telekinetically. Move.'

'Do it, Jarran,' Kett ordered.

'You don't get to tell me what to do, brother,' Jarran said, not taking his attention off Mina's face. 'We're both only in this mess because of you and Alere. Back off and shut up.'

Kett's jaw clenched but he stayed silent.

Jarran felt Mina's pulse. 'Come *on!*' He pumped again.

Alere slumped, limp and silent. Kett laid his fingers on her neck. He raised fear-filled eyes to Corin's.

'I can't feel Alere's pulse, either.'

Jarran swore and pushed again on Mina's chest. She convulsed. Alere did, too. Both drew a deep, gasping breath. And another. Another, and they were both breathing normally.

Tali backed away, her arms wrapped tight around herself.

'Alere?' Corin asked Kett.

Kett touched her neck, his shoulders sagging. He lifted her hand to his cheek and kissed it. 'She's alive. Mina?'

Jarran nodded. 'But her pulse is weak. We should get a Healer.'

'We can't,' Kett said. 'We can't trust anyone.'

Jarran's gold-brown eyes glittered. 'You trusted Houlia. And you trusted *her.*' He jerked a thumb at Tali, who stood with her back pressed to the wall, trembling.

'That's different,' Kett said. 'I know them.'

'And Healer House knows Mina,' Jarran said. He raked Tali with a narrow look. 'And I know who I'd trust more at the moment. You almost killed her.'

'I…I didn't mean to,' Tali whispered. 'I told you I didn't know what would happen. I'm sorry.'

'Did it work? The separation?' Kett said hoarsely, staring at Alere's slack face.

'The tie is broken.' She held a hand over Mina's chest. 'I don't think they should ever try to re-connect, though. Mina's heart has been weakened by this.' She sent Jarran a quick, frightened look. 'If they re-connect and we have to sever the Bond again, I don't think Mina would survive.'

Jarran sank into the chair and covered his face with his hands.

Tali staggered and grabbed at the bedpost. Corin jumped to his feet, slipping an arm around her waist. Surprisingly, she leaned into him. 'Thanks. I'm exhausted.'

'I'll help you get to bed.'

She shot him a suspicious look.

'To,' he said, scraping his hair back wearily, 'not *in*.'

The xintou accorded that the merest flicker of a smile.

When he arrived back at Kett's bedroom, Corin found Jarran and Kett standing toe to toe, glaring at each other. Rather, Jarran was glaring, Kett had his arms folded and wore a familiar, steely expression.

Corin closed the door and checked on Alere and Mina. Both slept peacefully.

'Have I interrupted?' he said. 'I hope so. I do love interrupting. But if you'd like to fight it out, please go ahead. Because we need to fight amongst ourselves at the moment.'

Kett sent him a warning look. 'Now Mina and Alere are separated, Jarran thinks we should wake Alere and go straight to the Alcazar to get his daughters out.'

Corin raised his brows. 'Have you looked at her, Jarran? She's exhausted and we have no idea what effect cutting that Bond has had.' He pointed at the window. 'And it's the mother-of-all storms out there at the moment.' Thunder punctuated the silence as if to agree with him.

Jarran gave vent to a growl and stalked around the room, fists clenched. 'Neither of you has any idea what I'm going through, here.' He grabbed the bedpost next to Mina and stared down at the sleeping women. 'I was living a gouri normal life, with a family and a business. My daughters were safe and happy.' He threw his arms out. 'Then I'm thrown into this feihua and I seem to have no control whatsoever over what happens to me or my daughters. Or even Mina.' His expression softened to aching regret. 'I'm supposed to be Jun First. Don't I get a say?'

Kett rested a possessive hand on Alere. 'I do understand. Believe me.' He stroked her hair. 'But this isn't just about your daughters – although I know it is, to you. There's a lot more riding on Alere's shoulders. Corin's right. She needs to rest.'

With a shake of his head, Jarran took the Koh-Lin bracelets from his pocket and threw them onto the bed. Then he scooped Mina up. He sent a cold, hard look at Kett. 'If my daughters die, it will be your fault, Kett. You abdicated and left me in this hole. Remember that.' He stalked from the room.

Kett dropped onto the bed, staring at Alere's peaceful face.

'Hey,' Corin said, gently. 'He's just frightened. Don't let it get to you.'

'But he's not wrong.' Kett swept his hands over his hair and sucked a deep breath. 'We can't let her rest as long as she needs to. The executions are the day after tomorrow. Have a servant wake us an hour before dawn, Cor? We need to make plans.'

CHAPTER TWENTY-TWO

ALERE

Alere awoke to an unfamiliar room. She felt...wrong, lightheaded; missing something essential. All she retained were vague memories of excruciating pain and loss; no idea how she got here. She shoved the covers aside and swept beneath her pillow, coming up empty-handed. Where was her knife?

Her feet hit cold timber. She wore a thin silk sleeping-robe with nothing beneath. The yanstones were gone from about her neck. Looking frantically around, she saw none of her gear. Coals from a banked fire lit the space in a dim red glow. The room contained a few pieces of much-gilded spindly furniture, but lacked what she most needed: weapons. Wait...the fire...

'Are you alr—'

She snatched up a poker from the hearth and swung. An iron hand blocked her arm, wrenching it toward a lock behind her back. She shifted and turned, countering before her attacker completed the move. Breaking free, she struck again at the shadowy figure. Again he blocked, this time winding her into a sleeper hold. A muscular forearm lay against her throat. The familiar scent of his skin cut through reactive training, into the older parts of her mind. This was someone she knew. On tiptoe, coughing and gasping, she stopped struggling and tried to think.

The arm relaxed. Something pushed against her back, forcing her several steps away. Turning, she squinted at the illusion wavering before her. Kett. Dressed in loose silk trous he stood, bare-chested, poised for action, wary.

'Alli, drop the poker. It's alright.'

'Kett?' She rubbed her eyes. 'But that's not… where are we? You're meant to be in Chengdu. You can't be here. You're safe.'

The room shifted and blurred. She squeezed at her temples, groaning as her knees gave way. She dropped the poker, barely hearing the tinkle of bronze on the timber floor. Kett's arms caught her. She melted into him, breathing in the warm scent of his smooth skin.

Then she broke free and retreated, clutching at a couch back.

'Why are you here?' Angry tears drowned the room and she dashed them away. 'I wanted you to be safe. You shouldn't have come after me. I can't…care. It makes me too vulnerable.'

Her throat closed and she stared into the flickering coals in the hearth, hardly feeling their warmth, cold through at the thought of losing Kett as she had Gavon. Loss, dulled for so many days, burned again as sullen coals of grief in her chest.

A long silence followed, broken by the faint crackle of burning wood and the soft patter of rain on the window. Kett turned her gently around. She shook her head, wanting to reject him and send him far from harm; angry at herself because, as soon as his arms pinned her against his warmth, the strength to save him dissolved.

Instead she leaned her forehead against him. 'I don't understand. How are you here? I dreamed…wait... Tell me it was all a dream.' She remembered everything from the trip, but as though through someone else's eyes. None of it was good.

'No.' Kett put his thumbs under her chin and raised her face. 'I'm here and it wasn't a dream. We're in Madina, in Jiaoji House. I'm not leaving. I told you – we're bound, you and I. We're in this together, no matter what you do or say. My place is with you. Stop pushing me away. Unless…you don't love me?'

His grey eyes were full of such love and underlain by such deep-seated fear that she buried her face in his neck just to breathe him in again, and stroked the smooth length of his back to reassure herself of his solidity. The rasp of the stubble on his chin, the rough callouses on his fingers as they caressed her; those were too real to be a dream.

He carried her back to bed and cradled her close, beneath the covers. She concentrated on the explanation he whispered into her hair.

When he finished speaking she pulled back to see him clearly. 'Tali? Tali did this?'

His arms tightened. 'You were so close to Fusion that if we'd waited any longer you both would have died.'

'But why? She knew about Celia.'

A frown flickered across his brow then vanished. 'It seems she envied you your freedom.'

'*She* envied *me?*' Alere gave a bitter laugh. 'That's nicely ironic.'

'Ironic or not…' He kissed her. 'I, for one, am grateful. She saved your life.'

'And Mina?' She sought for the yanstones, yearning for the ever-present contact with her sister.

Only an aching void remained in the place where the stones' warmth and the awareness of Mina had been for so long now. *That's* what was missing; what was wrong. She sat up.

'No,' she muttered, touching her throat. 'This isn't right. I can't feel her anymore! She's gone.' Panic welled up, her heart racing. 'I can't tell if she's alright. Where's the necklace? Where's Mina? I need to know.'

'Alli.' He grabbed her upper arms and pressed her back onto the bed, keeping his weight on her when she tried to throw him off. 'Stop fighting me. She's alright, I promise you. She's asleep in the room next door, with Jarran. Look at me, Alli.' He gazed at her, worried, loving. 'You know I wouldn't lie about something like this. She's fine.'

His intensity finally got through and Alere made herself relax. He seemed truthful, but it was always hard to be sure with Kett. He lied rarely, but when he did it was impossible to tell.

Lowering himself onto the bed beside her, he caressed her cheek. 'I promise.' Then he kissed her and there was no hiding the honesty of that.

With a sigh, she stared at the silken drapes above, resting her still-aching head on his shoulder.

'It just feels so strange not to have her inside my mind anymore. It crept up on me, bit by bit, since even before Shanzhai. A little stronger every day and every time I used the yanstones.'

'Well…' The sound rumbled low through his chest. 'You're just lucky Tali separated you when she did.'

Alere lifted herself onto her elbow and regarded him. 'Am I? I'm not sure, Kett. There was something...' She gazed into the last glowing coals of the fire, trying to remember how it felt, beyond the immediate memory of pain and sadness. 'Something almost comfortable about it. The temptation to open all my wards to Mina and blend our minds together was…compelling…empowering, almost.'

'This from the girl who, at fourteen, was so desperate for freedom that she dressed as a dancer and tried to join the travelling purple caravan leaving for Jadid?' He smiled. 'Wouldn't Fusion be the ultimate loss of freedom?'

She ignored the attempt to lighten the mood, needing him to understand. 'I'm serious. I feel… incomplete now. Like part of me is missing. Maybe we are meant to be connected. Maybe I just didn't know how to manage it properly. If I could just—'

'Don't.' Kett's arm tightened around her. 'Don't try it again,' he said hoarsely. 'I waited too long for you, Alli. Don't do anything rash.'

She gave an uneasy laugh, unsettled by his display of emotion. 'You know me. I'm always careful.'

'Of *course* you are.' He kissed her forehead.

Alere listened to the steady thud of his heart, feeling secure and alive for the first time in days. Behind the heavy, white brocade curtains, dawn-light sent soft, grey fingers into the room. This idyll couldn't last.

'What day is it? The last few are a bit of a blur.' She rolled onto her back to stare at the ceiling again. 'In fact, a lot of the trip from Chengdu is a blur. I remember some things clearly – the mercenaries, Batu's death. Mina was so angry.' She shuddered. 'But the rest… It was strange, like…I wasn't really me. I've never felt so helpless and unsure of myself. Everything seemed frightening and overwhelming. Now I feel almost normal again.'

'I don't think it *was* entirely you. Mina, for all her sweetness and calm, is a lot more fearful than you are. You think fast on your feet. She doesn't cope well with sudden changes. I think those feelings were her personality bleeding into yours.'

It made sense and, if it was two-way, would also explain Mina's forcefulness in the village. But how did she live, so afraid and worried like that all the time?

'And it's Ithnan, the eighth.' Kett drew her back against him as she tensed. 'I know what you're going to say.' He caressed her cheek and neck, across her breast and the curve of her hip. 'But I think the world outside can wait just a little longer, can't it? In a short while we'll have to get up and decide what to do about Rohne and Nasra and Hassan. I know that.'

'But we should—'

'Alli.' He gently stroked her face, her hair, her throat. 'No matter what we do today and tomorrow, people will die. It could well be you, or me. Focus on us, just for a few minutes.'

She touched his lips, cold inside again at the thought of losing him.

He kissed her fingertips. 'I've missed you. You have no idea how scared and angry I was when I woke in Chengdu and you were gone. You're my only family.'

Guilt over her part in Radan's death stabbed through her heart. How could she ever tell him? She thrust it aside with a light smile.

'Angry I can understand. I'm sorry I did that to you. I was so afraid of losing you, it was the only thing I could think to do. But it was stupid and wrong and I regretted it the minute Dalor's chuan left the dock in Chengdu.' She kissed him and felt his instant response in the way his body shifted against hers. She leaned back, smiling. 'I've missed you, too. So much.'

'I was beginning to wonder. Hitting me with a poker is not a convincing way to show me.' He brushed her lips with a fingertip. 'That was much better.'

She kissed him again, lingeringly, drowning in the soft strength of his lips; the sensual sweep of his fingers on her skin.

Then she eyed him. 'Were you really scared for me? You're the bravest person I've ever met. I thought you'd trust me to handle this. Like you did when I went to Ven.'

'That was a bit different. He was never a match for you.' He tucked loose hair behind her ear. 'And it's not a matter of me trusting you, so much as you trusting me. You have a bad habit of thinking you have to do everything on your own. Loving someone means letting them in. Here.' He laid a palm over her heart. 'And letting them help you.'

Alere sat up. 'That's what Mina said, too.' She crushed the sheet in her fingers. 'But what if I don't know how? What if I *can't* let you…anyone in?'

Kett sat up as well. 'You just said before that I'm the bravest person you know. But I'm terrified of this as well. Loving someone *is* bravery. And being brave doesn't mean you aren't afraid. Courage without thought or meaning is just reckless stupidity. Brave people aren't fearless. They've just found something that matters more than fear. In my case, that's you.' He kissed her softly. 'When you're ready, you'll stop being afraid that I'll hurt you. Or that Mina will hurt you. You'll trust that we're trying our best and that we love you – even if we make mistakes. Then you'll let us in.'

Alere sighed and lay back down. 'Part of me still wishes you were safely out of this. Losing Gavon was hard enough. I don't think I could stand losing you.'

'You really expect me to leave you to face this sort of danger alone?' Kett hitched himself on one elbow and trailed two fingers down the length of her body. 'Besides, I think I could be in serious trouble right here and right now. What are you going to do about it?'

'You're trying to change the subject,' she objected as his hand slipped under her robe and caressed her stomach.

'Without much success, evidently.' He grimaced. 'Let it go, Alli. I'm here and I'm staying. Now, we have about half an hour before the servants come to wake us and we have to plan the downfall of another Jun. Do you really want to spend that time in an argument you can't win? Or is there something better we could be doing?'

Sensing a lost cause, Alere gave up.

She scanned the brightening room and flashed him a deliberate, sultry look beneath her lashes.

'If this is Jiaoji House, then this is the White room, number thirteen.' She rolled over, straddling his hips and sliding her robe off one shoulder. 'Shall I show you what I learned here?'

He groaned. 'You have no idea how difficult it was to walk you here every week and wonder what was going on behind these doors. It was pure huozui.'

'Can't have been all bad. From what the other students here told me…' she stroked his lips '…you knew exactly what was going on.'

Gripping her wrists, he studied her closely. 'Did it bother you?'

She smiled. 'No.' Hurt flickered through his eyes. She kicked herself for thoughtlessness and tried another tack.

'Kett,' she said gently, 'I knew you weren't serious about any of them. Besides, you were my shifu and my friend, and I was so angry with my lot in Xintou House that I had no headspace for anything else.' She kissed him softly. 'I honestly didn't know how much I loved you until I thought I'd lost you to Mina.'

He searched her face for something. Then his lips curled into a faint, almost-sad smile.

'Well, in that case…' He became busy with the belt on her robe. 'Perhaps I should show you what *I* learned, instead.'

At sunrise, Alere and Kett slid reluctantly out of bed and dressed. Alere hesitated over putting the yanstone necklace and Rafi's bracelet back on, but the aching need for them was irresistible. Her skin hurt, her bones hurt, her mind hurt without them. She picked the linked chains up from beneath her neatly-folded clothes in the drawer.

Nothing.

Heart pounding, she snatched up the pair of bracelets Rafi had given her and Mina, as well.

Nothing. No sense of warmth beneath her skin. No taste of iron and smoke. Most of all, no connection. No reawakening of her xintou powers. Her hands trembled. She threw the necklace linked to Rafi's bracelet over her head and slipped the twin-bracelets on her wrists. Then she fumbled amongst her gear for her weapons and yanked off the suede covers. But, even with both hands on their yanstones, there was nothing. Not a flicker of life, of fire, of…anything.

She sank to the floor, clutching the sheathed weapons to her chest. Bile rose in her throat and her skin felt hot and stretched too tight.

'Alli? What's wrong?' Kett crouched before her.

'They're dead,' she whispered. 'I can't…I can't *do* anything. The xintou powers. They're gone.'

She thrust the sword and dagger at him and he studied them. The gems still caught and held the flare of light, throwing it back in an eye-aching glitter as the sun rose and streamed in through the window. He rubbed his thumbs over the stones.

Alere tensed, but the familiar touch of his mind remained silent. She forced down a hopeless cry.

'What am I going to do?' She touched the scabbard. 'I can't…without powers I have no hope of beating Rohne and Nasra. I'm nothing.'

Kett put the weapons aside and drew her to her feet. He belted the scabbards to her hips.

'You are not nothing, Alere,' he said sternly. 'You're smart and you're a gifted warrior. And *we* will think of something, I promise.' He kissed her swiftly, hard. 'We have Tali as well, now. And we have the Xintou House girls we sent to Yasmin. *We* can do this. Together.'

He caught her close, but she couldn't stop trembling. A void now gaped where she once felt whole. She thought it was just the connection with Mina that had been severed. That, she could handle. But without the yanstones… She shivered, a cold sweat dampening her skin and clothing.

Kett held her against his side. 'Come on. You need food. We're meeting the others in Houlia's room.'

She let him lead her from the bedroom, but a vortex of doubt threatened to obliterate logic.

They joined the others in Houlia's rooms, where a large table had been set up to accommodate more food than Alere had seen in many days. Even the thought of eating nauseated her, but she had to.

When she entered, Saric gave her a shrewd look and then a wide grin. He swaggered over.

'Better, then?'

She forced a smile and resisted the urge to ruffle his messy, white-blond hair. 'Thanks. You alright? I mean…Wei and all?'

He scuffed a bare foot on the lush carpet. 'I miss her, but…' he grimaced '…her choice, right?'

Alere crouched and offered a hug. He hesitated, then wrapped his wiry arms tight around her and buried his face in her neck.

'Don't you leave me, too.' His words were muffled.

She said nothing, only held him tighter.

He pulled away, scrubbing at his face. 'Eat. You look like a stick.'

Corin, standing nearby holding a plate of eggs and fried rong, laughed. 'Fatherly lesson number two. Never comment on anyone's looks, unless it's positive. Manners, kid.'

Saric jammed a dumpling into his mouth until his cheeks bulged. He stared pointedly at Corin as he chewed, mouth open. Corin turned to Alere and Kett.

'The kid will kill me, I swear.'

'Literally?' Kett asked.

'Yes,' Saric said thickly, chewing on another dumpling.

'Probably. Lancha?' Corin held up an exquisite teapot decorated with cavorting red dragons.

Kett held out two matching cups and Corin poured the blue liquid.

'This is all a lot more civilised than the last week,' Kett murmured.

'Couldn't be much less. Jarran and Mina are here now, so we'd best get down to business. Several messages have come in from our contacts. The news is not pleasant. Do sit. Eat. You'll need it.'

While the others sat, Alere debated how best to approach Mina. The yanstones had to work again. The twin-bond must be the missing piece. But would Mina agree? Her sister was pale and drawn, her eyes dark-shadowed. She pressed at her left side and winced as she walked.

Mina paused, searching Alere's face. Then tears gathered and she held out her arms.

'I'm sorry, Alli,' she whispered. 'I'm so sorry. I had no idea.'

Alere gave Mina a quick, gentle embrace, mindful of her cracked ribs. 'I know. It's not your fault. It's mine. I should never have got you into any of this.'

Mina shook her head vigorously, her washed and re-dyed white-blonde hair falling softly over her shoulder. 'No. I chose to come. And I forced you to help with Batu when you didn't want to.' She frowned. 'But being connected to you made it all seem possible.

Logical. But then…' Tears shimmered again on her lower lids and she brushed them hastily away.

'It's alright.' Alere glanced across at the table, where the others were waiting. 'You were right. I was just being…' she frowned and rubbed her thumbs over the yanstones '…I don't know…influenced by the stones somehow. But…'

'I miss the connection,' Mina murmured. 'But I'm glad it's gone. I know you said it in anger, but you were right. I am afraid. Of so many things. Of being alone. Of being overwhelmed by…everything. If I could go home right now, I would.' She straightened and winced again. 'But I won't leave you to do this on your own. I have to face my fears, just like you do. And we must stop Nasra and Rohne. Whatever they're doing, I'm sure it's not right. Jarran says that somehow Nasra has dozens of twin girls working as xintou. They must be the twins from Hassan Wen-Gates's estate, but I don't understand what she's done to—'

'Mina,' Alere interrupted. 'I…I need something from you. It won't be easy, though.'

Mina kissed her cheek. 'Anything, you know that. Thank you for asking.'

'I need to reconnect us,' Alere blurted. She hooked a thumb under the yanstone necklace and showed it. 'They don't work any more. I have no powers. None.'

Mina retreated. 'No. I can't. I'll do anything else, but not that.'

Closing the gap, Alere gripped her arms. 'You have to. I feel so helpless. So ordinary and small. I can't go up against Rohne and Nasra without xintou gifts.'

'No!' Mina wrenched free and backed away. '*I* feel helpless when we're connected. Not your equal, just some power source with no choice but to feed you. If you wanted to use them to heal everyone, I'd agree. But you'll use them to kill. Nasra's a good person. So is Rohne. I grew up with them.'

'But you just said—'

'I said stop them, not kill them.' Mina clenched her fists. 'There must be another way. We just need to find out *why* Nasra's doing this. I'm sure we can talk to her. Tell her we can cure Rohne.'

'You can't be that naïve.'

'Wanting to understand people better is not naïve, Alere. In fact, I've changed my mind. I will re-Bond with you.'

'I—'

'But only if you agree to open yourself completely. You need to understand where I'm coming from, not just force your will on me. If you'll go into it as equals, and help me cure Rohne, I'll do it.'

'But we'd Fuse and die.'

'We might not. You don't know for sure.'

'And Kett said that Tali said your heart is weak. If we had to sever the Bond you wouldn't survive.'

'You weren't worried about that, a minute ago,' Mina said. Her eyes narrowed. 'It's a risk I'll take, Accept me as an equal. Love me and let me love you. Then I'll help. Because then I know I can influence you, too.'

Alere shivered, torn by conflicting desires. Her whole body longed for the warm strength and reassurance of the yanstones' power. And the intimacy of her connection with Mina was seductive, comforting. To be loved unconditionally like that; bonded so closely that thoughts and feelings were truth. But it also meant letting go of control; opening herself to judgement for her mistakes; exposing her deepest fears and secrets. Those were too close to the surface and too real to bear scrutiny. She would be judged and her unworthiness open for Mina to see.

'I…I can't!' Alere walked blindly away, her stomach roiling. Without the yanstones, she had no hope. But she couldn't pay the price Mina asked. Not and be whole afterward.

CHAPTER TWENTY-THREE

ALERE

Houlia caught Alere's attention and waved her over to where the House Mistress stood, feeding her pair of golden jin-birds. The Jiaoji House Mistress swept a shrewd gaze over Alere and nodded.

'You're looking better. How's your sister?' She fed one of the birds a tidbit of raw meat and crooned softly to it. The bird fed the piece to its partner, which accepted delicately.

'Alright, I guess.'

'Did you know,' Houlia murmured, feeding another piece to the birds, 'that jin-birds partner for life?'

'Oh.' Alere waited. Experience told her that many of Houlia's life-lessons were delivered in very obscure ways.

The House Mistress smiled. 'But their partner is their sibling. Sisters with sisters. Brothers with brothers. If there's no nest-sibling, then a single aunt or uncle steps in to fill the gap.' She caught Alere's startled look. 'Oh, I know what you're thinking. It's totally platonic. They mate with birds from other family groups but raise the chicks within their own family.'

'And?'

Houlia glanced across at Mina. 'And nothing can break the love a pair has. They'll find each other across a thousand gongli. They hunt together. They raise each other's chicks. They defend each other against outsiders. If one dies, the other often dies shortly after.'

Alere stared at the gold-furred reptiles. 'I have a female jin-bird in Shanzhai. Well, Lia did. I inherited it. But she's got no partner.'

Houlia laid a gentle hand on Alere's arm. 'She needs one. She can't live a full life without her sibling. Make sure you find her a partner when you get home.' She fed the last bits to the birds. 'Now. I'll leave you conspirators to plan Nasra and Rohne's downfall. I have a House to run.' She kissed Alere's forehead. 'Sisters are part of you. Don't throw away that partnership out of fear.' She strode from the room with a languid wave to Kett.

Alere hesitated, then hurried to the table and chose a seat next to Kett, as far as she could get from Mina. She avoided her sister's eye and folded her arms. Sibling-love was all well and good, but Houlia didn't realise what Mina was asking. Opening her wards completely? Full connection and allowing Mina equal control? Fusing? No. There had to be another way.

But what? How could she possibly succeed without the yanstones?

'So,' Corin began. He held up several pieces of paper. 'No flitters getting through, but we do have other means. Worst news: The Jun Seconds, Mistress Li, and Jarran's daughters are all on tomorrow's coronation execution list. Unless Jarran, Lia, Kett – and now Mina as well – give themselves up.'

Jarran made a strangled sound and covered his face. Mina wrapped her arm around his broad shoulders and leaned her head on his bicep.

'There are another ninety-three ordinary people, and four senior members of the Trade and Miner's Houses on the list.' Corin threw the paper down. 'Looks like Hassan's determined to rid the city of every petty criminal and political dissenter.'

'Yes,' Kett said. 'And, without the Xintou House law Mistresses, there's no due process. No impartial judges to Read accused criminals to see if they really are guilty.'

'And hence the blood runs daily in the Alcazar's courtyard,' Corin said. 'Houlia's spies tell me, if the gates weren't closed to people leaving, the city would be empty. Even Houlia's considering taking her staff to set up in Jiali or Shanzhai.'

Alere groaned.

Kett gripped her hand and added, 'She's afraid Nasra's erheyi girls will breach her wards and she'll betray us unwittingly.'

'What do we do?' Tali asked. 'We can't turn anyone in.'

'I can go,' Jarran said, raising his haggard face.

Mina sat up. 'I'll go with you. Maybe I can talk to Rohne.'

'It wouldn't help,' Corin said. 'They won't release your daughters. It's all four of you, or none. And you know gouri-well that they'd never release your girls, or Rafi and Petar. Don't be a shazi, Jarran.'

Jarran's shoulders slumped and he covered his eyes again.

Kett cleared his throat and slid a sideways look at Alere. 'We have more bad news.'

Alere tugged at a stray lock of hair over her ear and stared at the table. 'Cutting the Bond between Mina and I…it removed my xintou powers as well.'

'Gouri…' Corin collapsed in his chair, rubbing at the back of his neck. 'Can you re-Bond?'

'They really shouldn't,' Tali said hastily. 'Mina's heart is far too weak to handle the severance a second time. She needs time to recover strength.'

Alere looked away from her sister. Maybe…just maybe it was a neural overload, as Mina had said in the barn south of Dalcin. Maybe cutting the bond had burnt out…no, just temporarily overstrained the xintou parts of her mind. Alere clung desperately to the hope.

Corin spread his hands. 'I'm open to ideas. Anyone?'

'We should enlist the help of the Selb,' Tali said. 'You said they're here to help Alere and Mina? Get them to join up with Yasmin's army, rather than sitting there, waiting.'

'No,' Jarran said. 'The priority has to be getting my daughters out of the Alcazar. It could take all day to get the Selb to join up with Yasmin. We don't have that kind of time to waste. There's no guarantee Hassan Wen-Gates will stick to his side of the bargain. From what Houlia says, he's been executing people at random for days. I'll go get my girls on my own if I have to.'

'And what purpose would getting caught sneaking into the Alcazar serve?' Kett put in quietly. 'Your daughters need you alive. You have to stay as far away from Hassan as possible until they're out. If he catches you, you're all dead.'

'Give me a solution, then!' Jarran snarled.

'I agree we can't wait. We'll split up,' Kett said, still calm. 'The Selb expect Alere and Mina to lead them. But Alere should be with the group going to the Alcazar. She can't be a figurehead for the Selb *and* lead the rescue team to get Ashi and Rhea out of prison.'

'Why can't you lead the rescue team, Kett?' Mina said. 'You grew up in the Alcazar.'

'He was seven when he left.' Alere dismissed the idea. 'I was there recently. And I spent two weeks deliberately familiarising myself with the layout.'

'Trust me,' Kett said. 'It's important for several reasons. As for how she'll be in two places at once. I have an idea for that, too.'

'Well, I do think that's about got it.' Corin walked one more time around the two women, twitching a fall of gold silk into place on one and the set of a swordbelt on the other. 'You lot – what do you think?'

Alere glanced over. Saric reluctantly pushed his third helping of chun bing pancakes away, belched loudly and wandered across.

'Not bad.' He beckoned Alere closer and murmured into her ear. 'I still say this is a stupid idea. But no-one listens to me, do they?' She shushed him.

Jarran and Kett broke off their sotto voce discussion in one corner of Houlia's suite and reviewed Corin's work. Shoulder to shoulder the kinship between them was obvious. Even with different eye colours, they were unquestionably brothers. Kett a shade taller, leaner and broader in the shoulder; Jarran more muscular, more intense, quicker to anger and to smile.

Corin called Alere. Hitching herself off the wall, she caught a glimpse of herself in a mirror and shoved her hands into the pockets of her Trades-House-brown trous. With her hair hidden beneath a short, blonde wig and her face radically altered by makeup, she resembled none of her previous guises. Now she was an apprentice tradeswoman. A carpenter; which was fine as long as no-one expected her to use a hammer for its true purpose.

She surveyed the others and gave her approval. Tali stood, regal and entirely comfortable in the traditional gold of a xintou, her lovely face obscured by the half-veil and her long hair hidden under a pale silk headscarf. She masqueraded as Mina, in her guise as the xintou who freed the Melcori slaves.

Mina wore Alere's travel clothes. With her hair cut and dyed back to its normal shade of rich, dark brown, the only thing that gave her away was an air of nervousness. Otherwise, she was Lianna Koh-Lin, liberator of the slaves, Wushi Games champion.

Their plan was to send Tali and Mina to get the Selb moving. That should draw Hassan and Rohne's attention, providing a distraction while Kett, Saric, and Alere attempted a rescue of the prisoners. Alere and Kett were dressed as tradespeople and carried similar disguises for the prisoners. They intended to do the unexpected and take them all out through the front gate. A contingent of Houlia's staff, dressed in the orange runner uniforms from Dalcin, would form a second distraction. Hopefully, Rohne would remember Corin's proposal to disguise as runners to rescue Alere from Ven's camp in Shanzhai.

It could all go suilie, though, if Mina couldn't carry off her impersonation of Alere.

Alere drew Mina aside. Tali gave them space, moving to sit on the windowsill. She leaned out the open pane and watched the street below.

Alere examined her sister's white face. 'Are you alright?'

'I-I don't know.' Mina pressed at her stomach. 'I feel sick. And I'm scared, Alli.'

'We all are. Here. Just in case.' Alere produced the yanstone bracelets and clasped them around Mina's wrists. 'I'm not asking you to re-Bond right now. But if you get in trouble, reach out to me.'

Mina shivered and touched the stones before pulling her sleeves down to cover them. 'And you?' She pointed to Alere's neck.

'I have the Koh-Lin necklace and Rafi's bracelet.' She touched the dead gems around her neck. 'But I promise I won't re-connect unless you do. It's just so we can communicate if you need me.' She shuddered, aching to immerse herself in the stones' warm reassurance. She'd half-hoped that the act of putting the bracelets on Mina would bring back the silver-gilt power. But it didn't. She was still empty and cold. Soft. Her mind tumbled by uncertainty.

'I'm sorry I laid that ultimatum on you, Alli,' Mina said. 'But I needed you to know how important it is to me – not killing, I mean.'

'No,' Alere said. 'You were right. I can't help how I think and I don't understand how you think. If I could open to you without Fusing…I might. But I can't, so I won't risk it.'

'But what about your powers?'

She gritted her teeth. 'I didn't have them before I met you and I survived for twenty years. I'll manage. But I'm hoping cutting the Bond just overloaded my mind temporarily, like you said.'

'You could be right,' Mina said. She moved a step away and scrubbed her hands down her thighs. 'What if something goes wrong?' She glanced out the window. Part of the Alcazar's southern tower could be seen, hazed in purple smoke.

Alere turned Mina's face away from the window. 'I promise you won't have to be part of the action. Just convince the Selb to retreat around to the south of the city and join with Yasmin's men. Adding four thousand fighters to Yasmin's army could tip the balance in our favour.'

'But I don't know what to do, Alli!' Mina said. 'I'm not like you. I've never been strong and with our bond cut I don't even have the strength I borrowed from you.'

'Mina.' Alere sought for the right words. 'Do you remember when you were attacked here in Madina? The day we first met?'

'Y-yes.' She touched her throat, where a tiny, pink scar marked the memory.

Alere looked into her self that was yet not her self; her opposite. 'You showed far greater strength, compassion and calm under pressure than I did that day. You were strong long before us. You don't need to borrow anything from me.' She kissed Mina's forehead. 'You are better than me in so many ways I can't even begin to count them.'

'But I'm not. I'm not a warrior like you. I'm a healer.'

'Mina!' Alere gripped her sister's shoulders then stopped herself. Anger wouldn't help. She lowered her tone, bringing the emotion back to calm reason. 'It's not about being a warrior. It's about letting me do the right thing by you for a change.'

Her sister blinked at her.

Alere yanked off the hot wig and threw it aside, scraping back her hair. 'You were right, in the village. I *do* owe you.' She pointed south. 'I dragged you away from your home and I made you do unspeakable things that ran directly counter to your ethics, even though they helped thousands of people. And I've tried to justify it on that basis, but it was wrong, and you should hate me for it. Do you know what's really different between us?'

Mina raised one shoulder like a little girl waiting to be scolded, hopeful she won't be.

Alere pointed at herself. 'My whole life I've done things out of fear and anger. I was afraid of never being what I thought I was born to be. Afraid to leave the House and take the freedom I wanted, because that would be admitting failure. Afraid to *not* help Rafi in Shanzhai, and Jahil in Chengdu, because helping them was expected of me. I've been hard and tough, because I had to be.'

She took Mina's hands in her own. 'Everything I've done has been spectacular, but I've done it for the wrong reasons. Out of duty or to impress people. Or worse – out of rage. Everything you've done has been to help people because you love them. And that takes far greater strength because it goes unrecognised. You're gentle and soft, but you're not weak. You've helped me, now I'm asking you to let me help you.'

'But I don't understand! How is me pretending to be you on the battlefield, you helping *me?*' Mina snatched her hands free.

Alere stalked across to Jarran, steered him over, and planted him in front of Mina.

'Do you love him?'

Mina lit up, her eyes sparkling. She blushed and nodded. Jarran's black expression vanished and he caught her knuckles to his lips.

'Good,' Alere said. 'Because he loves you. He also loves his daughters. Rafi, Petar and Leah are all good people but – if I'm being honest – I hardly know them. I think I spoke with Petar and Leah maybe twenty times in the decade I lived under their roof. Rafi I've known a week or so. I'll try and save them because it's the right thing to do. Jarran's daughters – who I've met once – matter more.'

Mina frowned. 'That makes no sense.'

'Because they matter to him. And he matters to you. And you are fundamental to something in me.'

Mina's mouth softened and her gaze shifted to misty-eyed comprehension. 'Oh, Alli. I—'

'Don't, Mina.' Alere held up both palms and cleared her throat. 'This is hard enough. If I could save you this task I would, but if we're going to free the girls and the others, it has to be today. And it has to be you out there with the Selb.'

Still Mina hesitated. Jarran pulled her into his arms and whispered something into her ear. She leaned back, wreathed in smiles.

'Yes!' she murmured, then turned a dreamy look on Alere. 'Yes, I'll do it.' She kissed Jarran. 'And yes, I'll join with you in the hunli ceremony.'

Tali, seated at the window, leapt to her feet, her cheeks pale. She excused herself and vanished into the bathroom.

Saric groaned. 'Yeah, I think I'll be sick, too.'

CORIN

Lost in thought while tightening the girth on Tali's horse, Corin started when Saric appeared from nowhere to stand silently at his elbow.

'Gaisi, kid.' He tugged another notch on the girth. 'I think I need to take lessons from you. I've never seen anyone move as quietly as you do. Even Kett.'

'It's a gift.' Saric shrugged. 'Just thought you should know.' He jerked his chin toward where Mina and Alere stood, talking in the torchlit, flickering darkness beneath Jiaoji House. The rush and gurgle of stormwater through the tunnels obscured their words.

Corin surveyed them casually. 'What?'

'I might have been doing some eavesdropping earlier,' Saric said.

'I should hope so. And?'

'She's wearing the stones again.' Saric lowered his voice. 'And she got Mina to wear the bracelets. Mina's refusing to re-Bond. Alere tried to convince her.' He studied Alere again, 'I dunno. I've seen people who can't give up the jiu or the blackweed act a lot like this. Twitchy. Desperate.'

'Khara!' Corin finished with the buckle. 'Thanks kid, I'll talk to Kett.'

'He knows. Said it was her decision.'

'Gah!' Corin scrubbed at his scalp, undecided. 'Sometimes that man annoys the diyu out of me. He should just take them away from her.'

Saric gave a sardonic snort. 'Him and what army?'

'You do have a point.'

'Kett also told Mina and Alere all about that Lei someone journal-thing. The bit with the kid who died and killed all those people with his mind.'

'Ah. I'm guessing Mina wasn't too happy about that?'

'She cried and talked about Rohne.'

'She does that. Nothing seems to convince her that Rohne isn't the person she believes he is.'

'Well, if we're lucky, she's right and we're wrong.'

Corin sent him an ironic look. Saric grinned, wryly.

'Right,' Corin said, 'we're heading out. Watch Alli's back and take care of Jarran's girls. It'll be a good thing to have the next Jun First owe you.' He resisted the urge to haul his son into a hug. After a decent night's sleep, Saric was back to his cynical self and would most likely be embarrassed. 'Be safe, kid. And do make sure you're not picked up by the Alcazar weishi.'

Saric raised an eyebrow. 'More advice?'

'It's part of the job.'

'Who hired you?'

'Your mother.'

'Yeah,' Saric curled a lip, 'well she's dead, isn't she? And even she never tried to tell me what to do.'

With a grimace, Corin tried again. 'Look, kid, I've just got used to the idea of having you around, alright?'

'Oh, I'm hard to get rid of. Just ask Liu.' He cleared his throat and scuffed a toe on the filthy brick floor. 'You stick around, too, huh? I'm kinda used to you, as well.'

Corin watched Saric saunter over to Kett. Fatherhood was too much like hard work.

He turned to throw Tali into the saddle. She was watching Mina and Alere with a haunted look in her indigo eyes. Corin cupped his hands and helped her mount.

'Keep your head down while we're in the lower parts of the tunnel,' he advised. 'Otherwise that pretty gold silk robe will be ruined. The walls are nicely decorated in sludge. And do stick close to me until we get out of the storm drains. They're a bit of a maze.'

'Corin?' Tali hesitated, her eyes luminous behind the gold veil.

He smiled involuntarily. 'Shunu?'

She ignored the teasing. 'I'm…a little worried. It sounds silly, but I haven't even been outside the walls since I was nine.' She wiped her palms on her robe. 'I don't have a weapon, either. Are these Selb trustworthy? Are we sure this is the right thing to do? Shouldn't we, maybe, do some more planning…I don't know…this seems awfully rushed.'

Corin laughed. 'You'll get used to thinking on your feet if you hang around with Alere for long. Besides, *you've* got nothing to fear from the Selb. They practically worship the xintou. They won't touch you. And outside the walls is just like inside. Just bigger, cleaner, and it smells better.'

She sputtered a nervous giggle, covering her mouth to hide it; endearingly child-like. She was far too serious for her own good, most of the time.

'As for a weapon…' He dug in his pack and produced a small, double-edged dagger, about the right size for her, complete with calf-sheath.

In presenting it to her with a shallow bow, he dragged his fingertips across the thin, sensitive inner skin of her wrist. Her eyes flew to his and she flushed.

'Can you use it, though?' he asked.

She turned the dagger over. 'I'm guessing you take this sharp bit and stick it into people who are bothering you.'

'Something like that.' Corin plucked it from her, resheathed the blade then strapped it to her lower leg, deliberately letting his hands linger on her skin as he tightened the buckles. She sucked a quick breath.

He rose, appreciating the pink tinge to her cheeks. 'Make it a last resort. A weapon will end up in the wrong hands if you're not committed to using it.'

Her lips quirked into an excited little smile. She lifted the hem of her robe, admiring the zitan-wood handle laying along her shapely calf.

'Thank you. I love it,' she breathed. 'I always wanted to train like Alere did. Do you think maybe I could…No, I forgot…' Her mouth drooped and she gathered the reins.

'Hey.' Corin laid a hand over hers on the leather. She jumped but didn't withdraw. 'I think you can do whatever you want, when this is all over.'

She didn't meet his eyes, her cheeks flushing dark. She kneed her mare into motion and moved away.

Corin watched her go, uneasy for no reason he could pin down.

'Cor,' Kett said, appearing from the darkness.

Corin started. 'Don't *do* that. Between you and Saric, I'll die of a heart attack.'

The weishi gazed after Tali. 'Your job is to protect her, not seduce her. She's had a sheltered upbringing. She won't understand it's just a game to you.'

Corin gave him a cool look. Truth was, he often did these things out of habit, using every tool at his disposal to manipulate a situation. All the women he'd dallied with previously were either his unveiled jiaoji spies, or women who played the game as well as he did. He also never deliberately toyed with the emotions of vulnerable girls – and didn't intend to start now.

Regarding Tali's slender, upright figure, he threw Kett a grin. 'Y'know what? It's not often I get to say this, but you're wrong. I've been at this for ten years, so believe me.' He nodded at Tali. 'That girl is playing head games with *me*, not the other way around.'

At Kett's darkening scowl Corin held up a placating palm. 'Never fear. I know where to draw the line, my friend. It's whether she does that should worry you. You could start by asking how long she's known about the tunnel to Jiaoji House. And how many times she's used it in the past.' Enjoying Kett's startled reaction, Corin grinned.

He slapped Kett's shoulder. 'Be safe and do bring Alli and Saric back in one piece, please. I'm rather attached to both.'

Kett clasped his forearm. 'I will.' Then he hesitated, glanced at Mina, Tali, and Jarran who awaited Corin. 'But I can't shake the feeling I've missed something vital, Cor. There's something not right about this whole thing. Get them away the minute you see anything you don't like.'

'In that case, we shouldn't even leave the tunnels. I don't like much of anything about this.'

'Neither do I.'

'Tell Alli I'll use my yanstones to contact her in exactly one hour with a progress report. She'll need to open her wards. Good luck.'

'And you.'

CHAPTER TWENTY-FOUR

ROHNE

Are you prepared?

Rohne turned at his mother's quiet question, left the window that overlooked the northern city wall, and joined her at the fireplace. Somewhere, just inside that wall, half of Hassan's junren were massing to confront the Selb. Within an hour or two, they would have their first victory against those who stood in Nasra's way. Then they would rejoin the rest, outside the southern wall, and take on the Koh-Lin army, when they arrived, tomorrow.

Rohne held his fingers to the fire's warmth and studied Nasra's profile. They were in the suite she had chosen for herself. The most ostentatious and beautifully-decorated guest xintou suite in the Alcazar. All lush purples and golds, with heavy furniture and thick xiao-bearskin rugs. The luxury of it was in stark contrast to the small cottage in Gaton where he'd been raised. It made him uncomfortable, but she seemed to revel in it.

She bore an air of suppressed triumph that almost made him smile. She was so certain of success. He wasn't sure whether to be glad or irritated. Her plans – those she shared with him – were impressive and thorough. But she underestimated Alere. Nasra dismissed his objections, however, refusing to consider Alere as a real threat, especially against Hassan's army and the erheyi girls. He decided to give it one more try.

'I am prepared, Mother,' he replied formally. 'I know my job today. And I'll keep Hassan under control. Will you be ready here? I'm certain Alere or Kett will try to rescue our prisoners. It would be very much in their style. Predictably so, in fact.'

Nasra shrugged, complacent. *I'm counting on it. So much easier to have her bring Jarran and Kett to me, rather than trying to track them down in this glass-rabbit warren of a city.*

'And you're sure your men will recognise her. She's become quite adept at disguises.' Rohne scowled at the dancing flames.

My men know exactly what to watch for. Don't worry, love. You take care of Hassan and leave the rest to me.

'Very well.' He tucked his hands into the sleeves of his gold silk robe. 'But, if you let them escape, they'll join with Yasmin and encourage Madina to rise against us. That will make it much harder to bring this city under control.'

Nasra gave him a dry look. *Why do you think I've allowed Hassan so much freedom with his wholesale killings? The city's inhabitants are in no state to do anything but cower in their hovels for fear of being deemed unclean and dragged into the courtyard. As for Yasmin...* she made a dismissive gesture...*Even if Rafi reaches her, after today she'll be powerless to prevent the coronation. Once that is complete, we can finish her, Rafi, and any other Juns who object. Without heirs, the Seconds' lands will all fall to us and Mamlakah will be unified.*

'And how are we supposed to prove that Rafi has no heir,' Rohne asked acerbically, 'when the world believes Alere – who is quite alive – to be her?'

Nasra patted his cheek. *That, dearest boy, is why you're going out with Hassan today.* She screwed up her nose. *Yes, he needs a watchcat, but I also have it on good authority that one or both the Koh-Lin girls will be there today to rally the Selb into action. If it's Mina, bring her to me. Should Alere slip away today, Mina will serve as hostage. Alere may not exchange herself for Rafi, but she will certainly do so for her sister.*

'And at the coronation? What are the plans for protecting me and Hassan there? It's very open.'

Nasra smiled. *Only the best, of course. It will be a glorious day. The world will see you and be awed. The blood of those who object will be the red carpet upon which you and Hassan walk to the ceremony. A hundred heads will fall and silence dissent amongst our people. Trust me.*

'And Mina?'

She raised one shoulder. *If you still care for her, you can have her. I have no objection. In fact, it will lend legitimacy to our claim to the Koh-Lin lands. If you need my help in…changing her mind on certain matters, let me know. I can be quite persuasive. I should like to practice my skills on her.* She grimaced. *She always got on my nerves. I never understood what you saw in her.*

Rohne ground his teeth but said nothing. Of course Nasra would object to Mina. To the one person who ever showed faith and respect for him. The one person who had loved him when everyone else spat on him. He would not allow her to meddle with Mina's thoughts. He could do that, himself.

But it wouldn't be necessary, anyway. Mina would see his greatness, now. Her fixation with Jarran was just as fleeting as her interest in Kett. As soon as she was in the Alcazar, she would remember how much Rohne meant to her. How close they had been.

A servant arrived at that moment, murmuring a message into Nasra's ear. She left the room, with a reminder to bring Mina or Alere straight to her as soon as he arrived back.

Rohne considered her retreating figure. She "had it on good authority" that one of the Koh-Lin girls would be on the field of battle? Whose? What else hadn't she told him?

The constant, lingering ache in his head spiked into sharp agony for a moment and he had to lean on the wall, gasping, to recover. Jiche! What was *wrong* with him?

ALERE

After Corin and the others left, Alere followed Kett into the mouth of a tunnel running northeast in the direction of the Alcazar. It wouldn't take them all the way there, but they would emerge close, reducing the risk of being stopped in the street.

She'd reluctantly left her sword in her room. A Trades apprentice could hardly be seen carrying a large sword in public. Her dagger was acceptable. Few people walked abroad without something similar. Of course she also carried several other, more discreet, weapons – including the gold poison ring. But the absence of sword and bow left her feeling vulnerable.

Just before they entered the tunnel, Kett rounded on Saric. He crouched before the boy and pressed a small, folded piece of paper into his palm. Gripping Saric's thin shoulder, Kett stared intently into his green-grey eyes.

'You know what to do?'

Saric nodded, alight with excitement.

'Good. Give him the message. You'll need to cover ground fast. Don't waste any time and *do* remove any obstacles that might slow you down or give away your position. And by remove,' he said, smiling thinly, 'I mean the black feathers. You have about an hour, at the most, to get them into position. Go.'

Saric, with a quick salute and a wink for Alere, splashed into a tunnel running east, his little lantern bobbing as it dwindled into a distant spec. Alere gaped after him.

'What was that about? I thought he was coming with us.'

'He's not,' Kett replied evenly. 'And you need to get changed.'

'What? Why?' She twitched her costume. 'I spent ages getting this makeup on. I'm pretty much out of disguises, Kett. If not this, then what?'

'You and I both know the tradesman idea would never have worked. Whose benefit was it for?' Kett folded his arms. 'And, seven years old or not, I remember the Alcazar. I know you can*not* sneak out of the Jun First's bedroom, and through the main building, unnoticed – as you've told everyone you did. I think it's about time you explained *exactly* how you escaped.'

Alere stripped the wig off again, turning it over without seeing it. 'You're right. I knew this wouldn't work. I had to come up with something.' She checked the stairway leading into Jiaoji House. 'I just had a feeling. Someone was hiding something. Or maybe watching from inside the walls? It just felt wrong to give away all our plans.'

Kett gave a snort. 'I think we can safely say just about everyone here has secrets to keep, but I agree with you. Corin noticed it, too. Which is why he didn't object to the ridiculousness of the tradesmen idea. Saric thought the plan was insane, but I kicked his foot before he spoke up. Luckily, the others don't have his devious mind and couldn't see the flaws.'

'So, what's with the little side-trip for Saric?'

Kett regathered his pack from the floor and shouldered it. Then, reaching into a shadowy recess inside the tunnel mouth, he withdrew two long, cloth-wrapped bundles and handed them to her. She opened the first and revealed her sword and his. The second held her bow, quiver, and arrows.

She removed the trades toolbelt and strapped them on with a sigh of relief. She tucked her hair back under the wig, and reversed the distinctive Trades-brown jacket to show its nondescript grey lining instead. Kett did similarly and now they were just ordinary citizens, albeit with expensive weapons.

He waved her into the tunnel. Alere preceded him into the darkness, trying to stay out of the deep water that coursed through the drains after the storm the night before.

A few dozen steps onward – out of earshot of any House spies – she stopped. 'So?'

'Yes,' he replied. 'So?'

She huffed. 'Fine. There's a secret access tunnel leading from the Jun First's bedroom. Radan showed me. One exit leads to the cells, the other opens through the Alcazar's outer wall, into the alley near the stables and smithy. Happy?'

He laughed softly. 'Oh, yes. And you remember where the exit is?'

'I think so.' She cast her mind back. 'It was night and raining and I was terrified, so I hope so. And Saric?'

'Insurance,' he said, waving her on.

She grumbled but there was no point in nagging. He wouldn't tell if he didn't want to.

Twenty minutes or so later – it was difficult to judge time in the darkness – they emerged onto a back street through an access hatch in the ground. Heaving herself out onto the cobbles, Alere found the only threat in sight to be a zibal, scurrying along the gutter. The alley was eerily deserted. The nearby houses closed and dark. Kett emerged and they headed for the Alcazar's south wall.

Alere unslung her bow and nocked an arrow. In these long streets, curving around the Alcazar walls, they were likely to first see Hassan's men at a distance. It would be fatal to let one escape to raise the alarm.

A few seconds later, a three-man patrol emerged from a side street about thirty paces ahead. They examined Alere and Kett with suspicion, drawing their swords. After a quick exchange of words, one of them headed back the way they'd come.

'You take the messenger.' Kett threw a knife at the closer pair. One man fell with a cry, the blade protruding from his unarmoured thigh.

Swearing, Alere drew and released her arrow in a hurry. It was off-target. She released a second. A shout went up. The escaping junren leapt to one side. The arrow took him high in the right arm, instead of the back. He stumbled but staggered on. Almost behind the sheltering corner of the nearest dwelling.

A flutter of his cloak revealed he wore alzin armour. Another body shot was too much of a risk when she had time for only one more. The armour would stop her bronze tips. She drew string and breath together, anchored and released.

The point took him behind the knee. He collapsed to the ground with a scream, clutching at the leg. His cries would attract attention. She released a fourth arrow. It skewered the back of his neck and the yelling ceased.

Unspeaking, she and Kett dragged the three bodies through the unlocked doorway of an abandoned house. They stripped the bodies and bundled everything in a cloak, then closed the remains into a cellar. Two arrows were broken, but she retrieved and cleaned the others. The only other evidence was blood glistening on the street. Hardly unusual in Madina these days.

The disappearance of a patrol did, however, mean the clock ticked on their mission. According to Houlia's information, the Alcazar patrols reported back on the hour. It was ten past the hour now, so they had much less time than they'd hoped to get in and out again undetected.

'The entrance is this way.' Alere pointed at the Alcazar's massive, stone outer wall, just twenty paces away at the end of the side-street. 'The smithy and workshops will probably still be operational, so they're the next danger point.'

'Lead on.' Kett unsheathed his blades.

When they arrived at the wall, Kett kept lookout and found a place to stash the dead weishis' uniforms while Alere searched for the hidden latch. The street workshops were strangely silent but who knew for how long. Several precious minutes later, she found the latch. Pressing into the gap in the mortar, she called out to Kett.

She felt along the wall inside and found the lightswitch. Only one of four bulbs overhead worked, lighting just a small section of the narrow stone corridor with a dim, yellow glow that did little more than deepen the shadows in the corners. The hall smelled of dust. A thick coat of grime on the floor was disturbed only by her own, outgoing prints from two months before.

At the opposite end lay the door to the Alcazar cells. She doused the light and eased the eye-cover open with great care. The faint scrape still sounded loud.

Four of the five cells were occupied. A pair of mel-oil lanterns, hanging from hooks on the walls by the door, lent their flickering, smoky light to the scene. Overhead, the electric bulbs hung unlit. Either they were broken and repairs were beyond the current maintenance crew, or Nasra simply had a flair for the dramatic and preferred the ambience of flames.

One cell held Leah and Petar Ma-Safra, sitting in miserable silence, side-by-side on a wooden bench. Thinly-clad in a plain grey house-robe, Leah shivered and leaned into her husband. Her long, light brown hair escaped its plait and drifted around her drawn face.

A gentle, kind woman in her mid-forties, she looked a decade older. She gave a faint, hoarse cough. Petar kissed her temple. Age had thickened his middle and dusted his dark hair with salt. His ready smile was absent, replaced by a deep frown that sat ill on his round, cheerful countenance.

A second cell held Rafi, dressed in wrinkled, formal Koh-Lin dark green and silver, as though he'd been brought there straight from court or a function. He stood and paced his cell. In his severely-cut tunic and trous, with his close-cropped greying hair and scowling expression, he looked like a man ready to explode.

Only half-visible in the third cell, Jarran's two little girls lay, curled together beneath a thin blanket. The elder cradled the younger; both pale and waifishly pretty. The younger, Ashi, cried out in her sleep, tears sliding down her cheeks. Rafi stretched through the stout timber bars and stroked the tumble of dark curls. Ashi sighed and slept on.

The fourth cell was just visible from this angle, but little could be seen of the occupant. Just a tiny pair of feet, shod in gold silk house slippers, and the bottom of a heavy, gold-silk xintou robe. No movement. Was Mistress Li still alive?

Alere gestured to Kett. She stripped off her bow and quiver and laid them carefully on the ground as he first surveyed the room then pushed the eye cover into place again.

'I saw the foot of one guard, just off to the left,' she whispered.

'And I'm pretty sure there's one more,' he said. 'I heard something. We need to take them down together to prevent outcry.'

Alere palmed three throwing knives. He did the same. From a pocket, she retrieved a small sac of whiteseed oil with a tiny nozzle at one end: the friend of all xiongshou. Saric had handed it to her, without explanation, this morning. Four drops on the latch and both the hinges.

With great care Kett depressed the latch. Only the faintest, metallic click resulted, but it was enough to make Rafi pause in his incessant pacing. He glanced at the guards, then broke into an angry monologue, ranting at Nasra and Hassan, occasionally kicking the bed frame or the bars.

Kett used every covering noise to draw the door open a fraction as the ages-old hinges still stuck and squealed faintly. When the door was wide enough to admit Kett's broad shoulders, he and Alere slipped through. One guard got off his chair and stalked to Rafi's cell. Kett and Alere froze. Unless the guard turned around, he shouldn't see the door, but motion might alert him.

The guard thumped the pommel of his sword on the bars. 'Shut up old man. Cut the feihua. Your chouhuo of a daughter is not coming.' He dragged a finger across his own throat. 'Tomorrow it's all done for you and, as soon as we catch her, she'll go the same way.'

Petar, staring at Rafi in perplexity, glanced past and his gaze connected with Alere's. He shot to his feet and rattled his cell door. 'Well,' he said haughtily, 'until tomorrow, both of you and the other *two* outside should treat us with the care due to Jun Seconds. My wife is ill, as is Mistress Li. I demand you send a healer.'

The second guard emerged and pointed the tip of his ceramic sword at Petar's stomach. 'You're in no position to make demands, Jun Second.' He spat into the cell. 'As for your wife and the Mistress, we have orders to let them die if they will. Saves the executioner re-sharpening his axe. You and her kind have kept us in the dark ages. We'd be a lot richer – like old Earth was – but for you Juns and the House.'

'That's what this is all about?' Petar said. 'This world has no iron and barely a tenth of the other mineral resources Earth had. And those very resources destroyed Earth. That's why this colony started. Are you all blind zifts?'

The two guards exchanged amused looks.

'No iron,' the first said, 'that's a funny one. Biggest gouri lie we've all been fed. There's iron here. Blade that'll kill you tomorrow is made of Kalima steel.'

Just as Alere readied for the first throw, the outer door opened and the other two guards marched in, weapons drawn.

'What's all the noise about?'

'Now,' Kett commanded.

CHAPTER TWENTY-FIVE

ALERE

Alere's first knife and his flew in almost perfect synchrony. Aimed at the unprotected back of the guards' necks. Both struck true. Spinal columns severed, the pair collapsed like marionettes.

The other two junren gaped and turned. That exposed their throats. Alere and Kett threw their second knives. Alere's struck true, slicing jugular and windpipe. The man scrabbled at his neck. Blood pulsed through his fingers. He yanked the knife out and fell to the stone floor, gargling.

Kett's knife missed as the junren leapt to one side. He dived for the door, arms up to protect his neck. Kett threw his third knife. It lodged in the armpit; in the gap in the alzin armour. The man grunted and did the worst thing possible: pulled it out. He threw it expertly back at Kett, who caught the handle. Blood poured from the guard's severed artery. Alere's third knife sliced into his hamstring. He dropped to his knees, crying out. Kett strode over and silenced him.

Rhea and Ashi woke and sat up. Ashi opened her lips. Rhea slapped a palm over her sister's mouth, muffling the incipient scream.

'Good girl,' Alere approved as she hurried forward. 'Your father sent us to find you. Are you ready to go?'

Both girls leapt off the hard cot. Rhea whispered, 'But what about the other girl? The one in yellow they took away?'

'In yellow? One of the Xintou House girls? Who?' Alere glanced at the adults. Petar and Leah looked baffled. Rafi opened his mouth, slid a look at Petar, then closed it again.

'She was here when they brought us in,' Rhea said. 'But they took her away. Uncle Petar and Aunt Leah were sleeping so they didn't see her. I don't know her name.'

'They drugged us,' Petar said bitterly.

Rafi shook his head, his mouth set in a grim line. Alere's heart sank. Whoever the girl in yellow was, she hadn't been released safely.

She forced a smile. 'I'm sure she's fine. Let's get these doors open, shall we?'

Behind Alere, Kett closed the outer door and dragged the junrens' bodies across in front of it as a barricade. He tossed her knives back. 'Hurry. There's no lock on this side of the door.' Checking each junren, he swore again. 'No key to the cells, either. Have you got picks?' He pulled a set out of his pocket and went to work on the girls' door.

'Corin lent me a set, but you know I'm not great at it.'

'Lia,' Rafi said, looking at her intently. 'You're alright?'

She nodded.

'Lianna?' Leah's soft, incredulous question drew her. Alere reached through the bars to clasp the woman's thin hand. 'I hardly recognised you. Are you wearing some sort of makeup?'

'A disguise, shunu,' she replied.

'Yes, it's Lia.' Rafi looked a warning at Alere. So, he hadn't shared their secret with the Ma-Safras.

Alere sighed. After ten years away, Leah was unlikely to recognise her as Elmira's rarely-seen daughter, anyway. And Alere Connor was somewhere on the run, wanted for the murder of Radan Zah-Hill. Best to leave it that way. Lianna Koh-Lin had a chance at a life. Alere Connor didn't.

She set to work on Rafi's celldoor. 'Kett's going to get you out of there, shunu.'

'Kett?' Petar peered at the weishi, puzzlement shifting into astonished confusion. 'No! It can't be. Tekettan is—'

'Oh, it's him alright,' Rafi put in, glaring at Kett who swung the first door open and gestured to Jarran's two girls. 'He just keeps showing up.'

'Stop it, Rafi,' Alere snapped, trying to concentrate on the stubborn lock to his cell. 'If it weren't for Kett you wouldn't have an heir. Several times over. So just let it go.'

He pressed his lips together and folded his arms. The lock clicked and Alere wrenched the door open. Rafi snatched her into a brief, hard hug.

'Jarran? Mina?'

'We got them out of Chengdu.'

'Later, Lia,' Kett put in. 'There's no time. Thank you for distracting the guards, shenshi.' He opened the door to Petar's cell. 'Take the girls and go down the tunnel. You'll find an exit about thirty paces that way. Don't leave yet. There are patrols. Wait for us.'

Petar supported Leah, and Rafi took the two girls by the hands. Rafi's set expression spoke volumes for his state of mind.

'Shenshi Petar?' Alere whispered. 'Where's Elmira?'

Petar shoulders drooped. His eyes were bleak. 'She tried to protect us from Nasra. She confronted her mother, pleaded with her. Even tried to attack her, mind to mind. But it was no good.' He swallowed, his jaw working. 'Nasra accused her of betrayal. She…tried to force Elmira's compliance. When Elmira refused, Nasra's weishi drove a blade into her and left her to die in the hall of our house.' He cleared his throat. 'All the Jun-Bonded Xintou based in Madina are dead. And I heard from our cell guards that those out in other towns were slaughtered as well. I think only Valera of Melcor, Xiaan of Jadid, and Khia of Adeghal, still live. I'm sorry.'

Alere covered her mouth to stifle a cry. Her knees weakened and she had to lean against the bars. Elmira, dead. It couldn't be true. Her mind couldn't grasp the idea. Elmira's calm good sense and compassion. The memory of her callaflower perfume lingered. The soft comfort of her last embrace in the Ma-Safra's garden all those weeks ago.

'Lia!' Kett's harsh whisper helped her refocus and she wiped at her eyes. 'Have you heard from Corin?'

She dropped her wards, guiltily. 'Nothing. Is it time, though?'

'Yes. A little past.' He sent her a sharp look. 'There's something wrong. I know it. This has been too easy. Re-establish the Bond with Mina. We have to know what happened. Let Jarran know we have the girls.'

'But Mina won't—'

'You didn't need her permission the first time, did you? You must have connected when you first met her, without either of you knowing. Do it now.'

'But her heart!'

'We'll deal with how cutting the bond again might affect her heart, later. If we survive.'

He was right, but how would Mina react? Alere would be going against her express wish. But Corin should have contacted her by now.

She closed her eyes and imagined the silver-gilt thread stretching through the yanstones to Mina. Nothing. She tried again, searching for that surge of belonging and intimacy; aching for the ooze of golden strength that came with it. Nothing.

'I can't, Kett! I can't reach her at all. I thought both of us wearing the stones would do it.' She gripped his arm. 'What if it was something to do with Nasra or Rohne? I only used telepathy for the first time when I met them. Maybe it takes a true xintou to act as a catalyst for me and Mina?'

'I'll open Mistress Li's cell. Maybe she can help.'

Alere focussed again on her sister. Still nothing. She sucked a slow breath and got a grip on panic before it spiralled out of control.

'Alli.' Kett's soft call came. He stood beside Mistress Li's bed. He gestured Alere in. 'I don't think she'll make a trip through the storm drains. She's barely alive. She's asked for you. I'll keep watch by the door. Keep trying Corin and Mina.'

Alere sank onto the cot's edge and took the knotted, emaciated hand in hers. It felt like sticks wrapped in paper. Seeing her mentor's wasted face Alere bit her lip to prevent a cry of distress. Upset as she was at Mistress Li's manipulations and scheming, the woman had shown Alere great compassion and patience over her years in the House.

'Mistress,' she whispered, 'I'm here. What do you need?'

Mistress Li opened rheumy brown eyes, smiling faintly. 'You came for us.'

'Of course.' Alere stood. 'We'll get you out of here. The House needs you. Mamlakah needs you. You have to help me stop Nasra.'

She worked an arm beneath Mistress Li's shoulders and eased her upright on the bed. The scent of stale urine wafted from her stained robe. Mistress Li drew long, rattling breaths that seemed to afford her little oxygen and considerable pain.

'No, child. I'm not the one this Jundom needs any more. You are.' She coughed again, reached out shakily and patted Alere's cheek. 'I tried so hard to keep things as they were – as they had been for five hundred years – but I've failed. I haven't the strength to fight any longer. I must pass it on to someone younger and stronger. Here.'

She reached into her robe, scrabbling under the silk. Finally, she pulled forth a long golden chain and a pendant. Alere gasped as the light caught and the pendant flared into familiar, silver-gilt flames that flickered off the prison's coarse stone and smooth metal walls.

Set in a starburst of meteoric iron, a single, huge yanstone glittered between Mistress Li's gnarled fingers. Far bigger than any stone Alere had ever seen; palm-sized, it glowed with a dancing inner fire both hypnotic and strangely repelling.

Mistress Li dragged it over her head and held it out. 'This is the *shenhilya* – the spirit jewel. It has belonged to the Mistress since the House was founded five hundred years ago. We've always known about the yanstones. We know that combining them with meteoric iron unlocks a latent xintou gene or enhances an active one. This belonged to my ancestress, Kya, the first Mistress.' She stroked the stone with a lover's touch. 'The *shenhilya* is what unlocked the Edwards sisters' abilities. Through it, the Mistress can keep her xintou in control, ensure they stay on the right path. Communicate even over vast distances. With this yanstone, we have kept the colony stable and secure for five hundred years.' She coughed wetly.

Alere put her hands behind her back. 'I don't want it. I'm not Mistress and I don't want to be.' The old woman's legendary skills and her knowledge of the Jundom now had an ordinary explanation.

Mistress Li scowled and thrust the stone at Alere again.

'I don't want it!' Alere said.

'Oh, stop it, girl! I've told you often enough – important over what you want. This is more important than what you want. Of course you're not Mistress. But the shenhilya *must* be kept out of Nasra's hands and you're the only person I trust to do that. I was strong enough to prevent being searched when they brought me here. But I'm too weak, now. Take it!'

The full force of her authority and mind went into the command. Alere reached out, involuntarily, to grasp the chain. She nearly dropped it when she touched the metal. Even through the gold chain, the psychic connection clawed its way under her skin and burrowed into her mind like a parasite. Fire crackled beneath her skin and wormed its way into her flesh.

Bloodied iron and bitter ashes lingered in her mouth.

Great power existed here, but also many, many years of deviousness, ambition and twisted thinking. It contained the sum of all the women who'd worn it, their determination to keep Xintou House in control, to stabilise the colony. She shuddered then hesitated, staring at the stone's hypnotic, seductive glow. And yet…there was, at least, a connection. More powerful, even, than what she'd had with the Koh-Lin stones.

Perhaps, with this stone, she wouldn't need Mina at all. She itched to hold it. To feel again the xintou power pulse in her blood. But baulked at the sense of sheer, latent power buried in its gleaming lights.

She shook herself uneasily and tore a piece of cloth from the bed's thin blanket. Mistress Li was right in one thing: Nasra should not be allowed to have this sort of power. It would make her unassailable.

This stone, in Nasra's hands, would turn her – or Rohne – into exactly the tyrant predicted by Celia, Valera, and Qara.

She eyed Mistress Li. 'Is this why you've forbidden the copper-wire communications devices?' She frowned. 'And Miner House extracting iron from rocks and soil? Because you used this to control everything? Are you really so afraid of the future, Mistress?'

Wrapping the stone, she thrust it deep into a jacket pocket. Her fingers brushed something else heavy and metallic. Ah. The gold poison ring.

Mistress Li gave a breathy chuckle. 'Now you sound like Nasra. It's not change that's to be feared, girl, it's iron. If you understood your old Earth history, you'd know that most of their pollution and destruction came from the ready access to iron and the combustible products of ancient life. It drove industry, wars and death for thousands of years. I and my ancestors swore we would not let that happen to this colony.' She gripped Alere's wrist. 'Now you must use it to stop Nasra or everything we've worked for will be destroyed.'

'I can't, Mistress! I've lost my powers. We had to cut the Bond between Mina and I. Can you use that stone to reconnect us?'

'You cut the Bond?' A hint of the woman's old fire flashed across her wizened face. 'Stupid girl. The *shenhilya* is not enough on its own. Not against Nasra. And I can't re-Bond you without Nasra feeling it. Not here. You must find a way. It's vital!'

'But—' Alere began. A noise from beyond the door caught her ear. Kett signalled. Someone approached.

'Mistress.' Alere helped the old woman to her feet. 'We have to go. Someone's coming. Please. Walk.'

Mistress Li hobbled through the cell door to Kett. When he bowed to her, she smiled.

'Bring me that chair, boy, and put it here.' She pointed to a place before the empty cells and in full view of the guardroom door. Anyone entering would see the chair first. Kett obeyed.

Mistress Li eased herself into the seat with a popping of joints and a grunt of pain. Her nails dug into Alere's arm. Once seated, she straightened her spine, staring at the door with a reasonable semblance of her old authority.

'Now leave.' She flicked her fingers at the secret door then clutched at Kett's arm and gave him a piercing scrutiny. 'Wait. You need to know your place in this. Everything has been for a reason. *I* influenced Radan's Shangwei when Hanna made her kin-child laws and your life was in danger twenty years ago. *I* arranged for you to be placed in Weishi House. Then *I* picked you ten years ago to protect this child. You have discharged your duty well. I release you from your obligation to me. You are free to choose your own path now – once this little mess is cleared, of course.' She patted his arm and released him. 'Now go.'

'You—' He stiffened, the muscles in his jaw jumping. 'Why didn't you just *stop* the gouri laws? You had the power. Your Xintou could have prevented all of this.'

Her eyes narrowed. 'Don't you dare judge me, boy. You have no right. I did what was best for the Jundom.'

'I have every right, Mistress. And I owe you nothing.' He grabbed Alere's wrist. 'Let's go, Alli.'

The old woman ignored him and beckoned Alere close. Alere twisted free of his grip with an apologetic look. His jaw set, Kett stalked through the hidden exit. Alere bent toward Mistress Li.

'Listen closely, child.' Mistress Li scowled at her and coughed, each breath shallow and fetid with illness. 'It is Nasra who comes and you're not ready to confront her. I cannot best her, but I can hold her here and give you time to escape. Do *not* waste my sacrifice.'

'But,' Alere tried again, 'I don't know what to do! I'll never be a match for her. She's had years of training. Plus she has those erheyi girls. How do I beat them?'

'Stupid girl! Why do you think I chose you for the House? I've been training you for this very day. Re-Bond with Mina. Use that stone and the Koh-Lin stones.' Mistress Li frowned at her. 'There's one more thing. Twenty years ago, I knew something stirred against me, but I couldn't tell who or what it was. I thought Nasra dead. All the major Seeings of the last century have pointed to this time. The time of the erheyi. When a tyrant of unstoppable power will rise. Nasra.'

Her feeble grip tightened. 'But there were hints of those that could stop it as well. Every House Mistress has waited for some sign. As soon as the Koh-Lin Bonded Xintou told me of Sura's pregnancy with twins carrying the gene, I knew the time must be close.'

Someone rapped on the outer door, demanding entrance. Alere straightened, her heart pounding.

Mistress Li scowled and pulled her close again. '*I* nurtured the idea for the kin-child laws in Hanna. I needed to make sure Sura would be hidden from my enemies, so I could protect you girls. *I* made sure Elmira went home to Gaton for the birth. I made sure she placed you in the House. My only mistake was in underestimating Nasra's ambition and cunning. And Elmira's loyalty to her mother.'

Stunned, Alere said nothing, too horrified by the implications to even speak.

'I've been observing you, using the *shenhilya*, the last two months, Alere.' Mistress Li's fingernails dug into Alere's arm. 'Control your tendency to get emotionally involved and you can do what needs to be done. With that pendant – and Mina's help – *you* can best Nasra.'

She drew a slow breath and straightened. 'You owe me your life. Repay me by defeating those who would destroy the House. Now go!'

CHAPTER TWENTY-SIX

CORIN

'I have a bad feeling about this,' Corin said in a quiet aside to Jarran as they cantered toward the Selb. The camp was not the disorganised chaos he'd expected and that, for some reason, disturbed him.

Northeast of the city and spread out in neat rows, hundreds of campfires poured smoke and the scent of cooking meats into the cool spring air. Mingled with that was the less pleasant scent of sewage from the latrine area to the west. The crackling of flames, the buzz of thousands of conversations, the clink of weapons-training, the regular clang of smith-work, and the neigh of horses and che-ma, all added to the overwhelming sense of community and cohesion about this group.

Behind Corin's party, the city gates creaked open and rank upon rank of Hassan's junren filed out onto open ground, just visible as a growing black smudge against the city's high, golden walls. Black and silver pennants snapped in the light spring breeze. Bronze weapons flashed. Ceramics gleamed orange in the rising sun. The chink of bridle and bit resonated across the field, audible even at a distance.

Yet the Selb paid no attention. Not a head lifted, not a hand shifted, not a weapon moved. They went about their morning routine as though they intended to live in this campsite forever.

Corin regarded the nearest with interest. All the Selb wore variations on the same clothing: loose, long grey trous and a high-collared black, longsleeved shirt. Most carried double-bladed war axes of various sizes. A surprising percentage were steel-bladed. Where had they found so much iron?

He fingered the silver-metal axe pendant from Liu Gray.

'A really bad feeling about this,' Corin muttered to Jarran. 'Keep close to Mina and get her back to the House if you see even the slightest hint of anything going suilie'

Jarran acknowledged and urged his horse alongside Mina's.

At the sound of rhythmic stomping and shouts, Corin rose in his stirrups and peered across the camp. In a roped-off square of level ground, a dozen pairs of men and women went through training drills – a series of strikes, blocks and counterstrikes – with precise skill. The power and technique behind the drills spoke of years of practice. In another area, less-skilled combatants took lessons from masters dressed in black. Although many must be untrained ex-slaves, clearly many were not.

These people had supposedly come together for the first time, from all over the four Jundoms. Why did this camp feel less like a rabble of extremist radicals and more like a disciplined army?

Corin kneed his mount forward until he rode between Mina and Tali. 'You two alright?'

Mina's face was white, but she nodded, unspeaking. Tali wound the reins around her fingers, shifted in her saddle and squinted back over her shoulder at Hassan's army and the distant city. She turned forward, sitting straight and stiff. Below the veil her lips pressed together and her throat worked.

'I just want to get this done. I don't like this.'

'You and me, both.'

In the camp's epicentre, a large, tanned-leather khiba stood tall above all others. A small flag fluttered on the top: a grey double-bladed axe on a black background. Forty or so men and women knelt in silence before the khiba. All were dressed in the grey trous and black shirts, but with hoods over their heads. Beside every bent knee lay an identical steel axe. Each supplicant wore the distinctive band of braided black silk that Weishi House traditionally reserved for *jijin,* xiongshou masters. Corin was too far away to see the city colours twined into the black. Were they all from one city? It seemed unlikely.

A wave of silence followed as they approached the central khiba. People rose from their campfires, weapons ready, but with heads courteously bowed to Tali and her gold silk. The silence spread, then became a vast susurration as the words 'xintou' and 'erheyhi' swept along in its wake.

Mina hung her head, fiddling with her horse's mane. Jarran murmured into her ear. She flushed and straightened. With that hint of false confidence, she appeared more like Lianna Koh-Lin, Games champion.

'Hang in there, Mina,' Corin said. 'Remember we're just here to make them get safely out of Hassan's reach and joined with Yasmin. Let me do the talking.'

As they reached the outermost row of people kneeling before the khiba, one man rose and held his palms out. Over his shirt and trous he wore open, black robes, severe in their styling, but muddied at the hem. Around his throat a small, double-bladed axe pendant of some silvery metal gleamed dully. His wrist bore not only the black shuriken tattoo, faded and softened to blue by age, but also the black and silver braided ribbon of Madina Weishi House. His eyes were the colour steel and just as hard. His scalp was shaved bald.

'Molian.' He didn't wait for their reply. 'I am Zand. Our master requires you to wait until this ceremony is complete. Then he will see you. Do not request an alteration to that arrangement or you will not be granted an audience.'

Zand. Why was that name familiar? Who was this 'master'? Kett's question about the Selb's leadership came back to Corin. He was right: someone must have coordinated this. Corin shook his head. Lack of sleep had thickened his brain to sludge. He was missing something vital. It nagged at him like a splinter under the skin.

Whoever the Selb leader was, he or she needed to be open to the idea of joining with Yasmin's army. Otherwise, skilled as these people appeared to be, they would throw their lives away pointlessly if they confronted Hassan today with such disparate numbers. The challenge would be in persuading them to leave. The mark of a fanatic was righteousness. If the Selb were convinced they were on a crusade for Alere and Mina, they might be difficult to dissuade.

Unable to think of an alternative to waiting, Corin nodded.

A thin, tall man, his pale eyes burning with the fervour of a true obsessive, rose at the front. He wore plain black and the axe pendant, though it was larger and had the polished gleam of steel. His wrist bore the Weishi House tattoo. How had so many of this order infiltrated Weishi House without coming to Master Anh's attention?

The thin man's dark hair was shaved close to his scalp, leaving a shadowy stubble over his elongated skull. But a dark beard grew to his chest. From full, pink lips fell a chant in lilting old Mandrin. Corin tried to follow it, but only caught the occasional word.

Tali edged her horse alongside Corin's and whispered a translation.

'He's saying it's their destiny to free the world of tyranny. To set it back on the true way. That they must, as they always have, cleanse the world of those who would oppose the truth. That unworthiness can only be removed by steel.' She rose in her stirrups and sank back again. 'They're bringing out a prisoner. Someone he says is a spy and who does not walk the true way.'

'Ah,' Corin said, bile rising. 'Perhaps now would be a good time to look away, Mina. You too, Tali. This is going to get a little messy.'

A man was led out, struggling and cursing against his bonds as he was forced to his knees before the crowd. Corin gritted his teeth. The man was, indeed, a spy of sorts. One that worked for Houlia. A harmless sort who earned his main bread from selling flowers in the market square before the Alcazar.

'Can't we *do* anything?' Mina's strained voice reached him.

Corin muttered, 'Not if we want to get out of this alive. Fanatics aren't reasonable people. Just don't watch.'

A large, bearded man rose, holding a steel-bladed axe in thick fingers. He raised it high and the spy was forced to bend double before him. An unpleasant, ululating cry from the thin Selb leader rose with it, followed by weird, almost-inhuman laughter that carried no humour and gave no joy. An unpleasantly-organic sound followed, then a double thud as head and body fell to the damp earth. Mina gave a choked cry and covered her mouth, staring at her horse's mane. Tali muttered something comprehensively rude.

The fanatic said a few more things then bowed to the assembled crowd and dismissed them. Followed by Zand, he stalked over to Corin's party, expression solemn and fingers clasped over his stomach. As he approached, he gave them a cursory, almost disgusted glance.

'You will follow me. I will take you to the Master.' He strode toward the camp's outskirts, back the way they'd come, his black over-robe flapping about his booted ankles. Two men, watchful and carrying the ubiquitous axe, followed close behind.

Irritated and more than a little perturbed, Corin nudged his horse and the others followed suit. As they passed back through the massed Selb, their guide inspected each firesite, calling out instructions in a soft, flat voice. At each site, those encamped there leapt, without question, to do his bidding.

The more Corin saw of these people, the more dubious he was about enfolding them into Yasmin's army. Either their obvious fighting skill would be useful, or their fixation with worthiness would make them a destructive liability in the middle of an army who did not believe as they did.

As they passed the last campsite, Corin surveyed the horizon all around.

Thunderheads piled in the northwest, dragging a cool breeze from the south and threatening more rain later in the day. The same breeze threw dust and he coughed, squinting southeast. Something just beyond the line of trees, half a gongli or so in that direction, stirred dust. Possibly a herd of runiu, the main herdbeast in this area. The dust could cause a problem for both armies if it got too thick.

To the southwest, Hassan's troops marched closer. Close enough now that it was almost possible to pick out individual men in the lineup. Still, no-one in the Selb camp even bothered to look in their direction. Could the Selb be privy to some information; something meaning they wouldn't have to do battle with Hassan at all? But what?

The sun's position said it must be close to the hour and almost time to try and reach Alere for a progress report. Possibly another few minutes. Perhaps she'd encountered something to shed light on this.

A quick check on the two women showed Mina deep in quiet conversation with Jarran. Tali stared straight back at Corin, solemn behind the shimmering gold veil. He eyed her in question. She looked away, worrying at her lower lip.

Their guide and the xiongshou, Zand, stopped. Zand pointed wordlessly in the direction of a dozen horsemen, who stood in the middle of the bluegrasslands, facing Hassan's marching army.

Evidently assuming their job to be complete, the two Selb and their guards spun and hurried back to the camp.

Corin nudged his mount on.

Two horsemen sat slightly apart from the others. One – large and bearded – threw back his head, laughing. He clapped the second man – slighter and wearing a dark, hooded cloak – on the shoulder. The other ten horsemen waited a few paces away, in the attitude of weishi or mharebi; armoured and armed.

Corin slipped his thumbs beneath the suede covers over his sword and dagger pommels, stroking the yanstones' smooth, warm surfaces. He lowered his wards and stretched a thought toward the city, seeking Alere's mind.

Just as he touched the smooth black of her wards, the riders ahead turned. Mina gasped and stiffened. Tali gave a strangled little cry.

Thunder rumbled underfoot and overhead.

'Ah!' The bearded man inclined his head in casual greeting. 'You're here at last. Mina, so lovely to see you again. Won't you introduce me to your friends?'

His teeth gleamed white against swarthy skin. Muddy, blue-grey eyes were almost invisible beneath thick brows and heavy eyelids. Wrapped in a xiao-bear fur cloak and seated on the largest horse Corin had ever seen, the man was massive without a hint of fat or sloth about him. His hands were huge and clasped an axe so large it seemed unlikely any man could even lift it. Yet it bore the marks of use.

'J-Jada,' Mina stammered, her cheeks so blanched she must be close to passing out.

The man bowed in the saddle, leather armour creaking. He beamed. It was the smile of a man who knew he held all the advantage.

'Jada Marin-Kin at your service.' He gestured to the hooded man. 'And, of course, most of you know Rohne, my son.'

Rohne flipped his hood back, opening his black and silver-edged cloak to expose the gold silk robe he wore below. His amber eyes glittered with secret amusement.

'Khara,' Corin muttered.

CHAPTER TWENTY-SEVEN

ALERE

Alere hesitated. Someone pushed at the cell doors. Mistress Li frowned and waved her away. Alere snatched out the heavy gold poison ring and thrust it onto Mistress Li's knotted finger.

'Just in case,' she whispered. 'It's coated in si-xing. If you can kill Nasra now, you should.'

Mistress Li's lined mouth stretched in a thin smile. 'You always did want to take the shortcuts, girl. But I can see the sense in this one. Now, go.'

Alere was just a few steps from the secret exit when the main prison door pushed open and the weishi bodies rolled aside. She froze in a shadowed corner. With the hidden door closed, Nasra wouldn't find Kett and the others unless Alere betrayed their location.

Well! Nasra's mental voice was a shock, her anger an almost-physical force inside Alere's mind.

Alere checked her wards and found them solid. How was she able to hear the woman? Rohne had said only xintou could hear his mother if she wasn't touching them. Could the new pendant in her pocket have something to do with it? Had it re-activated her powers? Could she reach Mina?

No, it was too risky. Nasra might hear her thought.

I must admit, old woman, I am impressed. Where are they? Nasra's tone was cold and angry, but held overtones of worry.

When Mistress Li didn't reply, Nasra made a noise of frustration, snapped her fingers at a weishi and touched his arm.

Alere couldn't hear her mind-voice. Why? What did Nasra do differently?

He spoke to his men. 'Search here and the whole castle. Close the gates. They can't have got far. If you don't find the prisoners, you die, understood?'

A murmur of assent rippled through his men. Six entered the room, fanning out to search the cells and the adjoining rooms. Too many for Alere to take alone. She needed to hide. The corner in which she stood was no more than a niche, an odd shape caused by trying to fit square cells into the Alcazar tower's circular base. Shadowed and out of Nasra's line of sight, it would still take only a quick pass with a mel-oil lantern to reveal it.

The guards searched the other rooms and Alere used their sounds to cover her own. Pressing her back against one wall and her feet against the other, she wall-walked upward, toward the timber-beamed, web-infested ceiling. Her back slipped against the smooth metal surface. She splayed her hands, trying to get better purchase. Her feet caught and scraped against the sandstone of the other wall. She inched upward, muscles burning, legs trembling.

Nasra reappeared, walking around Mistress Li's chair, her focus on the old woman. Alere stopped. She could still just see the two women. A weishi passed beneath without looking up.

You know you can't hold against me. Nasra raised her gold veil and sneered. *Your wards are weak. You are weak. It's only a matter of time before we have the prisoners back.* She gave a silent, hissing laugh, more triumphant than amused. *I was so frightened of you when I was a child. I was four when I came to the House, terrified. My parents sold me to you, like a slave. Do you remember?*

Nasra dragged the chair and the old woman backward, bringing her into the glow of one of the wall-lanterns. Now Alere saw both women's faces as Nasra crouched. Mistress Li kept her attention fixed on her own hands, relaxed in her lap, ignoring her tormentor. The gold poison ring gleamed in the lamplight. Her hollowed cheeks were tinged pink over the parchment colour of illness, giving her the illusion of health. A knowing smile played on her lined mouth.

You could have treated me with compassion and love. Nasra spat at the Mistress' feet. *But all you cared about was making me conform to your precious ideals. And I, stupid child that I was, tried so hard. I gave almost forty years of my life trying to please you. Then you threw me aside for my own daughter! The second she was old enough you replaced me as Xintou to the Ma-Safras because I didn't agree with everything you taught. 'Clarity, stability, responsibility, and compassion'.* Nasra sneered.

What a joke. Stability is the only one you've ever been interested in. Now you've lost that. I run your House and this Jundom, too. My son is Bonded to the Jun First and together we will change this backward world for the better.

Mistress Li's eyes flew to Nasra's, horror in their cloudy depths.

Nasra's lips stretched wide in an unpleasant smile. *Now I have your attention. Yes, my son, the Xintou. Did his existence slip past you? Oh dear, how sad. Since I left the House, I have learned so much about xintou and what we can do. More than you've ever dreamed of. I can speak telepathically to anyone, any time – even if they are warded.* Her lips stretched wide in false sweetness. *And, I can do this.*

Mistress Li clutched at her skull. She gave a groan, slumping in the chair. A line of spittle slid down her chin. Alere bit her lip to hold back a cry of protest. Her thighs burned and her heart pounded.

Your wards are useless, aren't they? Nasra said softly. *All these years you've been teaching your girls to ward and yet I've learned how to pierce them with one thought. If I keep going, I can break your Inners as well. Drag out all the things you're afraid of. What do you think will happen to your precious xintou once my erheyi girls use this technique on them? Do you want to watch them all go mad with their own fears? Kill each other in a frenzy of hate?*

Nasra straightened, tossed her long auburn plait back over her shoulder, and paced around the chair once more. *Maybe I won't kill all of them, though. Maybe the younger ones haven't been so brainwashed as to be useless. I'm sure, with the proper demonstration of my powers – and Rohne's – they can be convinced to join me. What do you think of that?*

'I think…' Mistress Li's voice was breathy and rough '…that you're underestimating both me and my students. Your arrogance was always your biggest flaw, Nasra. But if you believe you can stop the inevitable from happening to your son, then your arrogance has exceeded even my expectations.'

Nasra slapped the old woman across the cheek, her face a mask of fury. *You will not speak of him. You would have killed him before birth. And for no reason. Male xintou are not the threat you teach. Not if you know how to control them.*

Mistress Li lifted her eyes. 'As I said, your arrogance will be your undoing. And his. What do you think he'll do when he finds out the truth of what will happen to him? Do you think he'll kiss and forgive you for your deception? Do you think he'll keep letting you control him? Have the headaches started yet?'

Shut up! Nasra slapped her again and this time Mistress Li's teeth were stained red when she grimaced.

Alere held her breath. Her arms trembled. Her feet and calves cramped. Her skin, clammy and cold, slipped on the metal, boots scraping on sandstone.

Nasra's brows drew together and her head snapped around. She took a step in the direction of Alere's hiding place. Alere held her breath, hoping Mistress Li would use the gold ring, but Nasra was just out of reach. The claw-like fingers of Mistress Li's other hand clutched at Nasra's wrist.

'Oh no,' Mistress Li muttered. 'We're not done yet, girl. You think you can win? I'm not your enemy. I never was. *You* are, you stupid girl. You're afraid you really are worthless; unlovable; and you're trying to prove you're not.'

She smiled again, pityingly. 'Your parents didn't sell you to me. Your muteness triggered your xintou gene early and your parents couldn't cope. You *murdered* them in a fit of uncontrollable rage as a child. Burnt out their minds.'

Nasra gasped. Then her eyes narrowed. *You're lying. I don't remember that.*

Mistress Li shrugged. 'I wiped it from your mind. But perhaps I was too compassionate in letting you live. I thought you could be rehabilitated. My mistake. You're still an angry child, lashing out at me for daring to discipline. But, by all means, try me, and we shall see. I still carry secrets, girl.' Her eyes glittered. 'Secrets I'll take to the grave. Secrets about how to cure your boy, even.'

You will *tell me.* Nasra bent over Mistress Li, her fingers curling into fists, her gaze focussed on the older woman.

Mistress Li gave a sobbing cry but never took her focus off Nasra. Her right hand rose, shaking. The gold ring glinted. Nasra caught the thin wrist and glanced contemptuously at the poison ring.

You must be desperate to think you could touch me with that. And I don't believe your lies. You know nothing.

'There's that arrogance again.' Mistress Li straightened in her seat. She sent Alere a quick, flickering look. *Go.* The single word pierced Alere's Outer wards.

Li tugged her arm free and dragged the ring's poisoned spikes down her own weathered cheek. The ring left two bloody scratches on Li's skin. She bared her gore-smeared teeth again and chuckled.

'It wasn't meant for you.' She slumped in the seat, breathing in quick gasps.

Nasra gave a strange, mewling cry, and tugged at the skeletal fingers locked around her wrist. Mistress Li cackled. Her bloody grin widened and she clung to the younger woman. Nasra glared at her. Mistress Li screwed up her dry-paper mouth in a pained grimace. Bloody froth bubbled at her lips. Her eyes rolled back. She released Nasra's arm and collapsed in on herself, convulsing.

Alere gasped, her grip on the wall failing. She slid to the floor, managed to get her feet down and collapsed into a roll as she hit the hard stone. An alarm cry went up and two weishi plunged into the room. With little space in which to swing a sword, Alere drew her dagger and a throwing knife. She deflected an overhead strike from one weishi. The steel dagger plunged through alzin, up under the second man's ribs, into his heart.

Nasra rounded on Alere, her face flushed and eyes hard.

Alere yanked the dagger free of the weishi's chest. She changed her grip on the throwing knife in her other hand and flicked it. Nasra swayed to one side. The knife flew past. It clanged off the wall and clattered to the floor behind her. The xintou sent Alere a scornful look that made her strengthen her wards.

To no avail. Nasra's drill-like intensity bored into her Outers. Pain blossomed, threatening to obliterate rational thought. How could she feel it, without her powers? Had the *shenhilya* done something to her mind? Alere gasped as the pain intensified. It would be only moments before the woman broke through. What had taken Celia several minutes to achieve would take Nasra only a few seconds.

Gritting her teeth, Alere blocked another strike from the remaining weishi and kicked him in the stomach to shove him off. Desperate, she snatched out her other throwing knife. Before the weishi closed again, she threw it at the lamp burning on the wall just beside Nasra. It punctured the mel-oil reservoir and sprayed the liquid over Nasra's back. Heat from the flame set the oil afire as it arced through the air. It caught on her robe's delicate gold silk. Flames leapt, licking up the cloth to Nasra's head.

The attack on Alere's wards ceased and she sucked a shaky breath.

Hissing, Nasra slapped at her clothing. Ornate toggles popped as she tore at the silk. Flames danced in her hair. The weishi facing Alere hesitated, looking at his shunu. Alere drove her dagger into his throat and he dropped without a sound. Mistress Li folded to the ground, her eyes open and blank. Her flesh shrivelled to waxen lifelessness as her essence slipped away. Four more weishi swarmed into the room, their focus on Nasra. They stripped the burning outer robe from her body and threw it to the ground.

Alere slipped through the secret door, closed it and slid two thick bolts into place. The stench of burning cloth and hair seeped beneath the panel. Through the thick timber, Nasra's muted grunts of anger were audible. A weishi yelled an order to find Alere and the prisoners. It wouldn't take them long to work out there must be a hidden exit.

She leaned her back on the door for a moment, drawing silent, shuddering breaths. Her knees and hands shook uncontrollably. Tears of rage and helplessness clouded her vision and tore at her throat.

Mistress Li was responsible for the kin-child laws. Responsible for mishandling Nasra as a child. Responsible for every gouri tragedy dogging her friends and family these last twenty years. All because she wanted Alere hidden away, to be moulded into some sort of agent of vengeance against the House's enemies.

Yet now Li was dead. By her own hand. Why? To stop Nasra discovering a cure for Rhone buried in Li's Inners? Had that even been the truth?

There was no way of knowing and Alere was left to deal with the aftermath of Li's deceptions, alone.

Kett appeared from the darkness and pulled her into a kiss that spoke eloquently of fear and relief.

She pressed against him, trembling. 'I can't believe she's dead. She sacrificed herself to save me. But the things she's done…'

'Li's death is nothing to cry over, Alli,' he murmured, grim. 'After what she just told me, I'm glad she's gone. I never understood why she instructed the Bonded Xintou to enforce those gouri kin-child laws. Made the Juns kill their own kin-children. I still don't understand. The world is better off without her. And without everyone who caused those laws in the first place.'

Alere broke their embrace, unable to look him in the eye.

CHAPTER TWENTY-EIGHT

CORIN

Corin tried again to connect with Alere. Her wards held firm. He glanced at Tali. Her cheek was pale, her eyes stark. She met his gaze, briefly. Would she be willing to stand against Rohne? He tried reaching her through the yanstones, but she was warded and refused to acknowledge his attempt.

'You didn't think you could use the Selb against me, did you Corin?' Rohne said pleasantly. 'Or that your little pendant would protect you?' He pointed to the double-bladed axe Corin had borrowed from Liu. 'I should thank you, and Alere, for freeing so many from slavery and bringing them all together. They might not be trained yet, but it will make defeating Yasmin's army so much easier.'

'Why should they fight for you?' Jarran growled. 'They've come to fight for Alere and Mina. To get Hassan off the throne.'

Jada Marin-kin chuckled, deep in his barrel chest. He reached inside his coarse shirt and pulled out a gold necklace. On the end of it dangled a small, steel, double-bladed axe.

'The Selb fight under my command. They have these last forty years. Alere called them to action, but I allowed it.' He slapped Rohne on the shoulder. 'They answer to me and I answer to this lad and his mother. And he's destined to change history. Guide humanity into a better world.'

'And what part do the Selb play in this grand plan?' Corin asked. 'You seem to have a lot of xiongshou on board. How much did you have to pay them?' Ah! Zand, that's where he'd heard the name. The signatory on the kill contracts for Kett and Alere. Weishi House's second in command.

'True loyalty cannot be bought, it is earned.' Jada smiled. 'The Selb have been the hidden army of Xintou House for five hundred years. The Mistress commands us. Our job is to work in the shadows when the House's talk and diplomacy fails to keep the world on the true path.' He shrugged. 'But now even the House has strayed too far. Mistress Li has failed. So, the House has a new Mistress.' He indicated the black army of the Selb behind them. 'And the world sees us, at last.'

Thunder rolled across the plains again. Corin tensed. Dust rose behind the trees just a few hundred paces away.

Jada flicked the reins on his huge black destrier and faced his captives. He spread his hands, holding both armies within his grasp.

'The time of erheyi is here.' He swept his arms even wider. 'But it's not about Alere and Mina. They've just been the spark. Nasra has planned for twenty-five years for this day. Erheyi is about the twins Nasra created. With them, and our steel to cleanse the unworthy, Nasra and Rohne will rule this Jundom and bring it back to the true path.'

'The Jundom won't bow down so easily,' Jarran replied. 'The people are smarter than that. They won't suffer a tyrant for long.'

Jada and Rohne both laughed. Jada wholeheartedly, Rohne with an ironic chuckle.

'You're a fool if you think that, boy,' Jada said. 'They've *been* under a tyrant for the last five hundred years. Mistress Li and her predecessors. The people are tired of stagnation and economic ruin. Do you really think they'll reject us, when we offer a bright future and more iron than they've ever seen in their lives? We're more like a benevolent dictatorship.'

'What's so benevolent about slaughtering thousands of people who don't believe as you do?' Jarran snapped back.

Jada's expression segued into the patronising. 'It weeds out the most strident dissenters and the rest are as herdbeasts. People want strong leadership. Left to themselves they flounder in miserable uncertainty. They don't want to have to think or decide. They'll conform. Then we'll have true freedom, true progress and true stability.'

'Freedom!' Jarran blurted the word, jaw dropping.

Corin wished he could reach the man to shut him up. His naivete would get them all killed. Arguing with a fanatic was madness. A fanatic wouldn't just defend their point of view. They would obliterate not only the objector, but even the memory of the opposing view. They'd wipe out family, village, culture and history, until anyone remaining alive accepted their leadership out of purely-human fear.

It was the religious wars of old Earth all over again.

Gavon had been right. Right not to trust the Selb. Right that humans were all kinds of stupid when it came to this sort of thing.

'Now.' Rohne nodded to the ten weishi nearby. One of them levelled a two-shot crossbow at Corin. 'My mother would like to speak with all of you and Jarran has an appointment with a rather large steel blade tomorrow morning. Shall we go?'

He took the reins from Mina's lax grip. 'There's no point in warding against me, Mina. I've had access through your wards since we were children. Jarran, just relax and this will be easy.'

Both Mina and Jarran took long, slow blinks. Corin watched in helpless anger as the spark of intelligence drained from Mina's expression, leaving her passive. Jiche! Rohne must be controlling them again, as he had in Chengdu. His own private puppets. Maybe giving Saric's blowpipe back had been a bad idea after all?

Alere. He tried her again. Still warded. What was she doing? Had she succeeded?

'Oh, Corin?' Rohne added casually. 'If you're wondering about Alere and Kett's attempt on the Alcazar then you can relax as well. My mother was waiting for them. I guarantee they are either dead or captured by now. But don't worry, you'll be with them, shortly.' He smiled in a friendly, easy way that made Corin's blood chill.

Corin forced a laugh. 'I wouldn't hold your breath. People have a habit of underestimating her.'

A frown flickered across Rohne's face and his eyes glazed for a moment. Contacting Nasra? Gaisi! Corin stifled a groan. When would he learn to shut up? He tried for Alere again. A measure of logic seeped through his fear. She couldn't be dead. Her wards were intact. But she could be imprisoned and he wouldn't know. Why didn't she lower her wards? Nasra's doing, somehow?

Another, louder, roll of thunder reverberated; continued. Jada straightened in the saddle. He scanned the line of trees not far away to the southeast.

Almost time.

Making a quick decision, Corin caught Tali's attention. He lifted his little finger. She sucked a quick breath, flickered a glance at Rohne, then nodded and lowered her Outer wards.

Be ready, Corin said.

For what?

A wall of men on horseback burst from the treeline. Galloping full-tilt toward them, sword raised and black-gold cloak flying, Kennor Han-Asad led a hundred or more junren in a screaming assault.

Corin grinned. Now there was a chance.

A frown twitched Jada's thick brows together. He waved three times. A warning cry went up from the Selb encampment and dozens of footsoldiers hastened to help their master. But Kennor was closer than the Selb army. The ten Selb already on the field turned in disciplined order and surrounded Rhone and Jada.

If Kennor could just keep Jada and Rohne occupied, Corin could get Mina and Jarran to safety.

A face appeared in the line of men riding with Kennor.

Tren. Farima's weishi.

Corin swore. The man was Selb and Kennor didn't know. How many of the Han-Asad junren Tren led were also Selb? This could go horribly suilie. As though it wasn't, already.

'Get out of here, Tali!' he yelled, hoping she'd obey. If she didn't, he had no way of protecting her. His priority had to be Jarran and Mina. More warriors ran from the Selb encampment. A black crossbow bolt whistled overhead, aimed at Kennor. Kicking his mount, Corin ducked low and pushed his horse into Rohne's animal.

A second bolt impaled Corin's left thigh. He swore long and loud. His horse jumped in reaction and skittered sideways, barrelling into Jarran's mount. Corin snapped the bolt in half, gritting his teeth against the excruciating pain. He snatched at the reins to Jarran's horse. Turning his own animal in a full circle, he interposed himself between Jarran and the crossbowman.

Kennor's men, yelling and thundering, swept around the little group in a confusing, dust-driven melee. They hacked into the Selb, mowing them down. Corin's heart leapt.

If they were quick, it might just work.

Jada bared his teeth and unlimbered his axe. It glinted in the dusted-orange sunlight. He cleaved his first attacker with a single, one-handed blow to the neck. He jerked the blade free. Shoving through the chaos of riders, he struck down two more men. He wielded the axe with the consummate ease of a practiced warrior, slicing through alzin and limbs. Then he aimed his mount for Kennor Han-Asad.

Corin struck down a Selb with an overhead sword-cut to the neck. He yanked his blade free and slashed at another. Blood sprayed and the Selb cried out, clutching at his shoulder. He flicked a black steel throwing knife. Corin ducked but the blade took him in the arm. He wrenched it out and tucked it into his belt. Hopefully it wasn't poisoned.

Rohne pointed at one of Kennor's men. A leather strap from the junren's armour wound itself around his throat, strangling him. He dropped his ceramic sword and scrabbled at his neck. He gave a choked gurgle, his eyes bulging. His body sloughed to the ground, one foot in the stirrup, his face purple. The horse skittered away, dragging the body out of the skirmish.

A flutter of gold silk caught Corin's attention as he searched for Mina. He raised his weapon, expecting Rohne. But it was Tali's horse dancing beside Mina's. She held Mina's reins. Mina sat rigid, staring blankly. Tali swayed in the saddle. Rohne's horse pranced on the other side of Mina, with Rohne calmly astride and watching Tali. He seemed almost bored as they fought a silent war. Tali thrust her veil onto her forehead. Her expression was grim and frightened. Then she drew a shuddering breath, appearing calm again.

Rohne's self-satisfied smirk stretched into irritation. 'You can't win, girl. Even holding Mina and Jarran I'm stronger than you.'

She faltered and gasped. Rohne used her moment of distraction against her. Dropping Mina's reins, she clawed at her skull. With a cry she slumped forward over her horse's neck. Corin kneed his mount, reaching out to grab Mina's reins. The horse jumped away. Rohne casually collected the straps, sending Corin a mocking salute. He nudged his horse closer to Tali's and reached for her reins as well.

Tali yanked the dagger from its sheath on her calf and slashed wildly at Rohne. He hissed and snatched his arm back. Blood seeped through the gold silk. His eyes narrowed and Tali screamed, the knife falling to the dirt.

Gaisi! Corin hesitated. He couldn't get all three of his companions to safety. Jarran's horse tossed its head, tugging at the reins Corin held. He snatched Tali's reins and kneed his mount sideways. The movement sent jagged spears of pain through his thigh. Something warm and wet dribbled into his boot.

Corin's horse reared and struck at a Selb horseman with its hooves, knocking the man off. Corin clung grimly on as the animal tried to avoid the fallen man and whinnied in distress. The Selb rose and rushed at Corin, sword swinging for the horse's neck. Corin kneed the animal sideways and hacked at the attacker. His steel sheered through the man's shoulder and neck.

All around, screams swelled. A pitched battle raged between Kennor's men and the Selb. Kennor's men had the upper hand. Selb fell under the swing of ceramic swords. Corin grinned fiercely. Kennor, an expert swordsman, engaged Jada.

The movement of horses separated Corin, Tali and Jarran from Rohne and Mina. Tali still lay half-unconscious over her horse's neck. Corin yanked at her reins and turned, trying to keep Kennor in sight. The Jun Third exchanged three good blows with Jada, managing to score the raider across the arm. He swung again. Jada swayed back and let the strike slide by.

He hurled the huge axe. The steel embedded itself into Kennor's chest and the Jun fell back over his horse's rump. Blood sprayed from his lips. Jada leaned over and levered the blade free. Kennor toppled to the muddy ground and was trampled into unrecognisability beneath the hooves of his terrified horse.

Swearing, Corin checked on Tren. Kennor's weishi stood in his saddle, peering at where his Jun Third had fallen. He gave that weird, ululating cry and a dozen or more of Kennor's men rallied behind him. Grim-faced, they rounded on the remaining Han-Asad junren. Blades rose and fell. A reaping of good men and women. A harvest of blood.

Corin hurled the throwing knife he'd taken earlier. It took Tren full in the throat and he slumped over his horse's neck, clawing at the blade.

Too late. Within seconds the meagre forces sent by Farima and led by Kennor would be slaughtered. Corin's heart fell with the slain.

He half-rose in the stirrups. Mina was too far away. Rohne held her reins. Hard as it was, he had to leave Mina behind and trust Rohne still had enough feelings for her to keep her alive.

He wrenched his horse's head southeast and kicked it hard. Tali's mount leapt into a gallop just behind, with the xintou clinging to its mane. Jarran's horse sat back on its haunches and reared. The leather tore from Corin's grip, burning across his palm. Jarran fell to the mud, where he lay still, staring blankly at the sky.

Corin glanced back as his animal pounded away. Rohne dismounted, still holding Mina's reins. All around him lay the mangled bodies of Kennor's men, broken and lifeless in meaningless sacrifice. Kennor's gold-lined cloak glimmered in the muck. Rohne gestured to Jarran. The man rose to his feet, slowly, jerkily, like a machine-man from the legends of old Earth.

Corin cursed. Now he'd lost both of them.

His next conversation with Alere and Kett would not be pleasant.

Except that he had no reason to doubt Rohne's word. They were probably caught, imprisoned with the others in the Alcazar.

He galloped on, hot liquid pooling in his boot. The landscape took on an interesting shade of sepia and tilted at an alarming angle.

Hoofbeats thundered after him.

Tali or someone else?

CHAPTER TWENTY-NINE

ALERE

Alere paced the austere room, watching dust swirl in the last bloody rays of sunlight that filtered through the enormous, stained-glass, western window. She walked the length of the great dining hall of Xintou House, barely seeing the window's beauty. Serried ranks of tables and benches stood empty for the first time in five hundred years, the ghost of young women's laughter haunting the room.

'Are you sure we're safe here?' Rafi asked her again.

'Yes!' she snapped. Since Xintou House was now empty and abandoned – even by Nasra's men – it was, as Kett pointed out, both an ironic and unexpected place for them to hide. It still felt…strange.

'The others should be back now,' she muttered. It had been two hours since Corin and Mina must have met the Selb. But there was no news. Unease roiled in her stomach. Something was wrong. She knew it. Even without the connection to Mina.

Nothing could be done until news came back from Corin and the others. Without access to either Houlia's or Corin's spy network, they had no idea what had transpired on the battleground north of the city. Had the Selb escaped? She hadn't been able to lower her wards at the appointed time, and Corin hadn't contacted her since.

Nearby, Kett flipped a page and frowned. The sun sank a little lower and haloed his dark hair in red. He sat at one of the long student dining-tables, bent over the Koh-Lin journal. Beside him lay a second, battered, handwritten book, and a Mandrin-Common dictionary he'd found in the jumbled pile of books in the library.

Impatience gnawed at her. She sat opposite Kett, in the seat she'd previously occupied at mealtimes as a student. He continued to read, apparently oblivious to her anxiety.

'What *is* so fascinating in that thing?' She tapped the Koh-Lin journal. 'You've told me everything in there. Col was a male xintou who went mad. Kya and Bree Edwards came back to the House and imposed the no-males and no twins rules. Their goal was to keep the Judom stable. What else is there? Shouldn't we be planning how to find Corin and the others? Or planning an assault on the Alcazar to stop Hassan's madness?'

He folded the book shut and slid it aside. He picked up the second, tattered journal and touched the ragged tears where pages were missing from the middle.

'This is the one Tali found. An account written by Yera, Kya's daughter. I was hoping it would shed some light on a few things in the other one. But all I can be sure of is an order for the House Mistress to watch for the appearance of someone very important.'

Alere swallowed hard, hearing an echo of Mistress Li's words.

Kett drummed his fingers on the tabletop and frowned. He flickered a quick look at Alere then went back to staring at the closed book. She grasped his wrist.

'What?'

'There's also a passage I asked Tali for a second opinion on. I read it one way. She had a different interpretation.' He indicated the open dictionary. 'Now, I'm fairly sure I was right.'

'Really? Tali was always the best in our language classes. I could never get my brain around Old Mandrin. All the inflections.'

'I know. Yet she read it as: *when the two are one, the time is near. The strong men in service to nature must rise in defence of the erheyi to wash away ignorance once more. Then the true guide shall teach all her will and the path will be regained.*'

'So?'

'She translated yinghan into *strong men* but it's more like *men of steel*. Which has a distinctively different nuance at the moment.' He swiped a hand over his hair. 'And she read zaohua as *nature* instead of *the mother of all*. And xituo as *wash* rather than *purge*. And there are a couple of other key differences, too.'

Alere spread her hands. 'But a lot of those old words have more than one meaning. Who's to say which is right?'

He put it aside and lifted the Koh-Lin book again, dusting flecks of gold off his fingers. 'True. And under normal circumstances, I'd agree with you.' His grey eyes hardened. 'But the differences are important. I read the passage as: *when the two are one, the time is at hand. The men of steel in service to the mother-of-all must rise in defence of the erheyi to purge the unworthy once more. Then the true guide shall subjugate all to her will and the path will be regained.*'

'Oh. That does sound…worse. Why would she translate it so differently?'

'That's what's bothering me.' Kett glanced at the bloodlight streaming in through the window. 'Especially given you and I both felt it necessary to hide our true intentions when we were discussing how to get into the Alcazar.'

Alere sucked a quick breath. 'What are you saying?'

'I'm saying that Tali conveniently couldn't find this dictionary when we came here before.' He laid a hand on the volume. 'And she suggested we go to the Selb. She also offered to cut the Bond between you and Mina. And said you shouldn't reconnect because of Mina's heart weakness.'

'Which none of us can confirm!' Alere pressed her palms to her temples. 'But she went with them. If she was betraying us, why would she put herself in the middle of a potential battle between the Selb and Hassan?'

'I don't know. It's all guesswork. I could be wrong.' He glanced at the sun again. 'But Corin and the others aren't back, yet. And they should be.'

'Houlia! Jiaoji House.' She rose from the table. Kett's fingers locked onto her wrist.

'You can't, Alli. If Tali betrayed us to Nasra and Hassan, then Jiaoji House is long-fallen.'

She sat back down with a thump, her heart sinking. 'That's why you brought us here, instead of there. But how will Corin know where we are?'

'I told Saric.'

'You suspected her and you didn't say anything?'

He sent her a level gaze. 'I had no proof. I couldn't warn Corin in case she Read him.'

'Where did you send Saric, then?'

'To Kennor Han-Asad. Waiting with his men in Plana, just east of the city. I told Saric to send Kennor as backup for Corin, just in case.'

'But they're still not back. What does that mean?'

'I don't know that, either. All we can do is wait.' His mouth twisted. 'And I know how much you love doing that.'

She ignored the jibe. 'What does that passage from the Koh-Lin manual mean?'

'They were the words of a Seeing by Kya Edwards. *Two are one* could mean you and Mina, but it could also mean Nasra's twins. Which would indicate the Selb – the men of steel – are gearing up to rise in *their* defence, not yours. The reference to a *true guide* must be this same prediction you've been hearing from various xintou the last couple of months. Referring to Nasra, I assume, given it says *her will*.'

'And the *mother-of-all*?' Alere opened the book and flipped through its pages, tracing the minute, beautiful script.

'That could either be a reference to Mistress Li, or perhaps Nasra.'

Lead dropped into Alere's stomach as she understood the full import of his words. 'You're saying the Selb could be working for—'

'Nasra and Rohne, yes,' he said grimly. 'Have you been able to reach Corin or Mina?'

'I tried. Back in the Alcazar. Nothing.'

'Jiangui! We need information. I'll go to Messenger House and get the runner-news. You stay here and protect Rafi.'

'But I—'

'Don't argue, Alli,' he said. 'We're running out of time and options. We might have saved Rafi and the others, but if Corin, Mina, and Jarran are taken, we're in no better position than we were this morning. Worse, in fact.' He strode out of the hall without a backward look.

'Where did Kett go?' Petar asked. He and Rafi sat at a table, barely speaking, picking at the remains of a meal. Petar had put Leah to bed not long before, having dosed her with medicines from the House healer's room. Jarran's two girls were with Leah, sleeping the exhausted sleep of the small and unaware.

'Out to get information,' she replied, and resumed pacing. Sunlight blinded her as she passed before the window and she stopped to consider it for the first time in many years. The ancient glass portrayed a stylised image of Kya and Bree Edwards, soulfully beautiful, gold-draped, holding their hands out in benediction above the heads of hundreds of kneeling people. Kya wore, around her neck, a starburst necklace. All these years, Alere had never really seen it, or wondered at its significance. No one had.

Right now, seeing their superior, pious expressions, Alere wanted to throw something through the glass; watch it rain as a thousand coloured, sparkling shards to the ground. Whatever stupidity convinced the sisters they had the right to play mother to the whole world?

The greatest irony was that every gouri class in the House preached the value of individuality and freedom. The care a xintou must take in her work so as not to manipulate her Bonded Jun, but only to guide and advise and inform.

When had '*clarity, stability, responsibility, and compassion*' become '*we know what's best for the whole world*'? How had Mistress Li been so blind to what people really needed: the freedom to choose? And how had she mishandled and misjudged Nasra so badly? Warped the child into becoming such a monster?

Alere extricated the huge yanstone from her pocket and partly unwrapped it, still reluctant to touch. Its milky-translucence glimmered, the internal fire dancing. A whisper of barely-heard voices urged her to deepen the connection; to draw strength and comfort from it; to use it to regain what had been lost and prevent what should never be.

Would it give her the power to reach Mina? Or Corin? Something about the yanstone repulsed her, even as it drew her, seduced her.

What should she do?

CHAPTER THIRTY

ALERE

She thrust the stone back into her pocket, shivering. Hopefully she would hear from Mina, soon. Or Corin. Surely, all it would take was Mina using the bracelets and their Bond would be re-established. Maybe, with the Koh-Lin stones, she wouldn't need to use the *shenhilya*. To use it would be to follow in Mistress Li's bloody footsteps. To become like her; to care less about individuals and more about some abstract, impossible ideal without understanding the purpose of that idea was to set people free.

She stared south, in the direction Kett had taken, unable to bear the thought of Kett's reaction if he found out Mistress Li had caused the kin-child laws just to hide and protect Alere and Mina. Everything that had happened to him – and every horrific ordeal in the last two months – was a direct result of those laws. Even Nasra's revolution may never have come to fruition if Alere hadn't killed Ven and opened the way for her to put Hassan on the throne.

So, what was the right course of action? How did she fix it? What was best for the Jundom and the future of Kalima? How did she repair the atrocities wrought by Mistress Li's arrogance?

In so many ways, she even empathised with Nasra and Rohne's desire to break the world free of the House's domination. Diyu, hadn't she spent ten years yearning for the exact same thing for herself?

But was the path Nasra offered any better? It had begun with such appalling violence, and she was so broken and bitter. How could Nasra steer the Jundom back onto the path of peace? Did she even want to? How would she react if Rohne died in the same violent manner as had the boy in the village? Or had she managed to control his degeneration?

And what if Mistress Li was right about iron? It was true that the rapid industrialisation of old Earth was due to their massive mineral resources. Would the same destruction happen here on Kalima if Trades House and Miner House succeeded in extracting iron from soil, rocks and the few meteoric iron sites? Could mankind be trusted not to destroy this world as they had their first?

An hour passed before the door handle rattled. Alere drew her weapons and stood before Rafi and Petar. The Jun Seconds rose. Kett slipped in and closed the door carefully.

He faced them and Alere's chest tightened. His eyes were steel, his face all hard planes and sharp angles.

'What?' she asked, breathless.

'Runners are announcing the news.' He limped to the nearest table and sank onto a wooden bench. Blood glistened on his black trous.

'You're hurt.' She reached for the stack of medical supplies she'd brought out for Leah, earlier.

Kett waved her away. 'It's not bad. Just a minor run-in with the city guard junren.' He smiled bleakly. 'Luckily Hassan hasn't replaced the shazis Kennor hired.' His jaw hardened again.

'Spit it out, boy,' Rafi said. 'What's the news?'

'I don't know it all,' he said. 'Only what the runners are crying out. Jarran and Mina are captured. Kennor Han-Asad and all his men are dead. The Selb army has joined with Hassan and will march tomorrow against Yasmin's forces.' He raised haunted eyes to Alere's. 'I'm sorry, Alli. Corin is dead. We failed. Hassan's calling for us to turn ourselves in. All four of us.' He nodded to Rafi and

Petar. 'If we don't, they'll execute Mina and Jarran at the coronation tomorrow. Which we know they'll do, anyway.'

'Corin? No.' Alere's knees collapsed and she sank onto the seat. 'I don't believe it.' It just wasn't possible. Surely she would have felt it? No, not with their tie cut and her powers gone.

'There are bodies on display in the square before the Alcazar.'

'Corin's?' Her heart stuttered.

'Couldn't tell.' Kett's jaw worked. 'Most were too…damaged to be recognisable. I saw Kennor's cloak, though. And there's more.'

Alere braced herself.

'Houlia, half a dozen of her senior jiaoji, and the Artist House Master were captured on the Jiali road, trying to escape the city.'

She covered her mouth to hold in a cry of despair.

He continued, his hands fisted on the table. 'At the coronation, there will be a hundred and fourteen executions. Mina and Jarran will be the last. Houlia and the Artist House master just before. And rumours I overheard in the market square say that Hassan and Rohne will be guarded by the Selb – who all apparently have steel weapons.'

'Steel!' Rafi groaned. 'Where did they get it?'

'There are other meteors,' Alere said. 'In the mountains near Gaton. Remember the valley we hid in, Kett?'

'Gouri. You're right.' He scrubbed at his face.

'But how did this happen?' Alere whispered.

'How did Corin and the others get caught?' Kett stretched his neck. 'I'm guessing the Selb handed them over. Assuming they do work for Nasra. Although, given how they worship xintou, perhaps not. Perhaps Tali did tell Hassan or Nasra of our plans. That would explain how Nasra knew to expect us. There's no news of Tali.'

Alere dropped her head into her hands. Corin couldn't be dead. He just couldn't. The black pit of grief threatened to consume her again. But this time there were no yanstones to draw it away and comfort her.

'Does it really matter who told Nasra?' Rafi put in. 'Any number of people knew you were in Jiaoji House. Silence is expensive. Betrayal is cheap. People will do anything to survive.'

'There was one other announcement,' Kett said, ignoring Rafi's bitterness. 'As soon as he's crowned, Hassan intends to declare war on Shanzhai. He'll use his army and the Selb to destroy Yasmin tomorrow, then march straight to Shanzhai for the iron.'

Rafi tipped back his head, driving his fingers into his hair.

'Oh, gouri!' Alere said.

'What?' Kett asked.

'Iron.' She swallowed down sick realisation. 'I gave the bracelets to Mina. Rohne has them, now.'

'Jiangui!' Kett closed his eyes, the shadows of pain and worry showing.

'Bracelets?' Petar asked. 'What…?'

'Never mind,' Rafi said, heavily. 'It just means we've lost one more advantage. Pete, you need to get Leah and Jarran's girls out of the city to safety.' When Petar protested, Rafi added, 'You've got your kin-son, Kenji, to think of. He's your Jun-Heir, Pete. And, if Jarran dies, Rhea is next Jun-Heir to the First. You can't let her and Ashi back into Hassan's hands. Get them all out of the city and into hiding until you get word from us. If you don't hear from us, then get Kenji and go over the border to Jadid. Prince Soran owes me for the Faktor incident so he'll take you in. Then, when Rhea's old enough to lead her own army, help her reclaim the throne.'

Petar hesitated, then struggled up from the table, exhaustion lining his face. 'I'll go wake them. We'll be safer moving in the dark. Good luck to all of you.' He scribbled on a scrap of paper torn from a book and passed it over. 'Rafi, here's where you can find us or send a flitter.'

His gaze lingered on Kett. 'Kett.' Petar hauled his nephew into a hug. 'I'm sorry I didn't know you were alive. Your mother… you have her eyes you know…and she would be proud of you, son.'

'Thank you, Uncle.'

Petar cleared his throat, nodded to all of them, and hurried to the door.

'Wait, Pete,' Rafi said. His shoulders sagged. 'I have to tell you. The young girl in the cells with Rhea and Ashi. The one you didn't see – who was taken away.'

'What about her?'

Rafi cleared his throat. 'Nasra was…talking to her when I was brought into the Alcazar.'

'And?'

'Nasra was…breaking her wards. Asking her if she knew where to find Kenji. The child was lying on the floor, screaming. She…died a few seconds later.'

'Kenji? But who would know—' Petar paled, turning a sickly shade of grey. 'No. Nasra wouldn't.'

Rafi nodded. 'It was Hallee. Elmira's daughter. Nasra's own granddaughter. I'm so sorry, Pete. If Hallee knew where Kenji is, you need to get to him quickly.'

Tears spilled from Petar's eyes and he swore beneath his breath. Footsteps dragging, he left the room.

Alere could barely draw breath. She turned to Kett. He gathered her close, his strength offering a comfort she couldn't absorb. Too many blows. Too many failures. Too many senseless deaths.

All because of her existence and Mistress Li's stubborn adherence to aeons old doctrines.

Hatred for Nasra burned dark in her stomach, smouldering. Even the small ambivalence she'd felt before vanished with this last piece of news. No good existed in Nasra or Rohne. No higher calling to try and improve the world. No possibility of their actions leading to something worthwhile. This was nothing more than twisted ambition, revenge and power-hunger. No-one with any sort of heart would do what she had done to her daughter, to her granddaughter.

'I…I can't see any way out of this, Kett. With the Selb, Hassan's army outnumbers Yasmin's. Nasra's men will have sealed the secret entrance to the Alcazar now. Corin's dead, and probably Tali, with him. Saric?'

Kett closed his eyes. 'Back in Asadia, Corin arranged for more men to join Kennor. They were Selb. I thought it would be alright. We didn't know…They would have betrayed Kennor. If Saric was with them…'

'No.' Alere backed away. 'No. It can't be.'

'We need to get out of Madina,' Rafi said, pacing. 'I need to get to Yasmin. We can withdraw to Shanzhai. Regroup. Make a stand there and find some other way to deal with Nasra and Rohne.'

'What?' Alere gaped at him.

'We have to,' her father said, grim. 'We owe it to our people, Lia.'

'What about Mina and Jarran?'

'I'm sorry.' His face was haggard. 'But I have to consider the whole Jundom. Get your things. We're leaving.'

CORIN

'Khara! Let go. I'm not going to fall over yet.' Corin pushed Tali's hands aside and braced himself against the brick wall, soaking in its heat, hoping it would ease the shivers wracking his body.

They were in an alley, somewhere in the small village of Plana. Having ridden hard for almost half an hour to get there, they'd given their horses to the first enterprising youngster Corin found, with instructions to ride them to the next village east before selling them and keeping the profit. Not questioning his luck, the boy leapt straight onto the animal and trotted happily off.

Saric appeared out of nowhere. He took one look, pointed at Corin's leg and pursed his lips. 'You're bleeding.'

'You don't say. Perhaps some more constructive help?' Corin looked down. Blood had soaked through the hastily tied bandage and tourniquet made from the tail of his shirt. His leg was numb, but if he released the sash, the wound bled too much. It took a lot of concentration just to walk and not collapse in pain.

'I won't be impressed if you die on me, too.' Saric sent him a narrow look.

Corin managed a smile and ruffled his hair.

The boy yanked his head away with a scowl but offered a shoulder to lean on. 'Where's Mina and Jarran?'

'Taken. Rohne has them. Knew we were coming.' Pain sluiced through Corin's leg and he vented self-directed anger by swearing eloquently. Tali, although apparently recovered from her mental contest with Rohne, remained silent.

'Made a mess of it, did you?' Saric said.

'Shut up.'

'Nope.'

'Surprised you weren't on the field with Kennor to keep an eye on me,' Corin said drily.

'Face-to-face fights are for zifts,' Saric replied. 'Give me a dart from the shadows any day.'

'Spoken like a true xiongshou.' Corin swore as his leg gave way and he half-staggered a few steps. When he recovered, he leaned again on Saric and squeezed the boy's shoulder. 'Thank you for sending Kennor. It was a good try. I'm assuming Kett sent you to meet Kennor?'

The boy nodded. 'What happened?'

'Some of Kennor's own men turned on him. My gouri fault.' Corin sucked a breath through gritted teeth. 'Can we talk about it later? I'm not enjoying having a bolt in my leg.'

'Corin,' Tali put in, 'we really need to get a healer. You've lost a lot of blood.'

Corin ignored her and addressed Saric. 'Anywhere around we can hide? I need to sit down.'

'There's a spot around the corner that's safe enough for awhile.' Saric jerked a thumb at the end of the alley.

'How long have you been here?' Corin had to concentrate on each step. The world was suspiciously fuzzy.

'Long enough to find places to hide. Here.' Saric led him to a sheltered niche behind a tavern. Tali trailed along in their wake.

'This smells delightful, like rotting fish and stale beer,' Corin said.

'Beggars and choosers and all that.'

Corin grunted and glanced at Tali. 'Better get rid of those robes, Tal. Too distinctive.'

She stripped off her xintou robes, bundling them into an overflowing waste bin. Beneath, she wore only yellow leggings and a yellow sleeveless tunic. Still too recognisable.

'Saric,' he said, panting, 'can you go find her something less noticeable to wear? And some wine. Better yet, jiu. There's a few coins in my purse.' He patted his shirt.

'Who needs money? Try not to die while I'm gone.'

'Right.' Corin waved vaguely at him. 'Do my best.'

The boy vanished down the alley.

'You should sit,' Tali said, tentatively.

'Oh, I will, but first things first. I didn't want to do this in front of him.' Corin gripped the bolt's broken end. Luckily, it was a small, smooth point, designed to pierce alzin, so he didn't have to push it through the muscle. Drawing three deep breaths, he bit on a mouthful of his sleeve and yanked the bolt free.

The world swirled around him in a red haze of agony and he groaned deep in his throat. He slid down the wall to sit on the filthy cobbles and put his head between his knees. He flung the bolt aside and waited for the dizziness to clear.

'Why won't you go to a healer?' Tali ripped two long strips off her tunic and made one into a pad. The other she wound around the injury, holding the first in place. When he released the tourniquet, his toes tingled but the pad soaked through in seconds. He tightened it again and swore.

'A healer would remember us,' he said. 'If Hassan or Jada has men out searching for us, they'll know I was injured. First rule of being on the run: if no-one sees you then no-one can sell you out.'

Corin stretched his legs out and rested on the wall, lightheadedness seducing him with promises of sleep. Shaking himself, he tugged the suede covers off his weapons and laid the pommels on his lap. Tali gasped at the display of yanstones. She reached for the stones' hypnotic gleam.

He gave her a wry grin. 'Besides, I'm counting on you to use these to heal me.'

'What?' She snatched her hand back. 'I'm nai-xintou. I only know how to manipulate DNA. Micro-scale telekinesis, not…that.' She gestured at his leg.

His head slipped and he forced it upright again, struggling to keep his eyelids open. 'Oh, don't you believe the House propaganda. I've learned a lot from Alere… the last few weeks. Pretty sure… you'll be able to do it.' He swallowed, riding a wave of pain and nausea. 'Or I can bleed out right here and… you'll be on your own. With Saric. He's xiongshou trained. But no Weishi house duty and honour feihua. No idea…what he'd do if he thought you'd let me die. Your choice.'

Her fists clenched. Finally, she made a noise of frustration, swore, and sat next to him with her back against the wall. He passed the weapons across. She took them in delicate fingers, gasping as Corin released their weight. They fell to her lap with a ring of metal on metal, loud in the alley's confines.

'Now what?' She extended a fingertip toward the stones. 'I don't know what to do.'

'Not… sure,' he confessed. 'I've never been able to do it. Seen Alli do it. Says she sort of… merges with the stones.' He grabbed her wrist before she touched them. 'But she takes the injuries onto her own body then heals herself.' He laughed breathlessly. 'She has a… bit of a hero-martyr complex. You don't strike me as that sort.'

He ignored the hurt look she sent him. 'Besides… you don't want this, trust me.' He indicated the bloodsoaked bandage. 'Neither do I, for that matter.' There was a loud ringing in his ears and he shook his head. The world spun. He swallowed down a flood of saliva.

'Well…' Tali bit her lip '…I did more nai-xintou classes than Alere. I think I understand the principle enough to apply it to fixing muscle tissue. I just don't know about this "merging". I've never heard of it and it sounds an awful lot like Fusion.'

Corin shivered as cold gripped his body. 'Apparently it's not. But you do…have to still be careful of that…possibility. Tal…you can't…wait any longer. Just try. Please.'

'Did…' She stroked the weapons in her lap. 'Did Alere and Kett get the people out of the Alcazar?'

'Don't know.' He groaned. 'But we probably shouldn't go back to Jiaoji House…in case it's been compromised. Clearly Rohne and Jada knew we were coming.'

She gave a low cry. 'You don't think they would hurt Houlia or her people, do you?'

'Yes,' Corin said, bitterly. 'Hassan, Nasra, and Rohne won't think twice about killing everyone in the House.'

Tali pressed three fingers to her mouth and swallowed.

'Houlia's smart, though,' Corin said. 'She probably left after we did. But, if you want me to help you find out, you're going to have to work fast. I don't feel…all that well.'

She swallowed. 'I–I'll try.'

Corin tried to pat her arm, but his hand was surprisingly heavy.

She closed her eyes and he dreamily admired her delicate profile. She laid her hands over the yanstones on his blades and his body jerked in reaction to the intimacy; to the sensation that she stroked his skin, but inside his thoughts, somehow. Then her mind was there in the silver-gilt black-nothing with him, reassuring, focussed, afraid.

With her work came pain.

Had he been a shazi to trust her?

Darkness swept in and the world wandered off somewhere else.

CHAPTER THIRTY-ONE

ALERE

'No,' Alere said.

'I beg your pardon?' Rafi raised his brows and folded his arms.

'I won't leave my sister.'

'You must,' Rafi said. 'Believe me, I don't want to, either. But we have a duty to our people.'

Alere drew herself up. 'I got her into this situation. Made her do things she hated. Pushed her away. I won't run when she needs me most.'

Rafi pointed at the Alcazar, visible through the northern windows. 'We're outnumbered and outclassed. There's nothing we can do! We must cut our losses.'

'Mina is not a nameless junren you can write off as a loss in battle.' Alere lifted her chin. 'This is my responsibility. All of it. More than any of you even realise.'

Rafi threw his arms out and gave a growl of frustration. 'Talk sense into her, Tekettan. You understand war. This one's unwinnable.'

'So does she.' Kett smiled grimly. 'And I'm with her, anyway. This began with me. With those gouri kin-child laws. It will end with me.'

Alere looked away, her breath catching.

Rafi laid heavy hands on her shoulders. 'Don't do this to me, Alere. I can't lose you, too. Not after all this.'

'This isn't about you, Rafi.' She pushed his hands off. 'Emotional blackmail won't work. Go, if you want to. But you'll have to get yourself another Jun-Heir.'

He paced the dining room, his boots echoing hollowly in the huge space. Then his shoulders slumped and he gave an ironic half-laugh. 'Corin warned me this day would come. When you would realise I need you more than you need me.'

'I do need you. I can't do this alone. Help us. You owe it to us.'

'How so?' Rafi glowered. 'How do I owe it to you to throw all of our lives away on a lost cause?'

'You,' she said evenly, 'and all the other Juns could have stood up to your Xintou and Mistress Li twenty years ago. Twenty Juns together could have stopped her and Hanna. But you didn't. And this is the consequence. You owe every kin-child who died or suffered in the last twenty years.'

Blanching, Rafi leaned on a table.

'Alli,' Kett said, low.

'No,' Alere said, waving him back. 'It's about time both of you admitted why Rafi hates you. It's because he knows he's partly to blame for what happened to you. To all of us.'

'Stop, Alli,' Kett said, gripping her shoulder. 'You know it's almost impossible for a Jun to ignore his Bonded Xintou's orders. That's why Xintou House training is so strict about not manipulating their Jun. Rafi couldn't have disobeyed her, even if he wanted to.'

'No.' Rafi sighed and jabbed his fingers into his short hair. 'She's right. The Bond isn't the same for everyone. Perhaps it's because I have the dormant xintou gene, myself. But I was always able to ignore my Xintou if I disagreed with her.'

Kett stiffened, frowning. 'You—' One hand dropped to the hilt of his sword. He took a step toward Rafi, who tensed, his eyes glittering.

'Kett!' Alere gripped his arm.

'Whether you believe me or not, I did try.' Rafi's mouth thinned. 'I tried to sway the other Juns. But only a few sided with me. The rest just…accepted the ruling, like it was perfectly ordinary to kill their own children.' He gave a half-gasping cry and covered his eyes briefly. 'So I stopped. I was young. Afraid they would all turn on me and I'd lose everything. I told myself backing down was the right thing to do. For my people.'

There was a long silence, filled with only the distant noises of the city outside Xintou House walls.

Then Rafi lifted his chin and threw his shoulders back. He looked at both of them squarely.

'You're right. I have hidden from this for too long. I can't keep backing down out of fear. I'll help.' He offered a hand to Kett. 'And I'm sorry for how I've treated you. And what you went through because of my fear twenty years ago.'

Kett hesitated, studying the older man, his face impassive.

'Kett?' Alere said. He had long wanted justice against those who carried out the kin-child laws. Believed the Juns and their Xintou untouchable. Would he kill Rafi, now?

He closed his eyes briefly and let out a slow breath. Then he took Rafi's hand. 'Thank you.'

Rafi cleared his throat. 'What do you need me to do?

'I'm not sure,' Alere said. 'Kett? He could join Yasmin. Use the Shanzhai army to distract Hassan's junren and the Selb while we try to save Mina and Jarran.'

Rafi's frown deepened. 'We're badly outnumbered. And if the stories about those erheyi twins are true…'

'You have the Xintou House girls,' Kett put in.

'Untried children! Even if we succeeded in holding out against Hassan's army, Alere has no powers to use against Rohne and Nasra. And this might be for nothing, anyway. We don't even know for sure if Mina and Jarran are still alive.'

'True,' Kett said. 'Alli, have you tried to reach Mina?'

'Not since we were in the Alcazar – before we released everyone. I couldn't feel anything. I've lowered my wards a few times, here. Still nothing from her or… Corin.' She swallowed against a lump in her throat.

'Try reaching out to Mina again,' Kett said. 'Maybe you were right. Maybe the connection to the stones needed a kickstart from a full xintou. You spoke telepathically with Mistress Li, didn't you?'

Alere shuddered. 'And heard Nasra. But that was them connecting to me. I'll try.' She gripped the yanstones on her weapons and focussed on those around her neck.

Nothing. Not a whisper. Not even a sliver of the golden strength she was so used to.

'Alli?' Kett ran his hands down her arms.

Her throat closed and she thrust him aside with an inarticulate cry. She kicked at a heavy wooden bench, toppling it with a crash that reverberated around the dining hall.

Kett groaned and caught her close, holding her tight when she struggled to free herself. 'Stop, Alli. It's not the end of the world.'

She pushed free. 'How am I supposed to go against Nasra and Rohne alone without any powers? I can't even tell if Mina's still alive!'

He held her face in his hands and forced her to meet his steady gaze. 'You're not alone. We're all in this. You didn't have xintou powers for twenty years. Think like a weishi, Alli. Rohne and Nasra are xintou. That's our advantage. They don't think in terms of warfare strategy and tactics. We just need to find a way to level the playing field again.'

Alere broke free again hugging herself to stop the shivers that wracked her body. Nausea knotted her stomach. Would she *never* feel that silver-gilt strength surge through her bones and flesh again? She *needed* it to win. Needed it to feel whole. Connected. Worthy.

Her hand crept toward the *shenhilya* in her pocket. Tainted though it was, perhaps—

'Alli?' Kett's thoughtful question pulled her back. 'Does…did Mistress Li keep fanghu in her office?'

'Not since I put it in the water to shut down everyone's xintou gifts that time. Why?'

'Gaisi! Istilqa it is, then.' He pulled a green-feathered dart out of his belt. 'I got some from my old quarters when I was out.'

She frowned. 'What are you thinking? There's no way we can get close enough to dart Nasra and Rohne. And remember Rohne's telekinetic. He could just stop it.'

'I know, but—' He paused and looked toward the door.

Alere held her breath. 'I heard it, too. A voice in the hall.' She drew her sword. 'You go through the kitchen to the other exit. Get behind them. Rafi, go with him but stay in the kitchen.'

Her father scowled. 'I'll stay and fight.'

'It could be Corin. And Tali. She doesn't know you're here. You should hide until we know whether we can trust her.'

Kett and Rafi headed for the kitchen. Her father cast a worried, warning glance back over his shoulder. Alere took up a place behind the main entrance to the great hall, her weapons drawn.

ROHNE

'She's at my gate!' Hassan rose from the dinner table, throwing his napkin aside as he strode to the window to fume at the darkness. 'Tomorrow is *my* day and Yasmin Koh-Lin is almost at my southern gate, with an army, to ruin what I've worked twenty years to achieve.'

What we've *worked for.* Nasra's thought speared through Rohne's Outers.

He flinched under the lash of her anger, even though his mother's ire was self-directed. He rested his aching forehead on one hand as Hassan and Nasra's argument swirled around him. Nasra's skill in getting through everyday Outer wards was such now that even he couldn't block her out. Each time she let her temper get the better of her, it flayed his mind a little more. He could barely stand to be near her.

She and Hassan had argued almost incessantly since his arrival back from the field that afternoon. Hassan ranting at the loss of his prisoners; Nasra lashing back in defensive anger. Now Hassan had little leverage over Yasmin and none over the escaped Xintou House women. At large, Petar could raise his own army to support the Koh-Lin's. With Jarran's daughters released, Hassan's claim to the throne was on shaky ground.

'We'll stop them, shenshi.' Jada's rumbling bass rolled out as he stabbed a piece of roast runiu meat with his dagger and relaxed back in his chair. 'Leave it to me. The men are ready. We'll march out in the morning and engage them before they know what's happening.' He took a bite and pointed at Hassan with his knife. 'With the erheyi girls and my Selb it'll be over quickly. We'll be back in time to keep control of the crowds for your coronation – with Rafi and Yasmin's heads as a gift.'

'You have steel?' Hassan demanded, hands wringing the neck of an imaginary enemy. 'You must have steel to do it right.'

Jada exchanged a tolerant glance with Nasra. 'Yes, shenshi, we have steel a-plenty.'

'Good, good.' Hassan wagged an admonitory finger. 'Steel is the key to everything. Go prepare the junren. Make sure they know how to cleanse this rabble properly.' He smirked. 'And yes, bring me Rafi's head.'

Unable to stand the unwarded emotions leaking from the man's cess-pit mind, Rohne left the table with a muttered excuse and headed for his room. Its shielded walls would protect him and also give him the chance to experiment with Mina's bracelets.

Rohne.

He stopped and his mother's light, hurried tread approached from behind.

'What, Mother?' He didn't even bother to turn. 'I'm tired and I suspect tomorrow will not go quite as easily as either Jada or Hassan seem to think. I'd like to retire.'

She laid a palm against his cheek. The veil and a gold silk head-covering lent her an air of mystery and hid her singed hair and blistered cheek. She lifted the veil, worry lurking in her blue eyes.

You aren't well. It was a statement, not a question.

'Just a headache.' He brushed her touch aside. 'I'm sure it will clear once tomorrow is over. I just need to rest. I haven't been sleeping well and Hassan's mind is…unpleasant to be Bonded to. The man is a zift and unworthy of the First title. How long will I have to put up with him?'

Not long, love. Just until we've quelled the rebellions. His people are loyal and his junren well-trained. After that we'll…find another solution. She reached up again, this time with both hands. *Hold still. Let me—*

Rohne yanked her wrists away. 'Why?'

She froze.

'Why do you do that?' he repeated. 'Ever since I was a child. Every night before I went to bed you would put both your hands on my head and bid me be still. Why?'

I... Nasra smiled condescendingly. *I'm your mother. It's a gesture of affection, nothing more.*

Rohne glowered. Surprisingly, she stepped back, a flicker in the blue depths of her eyes confirming his suspicions: she feared him.

He kept his voice quiet and even. 'Tell me the truth. You're one of the least affectionate people I know. So what is it? Tell me.' He advanced and she retreated. 'What is it about male xintou that frightens everyone?'

She hesitated, then gestured dismissively. *Nothing. It's just propaganda by the House. Five hundred years ago, Kya Edwards's son died in an accident. In her grief, she forbade males from studying at Xintou House. Over time, that story was distorted into lies by women who had a vested interest in keeping power over the House and the Jundom. Male xintou are stronger and women are threatened by that.* She placed her palm on the side of his head and stroked his temple with her thumb. *Go and rest. Morning will bring light into darkness. Remember, yours is the power to change the course of history. To be humanity's guide. We'll do it together.'*

His headache eased.

She blew him a kiss and walked away toward her own chamber, spine straight. Rohne concentrated on relieved and accepting thoughts until the door to her shielded room closed behind her. Then he spun on his heel and strode in the opposite direction, his quick footfalls silent on the worn, black and silver carpet.

If she wouldn't tell him, there was someone else who would.

ALERE

The great zitan-wood double doors creaked open and a blond head poked through. Saric caught sight of her. Alere held her breath in impossible hope.

'Hey.' He glanced back over his shoulder. 'She's here. Not dead. Looks a bit annoyed, though.' The doors opened further and Saric sauntered in.

'Well, that makes two of us,' Corin's exhausted voice echoed in the hall. He limped through the doorway, supported by Tali, his left leg bandaged and bloody.

Alere covered her mouth, muffling a half-sob. She wiped at her eyes with trembling fingers.

'I,' Corin continued, 'have had a particularly trying day. Turns out the Selb are working for Nasra and Rohne, under the command of Jada Marin-kin. I contributed to Kennor Han-Asad's very messy death. And our dear friend Liu Gray, in Chengdu, also wore the double-bladed axe pendant they all seem so fond of.' He stopped and spread his arms wide. 'We, my friends, have enabled this gouri revolution and I'm not excited by our prospects for ending it successfully – or alive.'

He let go of Tali and smiled at Alere.

Alere threw her arms around him, her heart too full to speak. He smelled of leather, sweat, blood, and mud, but his heart beat strongly beneath the alzin armour and leather. He held her and kissed her forehead, his green eyes shadowed with pain and lightened by relief. 'I'm glad you're alive, at least,' he said. 'Rohne tried to make me believe you'd been caught. I laughed. He wasn't impressed.' He grinned and limped over to sit at the table. 'Where's Kett? That speech needed a bigger audience. And a bigger reaction.'

A soft *phuut* sounded. Tali yelped and pulled a green-feathered dart from her throat.

Kett emerged from the shadows behind her.

'Why did you do that…?' She blinked, long and slow. 'I…I can't…Why?'

Corin eyed her with an expression of mild amusement. 'You can't be surprised, Tal. You did give us up to Rohne and Jada, after all. I'm astonished those feathers aren't black. Kett must be so glad to see me it put him in a good mood.'

'I am,' Kett said, clapping him on the shoulder. 'But if you knew she'd betrayed you, why the gouri did you bring her here?'

'After messing up so badly with Shasa, I thought I should give Tal the benefit of the doubt.' Corin pointed to his leg. 'After all, she did try to fight Rohne and she did heal my leg.'

Tali gave a whimper and folded to the floor, her eyes closed.

Kett leaned down and murmured into her ear a Suggestion to tell the truth.

'Now, we need to get out of here.' He eyed the entrance. 'Just in case giving her the benefit of the doubt is your worst idea, yet.'

'I do believe I'm offended,' Corin said. 'But I take your point.'

Saric asked where the kitchen was, vanished and came back a few minutes later with Rafi and a platter of breads, meats and water. After remarking acidly on the lack of wine in the House, he thunked the plates onto the table, split the food into thirds, pushed some to Corin and some toward an empty seat near Tali, who still slept on the floor where she'd fallen. Then he dropped onto the bench and inhaled his food with the single-minded intensity of a growing boy who'd not eaten in many hours.

'Corin,' Rafi said, gripping his shoulder. 'I'm glad to see you.'

'And you, shenshi,' Corin said. 'Do sit, all of you. You're making me tired with all that hovering. I'm fine. I had too much blood in me, anyway.'

'Tell us,' Kett said.

'Succinct as always. Very well.' Corin drank a large mug of water, then talked.

Alere sat, listening to his recounting of the battle; of Tali's attempt to rescue Mina, her fight with Rohne and her work to cure Corin's injury.

'So you did suspect her?' Rafi put in. 'Before you even left Jiaoji House? I must be getting old. You're all mad to have even tried it.'

Corin waved a hunk of bread. 'It was pretty obvious Alli and Kett weren't going to use that ridiculous tradesman disguise. But I wasn't sure who to suspect – until I saw Tali's reaction to seeing Rohne and Jada. Or, rather, lack of reaction.' He frowned down at the unconscious girl. 'The question is: why? And what do we do with her, now?'

'And where do we go from here?' Alere put in. 'Where is safe from Rohne and Nasra?'

Kett's gaze grew distant. His lips curved in a wry smile. 'Weishi House.'

Corin raised his brows. 'Now who's got the worst idea, ever? With half the *jijin* xiongshou turned Selb, Weishi House is a ziftish place to hide.'

'Exactly,' Kett said. 'Alere, get our gear? I'll carry Tali.'

CHAPTER THIRTY-TWO

CORIN

With the streets of Madina practically deserted, it took very little time to get to Weishi House. Corin limped along as fast as he could, irritated by his weakness. The yanstones had healed the leg injury, but apparently it took more than that to replace the blood he'd lost. Wine would be good. More water, at a pinch. Food and sleep, too.

He grinned mirthlessly. All likely to be in short supply for the next day or so.

Ahead, Saric turned back and waved him on. Corin lengthened his stride and glanced uneasily around the half-deserted city. Burnt-grey afternoon light raked across empty houses and windswept cobbles. Windows and doors were closed tight, as though hiding from Hassan's madness would negate its power. Here and there, the old three-circle/triangle kin-child symbol had been painted on houses that were burnt or had their doors broken down. Behind the windows of intact houses, curtains twitched and eyes watched. Corin scowled.

When they arrived at Weishi House, Kett paused in the shadow of a towering thorn-tuft tree opposite and studied the complex of buildings. A three-man Alcazar patrol marched past a block away and Kett gestured Corin and the others back, out of sight.

'The House is quiet,' he said.

'I noticed that the other day.' Alere glanced up and down the street. 'Only about a third of the xiongshou were in training. No-one was using the training walls. It was creepy to see it so empty. Why, do you think? Surely they can't all have gone over to the Selb?'

That was a terrifying thought, but one Corin considered quite likely, having seen so many in the tent city. He refrained from saying so. Things were bleak enough, already.

'Perhaps they've left for other cities,' Kett said. 'Or hired out as ronin to various Juns and merchants until things settle down. But let's go the back way. I want to see Master Anh without too many people knowing.'

'There's a back way?' Corin raised his brows. He thought he knew most of the secret entrances in Madina. To have missed the one into Xintou House – and now one into Weishi... He really wasn't doing his job well.

Kett nodded. 'Anh showed me when I was seven. In case Hanna's people came for me.' He vanished into a small alley between two shops. Corin and the others followed, edging sideways between the rough brick walls, kicking aside years of blown leaves and discarded rubbish. Kett emerged into a forgotten space between four buildings and hauled up a wooden storm-drain cover. He laid Tali on the ground and dropped into it. Rafi and Alere lowered Tali down to him.

Alere and Saric followed, with Corin last, climbing more slowly down a slimy wooden ladder and closing the cover behind.

A faint grey light filtered in somewhere ahead, a beacon.

Kett led the way. 'Watch the floor. It's uneven here.'

In the dark it felt like an hour but was probably more like five minutes before they climbed another ladder. Once aboveground, Kett – with Tali over his shoulder – barely fit in the cramped space between the timber and bamboo interior walls. He curled Tali into a ball on the dusty floor, slid back a peephole and checked inside Weishi House. Then he pushed the door gently open and eased out of the secret passage. Alere followed, dagger at the ready. Corin slipped out behind her.

'I was wondering if you'd show up, Kett.' A mellifluous voice rolled through the dim-lit room.

Alere and Corin spun.

Anh stood nearby, a one-shot crossbow cocked and aimed at Alere. Kett stepped in the way. Corin thrust her back and added his bulk to Kett's.

'Master Anh,' Kett said. 'I trust you're not intending to shoot that?'

'Well, there is a kill contract out on you. From the new Jun First, himself, no less.' Anh smoothed fly-away greying hairs back from his lean face and eyed Kett speculatively.

'And?' Kett said, his fingers curling around his sword hilt. The secret door creaked. Saric's blond head appeared, blowpipe at the ready. Kett held out a palm to halt him.

'I have notoriously bad eyesight,' Anh said. 'Can't see you at all without my glasses.' The House Master laid the crossbow on his massive black kellwood desk. 'I just didn't know who was coming in that way.' His mouth thinned. 'I can't tell who to trust in my own House these days. Tell your friends to come in.'

A half-grown black and grey xiao-kitten, curled up in a basket in one corner, cracked an eyelid, yawned, stretched and went back to sleep. Apart from the cat-basket, four chairs and the desk were the only furniture in the room. Nothing that could be used as a weapon lay easily within a visitor's reach. The walls were bare, stark, and white. Two doors. Bronze bars sealed the one, small window that overlooked the training courtyard. With the window closed, the room smelled strongly of jiu and fear-sweat.

Anh sat and threw back a glass of something clear. Jiu by the smell of it. He swallowed, his eyes watering. 'But you can't stay long. There *was* a kill out on both of you. I didn't know about it, by the way. But that was revoked. Now there's this new one on Kett.

And one on someone named Corin Mal-kin, who I understand is a friend of yours.'

Corin raised a hand. 'That would be me.' He sank into one of the chairs and helped himself to a shot of jiu, coughing as it dissolved his oesophagus. 'That's disgusting. Was it distilled in an old shoe?'

'You're welcome,' Anh said tartly.

Rafi appeared, carrying Tali.

Anh bowed. 'Shenshi Koh-Lin. Good to see you're not as dead as I expected.' He held out both hands to Alere. 'And you, my dear girl, are—'

'I see you've met my daughter, and Jun-Heir, Lianna,' Rafi cut in.

Anh hesitated for only a second, then bowed. 'Of course. And that explains a great deal, now I think about it. Come.' He indicated the chairs. 'Sit where you can. Your unconscious friend will be quite comfortable on the floor.'

Corin grinned, liking the Weishi House Master more each minute.

Rafi laid Tali on the floor and straightened her dusty grey robe precisely. She slept on. Saric slouched into one of the chairs, ignoring Rafi's cool glare.

Anh waved another glass of jiu at Alere. 'Zand, my second, signed a capture for you, Alere. Or rather, for Lia Koh-Lin. Now he's disappeared and I can't revoke it because I don't know who paid for it.'

'Disappeared?' Kett frowned.

Anh scratched at his silver, three-day growth of beard. 'A third of my people have just gone. Most are *jijin* xiongshou. And everyone I send to look for them disappears as well.' He threw back another shot of jiu.

'They're working for Nasra and Rohne,' Corin said bitterly. 'Including your second, Zand. Lovely fellow. The Selb army is stuffed with elite weishi.'

Anh swore comprehensively. 'I turned a blind eye to their gouri faith because they were extraordinarily good xiongshou. I should have known better. Fanaticism breeds stupidity. Or the other way around, perhaps. Always has.' He sucked a deep breath. 'But you didn't come to hear my woes. What do you need?'

'Do you still keep fanghu?' Kett came straight to the point.

'Not much,' Anh said. He picked out a large bronze key from a ring on his belt and unlocked the bottom desk-drawer. Within stood dozens of glass jars of liquids in various colours. Each one meticulously labelled with the name of a poison, sedative, or serum. He pulled out a tiny jar containing a fingerswidth of thick yellow liquid.

'Enough for three darts, I'd say. Why?' He dropped it into Kett's open palm.

'Probably best you don't know. You should get out of town if you can, Master.'

Anh gave a weary smile. 'You know I won't. Not while my people are protecting families that need us. And I suspect you'll need us as well. Tomorrow, perhaps. I'll have loyal people ready. If I can find any.'

Kett gripped his Master's arm. 'Thank you. I didn't want to ask, because we can't pay.'

'This goes beyond money, lad. Need anything else?'

'Can we use your office for a…meeting?' Kett nodded at Tali. 'We need to ask her some questions when she comes around in a minute.'

'Of course.' Anh rose, collected his crossbow and bolts, and straightened his wrinkled black weishi clothing. He swayed. 'I shall…' he waved the crossbow vaguely '…inspect a few things downstairs. Clean house. That sort of thing.' He sauntered from the room, moving carefully. The xiao-cat sprang from its basket and strolled after him, yeowling.

Kett locked the door and checked behind the second door – which led to a small bathroom.

Tali stirred, groaning, her fingers scrabbling at the floor. Kett hastily tipped three doses of fanghu into three darts and screwed on the feathers. He jabbed one into Tali's neck. She flinched and gave a slurred cry.

'Help her up, someone?' Corin said.

Kett hoisted Tali bodily into a chair at the end of the desk. She squinted against the late afternoon light.

'So!' Corin said brightly. 'Care to explain?'

'Where am I?' She frowned. 'This isn't Xintou House.' Her eyes widened. 'I…I can't Read anyone. What did you do to me?'

Kett held up a yellow-feathered dart. 'Fanghu. No-one can Read you, but you can't communicate with anyone, either. So your immediate survival depends on answering questions quickly and truthfully. Why did you betray Corin and allow Mina and Jarran to be captured?'

Corin ground his teeth. The bitterness of failure tasted worse than the jiu.

Tali pressed her fingers into her temples. She shut her mouth, her jaw clenching as she fought the istilqa Suggestion to speak truth.

'I can't!' she blurted. Her desperate gaze fell on Rafi. 'Shenshi Rafi! Where are the others? From the Alcazar?' She grabbed his wrist. 'Where are they?'

Rafi withdrew his hand, his expression cool and distant. 'I don't think you're in a position to ask questions. Why did you betray Corin and Alere?'

'I…' Her fingers curled into fists on the table. Rafi repeated the question. She pressed her lips thin, resisting, her dark eyes glittering. Then the words burst from her like water through a broken dam. Tears followed, sliding unchecked down her smooth cheeks.

'Nasra kept me aside when she took the House. She made me watch as she murdered the senior xintou. Then she said if I helped her she'd let my…' she clenched her teeth but the words spilled free again '…my House sisters go free.'

'But they were just being held in their rooms,' Kett said, frowning. 'You must have known she'd only kill them if they didn't join her. Tell us the truth, Tali.'

She let out a sound of frustration. 'I tried to warn Alere. Mistress Li had told me you were in Chengdu. I didn't know why she'd told me. But when the House fell, I knew it was so I could warn you. I sent a letter.'

'Or,' Alere shot back, 'Nasra could have told you to send it.'

'I could have let you and Mina die in Jiaoji House,' Tali snapped. 'But by then I knew what a mistake I'd made.'

'Really?' Corin said drily. 'So why the betrayal today?'

Dark lashes swept down, hiding Tali's eyes. 'Don't…I can't.' She bit her lip until blood trickled down her chin. 'She'll kill her. I can't!'

Corin, Alere, and Kett exchanged confused looks.

Rafi leaned forward. 'Who is Nasra holding that you care about, child?'

'Oh, Tali.' Alere groaned, her eyes huge. 'Was it Hallee Connor?'

Corin searched his fuzzy mind for a connection. Hallee Connor? Ah, Elmira Connor's gene-daughter. Alere's sister.

Tali nodded, the tears overflowing again. 'Please tell me you got her out? When she came to the House I offered to be her senior mentor. I wanted to help her because I'd never been able to help you. And I came to love her so much. But Nasra...' Her gaze flew to Alere. 'You said *was it* Hallee. Does that mean you got her out with the others? Or...'

There was a moment's tense silence then Rafi cleared his throat. 'I'm sorry. Nasra killed Hallee. Days ago. I witnessed it.'

With an anguished cry, Tali ran into the bathroom and slammed the door. Deep, wracking sobs could be heard, even through the thick timber. Something thumped the wall. Corin half-rose.

Alere touched his arm. 'Leave her for a few minutes.' Her expression was as blank and calm as Kett's.

Corin eyed her. 'How can you be so calm?' he asked. 'Hallee was your sister.'

Alere swallowed, her cheeks pale. 'Foster sister. She was two months old when I left the Ma-Safra house to come to Xintou and I haven't seen her since.' She stared up at the dark timber ceiling. 'And I'm not calm so much as...so angry I'm beyond tears or tantrums and out the other side.'

The bathroom door creaked open. Tali emerged, wan and red-eyed. She dropped back into the chair, swiping at fresh tears and avoiding their looks.

'I've been such a gouri shazi. I believed Nasra...No. I *wanted* to believe her. She was xintou. Clarity, responsibility, compassion and all that. Has it all been a lie?' She indicated the whitewashed, dim-lit bathroom. 'Everything the House stands for?'

Corin rested a hand on her shoulder and she didn't flinch away. 'Believe me , I do wish I could give you a straight answer. I just know we're all caught in the middle of a war between Nasra and Mistress Li that started before we were born. And they've used people like pawns on a qi board.

Kett leaned in, catching her eye. 'We've all lost people. The question is, where do you stand now? And what are you prepared to do about it?'

'You would trust me to help?'

'Is that what you want to do?'

'I...' Tali stared at her own hands. 'Yes. I think it is.' She glanced at Corin, blushing. 'But how could you trust me now?'

Kett straightened. 'Prove it. Let Corin Read you.'

Tali's eyes widened and she swallowed. Then she lifted her chin, her expression determined. 'The fanghu has worn off.' She swivelled to face Corin. 'I've dropped *all* my wards. Read me. Read that I won't betray you again.'

'It could be a ruse, Cor,' Rafi said.

'I don't think so, shenshi.' Corin shifted his chair closer, until he and Tali were eye to eye. He laid his hands on his yanstones and slid into contact with them.

'Careful,' Alere warned, one hand on her dagger. 'Don't go too deep or you risk Fusion.'

He nodded curtly and extended a careful thought. This was not his area of expertise. Even a bit. As he slid into her mind, Tali gave a whimper and closed her eyes, her face pale. Corin frowned. Sweat prickled on his back and his shoulders ached with tension.

Slowly, carefully, he sifted through her memories, burrowing deeper. She had a highly organised mind. Disciplined. Was that common amongst xintou? He suspected so. Ah... there. Her memory of Nasra's arrival was a vivid bruise; a mess of near-incoherent fear and anguish amongst the orderliness of her other thoughts.

Her first ever experience with death and it was to watch a dozen women she loved and respected slaughtered before her while she stood by, helpless. Forced to make an impossible choice. The links to those memories were so strong he wondered how she could sleep at night. And the guilt. Over their deaths. Over her betrayal. Over her survival. Guilt was a black fog that shadowed every waking moment.

Then, for some reason, his face appeared. His smile. His laughter. His eyes glinting warm at some shared joke. And every time it did, the blackness lifted and her thoughts became tinged with a small measure of hope.

Humbled, Corin withdrew. He studied Tali's exquisite face and touched her cheek, lightly, softly. She jerked back, her eyes snapping open.

'She's telling the truth,' Corin said, his voice rough. He cleared his throat. 'She did the best she could.'

Tali flushed and her shoulders relaxed.

'See. Told you she was worth the risk.' Corin smiled, yawned, and leaned on the desk, his head on a fist.

Kett hesitated, then pushed the gold-covered Koh-Lin journal across to her, finger on an open page. 'Can you give us a translation?' He tapped it. 'A true translation.'

She bent her head to read.

Corin yawned again, watching her lips move as she silently translated the text. 'So. What are our plans, exactly? I mean, Mina and Jarran are hostages. The Selb is a fanatical secret army, run by Xintou House. Nasra and Rohne've taken over the House and the Jundom, having killed pretty much anyone in Madina who objected. And Mistress Li has died and left us to clean up her mess.' He glanced around coolly. 'Have I missed anything?'

'Yes,' Kett said. 'Hassan is also clearly Selb. And, possibly, Liu Gray of Melcor. The other thing that concerns me is the amount of steel in Jada's possession. If Hassan commands a Selb army of that calibre and armed with steel, Yasmin's junren won't stand a chance on the field, tomorrow.'

Alere cleared her throat and sent a significant look at Saric then tapped her own chest and eyed the double-bladed axe pendant hanging around Corin's neck.

'Ah,' Corin said. 'Of course.' The last thing they needed was any plans leaking to the Selb, if Saric was a spy for Liu.

Saric glared. 'Not blind, you know. I'm not with the Selb and nor is Liu.' He put his feet on the desk and picked at his nails with a shuriken. 'He's too smart for that stuff. He was made an honorary Selb a year or so ago because he'd helped so many of their slave-get escape. Bet you a thousand tiebe he thinks they're zifts.'

He returned their scepticism with a shrug. 'I know he helped army-up the Selb, but Alere asked him to. Why would he swap one mad ruler of Mamlakah for another? Believe me, he doesn't know what they're all about.' He snorted. 'When I see him next, I'll give him a hard time for being such a zift.'

Corin sent him a speculative look. Could the boy be trusted? Had he been spying on them all along? Alere raised one eyebrow at Corin. He sighed. He didn't really want to know if his son was lying, but there were bigger things at stake than his hurt ego. He slid his hands to his weapons and connected with the yanstones' welcoming warmth.

Saric's feet dropped to the floor. He snatched up one of the two yellow-feathered darts on the desk and jabbed it into Corin's arm.

'Ow!' Corin yanked it out and brandished it at his son. 'What the gouri…?'

'I know that look. You were Reading me,' Saric snarled. 'You don't get to give me all that fatherly feihua about caring and being responsible for me, then not trust me. Do it again and I'll go back to Chengdu. I don't need you, old man.'

'Old man!' Corin gave a wry half-laugh and scrubbed at the back of his neck. 'You do realise I'm only twenty-six?'

'I don't care.' Saric's grey-green eyes sheened with swiftly-hidden tears. 'Trust me and stop telling me what to do, or I'm finished.'

Corin opened his mouth. He looked at his son, wanting to believe him. But years in this game had taught him most people were self-serving. Especially when it came to survival. Normally, he just assumed everyone was lying. The rare moments he trusted people he didn't know well almost always came back to bite him. First Shasa, then Tali. But they'd had good reasons.

Did he dare risk trusting the kid? He glanced at Alere, who shrugged.

'Fine, kid,' he finally said. 'I'm sorry. I can't guarantee I'll get it right, but I'll try. Just don't make me regret this.'

'Good.' Saric sniffed. 'You're not too bad when you forget you're my father and act like a normal person.'

'High praise, indeed,' Corin replied. He looked to Kett. 'Please tell me there was no istilqa in that dart? I'd rather not give Saric the chance to Suggest something unpleasant.'

Kett smiled. 'No, unfortunately.'

Alere picked up the one remaining fanghu dart and swore softly. 'Two would have made life much easier tomorrow.'

Corin lifted a brow. 'What for?'

She gave a half-shrug. 'Protection against Rohne and Nasra Reading me.' She rubbed her thumbs over the yanstones in her weapons and a fleeting moment of fear flickered across her face. 'Without fanghu or the yanstones… I just don't have a lot of options.'

'Perhaps. But it was worth it to watch that little interaction. We should—' Kett's head snapped around.

The faintest brush of cloth against wood sounded outside the door.

CHAPTER THIRTY-THREE

ALERE

'Kett?' Master Anh's whisper outside relieved the sudden tension. Alere relaxed.

Rafi unlocked the door and Anh strode in. He held his empty crossbow and retrieved four more bolts from his desk. Blood streaked his face. 'Time for you good folks to leave.'

'Master?' Kett frowned, his sword half out of its scabbard.

Anh nodded at the door. 'We're about to have visitors.' His eyes hardened. 'They killed my gouri xiao-cat. Needless to say, I'm unimpressed.'

Straightening, Kett drew his sword. Steel slickered against leather. 'Not a chance, Master. Rafi, get Tali out of here.'

Anh glanced at Rafi. 'When you get into the stormdrains, head west and take the third turn north. You'll find a bolt-hole set up for just such an occasion. Not exactly luxury, but safe enough for a few hours. Go, shenshi. I'd rather you weren't here. Weishi House is a-political. I'm not supposed to take sides.'

Rafi nodded and hauled Tali through the secret exit. Corin limped over, shut it behind them, and drew his weapon. Saric pulled out his blowpipe and crouched behind the desk.

Alere drew her dagger and wished for the yanstones' calming influence. Without them, her hands trembled and her heart raced. She sucked a slow breath.

The door burst open and eight masked xiongshou crowded in. Anh pulled the trigger. A black bolt skewered one man's shoulder. He wrenched it out and threw it aside without pausing.

One xiongshou raised a blowpipe. Alere flicked a pair of knives. The first went at his head. A distraction He caught it. The second knife went into his inner thigh. Blood poured out, the femoral artery cut. With any luck he would bleed out in five minutes. His blowpipe clattered to the floor, together with a green-feathered dart. Capture order, then. For who?

A black-feathered dart appeared in the largest man's neck. He gasped, yanked it out, and collapsed, half-out the door, convulsing.

Kett snatched up one of the heavy armchairs and hurled it into the six remaining attackers. They leapt aside and it crashed against the wall. Alere flicked a third and fourth knife. One found a knee and one a forearm. Both were immediately flung back at her. She caught one and ducked the other. It clattered off the wall behind. Anh yanked open a drawer and flung down a round object. Alere squeezed her eyes shut.

The flashbomb turned her eyelids white-red. She opened them and coughed, squinting against the red smoke that filled the room. One of the weishi vanished out the door.

Rolling over the desk she sprinted after him. If any reported back to Rohne and Nasra, everyone in Weishi House would be endangered.

'Alli!'

She ignored Kett's call and ran on, through Weishi House's twisting dark corridors, chasing light footsteps. She skidded to a stop in the narrow hall between the students' bedrooms, listening. No footsteps. Weishi House was a maze of hallways. Had she lost him?

A black-clad body leapt at her, hands grasping. No weapons. She sidestepped but there was no space to move. A hand snagged her shoulder and his foot swept her ankle. They fell together. She landed on her back, half underneath his heavy body. The dagger clattered from her grip. He pinned one arm to the floor and tried for an armlock. She squirmed until she got her legs around his hips and hooked her ankles together behind his back. He punched at her face. She blocked and wrapped one arm around his neck, closing the gap, protective. He slammed her hard against the wooden floor. Gasping for breath, she clung tighter, giving him no space to strike.

He wormed a forearm between them and pushed against her jaw. Excruciating pain lanced through her head. Red lights flashed behind her eyes. She punched into his liver. He jerked and swore but didn't relent. His fingers fumbled at his belt. If he was going for a dart she was done for. She yanked out her last throwing knife and drove it into his jugular. He choked a gurgling gasp and fell off her, his fingers clawing at the knife. Blood spurted, glistened on his black clothing and pooled across the floor. He slumped into stillness.

She pulled up his mask and froze. She knew him. A weishi she'd trained with, often. Her stomach heaved. She pressed a hand to her mouth and looked away. She shouldn't have killed him. He was on a capture order.

What was this war coming to? Pitting friend against friend, student against Master.

Leaving the body, she raced back to Anh's office, her heart pounding. Was Kett alright? She leapt over one body in the hall, slid around the corner and grabbed at the door frame.

Of the attacking weishi, only death and blood remained. Six black-clad bodies lay sprawled about the room. The haze of red smoke still hung on the ceiling, shading the lamplight carmine.

Kett leaned against a red-spattered wall, his head hanging, blood dripping off his knife. Corin and Saric held up each other, both panting and stained with blood. A bruise showed purple on Saric's flushed face. Corin bared his teeth in a hissing groan and pressed at his ribs. Anh, his hair smeared with gore, staggered to his chair and sank into it. His hands trembled as he poured a glass of jiu and drank it down.

'Alere?' Kett turned, his expression anxious.

'I'm alright. You?'

He nodded, his chest heaving. Blood stained his right sleeve but the cut on his arm didn't seem deep. 'Did you get the last one?'

Alere nodded. 'As long as there were only eight. But we should go, just in case.'

Master Anh reached down and ripped the mask off one of the xiongshou. He sighed. 'She was one of Zand's cadre.' He tore off another and checked pockets, pulling out a folded scrap of paper. 'Him, too. Gouri! This is a capture order for me, signed by Zand. I trained that man since he was ten. How dare he turn on me this way? What the diyu is going on, Kett?'

Kett toed two of the fallen. 'They're all dead, so we can't ask. We have to go. We'll send word when we need you.' He picked up one of the dropped blowpipes, and several black-feathered darts, and tucked them into his belt.

Anh waved them out. 'Go, lad.' He raised a fresh glass of jiu in homage. 'I'm going to drown my sorrows for a little while, then I'll take those still loyal and follow you into the storm drains. We'll be at the coronation.' He bared yellowing teeth. 'And I think I'm looking forward to it, now.'

Kett upended a splintered wooden crate and laid out a map of Madina he had brought from the Xintou House library. 'Corin, what was the latest on Yasmin's position?'

With a groan, Corin sank onto another crate. Alere dropped her pack and prowled around the claustrophobic, brick-lined room. Tucked away in the storm-drain system beneath Madina, the tiny room held nothing but three rickety canvas cots, three crates and a few lanterns. Water dripped and glistened, blood-red with algae, down the walls. The stench of mould and rotting refuse was almost overpowering, the cold air still and thick. Saric kicked a wriggling red salamander out the door into darkness. It splashed into the drain water and something squeaked. Tali jumped and rubbed at her arms, glancing apprehensively at the opening.

Corin repositioned a mel-oil lamp so more light shone on the map. 'Yasmin should be just south of the city if she stayed on her previous course and speed.' He pointed at an open swathe of land outside the city limits. 'But how does that help? We can't let them face Hassan and the Selb on open ground tomorrow.'

Rafi paled. 'My wife has no experience leading an army and no idea of the odds against her.'

'You're right, shenshi,' Kett said, placing a broken piece of brick on the map to hold it flat. 'We need to take the Selb out of the picture. Let's assume Jada will bring them through the city to join the rest of Hassan's army, already waiting. Marching them around would take too long. He'll have to move them through this part of Madina.' He indicated the Zalam area. 'Have you ever heard of urban guerilla warfare?'

'No.' Rafi glowered.

'These parts of the city inside the wall were planned.' Kett smoothed the map again. 'Not haphazard as people think. And planned by someone not as idealistic as the rest of the colonists. The designer laid out the streets around the Alcazar to be a defensible, confusing maze. Only the main north-south and east-west access roads are straight. Normally, the advantage in urban warfare lies with the inhabitants. But if the invaders know the key to the maze, and the defenders are unfamiliar with this sort of warfare, then the advantage changes hands.'

Alere peered at the map, hope rising. He was right. Close fighting in narrow streets favoured those who knew the terrain and the tactics of such warfare. It allowed small groups to defeat larger ones.

They needed to fight the Selb inside the city, not out on the open plain.

'I see,' Rafi said. 'But we have so little time. How do we teach them this style of fighting and what's the goal of it? Are we to kill or capture? What about civilians?' He paused and stared at the dark, vaulted ceiling. 'Wait.' He turned suspicion on Kett. 'If the Selb leaders are elite weishi, won't they know all this, too? How do we know *you* aren't part of them?'

'Shenshi.' Kett's voice was low and even. 'Are we back at this? As I've said before: if I truly wanted the Jun First throne, or to displace you, I could have done so years ago. Radan would have welcomed me back with open arms.' He leaned forward, a mere handspan from Rafi. 'Now, if you have nothing useful to contribute, you will oblige all of us by shutting up.'

A long, cold silence followed, full of unspoken rage from Rafi. Saric snorted a laugh and Corin cuffed him lightly over the head.

Alere gripped her father's wrist. 'Believe me, Rafi, Kett is not your enemy, I promise. He's also not your usual weishi. Most of them rarely even open a book, let alone the oldest ones where he learned about this style of warfare.'

Rafi looked back and forth between her and Kett, eyes narrowed in flowering suspicion. He dragged his fingertips across his forehead, lips clamped tightly together.

'I apologise. Again.'

Kett indicated the map. 'We have a lot to do. We'll need to split up.

'Oh!' Tali had been reading the Koh-Lin journal and flipped the page so Kett could see. 'Did you read this part? About how they tried to cure the boy?'

'Yes. I don't understand the xintou techniques they were describing. That's the part I was hoping you'd read. What does it mean?'

'They started off by trying to do what Mina did – create a control-gene so the boy could manage his powers.'

'But?' Alere asked.

'He was already unhinged. He resisted. They failed.' Tali flipped the page. 'Even with both Edwards twins working together, they didn't have enough power to contain him and perform the procedure. So instead they tried to switch off the trigger gene. He would at least live a normal life.'

Alere gasped. 'Is that possible?'

Tali nibbled at her lip. 'I'm not sure. They lost control of him before they could finish. That's when he killed everyone in the village. Oh.' She shuddered and her mouth drooped. 'Lei Koh-Lin had to kill him. Stabbed him with a steel dagger. I think that might be where the Selb get their idea about steel being needed to cleanse the impure.'

'Makes sense,' Corin said.

Tali's eyes widened. 'And this part about the twins Fusing to—'

'Tali!' Kett's voice cut across hers and she shrank away.

'What?' Alere asked. 'What about Fusing?' Kett looked away. 'You have to stop protecting me, Kett. If there's anything in there that can give me an edge, I need to know.'

'No,' Tali said. 'He's right. It's not worth it.'

Alere glared at both of them. 'Tell me.'

Kett sighed. 'Very well. When Kya and Bree Edwards were trying to save Kya's son, they used something called a *shenhilya*.'

He lifted troubled eyes to hers. 'Kya believed that Fusing – either with each other or with the *shenhilya* – would provide enough power to cure him or switch the gene off. Bree refused to try.'

Alere stilled, trying to keep shock from her expression. She resisted the urge to touch the heavy yanstone pulling at her pocket. Would holding it, giving herself over to it…would that kickstart her powers again? Did she dare when it felt so…seductive; so powerful?

'Fusing. No. It's fatal.' She pulled at a lock of hair tickling her neck.

'I know. And we don't even know what a *shenhilya* is. Plus you don't have the xintou gift now. That's why I didn't want to say anything.' He gripped her hand so hard the knuckles ground together.

'Why were they trying to save the kid, anyway?' Saric said caustically. 'Sounds like a ziftish thing to do.'

Corin eyed him. 'No idea. Why would any parent want their brat kid to stay around?'

Saric grinned. 'Charm and good looks?'

'There's something about that back here. I skipped it.' Tali flipped back a few pages. Her fingers stole to her mouth. 'Oh, no.'

'What?' Alere peered at the page.

'I recognise this phrase.' She pointed. 'The first part says that the Edwards sisters thought male xintou had the potential to be more powerful than females. They just needed more power to stabilise one. And they thought they could achieve that through their own twin-bond and the *shenhilya*.'

'We already know Rohne can do more than most,' Alere said.

'But then it says they thought a stable male xintou would have the power to change the course of history and to guide humanity into a better world.'

'So?'

Tali raised frightened indigo eyes to Alere's. 'Out there today, that Jada Marin-kin man. He said Rohne would change history and guide humanity to a better world. Those exact words.'

Alere exchanged a horrified look with Kett. 'Rohne said Nasra had a huge library. What if she had a copy of the journal? What if she's used the Edwards sisters' ideas to stabilise Rohne all these years? Until she could find the power to make it permanent. Maybe that's partly why she created the erheyi girls – trying to replicate what the Edwards sisters were doing?'

'Makes a kind of twisted logic, I guess,' Corin said.

Alere gasped. 'You said all the erheyi were teenagers!' She pressed a hand to her lips. 'Nasra is nai-xintou. She was there when Mina and I were born. *Our* latent xintou genes gave her the idea. Oh, gouri!' Her knees gave way and she collapsed onto a crate.

Kett squeezed her shoulder. 'Don't, Alli.'

'Did it work?' Corin asked. 'Do you think Nasra managed to stabilise Rohne permanently?'

'No.' Alere sucked a breath, quashing the flare of guilt. 'Mina said Rohne was getting bad headaches all the way to Chengdu. It's one of the symptoms.'

'The journal has detailed instructions on how to shut the gene down,' Tali put in. She grimaced. 'But it needs the twin-bonded minds to make it work. One controls the patient and funnels power, while the other does the nai-xintou DNA work. So, I can't do it.'

Everyone looked at Alere.

'I can give you the instructions,' Tali said meekly. 'But you need Mina.'

'So, this will only work if I re-connect with Mina and get our powers back?' Alere said. 'Does the journal mention yanstones?'

Tali re-read a few pages. 'Not that I can tell. Kett? You've read it more thoroughly.'

'No, I didn't find any reference, either. Why?'

'Nothing,' Alere said, acutely conscious of the Xintou-House stone pressed against her thigh. That had to be what Mistress Li intended. She wanted Alere to use the power of all the yanstones, including the *shenhilya*, to shut down Rohne's xintou gene. With the Koh-Lin necklace and Rafi's bracelet, Alere now had more yanstones set in meteoric iron than had ever been available to the Edwards sisters. The extra power could be the missing ingredient.

And with that additional power, Fusing shouldn't be necessary. As long as she used the *shenhilya*. But would that work? Would it re-start her gifts, even without Mina? There was only one way to find out.

Sucking a deep breath, she slid one hand into her pocket and pulled the *shenhilya* free of its cloth wrapping. Turning away from the others, she closed her eyes, steeled herself, and gripped the stone with her hand.

A faint tingle as energy burrowed under her skin, leaving the taste of burnt wood and quenched iron in her mouth again. She tried to reach Mina. Nothing. She opened all her wards, right to the Inners. Still *nothing!* Not even a connection to the Koh-Lin necklace at her throat. Bitter disappointment drove a fist into her stomach, leaving her sick and weak-kneed. She released the stone.

There had to be a way to get her xintou gifts back. She had no hope of defeating Nasra and Rohne without them.

And, if that journal was right, she needed Mina in order to stop Rohne. So how did she re-Bond? The answer had to lie with Mina. She must have to be close to Mina, touching the stones, *and* with Mina's wards lowered. It was the only thing that fit. The only thing she hadn't tried. But would Mina even agree?

She returned to the discussion and interrupted Corin's questions to Kett about guerrilla fighting.

'Only one problem with the plan to switch off Rohne's abilities by re-Bonding Mina and I,' Alere said, brusquely. 'Even assuming I *can* re-Bond, Mina won't want to shut down Rohne's abilities. She'll want to try and cure him. And what about her heart? Was that even true?'

'No,' Tali said quietly. 'I'd been instructed to cut your tie and stop you re-bonding.' She touched the Koh-Lin journal. 'At least now I know how Nasra knew about it.'

'What choice do we have?' Kett said. 'You'll have to force Mina to re-Bond. Rohne has to be neutralised, one way or the other.'

'Which makes me exactly what she said I was becoming,' Alere said. 'As much of a monster as Ven, or Hallon, and even Nasra. Someone who forces their will on people. Takes away their freedom of choice.'

Kett grimaced. 'I'm sorry, Alli. But we can't let Mina's Healer ethics and her rosy view of Rohne get in the way of this. If we can't stop Nasra and Rohne, they will crush every ideal of freedom and peace this colony stands for. This is the start of a new religion. One that worships the rule of strength by steel. Controlled by the power of male xintou. A tyrannical power that will manipulate the very thoughts in people's heads.' He swiped a hand over his face. 'One of them will be the tyrant you've been warned about three times, now. If Rohne and Nasra win, ours is the last generation that will know freedom of choice in any form.'

Sickened, Alere strode away. Her aimless, hasty steps took her to the arched doorway and back. She drew long, slow breaths, trying to calm her mind and heart.

'Alli?' Kett's warm hand stroked her back and she repressed the urge to throw herself into his arms. It would solve nothing. No amount of bemoaning would. She needed action.

And she needed to be more powerful than Nasra and Rohne. She had to reconnect with Mina. To use her own sister, even though it would probably destroy both of them if she couldn't control it and they Fused.

When the time came, she would let the yanstones in. This time she was resigned to what they would mould her into. Jarran had been right. Someone dispassionate had to make these choices. She would need to be that person – that weapon – in order to force Mina's compliance.

If the Bonding worked.

There were no guarantees. She couldn't assume it would. She needed another option as well.

Certain of her path now, she accepted her fate. She was done with fear. Done with hesitation. Done with worry about how her actions might affect those close to her. That was for later. Right now, only Nasra, Rohne, Hassan, and Jada mattered. Only their deaths would guarantee the safety of everyone, and everything, she loved.

Straightening, Alere spoke calmly. 'I'll be alright. Continue the briefing. We need to get this done, Kett.'

He scrutinised her, a flash of worry in him. Reassurance would have to wait. She had a job to do and she now knew exactly how to attempt it.

Corin held up a hand. 'Anyone else hear that?'

They all fell silent, every breath held.

'Voices.' Saric cocked an ear. 'Back toward Weishi House. Five, at least.'

Tali's gaze unfocussed. 'He's right. Five weishi with very strong wards. No. More. A lot more.' She shivered.

Corin rose. 'Time to move again. We can't be sure if they are Anh's men or Rohne's.'

'Where?' Kett asked, folding the map and stuffing it into his pack.

Alere collected a lantern. Saric snatched up another.

Corin led the way. 'Follow me.'

PART IV – Time of the Erheyi

CHAPTER THIRTY-FOUR

CORIN

Corin hauled himself up the stout wooden ladder, hoping his hunch was correct. He was filthy, cold, exhausted, and hungry. They all needed somewhere safe to plan or this ridiculous venture would be over before it began. At the top of the ladder, he pressed a catch and a small door swung soundlessly outward. He crawled into open air and breathed deep.

The open courtyard lay empty and silent. To the west, the sun was a firey ball on the horizon, just glimpses between the outbuildings; bloody light reflecting off the great house's west-facing windows; the shadows steel-blue and cold.

Alere and Kett emerged, weapons at the ready. He waved them aside and used a wall to push himself upright. Every muscle ached and he wanted to sleep for a week.

Rafi straightened and pressed at his lower back, groaning. He gazed around, his brows rising. 'We're—'

Corin laid a finger to his lips and whispered. 'Wait until we're inside. The neighbours think the owner is away, remember?' He kept to the shadows and made his way to the back door. It took only a few seconds to pick the lock. Rafi eyed him wryly.

Inside, the house waited, dark and chill, heavy with the smell of absence and abandonment.

'Where are the staff?' Rafi whispered.

'Houlia said,' Corin murmured, 'that, after the Alcazar raids, the staff shut the place up and went to stay elsewhere.'

'Where are we?' Tali asked, tiptoeing behind them down a long, gloomy hall.

Corin opened a door and set his shuttered lantern on the enormous dining table of plain blackwood and red zitanwood. He and Rafi hurried to the four large windows and drew the heavy velvet curtains closed. Then Corin opened the lantern enough to see the room. High ceilings; regal portraits of people wearing old-fashioned clothing adorning each wall; a bamboo floor silenced with silver-threaded, deep green rugs.

'Welcome to Koh-Lin House,' he said quietly.

'Are you *mad?*' Alere hissed. 'Houlia said Nasra's people have checked here three times since she came.'

He grinned. 'Exactly. Three's the magic number in people's heads, I've found. They won't come again.'

She sent him a disbelieving glare.

'Let's not waste time, just in case.' Kett lit three small candles and placed them in the middle of the table, bringing little pools of golden light into the darkness. They couldn't risk switching on the great, overhead electric chandeliers. They all crowded close as Kett traced over the map again.

'It's just fallen night and we have until dawn to get in place. Saric, you'll liaise with Corin's spy network to spread the word. Then go to Messenger House. Get them to use the new copper-wire communication to warn Petar's people in Jiali about the Selb. Flitters will be restricted, but I don't think Nasra will know about the wires as that information hasn't been released to the public, yet.'

'Who are we spreading the word to in Madina?' Alere asked.

Kett frowned. 'From what I saw, the people are sick of the mass murders committed in Hassan's name. They should be willing to help us, or at least stay out of our way. But Hassan's army are half locals, with families, so it's a calculated risk. Rafi, you and Corin will go to Yasmin and brief her junren on what to do against Hassan's junren outside the city. Then Corin will bring a thousand back into the city, through the drains, to ambush the Selb.'

Rafi nodded. Corin sank into a chair and massaged the newly-healed bolt-wound on his leg. The night was going to be a long one. Perhaps a quick trip to Rafi's wine cellar might be a good idea.

'Tali.' Kett addressed the xintou. 'Where do you stand? Are you with us?'

'This is my fight, too.' She threw back her shoulders. 'It's my city and my people. The House was meant to protect and guide people, not control and murder them. What do I do?'

'You'll go with Cor and Rafi to join Yasmin. Take charge of the xintou girls. We'll need them for two things: communication and to handle those erheyi girls. Split the youngest xintou up and put them in safe rooftop vantage points around the city to help our leaders communicate. The older ones will need to deal with whatever the eleven pairs of erheyi can do.'

'Nasra has taught them a technique,' Alere put in, shivering, 'for drilling straight through Outer wards in seconds. Tell them to be ready for that. There's no protection so you have to strike first and fast.'

Tali blanched. Corin gripped her hand and she gave him a small, grateful smile.

Kett rubbed at his face. 'You'll be at a disadvantage – the twins have trained for this. Xintou spend their whole lives being told *not* to use their skills as weapons. But Alere can help you come up with some pretty devious options.'

Alere's dark eyes blazed. Corin grinned. He suspected Tali would find many of her ideas appalling. It would be a matter of convincing the xintou to break their training. Who they would be afterward was a matter for speculation.

Rafi looked shrewdly at Kett. 'And you, Tekettan? Since you're the best qualified to lead my army, is that your part in this?' He restlessly wiped at the map, as though obliterating the city.

'No. Helping lead Yasmin's army is your job, shenshi,' Kett said, his tone still respectful. 'Mine is protecting Alere, as it's always been.'

'Protecting her while doing what, exactly?' Rafi scowled back and forth between Alere and Kett.

'I,' Alere said into the thick silence, 'have to be at the coronation. I have to re-Bond with Mina and get her and Jarran free.' She pushed back from the table and stood, poised as if ready to escape the inevitable argument. 'Before you all get protective, I'll stay in the audience. I'm sure I can reconnect with Mina once she sees me. She'll let down her wards.'

Corin gazed at her suspiciously, misliking the innocent tone.

Rafi scowled. 'You should have at least a few weishi with you as protection.'

'I can hide in the crowd better on my own. Kett will get Jarran free. But it's my responsibility to put a stop to Rohne and Nasra. I'm the only one who can. I know that now.' Her hand slid into the pocket of her trous and she looked away.

'What about Rohne?' Rafi asked. 'What about his powers with the stones in Mina's bracelets?'

Her chin came up. 'I'll deal with it.'

'*How?*' Rafi slapped his palms onto the table.

She sent him a cold glare. 'I just will.'

Corin leaned back, smiling grimly. He knew that look. Rafi had no hope.

Rafi frowned at her for a few moments, then seemed to fold in on himself. 'And I can't stop you, can I? Very well.' He sank back into a seat, appearing to age a decade in a few seconds. 'Kett, what do we do?'

'I'll go speak to a man I know in Trades House.' Kett tapped the map. 'He owns a building business. Teams can saw through half a dozen of the thorn-tuft trees along the main street.'

'Those trees are five hundred years old!' Tali said.

'And this is the reason they were planted,' Kett replied sharply. 'To use as timber-fall traps. The thorns in the canopy leaf-tufts will spray out on impact as well. That should drive the Selb into the side alleys. Corin and his contingent of junren will be waiting for them.'

Corin groaned. A *really* long night.

Kett continued. 'Cor, your job will be both containing the Selb, and providing a distraction while Alli and I get Mina and Jarran free. So *do not* let them out the south gate.'

'What do we do with prisoners?' Rafi said.

Alere traced her finger along the Zalam streets to the riverside docs. 'There are a lot of abandoned warehouses in that area. Wouldn't take many guards to keep them in.'

'Good thinking. The fewer deaths the better.' Kett nodded.

Alere pointed at the main street. 'But what about the elite *jijin* xiongshou squads of Selb? They'll be riding point and rear, and guarding the erheyi. At least, that's how I'd do it.'

'Agreed,' Kett said. 'Which means they won't be caught in the timberfall we aim at the main body of Selb junren. And we can't afford to let them escape. Rafi?' He eyed the Jun Second. 'Was there any gunpowder left after you blew the bridges in Shanzhai? Would Yasmin have brought it with her?'

Rafi straightened. 'Yes, on both counts. Six barrels. Why?'

'I think,' Kett said grimly, 'some booby traps are in order.'

Corin laughed.

'Alere!'

She turned at Corin's call. Her face was half-shadowed in the bloody moonlight.

An hour of planning and arguing later, and Corin, Alere, and Kett stood in Koh-Lin House's courtyard and farewelled the others. Full dark blanketed the House, inside and out. The buildings were closed and vacant again as everyone left on their various tasks. Corin limped over. His bootheels echoed too loudly in the empty space. He snatched her into a tight hug for a long moment, treasuring the lithe warmth of her one last time. Then he held her away.

'Y'know, I get that you have to be the one to deal with Nasra and Rohne, I do.' He eyed her narrowly. 'But why at the coronation? I mean, I can see the appeal. It's got nice drama and timing to it. A big stage with lots of witnesses. But, despite past evidence to the contrary, you're not a showman. Couldn't we just arrange a discreet little assassination behind closed doors for Hassan? Then quietly crown Jarran and cut their feet out from beneath them that way?' He wanted her as far away as possible from Rohne and Nasra. Being at the coronation was insanity.

Alere shivered. Her breath frosted as she spoke, 'You're right, it's not about the show. Although doing this publicly means less misinformation afterward. Believe me, when I was in the Alcazar this morning I thought long and hard about using the hidden door to Hassan's room to lie in wait for him. And maybe I could have. I might even have been able to hide long enough to get to Rohne or Nasra, but probably not. Especially if Rohne had the bracelets when he got back from meeting you. Even if I'd killed one of them, you'd still be left with the other. Plus, Hassan, Jada and all the Selb.

'No.' She pushed her fingers into her loose hair. 'The coronation's the only place they'll all be together, and vulnerable. And with you and Rafi taking some of the erheyi girls out of the picture, I won't have to deal with all of them. I have to get close enough to Bond with Mina again. I can't do it from here. I've tried.'

Corin screwed up his nose. 'Surely they'll have more security at the coronation, not less. How will they be more vulnerable?'

'I don't mean physically vulnerable. Rohne and Nasra are overconfident.' She paced a couple of steps in each direction. 'Rohne wants recognition. Nasra wants to show she's in command of the xintou and the Selb. To show she can destroy anyone. I have to convince the people watching the coronation that she's not in control and the Xintou are not to be feared.' She kissed his cheek. 'I promise I'll stay hidden in the crowd.'

Corin sighed. 'This is a gouri suicide mission, Alere.'

'Yours or mine?' she asked, her smile wavering.

'Yes.' He strode away, his heart leaden.

CHAPTER THIRTY-FIVE

ROHNE

Two levels below his room in the Alcazar's south tower, Rohne paused outside a guest room. He waved aside the weishi standing guard and let himself in.

The room was dark and cold, lit by one, dull bulb flickering high above the bed. By its feeble light, he just made out the thick, dark-timbered furniture, deep blue soft furnishings, and two small pictures on the walls. No fire burned in the hearth and the room was stripped bare of anything useful as a weapon. A meal for one, untouched, waited on a low table. Draped across the couch, a plain white house-robe lay unworn.

Luna-Yi, full and fat on the eastern horizon, spilled blood into dark streets emptied by Hassan's curfew. Curled up in the window seat with her arms around her knees and her head resting on them, Mina gazed in silent melancholy across the dusk-shrouded, blood-washed city. She didn't even look around as Rohne closed the thick zitan wood door behind him and locked it.

'Why bother,' she said. 'All you have to do is *make* me stay. You don't need a lock or guards.'

'Mina…' He wasn't interested in arguing with her. He needed something from her and, although he could take it, it would be simpler and less painful if she co-operated.

Perhaps he just had to win her sympathy back.

She turned and dropped her booted feet to the floor, crossing her ankles and tucking her hands beneath her thighs.

'Don't, Rohne.' She stared at her feet. Still dressed in Alere's travel clothes she looked ridiculously young and vulnerable, her gaze full of resignation and pity when she finally looked up. 'Whatever you have to say, just don't. I don't want to hear it.'

He glowered. 'I haven't come to say anything. I've come to ask you a question.'

'Why even pretend to treat me like a real person?' She rose and tapped her temple. 'You can just take the answers, can't you? You don't need to actually talk to me. Go ahead. It's so much easier.'

'Mina—'

'After all, if you don't talk to me then you don't have to deal with all the messy, difficult emotions that go with being human.' She flung her arms wide. 'All the feelings you've spent your whole life trying to ignore by pretending you're so much smarter than everyone else who has them.'

'I don't think I'm—' Rohne began, resentment building fire in his stomach.

'Save it.' Her mouth pursed. 'I couldn't begin to count the number of times you've ranted at me over the years. Telling me what a shazi someone was because they were upset or angry at something you'd done. And you've always been so proud of your ability to keep people at arms length.' She folded her arms. 'Even me.'

'You?' He closed the gap between them and grabbed her by the elbows. 'I never kept you at a distance. You were the one who went off to Madina for years. You were the one who chose Kett, and Jarran, over me. I loved you, Mina!'

'I wish I could believe you, Rohne.' She indicated the room. 'But love doesn't do this. Love doesn't imprison and control.' Laying a palm on his chest she said quietly, 'All I ever wanted was for you to tell me what you *felt*. Not what you knew. Not why I was wrong and you were right. What *you* felt.' Her fingers curled into a fist. 'But you were so caught up in your obsession with being xintou, and proving yourself smarter and better than everyone, you couldn't just be…Rohne. You didn't want my love. You wanted my worship; my admiration.'

She gave a derisive laugh. 'Now look at you. Alone with Nasra in your steel tower, just as she always wanted. Are you happy? You've got all the books and money you want. Servants to wait on you. People to bow and scrape and admire your brilliance. And you can destroy anyone who disagrees with you like *that*.' She snapped her fingers. 'Isn't that what you wanted?'

'No!' Rohne glared. What right did she have to scold him or make him feel like he was some rebellious adolescent? 'I never wanted this. Nasra did. I didn't know she was going to do all this. I just wanted to be accepted for what I am and not feared.'

'You're lying.' She pressed her mouth thin. 'I can always tell. You knew about the twins and what they could do. She's obviously been training them for years. What did you think they were training for?' Mina stopped and pressed her fingers to her flushed cheeks. 'Jiche! I just remembered. When we first left with Alere and the four of us camped on the edge of Hassan Wen-Gates's estate. We joked about him and how all the twins on his lands were odd, but not dangerous. How you must have laughed at us. How superior you must have felt.'

'Nasra just said we were going to put Xintou House back on the right path,' he muttered, annoyed at the direction the conversation was taking. 'I didn't know.'

'And you never stopped to think about what that would entail?' Mina raised her brows. 'You had to be wilfully blind if you thought she could do that without bloodshed. I've been defending you to Alere and the others all this time. Telling them you're a good person. But I think they were right. You're just selfish and bitter and power-mad. What did Nasra promise you? Just the Bonding to the First?' She put her hands on her hips. 'Or the throne itself?'

He paused, anger derailed by the unexpectedness of the question. 'Why would she promise me the throne?'

Now it was her turn to stare at him, openmouthed. Then she gave a slightly hysterical giggle.

'She hasn't told you?' She laughed again, this time pityingly. 'Surely you've read enough of Sura's healer books to have picked up some genetics. Have you never thought about your parents? For years Jada didn't want to acknowledge you. Then suddenly he does. And you didn't find that strange? No.' She wiped her hands down her thighs. 'I suppose not. You were so contemptuous of the villagers when they teased you as a mother-kin child. So quick to rub their noses in it when Jada acknowledged you. I suppose you wouldn't want to question it.'

Rohne grabbed her shoulders, shaking her. 'What are you talking about?'

She shrank away. 'Your eyes, Rohne. What colour are they?'

It took several seconds for her words to have meaning, then it hit. He released her, staggered back and collapsed onto the couch. How had he missed it? His eyes were amber. Nasra's were dark blue and Jada's were blue-grey. Blue was recessive. It was almost impossible for them to have a brown-eyed child, even with a nai-xintou to tweak the genes. Khara! Mina was right. He hadn't wanted to see it. He pressed his thumbs hard against his temples as the throbbing returned five-fold.

A stronger overhead light flicked on and he squinted against the glare. Mina removed a small painting from the wall and shoved aside her meal to lay it on the table before him.

'Look,' she ordered. 'Look and tell me you don't see the resemblance. Your eyes, Hassan's, Jarran's they're all the same shade of golden-brown. That's Radan Zah-Hill at about your age.'

Reluctantly, he studied the picture. She was right. The eye colour and shape were identical, as was the nose. Radan's hair was black, his was auburn, like Nasra's. But she was vain about that and would have duplicated and kept that gene. The rest she hadn't cared enough about to change.

Mina knelt before him. She turned his face so he had to meet her gaze.

'She planned this, Rohne. Twenty-five years ago. She planned you. She seduced Radan to produce you and she planned this whole coup. She's manipulated all of us for her own twisted reasons.' Tears welled again and her lip quivered. 'Now she's going to make you murder your own brothers. Jarran and Kett are both your half-brothers. Jarran's little girls are your nieces. Is that who you want to be? A murderer? Because that's not the boy I grew up with and loved.'

'No!' He hurled the painting across the room. It smashed against the wall, the canvas tearing and the timber frame snapping in two. He stood and headed for the door. 'You're only saying this because you want me to save Jarran,' he snarled. 'You don't love me and you never did. You pitied me, like everyone else in that gouri backward village. You—'

A sword of pain sliced through his skull from temple to temple. Knees buckling, he fell against the wall, gasping.

'Oh no!' Mina held him up as the pain peaked and ebbed, leaving him breathless and sick.

He opened his eyes to find her gazing fearfully at him.

'How long have you been having headaches? Tell me,' she demanded when he hesitated.

'Since not long after we left Gaton,' he admitted. 'They've been getting worse.'

'Oh, Rohne!' She guided him to a chair. 'I'm so sorry. I was hoping she'd found a way to make the stability permanent.'

The ache waned and became bearable again. 'What do you mean?'

'Here.' She raised her face. 'Take the memory. It's what happened on our trip here. It will happen to you, too, if you don't get help. I don't have the skill but maybe Nasra does.'

Rohne hesitated, suspicious. After all he'd done she was still willing to try and help him? Why? Was it some kind of trap? He saw nothing but concern in her. Worry about him and a hint of resignation. She'd never been one to hold a grudge or stay angry for long. She had always forgiven him the many times he'd lost his temper with her over the years.

More fool her.

He wrenched the memory from her. She cried out, whimpering as he dug deeper and tore out every minute detail of the child's death. When that was done, he found the memory of Kett's briefing on the Koh-Lin journal. Ignoring her pained protest, he sifted through the rest of her recent days. The process was much easier when she'd lowered her wards voluntarily. Easier for him, anyway. She still held something back; something locked behind a ward so deep into her Inners that he couldn't access it without risking Fusion.

He hesitated. No, it wasn't worth it. She couldn't know anything more vital than what he'd already seen in her memories: how to stem the progression of his malady. She and Alere had been close to an answer. With that knowledge and her yanstones, he could improve on their results.

When he had what he wanted, he released Mina and stood over her. She lay, curled on the floor in the foetal position, arms around her head. Tears streamed down her cheeks and she begged him to stop.

Tugging his robe straight, he bowed stiffly. 'Thank you. You've answered my question. But you were hoping to appeal to my humanity? Hoping I would help you stop Nasra. All you did was prove that I need her alive. And I have even more reason to stop Alere now, and none at all to keep you or Jarran alive.' He curled a lip. 'Especially now I know for certain you never loved me, and never will.'

'Rohne!' She grabbed feebly at his ankle. 'Please? I can help. Let Jarran go. I'll do anything you ask.'

He kicked free. 'You're pathetic, Mina. I don't need your approval or your love. Thank you for revealing my inheritance, though. I'll be pleased to take Hassan's place on the throne. The man is a hmar.'

Opening the door he sneered at her. 'Enjoy your last night. In fact, by way of thanks, I'll even send Jarran in. You can console each other before you die tomorrow. Sleep well.'

'Rohne!'

ALERE

An Alcazar patrol drove Alere and Kett into hiding after they left the Koh-Lin residence to put into place their part of the plans. They slipped into one of the small, damp recesses in the southern wall of Xintou House and paused to take stock of the street outside. A light drizzle of rain drifted from the sky and clouds scudded across to obscure the bloody moon. Kett dropped his bag at the back of the niche.

'Leave your gear here. We'll collect it on the way back.' He parted the thick curtain of black vines a fraction, then let them fall. The ten-man patrol marched down the street in the direction of the Alcazar.

When the patrol passed, Alere touched Kett's arm. He turned back, his eyes just a glint of light in the gloom.

'We've come full circle,' she said. 'This was where you first came to my rescue when I ran from the Alcazar.'

He took in their surroundings, his expression serious. 'Yes. And I'll do it again, Alli.'

'No.' She kissed him. 'You can't this time and I have a favour to ask.'

'Why do I have a feeling I'm not going to like the next words out of your mouth?' He gazed darkly down at her.

'Because you know me so well. After we get back from seeing your builder friend about the timberfall traps, let's get a couple of hours sleep.'

He kissed her forehead. 'That doesn't sound so bad.'

'Then...' She ran her hands down his arms, feeling the tension there. 'We'll need to be in position before dawn.'

'Agreed,' he said, palpably waiting for the rest.

'And tomorrow, when it comes time for me to confront Nasra and Rohne, you focus on getting Jarran to safety but don't...' she cleared her throat '...don't put yourself in harms way trying to help me. No matter what happens.'

Kett was silent for such a long time she almost broke her own rule in dealing with him and pressured him for an answer. At last, he sighed.

'Don't ask me to stand by and not help you.'

'I'm not asking.' She stroked his jaw, running a thumb over his lips. 'I'm telling you. Stay out of the way. If I'm going to do what needs to be done, I can't afford to be distracted by worry. You have your task. Don't try to help with mine as well.'

His mouth curved into a wry smile. 'And so the student outgrows the teacher?'

She chuckled. 'More like the student aspires to become anywhere near as good as the teacher and can't concentrate if the teacher is hovering.'

'Doesn't quite roll off the tongue so easily, though. Alli, I can't—'

'I'll be fine,' she assured him, hoping the darkness hid her doubts. 'I just need to be sure you will be.'

'Jiangui!' He hauled her close, his arms so tight she could scarcely breathe.

'You know I love you, Kett,' she whispered.

This time the silence lasted so long she thought he really wasn't going to reply.

'I wish you could Read me,' he said at last.

'Me too. Tell me.' Part of her didn't want to hear, in case she lost courage to do what must be done.

'I'm…afraid of losing you, Alli.' He rested his forehead against hers. 'I've been alone my whole life. Afraid to love anyone in case they left or rejected me.' He spoke slowly, haltingly, and she understood how hard it was for him to put these feelings into words.

'But I trust you,' he murmured. 'You're the one person who would never betray me.'

She didn't deserve his faith. She withdrew from the intimacy, from their physical closeness, unable to bear the knowledge she had, already, betrayed that trust. She had killed his father, and she had deliberately misled him – and the others – about what would happen at the coronation. But there was no other way. No other choice.

He frowned. 'You're holding back. What?'

'I…' She shook her head. 'I'll tell you later. We have to go, now.'

Kett grabbed her wrist. 'Promise? We can't have secrets any more, Alli. Not now.'

She pulled free and ran out into the street. He swore but his soft footsteps followed.

CHAPTER THIRTY-SIX

ALERE

The time to wake came too soon and Alere sucked in a slow breath. The clear white light of Luna-Er streamed in through a small skylight, faintly illuminating the familiar four white walls of her tiny room in Xintou House. That made it about two hours before dawn and time they moved out.

Her bed was too small for two people, so Kett had put two mattresses on the floor when they returned to Xintou House just after midnight. Their lovemaking had been fierce and poignant, desperate and full of unspoken fears and gratitude. Alere fell asleep content, with the spice of Kett's skin in each breath, his steady heartbeat in her ear and the warmth of his body fitted against hers.

Now she awoke, languorous, trying to hold onto the contentment. Perhaps she could just lock the door and keep the world out forever. Heavy-hearted, she looked up to find Kett regarding her, calm and serious.

'How long have you been awake?' She stretched, arching her back.

He traced a fingertip along the line of her cheek and jaw. 'Awhile. This mattress is amazingly uncomfortable. How did you stand sleeping on it all those years?'

She yawned. 'I guess I got used to it. Mistress Li didn't exactly encourage us to be soft. Did you sleep at all?'

Kett gathered her close. 'You had nightmares.'

'Which translates to "you kept me awake again".' She sighed. 'Sorry. Maybe, after today—'

'Jiangui, Alli! Don't.' He rose and dragged on a pair of trous, moving restlessly to the door and back again. Folding his arms across his bare chest he leaned against the wall, only to shove off again when she stared at him in bewilderment.

'Quit pretending,' he said. 'Don't you think I know what that promise last night was really about?' The moonlight cast deep shadows below his cheekbones and brows, lending his face an unusual severity. 'You don't believe there will be an "after today".'

Alere held back a defensive retort by sheer force of will.

'Please don't, Kett.' She scrambled up and sat on the hard timber cot, wrapping a flimsy house-robe around her nakedness, vulnerable beneath his unexpected display of anger.

'Don't what?' he growled. 'Be right? I've known you long enough. I can see it in you. Why do you doubt yourself so much?'

'It's not that…' She faltered, unable to put into words the extent of her fear: that she wouldn't regain her powers; that Mina wouldn't allow the Bond. Or that she would, and it wouldn't work, or wouldn't be enough. Or worse, that she would but only in Fusion would they be strong enough to overpower Rohne and Nasra.

No matter what the outcome, confronting Rohne and Nasra would be the end for her. And, probably, for Mina as well.

Kett stilled. 'Gouri. You don't believe you can beat Nasra with the yanstones. Even with Mina's help.'

She averted her face.

'No, that's not it.' He gave a disbelieving laugh. 'I can't believe I missed it. You don't even think you can regain your powers.'

'Kett…' But there was really nothing she could say.

He scraped back his hair and closed his eyes briefly. 'You never intended to stay in the audience at the coronation. You think the only way is to plant a blade in their gouri hearts. And the only way to get that close is to surrender to them. Which means you'll be too close to

Rohne and the Selb weishi. You can't take them all on and win.' He flung an arm toward the Alcazar. 'Those *jijin* xiongshou are the best of the best. Two or even three and you might have a chance. But not more. Especially if you're dealing with Nasra and Rohne as well. This is suicide.'

Alere shot to her feet, clenching her fists by her sides in an effort not to lash out at him. 'Don't you think I've tried to think of some other way?' She gestured vaguely. 'Some clever trick like I did with Ven or in the Games. I can't *think* of anything else! I *have* to surrender. It's the one chance I have, slim as it is. The only chance of killing Nasra and Rohne, and freeing Mina and Jarran.'

'No!' He grabbed her by the shoulders. 'No, Alli. I've stood by you for ten years. Protected you. I've held my tongue when you've risked your life over and over these last two months. I can't this time. There's got to be another way.' He laid his forehead against hers. When she wrapped her arms around his waist, he buried his face in the curve of her neck and shoulder and murmured, 'Please, Alli? I can't order you any more, so I'm asking. Don't surrender. Don't get near them.'

He pulled her close. She lifted his chin and saw the faintest sheen of tears in his haunted grey eyes. Half-blinded by her own grief, she shook her head.

'You know there's no other way, Kett. I can't be sure of getting my xintou gifts back – even assuming Mina even agrees to re-Bond. But if she does, the only way my powers are strong enough is if we're practically Fused. And I don't think I could stop Fusion if things go badly and I need more power. I can't risk Mina's life like that. I've forced her to kill too many times. I have to try another way.'

'But you'll risk your own.'

'Yes. And before you insist on surrendering yourself, too…you can't.' She swallowed down the urge to ask him to run, to leave, to be safe. He wouldn't listen. 'You need to get Jarran to safety. I'm counting on you. Don't try and help me. Don't split my focus. Promise me, Kett.'

'Don't deny me the right to stand by you,' he whispered. 'Not now. If there's a chance you could die, I should be there.'

'I wish you could be. More than anything. You're the only one I trust to have my back. You always have been.' She cradled his face in her hands and kissed him, lingering, tasting the salt of his fear and sweetness of his love. 'But I also want you to live and we both know how this will probably end. Don't sacrifice yourself as well, Kett. You deserve to live free after hiding for so long. And…' she hesitated '…I know you don't want to hear it, but if Jarran dies, you're the only one strong enough to lead the Jundom. His girls are too young. You'll need to be regent for Rhea.'

'Gaisi! Alli!' He thrust her away. 'How many times do I have to say it? I don't want the throne. Even a regency. This whole gouri mess is because I stood in the way of Ven for the throne. If Hanna hadn't created those kin-child laws none of this would have happened. I should be—'

'Enough!' Alere's voice broke. She knew what she had to do to convince him. The words almost closed her throat. She dreaded his reaction, but this was the only way. 'This is *not* your fault. It never was. It has always been because of me.'

'How? You weren't even born when Hanna created the kin-child laws.'

She folded her arms and stared out at the cold moon, wishing for another path. 'In the Alcazar cells, Mistress Li told me the truth. When Sura was pregnant, Mistress Li decided Mina and I were important.' She gave a bitter laugh. 'More important than anyone, apparently. That we were, somehow, the key to stopping this tyrant everyone saw coming. Li wanted Sura in hiding to protect us. So she manipulated Hanna into making the kin-child laws. All those children Hanna murdered? Not because of you. Because of me.'

Alere rounded on him, glaring. 'You want to kill everyone who had anything to do with the kin-child laws. Well, that means me. And Mina.'

'Alli,' he whispered the word, his face grey.

She sucked a deep breath. 'The erheyi twins? Nasra got the idea from Mina and I, remember? And Radan's death? I did that. I killed your father, Kett. To protect the secret of the iron from Celia. The secret Mistress Li had told Radan because she wanted him to give *me* the yanstones in Corin's dagger and Sura's bracelet. She wanted me to have xintou gifts. Then she wanted me to go to Rafi and help him kill Hanna, Ven, and Celia.'

Alere scrubbed at her face. 'Mistress Li groomed me to kill the "one" everyone's predicting will destroy the House and subjugate the world. And that "one" turns out to be Nasra. Or Rohne. I don't know. At this point, I'm intending to kill both.'

Kett paled and retreated a step. He leaned on the wall and swiped a trembling hand over his mouth.

Part of her hoped he would say it didn't matter. That he still loved her, in spite of everything. But he didn't. He stared at the floor and wouldn't even look at her.

'All of this,' she continued, her voice cracking. 'It's all been about the iron and about Mina and I. Not you. I'm the one who caused this, so I need to finish it. So please, just do what I ask.' She glanced out the window at the moon. 'I have to get into position. Do your job. Get Jarran to safety.'

Without looking at him again, she snatched up her clothing and weapons and ran from the room. He called her name, but she ignored it and brushed away hot tears as she ran down the long, shadowed corridors.

Stopping just inside one of the small side exits, Alere put her back against a wall and covered her mouth to keep in a cry of despair. The look on his face. The hurt she had inflicted on him.

What had she done?

She stared at the closed outer door but couldn't force herself to open it. What if this was the last time they were together? What if she died? Or he did? She would regret this. And wouldn't he feel the same way? She knew him. Knew how he thought. Knew it took him time to process new information and she'd just thrown Mistress Li's confession at him to push him away. To save him.

But wasn't that what Mina kept saying she did wrong? Jiche! Would she never learn?

She dressed and sprinted back up the hallway, taking the stairs two at a time.

'Kett!' She reached the door to her room. It was empty. His gear and clothes gone. Her heart sank. There was no time to follow him as their parts in the plan meant they had to be in different places before dawn.

She turned from the room, heart-heavy.

Kett stood before her in the grey-lit hallway, his eyes dark-shadowed, his mouth set thin. 'You came back.'

She hesitated, then caught his strong, calloused fingers in hers. He let them lie without holding hers. But he didn't pull away.

'I'm sorry. I'm a shazi,' she said. 'I shouldn't have pushed you away. I keep doing that and look what happens? Mina was right.'

'Alli, stop.' He snatched his hand back. 'I have something to tell you, too. You keep blaming yourself for Mina leaving Shanzhai. But that was my fault. She came to me the morning of the battle against Celia and Hanna. She wanted to know if I loved her.' He closed his eyes briefly. 'I said I didn't. She left in tears. Then Rohne came and berated me for hurting her. We argued. I told him Mina didn't love him and he should leave her alone or I would make him. He must have gone to her and offered to take her away. To spite me, I think. Trying to prove himself to her, as well.'

'Oh, Kett. No. She doesn't blame you. I promise.'

He grimaced. 'The point is, you weren't the only one with secrets. Yours were just a bit more—'

'Horrible?' she said, managing a weak smile. He opened his arms and she stepped into them, her heart swelling with gratitude. 'I'm so sorry, Kett. I was so frightened to tell you about Mistress Li. And Radan. I was afraid…'

'I'd stop loving you?' he murmured against her hair. 'You think I'm that shallow?'

'Radan was your father, and I killed him.'

'You were protecting the secret of the iron.' He gave a soft, broken chuckle. 'And he really wasn't a very good father, if you think about it.'

'But what about you killing people who were to blame for the kin-child laws?'

He searched her face. 'Really? You weren't even born. You can't possibly think I'd blame you for Mistress Li's bizarre interpretation of a five-hundred-year-old Seeing.'

She smiled. 'I suppose, when you put it like that.'

'Shazi,' he said, and kissed her. She melded herself against him, kissing him back with fierce intensity, desperate to remember his strength, his warmth and the depth of his love.

She broke the kiss at last. 'You still can't come with me, you know. Up on the stage, I mean.'

He sucked a quick breath, the frown returning. She touched two fingers to his lips.

'But you'll be close by, won't you?' she asked. 'You'll have my back?'

His grimness softened and he nodded. 'As close as I can. But can we work on a fall-back plan, in case the old blade-in-the-heart thing doesn't work? Rohne will be expecting it.'

'I'm listening,' she said cautiously.

'The yanstones.' He held up a palm when she started to protest. 'I know what you said about Fusing. But remember the other gifts it gave you? If re-Bonding with Mina – without fusing – gives you those back, then that gives you the lightning to use.'

'I suppose.' Her ability to draw down lightning and to burn minds had only come with a strong connection to Mina. Rohne wasn't aware of those gifts, so if she could re-Bond, and get hold of her weapons, she might be able to surprise him. There were a lot of "ifs" in that plan, though. And Mina would have to agree, which was unlikely.

'They won't let you on the stage with your sword or the yanstones.' He frowned. 'How were you even planning to kill Rohne, anyway?'

She extended a foot and triggered the blade in the sole of the stolen boots from Dalcin.

He raised his brows. 'Possible. Not a great plan, though. I know how we can get your blades and the yanstones to you once you're on stage. You'll need Saric's help. And some smoke bombs.'

She grinned. 'That will make him happy.'

He stared as though memorising her face. 'We can do this, Alli. Together.'

She nodded. 'But Kett? If I do fall, promise me you'll find someone else? Don't be afraid to love someone just because they might leave you one day. Everyone dies. Loving someone is still worthwhile.'

His throat worked and jaw muscles jumped. 'Yes, it is. But I want that someone to be you.'

Then he let her go.

CORIN

'Here they come.' Tali peered around the building's corner.

The sound of marching followed her words. The first of Hassan's Selb army appeared in the street and headed for the southern gate four blocks away. Close to four thousand junren moved through the city, eight abreast in tight formation. They were strung out along the length of the main street between here and the Alcazar.

'But it doesn't seem like—'

Corin grabbed her shirt and hauled her away. 'Keep your gouri head out of sight, Tal. The whole point of an ambush is *not* being seen first.'

She flushed. The sun, peeking out below heavy grey clouds for a moment, sent glorious, dust-glittered shafts of light between the buildings and fired her hair to burnished copper. She, along with all the Xintou House girls, now wore plain clothes, so they wouldn't be obvious targets. Even in brown and grey, oversized trous and tunic, she was still beautiful.

'And your job,' he added acerbically, refusing to be distracted, 'is to co-ordinate the xintou. You're not supposed to be here. You should be back with Yasmin, out of danger.'

She screwed up her nose. 'I could hardly send twenty-six teenage girls into battle and stay back where it was safe.' A hint of mischief gleamed. 'Besides, I promised Alere I'd look after you.'

'You prom... gah!' Corin gave a groan. 'Save me from managing women. Look.' He let her see the gravity of his next instruction and she sobered. The staccato thud of marching feet came closer. 'You've never been in anything like this. The next while is going to be worse than you've ever imagined. I'll do my best to shield you, but you *have* to do exactly as I say and you need to keep your girls in line. You lose self-control to fear and they will, too.'

He waited for her nod. 'See this house?' He jerked a thumb at the open door behind. 'It's the safest place to be if things go suilie and something happens to me.' He ignored her quick gasp. 'If I fall, hide. With any luck any junren who search the place will think you live there and leave you alone. If they don't, use that replacement knife I gave you. Don't hesitate. Defend yourself. Got it?'

'But I don't need—' She stopped when he glared at her.

'Good.' He gentled his tone. 'Now, find out from your girls whether they've spotted the erheyi women. We need to get the archers ready. As soon as we have word that all the junren and the erheyi are in place, give the rooftop girls the go-ahead. Don't wait, Tal. Just do it, even if you haven't heard from Alere. If they open the southern gate and escape we'll have blown it.'

She nodded and sent out his commands. 'The girls I left with Yasmin say there are three pairs of twins with Hassan's army south of the city. And there are eight pairs in the city, walking in the middle of the Selb army. Everyone is ready, Corin.' She shivered and glanced at the heavy sky. 'But it looks like it could rain.'

Corin rubbed his hands together. 'Excellent. Rain adds to the confusion. And it sounds like all eleven pairs are accounted for and there won't be any at the coronation. Alere has a fighting chance. Right. Time to get moving.'

A frown creased Tali's forehead. 'But I'm not sure that—'

'Ya.' He waved her objections aside. 'We're all worried.' He drew his sword. The yanstones' power thrummed through his arm, surprisingly strong. 'Right. Wait five more minutes for Alere to contact you. If she doesn't, then give the signal, anyway. I have to go talk to the shangwei.'

As he slipped back down the street, she called his name in overtones of fear and frustration, but there was no time to go back and soothe her apprehensions.

CHAPTER THIRTY-SEVEN

ALERE

The lead up to Hassan's coronation was a masterful performance, guaranteed to put fear into the attendees. Hiding in plain sight amongst the subdued crowd of Madina citizens, Alere silently applauded Nasra's dramatic skill as the morning unfolded. But every moment hardened her resolve. There could be no redemption for someone who condoned this.

The sun rose, a feeble pink disc hidden by thick clouds. As a fine rain misted rainbows across the city, the supposedly-unworthy were led, one by one, onto a scaffold about twenty paces from the Alcazar gates. The great double-bladed axe rose and fell. Head by fallen head, thirty-two ordinary people and one Merchant Master died beneath the steel blade of Hassan's obsession, with more to come.

Tension and fear held the waiting audience in coiled silence. The crunch of steel axeblade against bone and timber made a slow, rhythmic counterpoint to despairing wails of the condemned awaiting death.

Blood filled the gaps between cobbles, creeping in crazed lines toward the crowds lining the western side of the square. The metallic smell overpowered even the fear-stink of sweat, and the stench of vomit and piss from those overcome by nausea and fear. Clouds of tiny swamp-midges swarmed in the courtyard, attracted by fresh blood. The crowd slapped and scratched.

It took all of Alere's self-control to stop herself from trying to rescue the condemned. Saving them would be pointless self-sacrifice. Important over what she wanted. But the end game was small consolation when innocent blood glistened dark in the morning light.

Looking away, she stood on tiptoes and peered at the stage. Placed about thirty paces from the gate, it dominated the massive square before the Alcazar. Black silk skirted the timber stage and, on the platform, stood the pavilion Alere had last seen on the fields outside Shanzhai. The walls were rolled up, so only the peaked black and silver roof was visible. But she shivered in recollection. The healed whip-marks on her back itched.

Before the stage, stood rows of mismatched benches and chairs, aligned on either side of a long, midnight and silver carpet that led up a short flight of stairs. At the carpet's end, beneath the canopy, sat the Jun First's great Steel Throne. Made from solid steel plates, the throne looked as uncomfortable as it did ugly. The only softness about it was a short, pleated skirt of black and silver silk hiding the legs. The thing must weigh a ton.

Another head fell. A much-admired master of the purple Artist House. A faint moan swept through the crowd. But whispered conversations were shortlived.

A tall fence of interlocking bamboo poles stood between the seats and the rest of the courtyard. It kept the common people out – and penned the invitees into a cage. Inside, men in sober robes fingered daggers on their hips. Women shifted uncomfortably in their heavy, bright silks, many wearing the gauzy half-veils that were almost out of fashion. Perhaps hoping to obscure the horrors. Or at least hide their reactions. Children were noticeably absent.

Beyond the cage was a wide, clear path, then a wall of black-and-silver-clad weishi facing outward, holding back the crowd. They were more for show than crowd control. The onlookers were not in any mood to attack Hassan. Fear swirled from them like smoke.

A huge watch-xiao-cat prowled past, close to where Alere stood. Irritable in the daylight, it sniffed at the crowd, growling low in its throat and pulling restlessly at its harness. Half a dozen weishi followed huge watch-xiao-cats, barely holding the beasts in check. Onlookers shrank from occasional flashes of long teeth.

The Alcazar's great gates swung dramatically open, taking everyone by surprise. A low muttering rose from the crowd, silenced by glares from the weishi lining the walkway. Mina and Jarran were marched out first, followed by Houlia, and the rest of the condemned.

Mina and Jarran appeared to be in control of their own actions. They held hands and walked calmly in the centre of a dozen weishi. They seemed more resigned than defiant. Mina rested her head on Jarran's shoulder.

Jarran slapped at his neck, scratched and checked his fingers. Mina looked questioningly at him. He murmured something and kissed her temple.

Alere's heart contracted and she suppressed a smile. 'Well done, Saric.'

Hassan emerged, followed by Rohne and Nasra, both resplendent in shimmering gold xintou robes. Hassan wore a black robe embroidered with glittering geometric patterns made of thousands of silvery beads. If they were steel, then the robe must weigh heavily on his shoulders. Perhaps it accounted for his slow pace as he strolled around the courtyard, waving regally to the frightened crowd. A thick, resentful silence followed him, broken only by the creak of leather armour, the snarl of a cat, and the occasional cough or slap.

Behind Nasra and Rohne walked six young women, all between about fifteen and nineteen. Three pairs of identical twins. The rest must be with the armies. All wore matching tunics of pale yellow, like apprentice xintou, and matching expressions of blank, mindless compliance. Was Nasra forcing these girls to obey or were they so brainwashed they co-operated willingly, thoughtlessly? Surely even Nasra couldn't control eleven pairs all the time?

Behind them glided twelve Selb weishi, each in the grey and black trous and hooded shirts Corin had described. Each carried on their back the double-bladed steel axe; and on their wrists the braided black silk of a *jijin* xiongshou. Each watched the crowds with sweeping, intense focus. Jada Marin-kin was noticeably absent. Zand, Weishi House's second in command, led them, his bald scalp gleaming in the sunlight.

The procession passed by. Alere shifted out of their line of sight and concentrated on awed thoughts. She didn't breathe out until they were past and onto the long black carpet.

She froze again as the Selb weishi approached the stage. Would they check beneath? If they did, Alere and Kett's plan was undone. The weishi split up. Half took up guard positions on the ground around the front and sides of the stage, facing outward. The other half mounted the steps and spaced themselves evenly around the front and sides of the platform.

Again, Alere released a breath, trying to control the trembling in her hands.

The rain thickened and turned chill. Thunder rumbled overhead. The audience hunched into each other, miserable and shivering.

Zand nodded to the weishi guarding the prisoners. The executioner beckoned the next prisoner up to the block. Three more and it would be Houlia's turn. A quick glance at the sun's faint glow gave Alere cause to frown. The timing might not work. Well, she couldn't wait any longer.

Hassan's party stepped onto the stage and Hassan sank onto the throne, spreading his glittering robe neatly across his knees. The Jun

First's chief administrative officer launched into what promised to be a fulsome, false and dull welcome speech.

In the background, the steel axe rose and fell, punctuating the speech with blood and the thud of another fallen head. Alere swallowed. Two more before Houlia. There was no more time.

She threw back her shoulders and brushed damp hair from her face.

The two weishi standing at the entrance to the seated area were Anh's men. At her soft request, they parted and let her through. Muttered comments followed as she emerged onto the carpet. Weishi looked askance at each other, some hesitantly drawing weapons, others looking to the stage for instructions.

Behind her, the crowd shifted in waves as people pressed forward. Whispers gushed like steam and dissipated in the cold, tense atmosphere.

Alere strolled forward, raising her hands to show they were empty. She walked carefully, hiding the limp caused by the Xintou House *shenhilya* yanstone tucked inside her boot, under the arch of her right foot.

On the stage, the speaker's voice melted into silence.

People stirred and asked each other whispered, unanswerable questions. Tension and confusion mounted around her with each step.

She continued toward the stage, her booted heels silent on the thick, dark carpet. A storm-gust tossed hair into her eyes. Banners fluttered and snapped wetly in the silence, startling people transfixed by her progress. Rohne's straight dark brows lifted. Nasra's thin-lipped mouth stretched wide in triumph. She touched Zand on the arm. He waved imperiously to those guarding the prisoners.

Mina and Jarran were dragged forth and thrust onto the stage. Four Selb weishi took up close guard positions around them. Mina shook her head, her lips moving in a silent plea for Alere to leave. Alere ignored her.

Hassan scowled as she approached. He waved two weishi forward. Pre-empting their search, she tugged off her soft woollen cap and tossed it to the ground before the stage. Next, she stripped off her jacket and threw that. It vanished under the black cloth edging the platform, taking with it all the yanstones except the *shenhilya.*

Vulnerable and exposed, she now wore plain clothing identical to the travel garb Mina had been captured in – sturdy brown, longsleeved shirt and thick, dark trous. It may lead to an opportunity to get her sister to safety. Alere needed to use every advantage possible. Things were about to become…challenging.

She lifted her arms higher. 'Let Mina go. I surrender.'

Two Selb weishi glided closer. They took hold of her arms in bone-grinding grips. She gritted her teeth and didn't resist. Her fingers numbed and shoulders ached as they applied a painful lock. A third patted her entire body with painstaking thoroughness, even searching through her hair, between her legs and under her breasts. She tolerated the search without changing her expression of bored amusement.

In truth, her biggest fear wasn't what one of them would do. Her biggest fear was that, without the yanstones, she wouldn't be able to tell if Rohne or Nasra attacked her wards. If they broke her wards too soon, Corin and his plans would be jeopardised. As would Kett's position.

This was the riskiest moment in her whole plan. Well, apart from the high probability of everything going suilie.

She kept her breathing even as the weishi patted down her calves and reached her feet. Her boot-dagger was a weapon used by the Weishi of Adeghal, but not common elsewhere. He wore the *jijin* wrist ribbon twined with the purple of the Jadid Weishi House. Would he find it?

He slid a finger into the top of each boot, feeling around the inside at her ankles.

He rose, his dark eyes flat, and nodded to Zand.

Hassan leaned back in the Steel Throne. He eyed her with evident confusion as the weishi half-lifted, half-dragged her up the stairs. They released her at Rohne's gesture. She massaged life back into her wrists. Rohne swept her with a scornful sneer.

'What's going on?' Hassan thumped a fist on the Steel Throne's arm. 'Someone tell me what's happening. Nasra?'

She touched his arm and his frown changed to narrow-eyed confusion.

Rohne sent a quick look at Nasra then dragged Alere off to one side. 'Where's the necklace, and your swords?' His nails bit into her arm.

'Did you enjoy torturing that information out of Mina?' She shook his grip off and folded her arms. 'You didn't know they existed when you left Shanzhai. The only way you can know about them is from Mina. Did you like hurting her? Is that who you are now?'

He ground his teeth together, lips white and close-pressed. He kept control, but his voice shook when he asked again.

'Where are they? Tell me and she'll live.'

She curled a lip and measured his ire closely. She needed to be careful not to overdo it. Not yet, anyway. 'Why on Kalima would I do something as stupid as bringing them with me or telling you where they are? I've hidden them, of course. You won't find them, ever. You have me. Let Mina go.'

He laughed, incredulous, bitter. 'You're not that naïve. Whatever you're planning, it won't work. You really think you can beat me with no yanstones or weapons? What are you going to do, scold me to death?'

Alere shrugged. 'Are we having this little private chat because you haven't told Nasra about the stones? Shall I tell her for you?' She checked on Nasra who listened with badly-concealed impatience to Hassan's conflicting orders to stop everything yet still proceed with the coronation.

Rohne's fingers clamped onto her arm again. She directed a cool stare at him. He held out one wrist and flipped back his sleeve, showing the Koh-Lin bracelets, linked together on his forearm.

'Even with just these I have enough power to go straight through your wards, you know. I can just *take* the information I need.' He bared his teeth, feral and triumphant.

But he couldn't hide an involuntary twitch of pain. An air of desperation hung about him.

'Go ahead.' she said politely. 'Unless it hurts too much these days and even Nasra can't help you anymore.'

He flinched.

'So, it's true,' she said. 'And *you're* hoping more stones will help you control what's coming or even fix the missing gene. Sorry.' She twisted her wrist free. 'You're going to drown in excruciating pain, with a thousand voices screaming in your head, until you can't stand it any longer and you kill yourself to escape. That's your fate.' She raked him with sneering disdain. 'In the very near future by the looks of you.'

Anger flared red in his eyes but he merely snarled. He needed a bit more of a nudge.

'Or,' she added, 'you can let Mina and I switch off the gene altogether. We know how. So does your mother. If you lose control, she'll do it. She's just using you to get what she wants – control. Power.'

'Liar!' he growled. 'She knows male xintou are the future. She's worked my whole life for this moment. She needs me.'

'If you say so.'

He lashed out with a full-strength, open-palmed slap to the cheek. Alere saw it coming but allowed it to connect. She turned aside at the last second to ease the worst of the impact. She cried out and collapsed to the floor at the back edge of the stage. Blood's hot iron filled her mouth. She spat it back at him.

'Boy? Rohne.' Hassan chose that propitious moment to distract Rohne. 'What's going on here? Who is that woman?'

Alere covered her face, pretending to cry, and peered through her fingers. Only two Selb weishi watched her. She stayed on her side and slowly extended her feet and ankles out over the back of the stage. Then she let her hands fall. She lifted her head, stilled and looked past the watching weishi at the audience, widening her eyes and letting her mouth drop open. They spun to look behind, studying the crowd intently.

An old trick, but reliable.

Warm fingers gripped her calves, then the Koh-Lin necklace stones pressed against her ankle, so hot as to feel cold but, somehow, neither. A soft click as the necklace catch clipped shut. Then Rafi's bracelet – unhooked from the Koh-Lin necklace – dropped into her pocket. Courtesy of Kett, hidden beneath the stage since before dawn.

Now she needed Mina to wear Rafi's bracelet and allow her to re-Bond. And somehow get the *shenhilya* stone out of her boot. And get closer to the Steel Throne. Then she had a chance – a slim chance – at challenging Nasra, Rohne, and their apprentices.

Alere forced her racing heart to slow. She took a deep breath and held it for a count of four, controlled her blood's rush and jitter. Now would be a great time to access the yanstones' soothing reassurance.

She rose, keeping her hands visible to the weishi guarding Mina and Jarran. They watched her narrowly, hard and uncompromising. Zand was one of the four. His steely eyes never strayed.

She edged across to stand beside Mina. Under the guise of giving her sister a hug she slipped Rafi's bracelet from her pocket and hooked it around Mina's wrist. As the clasp clicked shut, Mina gave a heavy sigh. Then she pressed Jarran's palm to her cheek, and disengaged from him. He opened his mouth, glanced bleakly at Alere and then away again. His expression hardened to something beyond acceptance.

'We have to re-connect, Mina,' Alere whispered. 'I'm sorry. It's the only way I can have the power to protect you against Nasra and Rohne. And against the erheyi. I need to know if our wards are holding.'

Mina bowed her head. 'You won't kill him with the stones, will you?'

'I...I can't guarantee it. We'll try to fix him if we can, I promise.' There was no point in telling Mina her main aim was to kill both mother and son by running a steel sword through them.

Mina hesitated. Behind them the axeman's weapon fell again and a whispering groan swept through the watching crowd. Alere glanced over her shoulder. Houlia was next.

'Please, Mina? I can't do this alone.' Would it work, though? Doubt slivered through her stomach.

'I know.' Taking Alere's hand, Mina sucked a deep breath. 'I'm ready.'

Trembling, Alere opened to the stones. Nothing. She held back a scream of frustration. How was that possible? She'd been so sure. She looked at Mina. Her sister's cheeks were pale, her eyes downcast.

'You have to open your Outers, Mina.'

Mina pressed a hand to her stomach, glanced once more at Jarran, then gave a small nod.

Alere almost cried aloud as the silver-gilt warmth welcomed her back, engulfed her, soothed her fears, buried her guilt beneath power and acceptance. Voices whispered reassurance in words she couldn't quite hear. Honeyed heat glissaded across her skin and soaked into tired muscles, renewing strength and hope.

Mina gave a tiny, choked cry as Alere re-forged their link.

The massive House stone in Alere's boot tingled against her foot. A flare of electricity crackled across her skin and wormed beneath her flesh, into her thoughts. Smoke and iron filled her mouth, more powerful than ever.

Then Mina opened all but one of her deepest Inner wards. Alere did the same.

Incandescent, Alere's and Mina's minds entwined: the hard with the soft; iron and carbon.

Now they were ready. Now they were gangzhi.

Steel. A weapon with which to end this war forever.

CHAPTER THIRTY-EIGHT

ALERE

Rohne broke off his conversation with Hassan and glanced back at Alere and Mina. He took a half-step in their direction, his brow blackening. Hassan latched onto his wrist. He peered around the throne and tugged on Rohne's arm with the open-faced joy of a child who's discovered something important for himself.

'I recognise her now! She's that woman…that merchant woman who came to my estates.' His brow clouded, confusion replacing lucidity again. 'Wait. There are two of you! But you're not my girls. What are you doing here? You're interrupting my coronation. Jilla?' He pushed a thumb into one temple. 'No, that's right. Poor Jilla's dead, isn't she? Rohne. What's this woman doing, interrupting my coronation? Get rid of her. Both of her.'

Rohne bowed. 'Yes shenshi. Leave it with me. I'll take care of it.' He wrenched his wrist free and gave Nasra a jaded glance. 'Mother, can we be done with this farce now? Finish him. He's served his purpose and is, quite frankly, giving me a headache.'

Nasra sent her son a sharp look and pursed her lips. She nodded to Zand. The man bowed and strode to the throne. He hauled Hassan up by the shirt front, drew Hassan's own steel dagger and drove it into the Jun's heart.

Hassan, who'd done no more than open his mouth in confused protest, staggered away. He stared at Nasra and Rohne in horrified incomprehension. He gaped at the handle protruding from his chest, tried to grab it and failed as his foot missed the edge of the stage. Arms flailing, he toppled onto the stones below. The impact drove the knife through his chest. The blade tented the thick, ornate robe for a moment before the razor point sliced through. Black silk billowed and collapsed around his inert body.

A scream of terror rent the clear morning air and broke the crowd's shocked stasis. People leapt to their feet. They pushed and jostled each other. More rose, tipping chairs over and shoving one another to the ground in a mad rush to get away from the stage. Many, though, stayed in their seats, clinging to each other, frozen, wide-eyed.

Lightning crackled across the sky, chased by thunder that rumbled through Alere's chest. Tiny hailstones clattered to the cobbles and bounced.

Panicked people pushed at the bamboo fence until it fell under the pressure, trapping several dozen weishi beneath. The outside crowd caught the infection of fear and scattered, making for the three streets opening onto the square.

Weishi guarding the street exits drove them back with steel. Slaughtered them indiscriminately. Xiao-cats lunged. Three pulled free of their weishi handlers and leapt into the crowd. Screams took on the shrill note of agony as the cats' sabre fangs slashed through flesh and bone. The Madina citizens piled up against each other in the middle of the square, unsure which threat to fear. They ran, stopped, then ran again like a shoal of fish being hunted by a straight-eel.

Into this chaos, Saric added his measure. Throwing red-tinted smokebombs in all directions, he weaved in and out of the stampeding crowd. He used them as cover. Three Selb weishi around Alere and Mina collapsed, scrabbling at black-feathered darts lodged in their flesh. Zand ducked. The dart meant for him skimmed past Alere's cheek. More weishi leapt onto the stage.

Alere was about to alert Tali and Corin when the ground beneath her feet trembled. House windows around the square rattled and cracked. A shockwave thudded through her body, followed by two more. Lightning crackled and thunder rumbled. Smoke swirled into the air over the Zalam area, rising grey and thick above the buildings.

At her nod, Saric threw another smokebomb. It impacted the hat Alere had tossed to the ground, triggering a reaction with the chemicals inside. A huge, red cloud billowed, obscuring the crowd. The wind pushed it, enveloping the stage in thick smoke.

Time to move.

CORIN

Cobbles beneath Corin's feet jumped and glass showered into the main street. Screams tore through the silence that followed. The sky opened and hailstones pinged off roofs and cracked against glass.

'Right.' He grinned at Tali in anticipation of the battle-rush. 'As soon as the other powder kegs blow, tell the girls it's time to drop the trees, loose arrows and get ready for deserters. Remind everyone to kill the *jijin* xiongshou and take the rest of the Selb prisoners.'

Two more bombs went off, further away, rattling windows and causing slate tiles to slither off roofs and shatter on the roads. Grey smoke and dust billowed and swirled.

He peered around the corner, but understanding the chaos through the smoke was nigh on impossible. Screams of ear-tearing agony and fear sailed out. A babble of conflicting commands rose from officers trying to wrench order from disaster. The oddly-pleasant smell of gunpowder caught in his nose. It almost masked the sharp scent of urine and faeces as junren reacted in purely human ways to an experience unknown on Kalima.

Pale and shaking, Tali sent out the order to those of Rafi's men who waited on the surrounding rooftops. A dozen thorn-tuft trees, cut almost through at the base, were sliced free of their anchoring ropes. They creaked, tilted, and scythed through the smoke. The logs fell and ploughed through the milling mass of fighters pinned in the causeway. Foot-long thorns fired into the Selb. The wet slap of timber on soft bodies; of bodies against hard stone; the crack of skulls and bone snapping, turned hot triumph into the bitter ash of reality. Corin swallowed it, setting his teeth against the cut-off screams, and the chorus of despairing sobs and pleas for help.

Then the sky darkened as arrows rained from the rooftops the length of the street. Excitement faded before gory realisation. This was too much like the Chengdu Games for his liking: mass-killings of men and women whose only real fault was to be the pawns of Juns and madmen.

It needed to end, and fast.

The hurried slap of booted feet foretold the appearance of the first of the Selb junren escaping into this particular alley. Gaisi! Too late to get Tali out of sight. Three men, wild-eyed, bloodied and soot-smeared, in Selb black and grey, rounded the corner. They skidded to a halt and raised ceramic and bronze weapons in automatic self-defence when they saw Corin and Tali. Then, taking in the empty street behind the pair, the trio regained confidence.

Corin was happy to let just three go by in peace in order to keep Tali safe. The rearmost man shouted out to someone behind. Within seconds, dozens more junren appeared out of the haze. Too many to let pass. Limping, carrying broken companions, they searched for a way out of the nightmare.

Now he had to move things onto the next phase. That meant stalling until enough junren joined them to make it worthwhile. He thrust Tali into the shadowed doorway and warned her to stay put, ignoring her protest. He stepped into the street, steel drawn. Hail stung his neck and arms.

'Sorry folks, this street is restricted.' He nodded at the leader. 'You'll have to go back.'

The man, his smoke-reddened blue eyes startling against blackened skin, didn't even bother with a verbal response. He threw himself forward with all the mad ferocity of someone pushed past their limit. His bronze axe swung in berserk, adrenalin-fuelled strokes.

Corin side-stepped the attack. He ended it with a surgical slice to the back of the man's neck. The junren collapsed, limp and gaping like a fish, spinal cord severed. His weapon clanged onto the cobbles. Life faded from his staring eyes.

A moment of shocked silence followed. Then a deep-throated growl arose from the remaining Selb. They focussed all their fear, and anger onto Corin, and advanced.

Swearing eloquently, Corin set himself for the onslaught. He loosened his neck and shoulders and shifted his balance to allow for the uneven, slippery cobbles underfoot.

A muffled shriek from nearby dragged his attention to Tali. Hauled bodily from the doorway by a Selb woman, Tali skittered on tiptoes into the light. A bronze knife pricked blood on the smooth skin of her throat. The woman held Tali's hair fisted in her hand.

'Get out of our way or we'll kill both of you,' she growled. Smeared with dust and blood, her face was contorted into a feral snarl of hatred. 'Gouri traitor!' she spat. 'We'll kill you anyway, you stupid Shanzhai hamagi.'

She shortened her arm to plunge the blade into Tali's throat. Tali's nails scrabbled at the woman's besmirched face. Her fingertips contacted skin and the Selb gave a strangled cry. The woman dropped the knife, releasing Tali's hair to grab at her own head. Sinking to her knees she stared at Tali in blank horror, whimpering.

Tali placed her palm on the woman's forehead as though offering some sort of blessing. Blood seeped scarlet from the woman's eyes and nose. Bright new rivulets trickled over dirty skin to drip off her sharp chin. She let out a screech, that began low, spiralled up, and shredded her larynx until blood frothed at her lips. Then she toppled over. Twitching, she stretched splayed fingers toward her comrades. They shrank away in open horror and she relaxed into death. Her blood mingled with rain on the wet ground.

Tali smoothed her ruffled hair, and stepped across to join Corin. Regal grace hid whatever emotions underlay the ice of her expression. The Selb junren retreated, regarding her with superstitious fear.

Corin lifted an arm. With a whisper of cloth and leather, some fifty of Rafi's men emerged from the shadows and doors. They formed a blockade in the narrow alley, standing between the Selb and freedom.

Corin caught the attention of the Selb group's leader. 'Like I said, this way is closed.'

The man half-turned back to the main street's fearful chaos. He hesitated. Then dozens more refugees emerged from the smoke, many hale and carrying weapons. His expression firmed into decision. He screamed the order to charge and waved his men into battle.

'Khara!' Corin grabbed at Tali's wrist and dragged her back, into the protection afforded by Rafi's men. She protested, trying to wrench free. The first line clashed in the alley's narrow confines. From windows above, five archers shot into the oncoming ranks of Selb.

Corin yanked Tali into another doorway and pulled her into the house, slamming the door.

'Stay here and cut out the heroics!' he snarled, keeping half an ear open to the sounds outside, trying to judge the skirmish's progress.

She tried to shove past him as the clash of metal and the screams of battle increased. 'But I can help, you saw that.'

He clamped onto her shoulders. 'No.' He pointed at the door. 'This is a planned retreat down this street, remember. We're drawing them in; splitting the main force up into small enough groups that we can handle them. We need you to keep the lines of communication open. Your death would be pointless and would jeopardise the whole campaign. Can't you get that through your thick skull?'

Tali's lovely mouth took on a mulish set. 'But—'

'Tal.' Corin strove for patience. 'You just killed that woman. No matter who you are, that's transformative. We can't afford for you to lose it now. Leave the killing to me. Help keep our people alive, instead.'

She blanched and her hands shook. She pressed one to her lips and one to her stomach. Something crashed against the door beside them. She jumped and shrank away. Corin judged it time to refocus, before she drowned in remorse.

'Now.' He cupped her jaw, forcing her to meet his gaze. 'Hold it together. Check on the others. They need you. See if the other ambushes are going to plan.' He cocked an ear at the door as the sound of fighting shifted further along the street. His squad was led by one of Rafi's best weishi, so they didn't need him.

Her eyes glazed as she communicated with the other xintou. She refocussed on him.

He gave her an encouraging nod. 'We'll have this sewn up in the next hour or so, and—'

'W-will you sh-shut up, you arrogant hmar!' Tali's teeth chattered as she wrapped cold, still-trembling fingers around his wrists and pulled them away from her face. Her short nails dug into his skin. 'I've been trying to tell you something, but you keep cutting me off.'

'Fine. What?'

Outside, the quality of the battle-noise changed. Screams of pain took on the higher, more frantic tones of fear and the groans became those of despair. Corin tore free and wrenched the door open. Stepping over a body, he peered down the street. The rain thickened, interspersed with fist-sized hailstones that smashed windows and exploded into ice-shrapnel. What was happening in the confusing melee of people and weapons?

Corin leapt onto a low wall between two adjoining doorways. He strained to see over the heads of his own men, and the now-hundreds of Selb troops, still clashing in the constricted space. The full ambush launched and more green-clad Koh-Lin men swarmed from their hiding places. Pinned between two forces, with archers targeting the mass of grey-and-black in the middle, the Alcazar junren had no hope of success.

Corin laughed.

Tali tugged at his sleeve like a child. 'Would you *please* listen?'

He frowned down at her. 'I am. What?'

CHAPTER THIRTY-NINE

ALERE

Alere triggered the knife in her right boot and lashed out at the Selb weishi nearest. The blade dug deep into his thigh. He grunted, swore and reached for his axe. His fingers missed and he staggered, falling to one knee. He collapsed, twitching and frothing. The si-xing on the blade. Good. If she was in luck there would be enough left to take out one more.

She looked around for Zand, but he had vanished into the billowing red smoke. Beyond the pavilion, hailstones shattered on the ground, spraying ice chips in all directions. Hailstone rent a hole in the cloth overhead and exploded on the wooden stage. Mina screamed and ducked.

A Selb xiongshou ghosted into view, steel axe raised in two hands. Alere waited until his forward momentum and balance were exactly right. Then she swivelled aside. The axe skimmed past her shoulder. She jabbed the boot-knife into his calf and sliced, severing the Achilles. The small blade snapped off. She swore.

His leg folded. He fell, rolled and regained his feet in a second, most of his weight on the sound leg. He was still dangerous and she couldn't afford to look away. He reached behind, to where most xiongshou carried their throwing knives or shuriken. Jiche!

He drew back his arm, ready to throw. There was nowhere to take cover. Could she reach him in time? It would only take one scratch of a poisoned blade and she would die. He grabbed at his throat. His eyes rolled back and he sank limply to the stage. The knife tinkled onto the timber. Blood frothed at his lips as the si-xing on her blade belatedly did its work.

Alere breathed a sigh and scanned for the next threat.

'Jarran!' Mina's frantic cry drifted with the smoke.

Alere grabbed her sister's wrist. 'Shut up, Mina. Kett has him. That's his job – keeping Jarran safe. He'll be fine if you help me take care of Nasra and Rohne. Got it?'

Drawing a deep, sobbing breath, Mina nodded. A body flew past, out of the densest smoke. It landed brokenly on the stage. A Selb weishi, his throat sliced through. Blood poured onto the rough timber. He gargled and clawed at his neck, staring into terrified awareness of death to come.

'There.' Alere pointed to the gaping wound. 'That's Jarran's handiwork. He's using the karambit Kett brought for him. He's alive.' She grabbed Mina's face and forced her to look away from the dying man. 'Focus here now, Mina, and we may just get through this alive, too.'

Mina first shook her head then nodded. She covered her mouth and gave a slightly hysterical, smothered cry.

Taking that as assent, Alere collected two throwing knives and two throwing spikes, the only visible weapons on her closest victim. The axe was too large and heavy for her to wield. She extended a hand to Mina, who grasped it. Together, they crept through the smoke, toward the Steel Throne, where Rohne had last been standing.

The clash and clang of weapons, invisible beyond the obscuring cloud, testified that Master Anh's loyal students had engaged the Selb weishi – hopefully long enough to allow Kett and Jarran to escape. And long enough for Alere and Mina to neutralise Rohne and kill Nasra.

Somewhere in the smoke, a xiao-cat yeowled. Alere shivered. Lightning slashed across the sky, illuminating, blinding.

She kept a tight grip on Mina's fingers as the Steel Throne appeared through the dense red smoke. It stood empty. Almost close enough. Alere hefted a throwing knife, searching for Rohne and Nasra. If they left the stage and returned to the shelter of the Alcazar, this day was done. She would need to fight her way to safety and start all over again to find a way to defeat them.

That couldn't happen. Too many had died already.

The cloud vanished, blown into nothing. Less than five paces away, Rohne and Nasra stood, side by side. Flanking them were the three pairs of erheyi girls, their faces blank, threatening in their very indifference. Around the pavilion, a bubble of clear air now existed, free of smoke, hail, and rain. Rohne's doing. Outside it, chaos raged.

Alere swore inventively. Mina's fingers gripped hers. Drawing strength from their connection, Alere let the yanstones around her ankle siphon fear away from both of them. Mina lifted her chin, calming into serenity. The taste of iron and woodsmoke overwhelmed the smell of blood. Warmth curled beneath Alere's skin and caressed her like a lover's hand.

'It's ok, Alli,' Mina whispered, straightening her back. 'We can do this.'

Rohne held up a hand. A tiny, black-feathered dart quivered, trembling in the air before him. He flicked his fingers and the dart shot away. It pierced the neck of a loyal weishi in combat against a Selb nearby. Seconds later the man collapsed, twitching.

'You can't possibly stand against all of us.' Rohne's tone was condescending. He smiled over his shoulder at Alere and Mina. 'Why waste your time resisting?'

Alere stretched her lips into a humourless grimace. Two of the erheyi xintou women attacked her wards, and Mina's, their thoughts as drills. Mina's distress bled through the connection. Her wards were weaker than Alere's. Mina's clutch tightened, grinding Alere's wristbones together. Drawing on the yanstones' golden fire, Alere grimly shored up both their wards.

Could she release fire into the erheyi girls' minds, as she had done to the mercenaries on the road from Dalcin? No. It took all her concentration to hold the wards against their attack.

But only a few more steps and she'd be close enough to the throne.

Rohne surveyed the still-crowded courtyard. Everywhere, small skirmishes filled the space with the clang and clash of steel on bronze; the cries of men and women in pain. The scent of blood, smoke, and fear grew thick. Not far away, a xiao-cat tore at the opened guts of a man in weishi black. Alere froze, then released a shaky breath. Not Kett. He and Jarran fought two Selb, further away.

'Mina.' Rohne glanced at her. 'I'll show you how serious I am. Jarran will join us and I'll give you one last chance to stop this. One last chance to save the lives of these people.'

He gestured, smiling smugly.

Nothing happened. Jarran, who fought grimly by Kett's side, continued the lethal swing of his arm. He sliced through the throat of a Selb, hurled him aside and turned on the next.

Rohne scowled, stretching an arm toward the Jun-Heir as though trying to physically pull him closer. Again, nothing.

Nasra stared at her son. *Control his mind! It's simple enough.*

While they were distracted, Alere flicked two knives and one spike in quick succession. If her guess about how the erheyi worked was right, then fatal hits could tip the balance. Her aim was true. One after another, three erheyi girls clutched at their throats. Brilliant red blood coursed down their bright yellow robes. One of each pair slumped to the floor, gargling incoherent pleas for help. Each living twin screamed and clutched at her sister, looking to Nasra.

The mental attacks stopped and Alere sighed. Mina sagged against her.

As with Alere and Mina, one twin on her own was powerless. Now they were just frightened girls, waiting for their mentor's guidance.

Nasra hissed and tore the veil from her face, throwing it aside. She slapped one of the living twins across the cheek and shoved another aside.

The fourth spike, Alere threw at Nasra. It halted mid-air and exploded into half a dozen bronze slivers of shrapnel. Rohne's lips peeled back into a snarl. The glittering pieces flew toward Alere and Mina.

Alere yanked her sister down, protecting Mina with her own body. They weren't close enough to be wholly sheltered by the throne's steel plating. Some of the bronze pieces pinged off it and tinkled musically on the timber. Alere flinched as a piece drove into the back of her arm. Another speared through her left shoulder, and another deep into her thigh. Beneath her, Mina gasped and jerked with each strike. Alere drew on the yanstones and put pain aside. The injuries were minor, the pain irrelevant.

She sat up, gauging the distance. Still too far. She needed to get to the throne, and she needed to keep Rohne distracted from her purpose. She sent a swift thought to Saric. Another smoke bomb lobbed out of nowhere and detonated on the stage, hiding her from Rohne's view.

'Still sure you'll win this, Rohne?' she taunted. She yanked the fingerlength slivers from her thigh, arm and shoulder and flicked them away. Rolling onto her side, she squirmed across the timber, heading for the throne, with Mina close beside her.

Rohne didn't speak, so Alere filled in the silence. She needed to know where he was. 'I don't see Jarran obeying you. Haven't you heard of fanghu? We darted him with it. I'm surprised Nasra didn't tell you about how it shuts down the telepathic receptors. You can't control a brain that can't receive your commands.' When he didn't reply, she forced a lighthearted tone. 'Face it Rohne, you've now lost three of your erheyi and your army is being slaughtered by ours in the Zalam streets. How's your head, by the way?'

Silence followed, apart from the sounds of battle and the drum of rain and hail. With her good shoulder finally against the throne, Alere scrabbled beneath the black cloth and grasped the cold, smooth shapes of her sword and dagger, hidden there. With a silent thank you to Kett, she withdrew them and hefted their familiar weight. A touch on the yanstones sent a shaft of pure energy through her body and she bathed in strength and certainty.

After a moment's hesitation, she passed the dagger to Mina. The injuries to her left shoulder and arm hampered movement anyway. Healing herself risked neural overload and she couldn't afford to lose consciousness. Mina held the dagger for a long moment, then shuddered. She tucked it into her belt, under her shirt.

The red smoke cleared again.

Alere surveyed the courtyard. Everywhere, Master Anh's weishi were gaining the upper hand over those marked in Alcazar or Selb colours. Not far away, Kett and Jarran fought as brothers, back to back, blood-spattered and grim. Blood poured down the left side of Kett's head. A crimson stain spread on Jarran's thigh.

She untied her boot, pulled out the wrapped *shenhilya* yanstone, and laced the boot up again.

The stone weighed heavy in her fist. She dropped it into her pocket, reluctant to unwrap it, yet. The other stones may yet provide enough power to finish this.

Time for the next phase.

'Corin would you get down here and listen to me?' Tali's hands were on her hips, her mouth mulish.

He jumped down off the railing. 'I do have a war to run, but fine. What? I'm listening.' He glanced back down the street. More junren on both sides were dying than he'd expected. The Selb were putting up a vicious fight. He frowned. There seemed to be more in the black-and-grey, now. How was that possible?

'I've been trying to tell you!' Tali said, gripping his arm. 'There's something not right. The men in the main streets can't have been *all* of the Selb troops.' She stared along the street at the fighting mob. 'There weren't enough. All my girls have reached the same conclusion.'

'Which is?'

'They were a diversion; a sacrifice. Not real Selb. Not real erheyi twins. Someone must have told the Alcazar our plans.'

Corin stilled, his heart skipping. 'What?'

Fearful certainty bloomed in her face. 'Every side street, every group of Rafi's men, every single one is reporting back. We're being trapped in our own ambushes.'

'Are you saying they sacrificed *thousands* of ordinary junren to reverse the ambushes? Gaisi!' He swallowed. What sort of mind did that? Who had the stomach to throw away so many lives?

Tali clutched at her head and cried out. 'No! Three more pairs of twins have appeared in Hassan's army outside. They're overwhelming my girls. And the real Selb are flanking Rafi's men on the plain.'

'Three more?' Corin swallowed. 'And if the others were fake, then…the rest must be at the coronation. Gouri! I'm a zift. I should have known it was going too well.' He slapped his forehead. 'And that's why they weren't carrying steel weapons! Alere! Can you reach Alere and warn her?'

'Oh!' Tali's eyes glazed. 'No. She's warding too strongly. And she's focussed on something else. She can't feel me.'

'What about Rafi and Yasmin? Are they alive?'

She nodded then flinched. 'But three of our xintou with them are dead. The others are in such pain. I can't help them! Oh, no.' She turned stark eyes on Corin and pointed down the street. 'Look.'

At the alley's far western end, more men appeared, marching in close formation, disciplined and ready…and wearing black and grey. Carrying steel axes. So many steel axes. Heart sinking, Corin checked east. Sure enough, a fresh force of unscathed, battle-ready Selb marched around the corner from the main street. Axes, swords and daggers flashed in the grey morning light.

In front strode a pair of gold-clad young women with matching expressions of superior disdain on their identical faces. They stopped, flanked by a dozen Selb weishi, before the stoop where Corin and Tali stood. The rest of their junren continued past, reinforcing their troops.

The twins surveyed Corin and Tali in a swift, detached assessment. Slender and clad in shimmering gold silk, with lustreless green eyes, they appeared no more than about fifteen. They carried themselves with the arrogance and certainty of adults with years of experience, seeming unfazed by the bloodshed and desolation around.

The rain and hail eased, leaving only damp, cold air whistling between the buildings.

'You will surrender to us.' The gold-clad girls spoke in unison, their voices almost indistinguishable in pitch and rhythm, flat and cold. They made a simultaneous, graceful gesture toward the weishi at their sides.

'Tali.' Corin hefted his sword, speaking in a low aside. 'Get into the house and find a back exit.'

When she didn't reply he risked a quick look and groaned. She sagged against the house's stone wall. Her fingernails drew blood from her scalp. Her gaze was fixed on the two xintou girls, her mouth agape in a silent scream of terror and agony.

Was it possible to strike a fatal blow at one before the Selb around them reacted? Would killing one twin stop the attack? A quick scan of the weishi put paid to that idea. Not only were they closer, but they all had weapons drawn and ready, their weight balanced, their attention fixed on him. No way to get within striking distance of the girls.

Despair rushed in to replace certainty. Along the street, his men fell beneath Alcazar swords, even those that saw which way the wind blew and laid down their arms. Hassan's junren showed no mercy. Steel rose and fell. Blood washed the street.

Pushed too far, these girls would kill, too.

'Alright.' He let his weapons dangle from his thumbs and held his palms out. 'Stop hurting her and let my men live. We surrender.'

The erheyi gave matching, wintry smiles. 'We don't need to negotiate. Their deaths are inevitable. Yours and hers are the only lives to be spared.'

Tali gasped, her shoulders relaxing as the erheyi released her. She sank to her knees. Sobbing, she wrapped shaking arms around her anguish and curled into a ball.

A weishi relieved Corin of his weapons and patted him down, finding the two other daggers secreted in his clothing.

Corin glared. 'Why? Why us?'

A heavy hand fell on Corin's shoulder and he flinched but couldn't pull free of that implacable grip. A large shape blotted out half the leaden sky.

'Leverage, boy,' Jada Marin-kin said with a rumbling laugh. 'We need something from Alere and Mina. You're going to help us get it.'

Corin swore. 'I had a feeling you were going to say that.'

CHAPTER FORTY

ALERE

Alere peered around the throne. Rohne and Nasra stood at the edge of the stage, gazing complacently over the chaos of blood and battle in the courtyard. Alere frowned. Why weren't they concerned? Surely they could see their people were being beaten?

Jarran and Kett still fought side-by-side. Black-and-grey uniformed bodies lay piled about them. Kett faced off against Zand, Master Anh's second. The Selb drew back his thin lips in a feral grin and flicked a shuriken. Kett ducked and sliced at Zand's thigh. The Selb danced back.

'Zand, you gouri hamagi!' Master Anh stalked through his men and hurled three knives at his traitorous employee. Zand spun aside and struck at his former master.

Kett left him to it and caught an axe-blow on his sword, protecting Jarran's back.

Movement nearby caught Alere's attention. Rohne turned and she could see his expression clearly. Wild delight. A kind of mad, inhuman joy glittered in his amber eyes and twisted his mouth.

Mina gasped and whispered. 'He's worse, Alli. I think using his gifts so much has sped up the deterioration. We have to help him!'

Beside him, Nasra cast frequent glances at her son, a frown pulling at her fine brows. Rohne laughed and threw his arms wide. Nasra's shoulders tensed. She grabbed Rohne's arm and spoke silently to him.

'Don't be ridiculous, Mother,' Rohne replied aloud. 'Why should I calm down? Things are going so well.'

So well? Alere checked the courtyard again. Most of those in Selb and Alcazar uniforms lay dead or dying. Master Anh's weishi had won the day. Three xiao-cats lay dead, the rest had vanished into the city. Onlookers cowered as far from the action as they could, huddled in tearful, horrified groups. Master Anh had Zand at swordpoint and the Selb raised his arms in surrender.

The rain and hail eased to a fine drizzle. The storm's rumbling growl moved east across the river, leaving the courtyard spattered with white ice chips and mangled, bloodied corpses.

What on Kalima was Rohne thinking?

She extended a thought, testing Rohne's wards and his state of mind. Ahhhh. Mina was right. Even with his wards in place, she could sense his mind's tattered, frayed edges unravelling. Soon he would spiral into the same dark-chaos that had claimed young Batu. If that happened, then Rohne – vastly more powerful than the untrained young boy – would take every mind in the courtyard with him. If not everyone in the city.

It was too late to fix him. She just needed to convince Mina. And Nasra. As soon as Nasra admitted defeat. Then they could work together to contain her son.

Resigned to what she must do, Alere withdrew from Rohne's mind. But a fine, golden thread stretched tight and pulled her up short. The thread held her in place, outside the safety of her own wards. It thickened and twined darkness around the part of her that existed in this psychic other-world. Alere struck out, trying to fight back, or to draw on the calming power of the yanstones. The thread prevented that, too. Every attempt to break free simply tightened it, constricting, cutting her off from herself and her sister.

The thread led back to Rohne. A connection he must have forged in Shanzhai when she'd opened her wards to him. Her uneasiness with his contact; his voice in her head in Chengdu. It was more than just telepathy. She should have trusted her instincts about him.

With a laugh, he pushed her consciousness aside and bound her into a corner of herself.

Then he occupied the space in her Outers, instead.

Helpless, unable to control so much as a finger of her physical form, Alere observed from a deep distance as her body rose and moved jerkily out from behind the throne. Her grip on Mina tightened. She stumbled along beside Alere, frantically trying to pry loose.

Rohne appeared beside her, triumph and agony warring in his face. He leaned close, his lips brushing her ear.

'Still sure you'll win this, Alere?' he mocked. 'Underestimated me, didn't you? How's your precious freedom looking now? After all, my army has just wiped yours out in the Zalam. Oh.' He made a moue and shifted her head, so she faced the milling, terrified crowds of people in the courtyard. 'You don't believe me? Watch.'

With an imperious gesture, and a swirl of his gold robe, he sat on the Steel Throne. Nasra, after a brief, almost-worried glance at her son, took her place behind his right shoulder, where the Bonded Xintou traditionally stood.

At the southern street entrance, the weishi and crowds parted. They stumbled aside to avoid the disciplined march of junren entering the courtyard. All across the space, skirmishes and isolated battles dribbled to a halt as combatants craned to see whose army approached.

A cry of despair rose from the crowd as the first black-and-grey uniforms came into view. They were led by eight pairs of gold-clad erheyi girls, marching in triumphant order. Behind them, prodded on by the swords of their captors, staggered the key members of Alere's team. Alere's heart stuttered at the sight of their battered, bloodied faces.

Corin, Tali, Yasmin, Rafi, and a dozen or more young Xintou House girls stumbled into a clearing before the stage. Their hands were tied, faces bruised, clothing torn and bloody. The younger girls sobbed and clung to each other. Rafi, Yasmin, Tali, and Corin set their feet and stared defiantly back at Rohne. Leading them, Jada Marin-kin, his teeth gleaming against his dark beard and skin, swung his axe leisurely. He planted the head on the ground with a ring of metal on stone.

He swept Rohne a deep bow. 'Shenshi, you see your enemies defeated before you. What would you have me do with them?'

Rohne made a languid, dismissive gesture. 'Take the other two prisoner first, then we'll decide.'

Nasra signalled to the erheyi girls, who strode to the stage. There they moved, in perfect synchrony, to face the crowd. Each pair raised an open hand then closed it into a fist.

Every weishi and junren loyal to Alere's cause collapsed in screaming agony. Fingers raking at their heads, backs arched, legs thrashing. Onlookers clutched at each other, tearful and almost beyond horror now. The gold-clad twins opened their hands and the tortured men and women slumped into unconsciousness.

Except Kett and Jarran. They, alone, remained standing. With half a dozen blades at their throats, they froze, surrounded by the enemy. The Selb marched the two men over to join Rafi and the others. And Saric? Where was he? Dead or unconscious?

Zand paused by Master Anh's sleeping form. He smiled thinly, picked up a dagger, and plunged it into his former master's neck. Then he wiped the blade fastidiously, collected his axe and strolled to stand beside Kett and Jarran. Master Anh twitched, convulsed, and bled out onto the cobbles.

Deep inside her own mind, still unable to retaliate, Alere shrieked her impotent anger. Beside her, Mina wept, her hand limp in Alere's grip.

Alere pushed fruitlessly at the bonds holding her mind firm. How could Rohne, with the pain he endured, have such strength? Gaisi! How had she been so blind and so arrogant? *Know your enemy* was one of the oldest maxims in the Weishi House, yet she'd assumed Rohne would be ignorant of so much he clearly wasn't.

She'd played right into his hands by doing exactly what he expected. He knew how much she valued her friends. He knew she would sacrifice herself rather than let Mina and Jarran be executed. He'd sucked her in, with this coronation charade, until she overcommitted and became overconfident. Then he took away her ability to either free her friends, or to give her life in that cause. He had hamstrung her with her own weaknesses, her own blind, duty-bound beliefs.

He also knew Kett, and how he thought. After all, they'd spent three weeks together, travelling as friends. The odds were, they had spoken of similar interests and books on warfare must have been discussed at some point. Hadn't Rohne mentioned reading the copious ancient books in Nasra's library? Some of them must have given common ground for conversation. Clearly, he'd understood Kett well enough to anticipate today's urban warfare and to spring his own trap.

But what could she do? She was helpless to even lift a finger. Her only hope was to act the instant he released her. If he released her.

Rohne rose from the seat of Jun First power and paced once around Mina and Alere, considering them dispassionately. He pressed a thumb to his temple and grimaced.

Rohne? Nasra voice echoed in Alere's mind. *Enough. We've won.*

He waved his mother away irritably. 'Not yet, we haven't, Mother. Now,' he said in a low, tense voice, 'we come to the real issue. Me.' He gazed into Alere's eyes and pointed at Kett and the others, standing silent before the stage. 'They will die right here, today, if you don't do as I say.'

Alere didn't reply. Couldn't. She couldn't even move her eyes to follow his motion. Every part of her itched to strike. To wrap an arm around his throat. To slide her blade into his ribs and let his life drained away until a corpse lay at her feet.

But…

When he released her, he would expect that. He knew she always reacted from her weishi training first. So she needed to be someone he didn't know; do something out of character. Kett had always said that one's greatest strength was also one's greatest weakness. She needed to turn that knowledge on Rohne. What was his strength? His weakness?

No. What was *her* greatest weakness?

Ah…

Alere kept the knowledge of what she had to do hidden deep behind her Inners, safe from Rohne's awareness.

At her side, Mina's shoulders sagged. Could she still hear Alere's thoughts? Mina cast a quick, fearful look at Alere, her lashes sparkling with unshed tears. Then she straightened her back and firmed her mouth into resolution. Alere, frozen still, couldn't even reassure her. Wouldn't have been able to, anyway.

'What do you want, Rohne?' Mina's voice was flat, drained of fire and life.

He loomed closer so only they could hear. 'First I'll take the sword.' He matched action to word and pried the blade from Alere's grip. 'And I want the necklace. I know you must have it. Then you two will work with Nasra and cure me. You were very close with that boy. I can't do it on myself.' He twirled the blade, admiring the slip of light along its length. He gave them a bitter smile. 'I tried.'

'And if we can't?' Mina asked. 'There's a way we can switch the gene off. Let me do that. You'll be alive, at least.'

'Alive isn't enough. I'm meant to be more. Male xintou are more powerful than females. I deserve this.' He indicated the Alcazar. 'If you try anything but the cure, I'll just kill you. You're no use to me.' He rested the blade's tip in the hollow of Alere's throat. At his signal, six Selb weishi laid their axes at the throats of Kett, Corin, Jarran, Rafi, Yasmin and Tali. The steel at Kett's throat drew blood, which trickled scarlet, staining his shirt. He didn't flinch.

'First, you watch your friends die,' Rohne said calmly. 'Then you watch every gouri person in this city die because, if I go, then I *will* take them with me.' He stretched his mouth in a snarl. 'You might even survive, given you can ward. But I doubt you'll enjoy living after you find yourself alone and responsible for a city full of stinking carcasses.'

Mina paled. Her fingers, still locked in Alere's, twitched. She glanced at Alere, then at the crowd before the stage. She bowed her head.

'The necklace is on Alere's ankle.' She touched Rohne's arm, hesitating when he jerked aside. 'But be careful. You may hurt her if you touch it.'

Rohne laughed. 'And you think *that* would discourage me? You're pathetic, Mina.'

He crouched before Alere and found the necklace around her ankle. Alere steeled herself as he fumbled with the catch. The chain slipped off her skin and into his hand. Breathless agony speared through her body as he caressed the glittering stones. Each sweep of his fingertips was a lash across her skin, more painful than Ven's whip or the tear through muscle of Hallon's kusarigama. Each touch drove steel spikes beneath her flesh, into nerves; into her mind, flaying her to the bone; to the Inners.

He released his control of her, but there was no chance to strike. She grasped at Mina's arm as her knees buckled and her mind succumbed to the torture.

CHAPTER FORTY-ONE

ALERE

'Stop!' Mina's plea was barely audible through the roaring in her ears. 'You have to stop, Rohne! She can't help if she's in this much pain. Give it back, please? Having more stones won't make any difference to what you're going through. But she needs them if you want us to help.'

The world vanished behind a searing red haze and Alere actually longed for death. She collapsed to the stage and wrapped her arms around her head. Someone screamed, long and guttural. Her.

Then the agony ceased. She was left panting, tears dripping onto the timber beneath her curled body. The cessation of pain was like a bucket of cold water. Her limbs shook uncontrollably in the aftermath. Mina clipped the necklace around her throat and helped her to her feet. Strength surged back. Gilded. Warm.

Rohne! Nasra's mental voice, tinged with fear, intruded on Alere's bruised mind.

Luckily, the rest of the mother-son confrontation took place in silence as Nasra touched Rohne's arm. That the conversation went badly was obvious from the flicker of expressions. Autocratic arrogance in Nasra's expression dimmed. Her mouth fell open and she gasped. Rohne looked at her from beneath half-lowered lids and curled a lip. His hands clenched to fists and he jerked his arm free of her touch.

Nasra looked back and forth between the sisters and her son. She stalked over to Alere reaching for the necklace, only to hesitate when Alere flinched away.

She peered at Alere and gripped her arm, nails digging into the flesh. *Is it true? Do the stones give you xintou powers? Can you use them to cure him?*

Rohne really hadn't told Nasra about the stones. Why? Alere pulled her scattered thoughts together. Where was this going?

I'm not certain we can cure him, Nasra, she said. *But we can try. We were close once before. With your knowledge of how to stabilise the protein creation, we might be able to do it.* She hid the lie deep in her Inners. It was already too late. But this might give her and Mina a chance to shut Rohne down.

Nasra hesitated. Rohne paced back and forth across the front of the stage, muttering and shaking his head, pressing his thumbs to his temples and glaring at the women. Out in the square, Master Anh's weishi began to wake and rise to their feet. The Selb weishi confiscated their weapons and herded them back, in with the silent, watching crowd.

And you would do that, for him? Nasra stared at Alere. Her grip tightened. *This is not how it was meant to go!*

No, we won't do it for him. Or you. I'd do it to save the people I love and the people of this city. He knows that. She held Nasra's gaze steadily. *But afterward, when he's cured, he won't need anyone anymore. He'll take these yanstones and nothing will be able to stop him. Not you, not me, not all your twins, either. What will he do when he breaks the chains of his flawed genetics and his need for your approval?*

Would Nasra admit she had made a mistake in birthing Rohne? Would she kill her son to save herself?

He won't. Nasra's eyes narrowed. *He'll listen to me.*

Are you certain? Alere said. *Because we can also switch the gene off altogether. He would be normal, but he'd be alive.*

Nasra's mouth curled into disdain. *Better off dead than* normal. *He's destined to change the world. To guide it into the future. With me at his side, we will bring true progress. He is the true guide foreseen for this world. Kalima will be a better place. Everyone will benefit.*

Pretty sure that's what the zifts on Old Earth said, too. Right before they wrecked the planet and our ancestors left.

Leaving that to sink in, Alere slid her hand into Mina's and her mind into their private connection. Drawing strength, just for a minute, from the warmth of Mina's love, she straightened.

You know what we have to do, don't you? Alere asked.

Yes. Mina's mental voice held quiet acceptance. *Even if we could cure him, we can't allow it. He's too strong. Xintou House wasn't perfect, but their teachings kept the xintou from becoming tyrants.*

Exactly, Alere said. *And all the Seeing's have spoken of the advent of someone more powerful than any xintou that's come before, and more tyrannical. We can't let that happen.*

After a long pause Mina replied, her voice even quieter. *No. I know.*

I know you still care about him. Alere squeezed her hand. *Are you sure you'll be able to help me, when the time comes? Nasra will be monitoring us, so we can't just outright stop Rohne's heart. We have to go through with the pretence of a cure. We have to let him break and contain him long enough for Nasra to choose his death.*

Mina pulled free and wiped a tear from her cheek. She cast a quick, despairing look at Jarran. He returned it with steady clarity. Alere couldn't risk looking at Kett for fear her resolve would falter.

I just don't know if we'll be strong enough. Mina sounded troubled. *Batu was an inexperienced child and he was almost too much for us. Plus our connection is weaker now, and we have fewer yanstones to draw on without your sword and the bracelets. How do we contain Rohne? I still have your dagger, but I don't think I can ...kill him. I just can't.*

Sliding cold fingers into her pocket, Alere touched the warm steel of the Xintou House yanstone setting. Power thrummed from the stone, coursing up her arm.

Leave that to me, Mina. Not wanting to reveal too much that might be Read by Rohne or Nasra, Alere cut off Mina's questioning thought.

She grabbed Nasra's wrist. *If we're going to do this, it needs to be now. By the feel of his mind, Rohne is at the threshold. He's also going to fight us, because the gene splicing hurts. You'll have to help us keep him in check.*

After a quick, mistrustful glance, Nasra returned to Rohne. He shoved her aside, snarling. Turning on the crowd, he released a wordless scream that carried a Broadcast of the fire in his mind. He threw his arms wide and an invisible force rippled out from the stage. People were thrown off their feet, tumbled, crashed against chairs, walls, and each other in a terrifying display of telekinetic power. Writhing on the ground, the unwarded groaned, cried out and grabbed at their heads.

Another guttural roar and the windows of every elegant house surrounding the Alcazar courtyard shattered. Glass exploded in glittering fireworks that rained down on the screaming onlookers.

Nasra dug her fingers into Rohne's hair and jerked his head to face her. She pressed her forehead against his. He clawed at her wrists feebly then settled, relaxing his restless, fluttering movements and his pained grimace. Like a docile child, he allowed her to lead him to the Steel Throne and install him on it. He laid Alere's sword across his knees, inspecting it with vague interest. Then he appeared to forget about it altogether. His grip loosened.

Slowly, the crowd clambered to its feet, the stink of fear a miasma thicker than fog.

Nasra touched Alere's arm, her nose wrinkling into a disdainful sneer. *I've stabilised him but it will only last a minute or two. He's far past my ability now. Here's what I do.* She flashed a subliminal image, too complex and detailed for Alere's comprehension, straight into her Outers. *Fix him!* Nasra gestured imperiously. *I did not work so hard for so long to have it all fall apart, now. Fix him or your friends die.*

Two pairs of the erheyi girls took up positions on either side of Alere and Mina.

Nasra smiled coolly. *And you'll die if you try anything except the cure.*

Alere and Mina moved next to the Throne. Nasra stood on the opposite side, watching both them and Rohne. Alere entwined Mina's fingers in her own, forging and expanding their bond until it almost blotted out everything else. She drew on the Koh-Lin yanstones, but it was not enough power to contain Rohne at his worst. Not even close. So she slipped the other hand into her pocket. She unpeeled the cloth and gripped the Xintou House yanstone.

The stone burned cold against her palm. Silver-gilt fire coursed through her veins, fiercer, hotter, and brighter than the sensation from the Koh-Lin gems. Confidence hammered through her blood, quenched fear, forged her will into compliance with the blaze of energy. The temperature around the pavilion plummeted.

All hesitancy and horror vanished. Sharp clarity of purpose replaced it. Every emotion melted away. Nothing could disrupt the path she must tread. No more doubt. Only the way and the purpose, carved into the stone's matrix by the certainty of the nine Xintou Mistresses who had carried the *shenhilya* over the last five hundred years.

Stability was the reason for their existence. Petty squabbles over the throne were irrelevant before the greater purpose: peace and constancy. Almost all that comprised Alere vanished before the conviction of those long-dead House Mistresses, swept into darkness by the light of their fire and the steel of their determination.

Alere's connection with Mina flared and deformed as their minds contended with the memories stored in the stone. Alere fought back, struggling to maintain identity, to hold onto the important, to push back the will of dead women. The thread connecting her to Mina became a lifeline. She snatched at it and hauled herself back into connection with Mina.

Alere and Mina's Bond held. The yanstone was hers to control, theirs to control, its power bottomless. Alere knew her destiny. Their destiny. Now she understood Mistress Li's actions and her attention. Now she understood who she truly was, and what inevitable part she played in all this madness.

Yet, she and Mina belonged to the stone: merely a vessel, a cup, a conduit.

No! Shoving aside the stones' intent, she clung to hers: freedom, self-determination, truth, love.

Freedom? What use was freedom and self-determination if the path the free chose led to destruction? What use truth if the listeners didn't understand it? Love? There were things more important. Love made one weak. It clouded the mind. Important over what one wanted. Therein lay the power to choose the right path. All else led to pain.

Their strength faltered. Their minds were absorbed and rooted in the silver-gilt fire of five hundred years of power; controlling and controlled by it, both. They were sidelined, yet willing participants at once. Clinging to awareness. Part of the insanity. Just a single, thread connected them, keeping one small part of their minds hidden from the sight of past House Mistresses.

The sum of all that power and ambition emerged through their bodies.

Two heads lifted and smiled across at Nasra. Alere-and-Mina spoke together, as one, entwined and entombed in the great yanstone.

'Now we can begin.' The Alere body snatched her sword from beneath Rohne's lax grip. 'But first, I need to make a few changes.' The Mina body mimicked her words precisely.

Colour drained from Nasra's cheeks. *Who are you?*

'I,' Alere-and-Mina said, 'am the Erheyi. I am the Xintou House Mistresses. The world will be healed again. Released from doubt. Directed to the true path. Steady and safe once more.'

She raised the sword.

CHAPTER FORTY-TWO

CORIN

Corin staggered to his feet and watched in helpless, angry confusion as Nasra placed her abomination of a son on the Jun First's Throne, and Alere and Mina stepped up beside it.

What were they thinking? Alere knew better than to accede to any hostage situation demands. Nothing she did would prevent Nasra from ordering the execution of every single person who resisted her rule.

What did Alere have planned?

Kett's expression was blank. His shoulders were relaxed, his wrists bound, his feet planted at shoulders width. In short, nothing about him spoke of a man about to spring into action. If Kett saw no opportunity to help, that boded ill for whatever he and Alere planned.

Corin muttered, 'What's going on?'

'Shut up,' Kett replied.

'We can't just sit here. What's Alli doing? Did she get her powers back?'

Kett turned bleakness on him. 'We failed. There's nothing we can do. It's up to her, now. If there's an opportunity, we take it. If not, we have to trust her.'

Corin spat an ugly invective and looked back at the stage in time to see Alere reach into her pocket.

The item she produced sparkled in the sun, its aching brilliance blinding. He squinted, trying to see. She hung it around her neck and tucked it into her shirt. With the light hidden, Corin saw her and the change shocked him.

The face was Alere's but whatever lay behind it wasn't. Somehow, the eyes were older, harder, almost bored; the shape of her mouth cynical. She tossed her dark hair back, smug delight flickering for a moment. Beside her, the girl who was – and wasn't – Mina made the exact same movement at the exact same time. Then they both raised their arms to the sky in triumphant exultation.

The sword in Alere's hand gleamed silver. Sparks coruscated along its edges. Lightning crackled and flashed from the yanstones in the pommel, stabbing to earth nearby. A shockwave slammed into Corin's chest and tiny stone chips peppered his skin. Brilliance left a trail of red burned into his retina. He had to blink to see past the glare.

Another blaze of light split the tumbled grey sky. He raised bound hands to protect his face as more stone flew. Screams of uncomprehending terror rose from the crowd. The nauseating smell of burnt hair and flesh wafted up. He gagged, staggering back as yet another flash whited out the world.

Beside him, he vaguely made out the dark shape of Kett, his wrists still bound, strangling a Selb weishi. Corin squinted against the light and belatedly seized the opportunity. He looped one arm over the nearest Selb's head, locking a sleeper-hold onto his thick neck and kicking the back of his knees to break his balance. A quick twist snapped his neck.

Slicing his bonds on the axeblade, Corin snatched up the weapon and three steel throwing knives. Not far away, half-hidden by the oily, stinking smoke, Tali, Rafi, and Yasmin stood protectively before the younger xintou girls. At Tali's feet, two Selb twitched and gargled on the ground, bleeding from every orifice. Two older teenage xintou appeared beside her. One fell, a shuriken lodged in her throat. Her House sister gasped, then rounded on the Selb who threw it. He clutched at his throat, mouth agape, giving a glimpse of black feathers lodged in his tongue as he dropped his blowpipe.

Something whistled past Corin's ear and he leapt aside. A Selb staggered by, scrabbling at a shuriken that protruded from an eye. Corin snatched yet another steel throwing knife from the man's belt. A well-placed kick at an ankle overbalanced him. He tripped on an overturned chair, fell on his stomach, shuddered twice and slumped into death.

A quick scan showed Saric, crouched behind the piled up bodies of three Selb, blowpipe to his lips and another shuriken in his fingers. Corin saluted. A few paces away, Kett fought, barehanded, against three armed Selb. He bled profusely from a superficial cut to the forehead.

Corin weighed the knife, called Kett's name and threw. Kett looked up and snatched the knife as it tumbled past. He jammed the sharp steel to the hilt, through his attacker's alzin armour and into the heart. Yanking it free he ducked beneath a swinging axe. A kick broke the second man's knee. The knife sliced across the throat of the third.

With a nod to Corin, and a glance at the stage, Kett collected an axe and swung it experimentally. He chopped through alzin to cleave another Selb almost in two. Zand stepped in front of him, smiling. Kett swung the axe. Zand swayed aside. His hand flickered, driving into Kett's ribs. Corin heard the crack. Kett gasped and pressed at his side. Corin took a step in his direction.

'Hold!'

Projected forcibly into both ear and mind, the command froze every hand in every skirmish. The power of that voice trampled resistance. Female, many-layered, ancient, angry and cold, it was impossible to disobey. Muscles refused to function. Those running from the violence fell over as their momentum carried them forward. The courtyard became a frozen tableau of death in every stage.

'Lay down your weapons and look at us.'

Every person did as directed. Even focussing intently on his wards did Corin no good. His knives fell. His body turned, puppet-like, to face the stage. From the strain on the faces of Tali, Kett, and Jarran, their resistance was equally as futile.

'Why do you still fight each other?' Alere-and-Mina spread their hands, sneering. *'You are petty in your squabbling for power. There is no need. The time of erheyi is now. It was not in these children.'* They indicated the blackened smouldering piles of once-human flesh – all that remained of the eight pairs of twins Nasra had created. *'The erheyi is us. There will be no more fighting for there is nothing to fight over. We will guide you now. Be at peace.'*

Corin shrugged. They were right. What had he been so worked up about? A beautiful day beckoned. The world was good. Nothing needed to change. It seemed silly to kill each other over something as trivial as who sat on the throne. He should go back to Shanzhai. That was an excellent idea.

Other fighters straightened, studying their injuries and bloodsmeared hands in confused, regretful wonder. Selb helped up injured crowdmembers and fallen loyal weishi. Onlookers chatted amicably with junren. How strange that they were injured. What had they been fighting over? People righted chairs, dusted one another off, and tended to injuries, laughing. Standing by her son, Nasra beamed at Alere-and-Mina and patted Rohne's arm soothingly.

Nearby, Tali blinked rapidly. Kett pinched at the bridge of his nose, deep furrows between his brows. Strange. Corin found the Selb who'd taken his swords and retrieved them. The man gave them over with a cheerful bow, like he'd just borrowed a tool from a friend.

Sheathing them, Corin swiped his thumbs over the yanstones and choked, his knees softening as the weight of memories flooded back.

Checking the stage, he sauntered over to Kett, trying not to attract attention. Kett had found his steel sword and sheathed it at his hip.

'Here.' Corin offered the sword-pommels to the weishi and braced himself against the too-intimate contact. Surprisingly, the brush of Kett's fingers on the stones produced only the faintest sensation, like a gentle pat on the back. Kett's gaze cleared and he looked beneath his lashes at the stage.

'We need to—'

'*No!*'

The voice inside and outside Corin's head was not Alere-and-Mina's.

'*This throne is* mine! *This Jundom is* mine *to guide, not yours. These people are mine to command and mine to destroy if I wish.*' Rohne, raw and primal in his rage, cast his mind out and wiped away the false complacency implanted by Alere-and-Mina.

'Khara!' Corin swore as confused anger resurfaced in the expressions of the Selb around him.

On the stage, Nasra gasped and pointed at her Selb. Four leapt toward Alere and Mina, who gestured lazily. The Selb collapsed, screaming, tearing at their heads until blood streaked their faces. They died, blood streaming from eyes and noses, bodies contorted.

Four more Selb went for Rohne and held him to the throne. He screamed and the four men flew backward off the stage. They crashed to the ground, limp and broken. Rohne rose and stalked toward Nasra, hands raised. She backed away, eyes wide, mouth agape.

Alere-and-Mina gazed at Rohne in supreme indifference. Corin hesitated. What was the bigger threat? Rohne, Nasra, the Selb...or Alere and Mina?

Near to Kett, Zand lifted his head, cold determination in his steel eyes. Unhesitating, Kett snatched up a dagger and slashed at the Selb. Zand blocked and drove an elbow into Kett's liver. Kett doubled over, gasping. The Selb hefted his steel axe and swung at Kett's neck. Corin took a step in his direction, but Kett drove a shoulder into Zand's chest, one foot hooked behind his ankle. Zand crashed to the ground, rolled over one shoulder and rose. Kett yanked out his sword and sliced across the Selb's throat in one smooth move. The Selb gurgled and blood spattered Kett's trous.

'You gouri...'

Corin spun at the sound of Jada Marin-kin's throaty roar. The huge, fur-clad Selb raider stormed toward Kett, his eyes blazing and enormous axe raised. Corin hefted his sword and dagger doubtfully.

'Together?' he said.

'Definitely,' Kett replied. 'You go left.'

'Toward the axe. Wonderful.' Corin circled, watching Jada closely. A flicker of movement to his right pulled his attention away. Another Selb. A woman. Small and quick. Gaisi! He blocked a lightning-swift dagger-strike and kicked her knee. The joint snapped and the woman screamed. Corin finished her with a thrust through the heart.

He glanced back at Kett. Jada had him on the retreat. Axe-blows raining so fast it was hard to see the weapon. No opening for a counterstrike. Kett edged back toward the stage, step by step, barely holding his own. The axe-blade skimmed his chest, slicing through alzin and cloth. A line of blood blossomed. Kett yelled and spun aside.

'Take this.' Saric thrust a black-feathered dart into Corin's hand and nodded at Jada. 'He's wearing too much fur and leather for the blowpipe. Can't see a bit of skin.'

Corin lifted the dart. 'I don't think one will be a big enough dose.'

'I know.' Saric held up another. 'You do one, I'll do the other. Twice the chance. Neck's the best place.'

'Oh, no you don't, kid.'

Saric raised a brow.

With a sigh, Corin nodded. 'I know, I know. Fine. Go. Try not to die.' He sheathed his sword.

'Get me up high,' Saric said.

Together, they ran at the fighting pair. When they were three paces away, Corin grabbed Saric under the arms and hurled the boy at the Selb leader. Saric landed on Jada's back like a sky-monkey. He jabbed the black-feathered dart deep into Jada's neck. The Selb roared and spun. Saric backflipped off and scuttled out of reach.

Kett drove his steel sword deep into Jada's stomach. Jada swung a fist backhand and connected. Kett fell, rolled, and rose again, shaking his head and blinking. His sword still protruded from Jada's gut. Jada stared at it, frowning. Corin dove and jabbed his dart through the thinner cloth of Jada's trous, into the back of his calf. He leapt to his feet and backed away, watching.

With a roar, Jada lifted his face to the uncaring sky and dropped to his knees, his arms upraised. In one last act of desperation, he flung the axe at Kett and laughed. Kett staggered aside, barely avoiding the steel blade. Spittle frothed from Jada's blue lips. His eyes bulged and he toppled sideways, twitching.

Kett and Corin hung back a moment, just in case. Saric strolled in and kicked the Selb's hulking body. He wrenched Kett's sword free and handed it over.

'Thanks,' Kett said, wiping it clean. He spoke to Corin. 'This isn't over, yet. We need to get that stone off Alere.' He pointed at the stage, where Rohne had his hands around Nasra's neck. 'And kill Rohne, before he loses—'

On the stage, Rohne released his mother. She staggered aside, one hand to her throat. Rohne grabbed at his head and shrieked a banshee's cry. The ground rumbled underfoot. Buildings trembled. Roof tiles slipped and shattered on the ground. Bricks bounced and shivered.

Black, searing, raging, blinding agony lanced through Corin's wards, swamping everything he was. It sucked him into a maelstrom of pain from which there could be no escape. Ten thousand minds screamed with him and plunged into the abyss of Rohne's burgeoning madness.

ALERE

Mina? Blackness; pain; anguish; despair. A swirling vortex of lunacy dragged at her as she sought solid ground; a path back to reason.

Mina! A thin, frayed golden thread, slack and tarnished by the sable torment engulfing the world, brushed her consciousness.

Alere?

I'm here. Find me.

The thread tautened, thickened. From within the impenetrable ink of Rohne's self-hatred, the soft, silver-gilt essence that was Mina emerged. For a long moment Alere and Mina clung to one another, anchored in the buffeting storm, gathering strength.

I'm afraid, Alli. He's too strong, even for us, even with the Xintou House stone.

I know. But what can we do? I was afraid of the stone. So I thought that was my weakness. I thought using the stone would give us the power to stop him, but it's not enough! I can't control it. I'm barely keeping us from Fusing. The Mistresses…they're too strong as well.

We have to stop fighting—

What? You want to give up and let Nasra win? Or let Rohne's mind destroy everyone. He's so powerful even those with wards will die. His telekinesis will level the city. Or do we just give ourselves up to the House Mistresses in the shenhilya? *I don't like any of those options.*

Let me finish, Alli. The House stone is controlling us. We need to turn that around. Mina's mind-voice sounded tired. *That was the lesson Qara and Mistress Li meant us to learn. Not how to kill or even cure Rohne. It's how to control this stone and use it to defeat him. The* shenhilya *is more powerful than either of us. Right now the stone is controlling us and holding him in check. We need more power to contain it.*

How? It can't draw on the Koh-Lin stones unless I let it. And I'm keeping them apart. Just barely.

Why don't you let it access the Koh-Lin stones?

I'm afraid, Mina. If I give it full access to them and me, we'll both be absorbed by it, too. We'll Fuse – with each other. With the stone. With all the stones.

I know, Alli. That's the answer. It always has been. We have to Fuse. Then, with the Koh-Lin stones, we'll have the power to control the shenhilya, *contain Rohne, and shield the people. To do that we have to stop fighting each other and ourselves.*

I don't understand.

We have to set aside ego, independence and fear. You've been so afraid of losing your freedom – your very self – to either our twin-

bond or the yanstones we almost missed the potential in them; in us. And I've been so afraid you would control me, I couldn't work with you. But we have to let all that go. We have to Fuse. You and I.

But we can't! That will kill us.

Alere, trust me. We can do this. You must let go of fear. That's all. And so must I.

But... what if we can't reverse it afterward?

We can't let that stop us. This is bigger than what I want or what you want.

Alere cast about in the timeless golden darkness, desperate for another solution. But there was none. Beyond the illusion of security generated by each other, the swirling tempest of pain carried the terrified cries of thousands of minds, slowly being drawn into the centre. Into death and oblivion.

*Alli...*Mina's thoughts entwined with hers, loving, frightened. *I'm scared, too. But it's also the only hope we have of protecting and freeing the people we love.*

Alere sought for resolution. Kett's quiet strength. Corin's laughter. Saric's mischief. All gone if she failed. She stilled and found the place where fear's claws dug deepest into her heart. Could she let Mina in so far? Could she bare herself? Did she have a choice?

Yes. Always.

She reached out to her sister. *You're right. Together we're stronger than the yanstone and with all the stones we can contain Rohne. Join me. Love me and let me love you.*

Wordlessly, that-which-was-Mina approached. The gilded thread thickened to a rope, then to an amorphous, shifting ball of shimmering light that beckoned and invited them into safety and strength, unity and potential. Mina opened her Inners.

Alere hesitated, then opened hers.

Minds melded. Painless, joyous even. Fusion felt not like fire, but more like the enveloping warmth of loving arms, inside and out. The blending of their soft and hard; their strengths and weaknesses. Creating a forged, tempered whole. No secrets. Old scars and traumas revealed themselves to be nothing more than false beliefs. Bitter memories of the past flowed free, released and healed under the influence of a loving other. After all, how could something existing only in memory have power?

At last, just one small corner of Mina's mind remained shuttered. Alere waited with tender patience, for time meant little here. Reluctantly, Mina opened that final Inner ward and revealed what she hid so carefully.

Ah, you've Seen this. The small part that was still just Alere recognised the image for what it was. *And?*

I don't know. Mina's reply was steady.

Well, I guess we'll find out. Come. It's time.

With the final barrier gone, their minds Fused in one glorious, silver-gilt explosion. They shattered the bonds entrapping them in darkness and flew free of both Rohne's torment and the constraints of the House stone.

CHAPTER FORTY-THREE

ALERE-MINA

Alere-Mina drew slow breaths of cool, blood-tainted air and straightened. The situation in the square remained unchanged, for only fractions of a second had passed. Every visible living person lay on the blood-spattered ground. They writhed in the throes of Rohne's agony, eerily silent but for the soft, shuffling sounds of their clothes on the cobbles and the occasional, sobbing cry. Beyond that, a heavy silence blanketed the city. Every mind sank into the black depths of his horror. Birds spiralled from the sky, horses and che-ma collapsed, legs thrashing. Enhanced by the bracelets around his wrist, Rohne's self-destruction held the whole city in thrall.

On the stage, only Nasra stood, unscathed, gaping in voiceless bewilderment at her son and the annihilation he wrought around her. Her throat was reddened, bruised by Rohne's attempt to strangle her. She looked up as Alere-Mina stood and her expression shifted into a kind of fearful hatred. Her fingers curled and she bared her teeth, hissing her displeasure and guilt.

This is your *fault. You said you could cure him. Do it. Now!*

Alere-Mina shook her heads, thinking as one, speaking as one, inseparably certain of her path.

'It is your doing, Nasra. Yours and the House's. Kya Edwards's fear of the future, of her sister, and of her son set the House on this path. Your rebellion against it became the yang to their yin. You've destroyed each other. Your son is both a creation of, and a victim of, your self-hatred and the House's fear. Every death today is on your head.'

Alere-Mina regarded Rohne as he lay, half-slumped, twitching and groaning, on the great Steel Throne. Drawing on the power of all the yanstones, she invaded his mind and created an impenetrable ward. A wall of such silver-gilt solidity that not even a fraction of his crushing insanity could slip out. It confined him to his own, disintegrating consciousness.

Freed, shaken and battered minds returned to bodies. The people of Madina climbed to their feet, clinging to one another, weeping. Tremulous questions were asked by minds too numbed and hurt to comprehend the answers, even if they got them.

The Mina body produced Alere's dagger from beneath her shirt. The yanstones set in the hilt flashed in the watered-orange sunlight. The steel blade gleamed, sleek and silvery.

No! Nasra pushed in between, protecting her son with her body. Her elegant features aged into sorrow. *I should be the one to put him out of his misery. Give it to me.*

'Mina!' Jarran's shout went unacknowledged as the Mina body passed the blade over.

With the knife ready, Nasra faltered. She stood over her son, gazing at his torment. Her lips thinned, her eyes narrowed. Her fingers flexed on the grip and she shifted her weight, back and forth.

His mind worsened, his body stiffening into seizure. A bloody froth formed at his lips as teeth shredded the skin.

'Give him mercy, Nasra,' Alere-Mina said impassively. 'Even I can't hold him if you don't. His mind is too strong. Already it fractures the wards I've put up. Let him go.'

I...I... Still Nasra hesitated, half-formed plans flashing across her Outers. She was easily audible to the Alere-Mina mind augmented by the Xintou House yanstone.

Nasra yet held out hope of retrieving her plan to run the Jundom and the House. Without the erheyi girls, without her son, without even Hassan as a puppet-Jun. She still stalled for time, hoping the savage, explosive death of Rohne's consciousness would destroy the Alere-Mina being. Give her the chance to rule uncontested. She would allow her son to die a horrific, agonising death in the hopes of ruling a devastated House and Jundom.

To prove her worth in some twisted way.

Dispassionate, Alere-Mina gathered the fire of nine angry House Mistresses, and the sum of all the yanstones, into her body. She drove molten heat into Nasra's mind. But the xintou's wards were strong. The fire slid off, dissipating like steam. Nasra rounded on Alere-Mina, the knife gleaming in her fist.

How dare *you?* Nasra snarled. *I am in control. I am the House Mistress. You are not even true xintou. Without those stones, you are* nothing!

'Maybe,' Alere-Mina replied, 'but with them we are more than you or your son could ever be. We are the future, not you. Not this pathetic boy you birthed in some warped attempt to impress Mistress Li.'

Nasra hissed and slashed at the Mina-body. The Alere-body deflected the knife-blow and struck back with a single, clinical sword thrust. The steel slid beneath Nasra's ribs, piercing her heart.

Nasra coughed, grabbing at the blade in her chest. Blood seeped through the gold silk and stained the blade. She took a half-step backward, dragging the sword from Alere-Mina's grip. Open-mouthed, she sagged against the throne. She coughed again, spraying blood onto the throne's steel plate. The dagger she held slipped to land in Rohne's lap. She folded to the timber floor. Blood oozed away between the slats. The sword fell sideways, slicing through flesh to clang against the wood.

On the Steel Throne, Rohne arched, his amber eyes flying open, mouth wide in a soundless scream. Clarity warred with madness and his mind fought the binding control of the wards. Hairline cracks appeared. His fingers clenched around the dagger's handle and he leapt from the chair, swaying. An animal snarl curled his lips back from bloodied teeth and gums.

Alere-Mina bled more power from the yanstones, reinforcing the silver-gilt sphere encasing his mind. Without it his wildness would again encompass the city. Perhaps more, with the grief of Nasra's death to compound it. He neared the end now, regardless. Weaponless, Alere-Mina could do little but contain him until it was over. His will could not best hers.

No-one's could. She was the stronger by far. With the stones' collective power, managed by their Fused minds, there was no contest. Her combined strength would bring the world out of darkness and into light once more. Guide them to peace and stability.

Rohne's animal eyes met theirs and narrowed. His grisly smile widened. He leapt. His fist flashed out. Alere's dagger glinted in the light.

Alere-Mina interposed her body. Rohne buried the dagger in her chest, slicing into the form of one; into the will of the two.

Every strength is also a weakness.

He laughed and threw his arms wide, leaving the blade deep in Alere-Mina's body.

Alere-Mina screamed and yanked the dagger free of herself, her other. Her hold over the stones and the wards faltered as duality waged war against Fusion. Darkness swamped the one-mind. Alere-Mina fought, struggling for each breath, each heartbeat, each coherent thought. The hearts beat but feebly.

The power of their fusion slipped and the world faded.

Blackness shattered the golden sphere imprisoning Rohne. His thoughts grasped at the one-mind. His face twisted, distorted by crazed, miserable realisation. His hands reached for her, clawing fingers drawing blood from her arms. Endless agony tore at her body and mind.

His mind battered hers, stronger by far in his madness; overwhelming her resistance, prising apart the unity that gave her strength. A few more seconds and he would prevail. Life drained too quickly from the body, and the ability to stop him vanished with it.

And, when she was gone, his mental implosion would take every living being into death with him.

Alere-Mina drew every remaining skerrick of power from the stones and held her wards against his attack. She lifted her head, gazed into the depths of his insanity and knew a moment's pity.

Then she plunged the yanstone dagger into Rohne's eye. With the full force of her grief, she drove steel and silver-gilt fire into the brain that threatened everything she loved.

All the energy of all the yanstones, conducted through the steel, exploded gold-fire into blackness. It shattered every facet of Rohne's warped mind into glittering shards of nothingness. Ending his madness forever.

Released from his attacks, she drew the dagger from Rohne's head and let it fall to the timber.

He staggered back and collapsed, broken, across the Steel Throne.

As cold crept into Alere-Mina's body, she sank to the floor, cradling herself. Slowly, she opened her eyes, gasping against the pain in her chest. Her own face leaned over her. Then she touched her own cheek and brushed away a hair from her own lips. Bit by bit, she tore free the Fused threads of her consciousness from her sister's; separating their minds into two again. Freeing them from the Xintou House stone.

'Mina!' Tears dripped from Alere's face onto her sister's, falling on to the soft smile curving that gentle mouth. Blood darkened the brown cloth of Mina's coarse shirt. Alere pressed at the wound, Mina's blood mingling with Rohne's as Alere tried to staunch the flow. 'Mina, no. Please!'

The yanstones. She could heal with them.

Even as she tried to settle her mind enough to draw power, Mina touched her cheek.

'Don't, Alli,' she whispered, her night-black eyes strained, her fingers trembling against Alere's skin. 'It was always meant to be me. I knew it.'

'No, Mina,' Alere sobbed. 'Don't say that. I thought it would be me. I was sure it would be me. You'll be alright. Let me heal you.'

Mina sucked a shuddering breath. 'You shouldn't. It's not right for us to have so much power. No-one should.'

'Afterward, I'll destroy the stones. All of them. After I heal you. I promise.'

'Alli! It hurts!' Mina's face contorted. Liquid pooled beneath her body.

Alere gripped the Xintou House stone. The seductive pulse of its fire flashed through her, seeking, controlling, reaching out toward Mina. That's all it would take. The stone would heal her. Reconnect them and the Koh-Lin stones, bind them forever this time. Inseparable. Powerful. Insuperable. Its warmth engulfed her, promising peace, safety, security. The stone knew how, now. The Mistresses had learned. They would never let go. They would heal Mina. All she had to do was open to the shenhilya.

Gasping, Alere released the stone. She screamed in frustration, tore it from her neck and threw it aside. 'Mina, I can't. We'd never escape. It's too strong for me, now.'

The Koh-Lin necklace! She reached for the necklace's silver-gilt comfort. But it, too, was tainted with the Xintou's bloody ambition, linked to the House stone, waiting to Fuse Alere and Mina once and for all. To hold them in thrall.

'Oh, Mina,' she whispered, aching, her throat so tight she could barely speak. 'I can't. If I use the stones to heal you we'll never be free. They'll use us to rule the world. I'm sorry. I'm sorry.'

Peace stole over Mina's face and she smiled faintly. 'It's alright, Alli. You're doing the right thing. Nasra and Rohne weren't the danger Celia and the others warned you about. It was us. We were the *true guide.* We would have destroyed everything we loved trying to make the world perfect.'

'I know.'

Mina drew a shuddering breath. 'It's best this way. Let me go. I'm not afraid anymore. Live for both of us now. Thank you, though.' She touched Alere's cheek again. 'For choosing to love me. For letting me in.'

Her gaze drifted to Jarran. She reached toward him. He limped onto the stage and crouched beside her, tears streaking his soot-stained, bloodied face.

'Mina.' His voice cracked and he kissed her forehead. 'Don't go. Don't leave me, please?'

'I love you, Jarran,' she whispered. 'But promise you'll find someone who can rule with you. I would have hated court life.' Her lips curved into a smile and Jarran gave a choked laugh.

'And I would have left it behind, for you.' He wrapped his arms around her and Alere and held them both, his shoulders shaking.

Tears blurred Alere's vision and she wiped them away, not wanting to miss a second. Kissing Mina's lips, she opened all her wards again and embraced her sister – mind and body. Aching, loving, entwined, Alere eased Mina's passing, walking with her as far as she could into the darkness. Mina sighed. Her eyes closed.

Releasing her at last, Alere returned to her own body, alone, and wept.

CHAPTER FORTY-FOUR

CORIN

Corin knocked on the door and let himself in at Kett's answer. He edged into the half-lit room and approached the bed.

Kett rose from his chair, rubbing his face and yawning. He returned Corin's rough embrace. With a quick glance back at Alere's still form under the blankets, he jerked his chin at the door to the adjoining room.

In the Koh-Lin's luxurious guest suite sitting room, Corin studied the weishi. Kett sank into an overstuffed couch.

'Don't start, Cor.' Dark circles shadowed his eyes and he'd lost weight. His face was drawn and stubbled with a three-day growth. 'It's bad enough I have Tali and Yasmin here every day, telling me to look after myself. I don't need it from you as well.'

'Fine.' Corin held up his hands in surrender. 'I'll tell you now you look like diyu, we'll consider the rest said and move on. How is she?'

Kett shrugged. 'It's been a week and she does little more than sleep. She eats and drinks – barely enough to survive – but never speaks. I can't tell if she hears me, either. No one knows what to expect. None of the healers or xintou have any useful advice. No-one's ever survived a Fusion before. Tali's been scouring the House library but nothing so far.' He sighed. 'I don't know what to do, Cor. She's slipping away, bit by bit. Like she doesn't want to live any more.'

'Well.' Corin pointed at him. 'Give her something to live for. It worked in Chengdu.'

Kett sat back, staring at the ceiling. 'Don't you think I've tried? Even with her weapons on her I can't seem to get through. It's not that she's warding, it's more like she's just not *there*.'

Corin rose and paced restlessly to stare out the window at the distant farmlands across the Kabir River. 'There has to be something we can do to bring her back, Kett. More yanstones?'

'I don't know where the Koh-Lin necklace and bracelets went after that day. Someone took them.'

'I don't know, either.' Corin rubbed at the back of his neck, squinting as the burnished afternoon sun slanted in through the tall, leaded-glass windows.

Kett grimaced. 'To be honest, I'd be reluctant to put them on her, anyway. What they did to her…'

Corin snapped his fingers and spun back. 'What about Elmira? Can she help?'

'What are you talking about? She's dead.' Kett frowned up at him.

Corin chuckled, glad to be the bearer of some good tidings in these dark days when everything seemed horrific. He'd spent most of the last week helping Rafi and Jarran to put out fires around Madina, both literal and figurative.

In the aftermath of Hassan's abortive coronation, the remaining Jun families were glad of Rafi and Jarran's strong, decisive leadership. Jarran, with Rafi's support and guidance, buried his grief, throwing himself into the business of welding the Jundom back together, rebuilding infrastructure and the economy. He'd already made great strides. His no-nonsense, empathetic style of leadership won him friends and allies in all sectors. Keeping busy seemed to help him cope with Mina's death.

'Elmira survived Nasra's motherly attempt at murder.' Corin jerked a thumb at the door. 'The servants in Petar's house whisked her off to Healer House as soon as Nasra left. The healer-surgeons patched her up. They've kept her in hiding ever since. She's well enough to go home now, but she's on her way here, first. That's why I came.'

'Gaisi!' Kett leapt to his feet, hope blooming. 'That's the best news I've heard all week. Watch Alli for me. I need to bathe.'

'Yes, my friend, you do.'

Less than ten minutes later, Kett emerged from the bathroom shaved and dressed in a clean, dark-blue robe. The first time Corin had ever seen him in anything but weishi black, by choice at least. The suite door opened at the same time. Elmira entered, leaning on Tali's arm, pale and thin, but steady. Her auburn hair was softly drawn back into a plait, making her look younger than her forty-some years. The light blue of her robe matched eyes shadowed with memories of pain and loss.

Corin bowed as Tali introduced him. Elmira inclined her head regally, glancing between him and Tali in knowing amusement. Tali, too, eschewed the xintou gold these days and wore a rich, dark red silk robe, embroidered with dragons and birds. It would be a while before the Gold of Xintou House could be seen abroad without causing fear and anger.

Elmira held out her thin, blue-veined hands to Kett and he gripped them gently, kissing her cheek. 'I'm so glad to see you, Kett. Take me to her, please.'

Kett led the way into Alere's room, throwing open the curtains and flicking on a light by the bed. Seeing her for the first time in full light, Corin bit back an exclamation of shock at the change. Her cheeks were hollowed, her eyes dark-shadowed, her hair tangled and dull.

Tali came to stand beside him, leaving Elmira and Kett speaking in low voices near the bed. Corin slid an arm around her waist, holding her warmth close and relishing the clean scent of her hair. She laid her head on his shoulder.

Their closeness was a new development, something formed in the coronation day's aftermath, when they'd both needed someone to talk to; someone with whom to thrash out the horrors of that day; someone who understood. It was possible it may not last, for they were opposites in almost every way, but Corin was content to let things develop as they would.

Given her upbringing, and the demands on her time as one of the few remaining Xintou House senior students, he was happy to take things as slowly as she felt comfortable with. At the moment, that meant little more than a few hours here and there, spent mostly in talk or hidden away in one of Houlia's rooms in Jiaoji House, trying to forget the world for awhile.

For now, they were both as happy as it was possible to be in light of recent events. They needed each other, and those moments of happiness.

Hearing raised voices, Corin kissed her gently and strode to the bed to mediate between Elmira and Kett.

'It's the only possible solution, Kett. You've tried everything else.' Elmira spread her hands. From them dangled the Koh-Lin necklace, Rafi's bracelet and the twin-bracelets, the yanstones flickering and sparkling in the afternoon light. 'From what little we can decipher of Yera Edwards' journal, part of the problem the Edwards sisters had was with their yanstone. I presume she meant the one Mistress Li gave to Alere.' She scanned the room. 'Where is it?'

Kett folded his arms. 'I destroyed it. Smashed it into dust with an axe the day of the coronation.'

'Destroyed it!' Elmira frowned. 'You had no right.'

'I had every right, Elmira,' he said coldly. 'I saw the corruption it wreaked on Mistress Li and on Alere and Mina. No-one is strong enough to resist it.'

Elmira rubbed at her forehead. 'You could be right. I wish we could have studied it, at least. Tali and I both feel Alere would fare better with these on. One of the reasons yanstones have not been utilised more, is that the wearer becomes dependant on them. And I believe that's the problem with Alere. She's worn these too long and *must* wear them now.'

'She's addicted to them?' Corin recalled Saric's offhand comparison of Alere's behaviour to that of a jiu or blackweed addict. He'd dismissed it then, but perhaps the kid was on to something.

Elmira nodded. 'In a way. But I think she could wean herself off them, over time. For now, though, let me at least try. What have you got to lose?'

Kett gripped the bedpost, his fingertips white. 'Her. Besides, I tried the stones in her weapons. They didn't work.'

'These are the ones she bonded with most strongly.' Laying gentle fingers on his arm, Elmira said, 'I promise, Kett, you won't lose her – unless you prevent this.'

Kett stared at Alere's drawn countenance for a long time, then his shoulders slumped. 'Very well.'

She held out the Koh-Lin necklace. 'Lift her and I'll put these on.'

Kett gently raised Alere. Her eyes drifted open but she didn't seem to recognise or even see any of them. Her head lolled onto his shoulder. Elmira clasped the bracelets around her wrists and the necklace around her throat, then stood back.

Nothing changed. Kett's mouth pressed thin and he flicked Elmira a cold look.

Then, slowly, colour seeped into Alere's cheeks. She stirred and squinted in the dusty afternoon glare. Her eyes, once more alight with quick intelligence, dimmed with recollection. She lifted her arm and cried out. She sat up, her fingers scrabbling at the bracelet.

'Get them off! The Mistresses...' Her voice cracked. A frown pulled at her brows. 'They're gone. The stones were linked. They were using these to control us as well. But now I can't hear...'

She looked around in bemusement then saw Kett and held her wrists out in mute supplication.

'It's alright,' Kett said. 'I destroyed the Xintou House stone. It can't harm you, now. But you have to wear these ones. Just for a while.' He swept her into his arms and cradled her on his lap, stroking her hair and murmuring reassurances.

'Mina,' she said brokenly.

'I know,' Kett replied. 'She's gone, Alli.'

'Yes. But no.' Her lips curved, bittersweet. 'She was right. There's still a little of her here.' She tapped her temple, then caressed the yanstones' steel and fire. 'And here. I'll be alright, Kett. She's still with me.'

He frowned. 'You have the xintou gifts? How is that possible?'

She shook her head. 'No. At least, it doesn't feel the same. I can Read you all, but it's weaker than when I was Bonded to Mina. Watered down. I can handle it.'

Tali approached them hesitantly. 'I can do a gene analysis, if you like? It only takes a second.' Alere nodded and Tali closed her eyes, running light fingers down the length of her body. Tali smiled in wonder. 'It looks like the yanstones are now acting like a trigger and control gene, even without Mina's presence. So you'll have those minor gifts each time you wear them. Though it could fade over time. I don't know. But you'll be alright.'

Kett took Alere's face in his hands and kissed her. He tucked her under his chin, resting his cheek on her hair. A sigh shuddered through his lean frame. 'Yes, you'll be alright.'

Elmira approached and Alere's face lit up. She held out her arms and the two women embraced, crying on each other's shoulders.

Corin smiled. Tali joined him and slipped beneath his arm again. She drew him to the door with a significant look at the couple. He nodded, glancing back, no longer feeling the ache of missing Alere. He was simply happy for them, now.

'I'm sorry,' Alere said, burying her face in Kett's shoulder again. 'I let the stone take us over and so many people died. And Mina died. I had to choose and I let her die when I could have healed her. This was all my fault.'

'Shhh,' Kett said. 'You did the right thing in the end. You made the right choice and none of this is your fault You can't be held accountable for decisions Mistress Li and Nasra made before you were even born. They were what brought us here, not you.'

She gave a watery laugh. 'This from the man who tortured himself and spent twenty years seeking redemption over exactly the same thing?'

Kett stilled and let out a thick breath. 'Perhaps you're right, Alli. I never made plans beyond killing those responsible for the kin-child laws and protecting you. Now...maybe there's more to life.'

Alere stroked his cheek. 'I hope so.'

He looked to Corin. 'Cor, do me a favour? In the other room you'll find my sword.'

Corin raised his brows. 'And?'

'Give it to Jarran.'

'What? Why?'

Kett smiled at Alere. 'It's the Zah-Hill family sword. Radan's Shangwei gave it to me when he hid me in Weishi House. That was when I decided my path was to protect other kin-children and get justice for them.' He drew a deep breath and released it slowly, cradling Alere close. 'I won't be needing it any longer.'

EPILOGUE

ALERE

Reining Rumi in at the top of Eagle Pass, Alere gazed west over the broad valley below. She tasted the cold mountain air, flipped up her fur collar against a sharp southerly wind, and glanced back over her shoulder.

'C'mon, you lot, it'll take us two more weeks to get home at this rate,' she called. She lifted an arm and Reya, the little golden jinbird, fluttered down from a nearby tree to land on her wrist. Reya squawked unmusically at her and hopped onto Rumi's head, settling between the horse's ears. Her partner, Lila, soared down and landed on Alere's shoulder.

Saric kneed his brutish beast of a horse alongside, swearing as it chewed on the bit and tossed its head.

'This gouri animal is determined to do what even Prince Soran's weishi failed to: kill me.' He jerked at the reins. 'You could have found me a better horse.' His voice was deeper than Corin's, now; his lightning smile equally as raffish. He'd long since given up trying to keep his unruly blond hair tied in a mawei and adopted instead the latest youthful trend of cutting it short.

Alere chuckled. 'It's hardly my fault we had to leave Jadid in a hurry. Why do you think I left Rumi in Newmec? I know your father's penchant for getting you both into trouble. I expected to have to leave everything behind.'

'Now *that*,' he muttered, 'is an insult. I'm perfectly capable of getting my self into – and out of – trouble, thank you.' He was taller than Alere and with a mature, dark cynicism far beyond his seventeen years. He bid fair to be a heartbreaker, if he wasn't already.

'Don't I know it.' She slapped him on the shoulder. 'At least I got that trade deal negotiated for Rafi before things went suilie.' She looked back again. 'What *is* taking them so long?'

Saric shrugged. 'Last I saw Kett was teaching Gavon how to throw those knives you bought him in Jadid. And my feckless father decided Ella needed to improve her pocket-picking skills.' He raised a brow at her. 'Explain to me again why you brought them along? I mean, you know I'd do anything for the little shazi's, but it was a long trip for a couple of five-year-olds.'

Smiling as Kett and Corin finally rounded the corner, Alere gave her twins a wave. Ella, sitting behind Corin, waved back, holding Corin's coin purse aloft. Gavon rolled his eyes and sniffed at her from his place behind Kett, flipping a knife with deliberate casualness. Both were red-cheeked in the cold wind, their dark hair curling wildly around sharp-chinned little faces, grey eyes sparkling and mischievous.

'Do you really think Kett would let them out of his sight?' Alere said in reply to Saric's question.

They wore matching, rough travel clothing, bore small bows across their backs and lethal, Shanzhai steel swords at their hips. They practiced daily with both, though Gav took it all much more seriously than his lighthearted sister. She had a natural gift, but rarely applied herself with any consistency. He trained with a focus and determination that levelled the field and made them, for the moment, equally matched. Kett was devoted to and proud of both and they flourished under his even-handed guidance.

When they came alongside, Kett leaned over and kissed Alere, ignoring Gavon's mock-gagging. Ella giggled.

'So.' Kett ruffled his son's hair. 'Looking forward to home?'

Ella groaned. 'Do we have to? Jid Rafi is sooo bossy and Jida Yasmin is always trying to make me practice dancing when I'd rather be training with you and Mother and Uncle Saric.'

'Well.' Alere tried to keep a straight face. 'You did have the misfortune to be born first, which makes you next Jun-Heir. Dancing is just one of the many unbearable things you just have to put up with.'

'Ha ha!' Gavon poked a tongue at his sister. She retaliated in kind, subsiding only when Kett gazed steadily at both of them.

'I confess,' Corin said, looking out across the hazy valley floor, toward the distant smudge marking Shanzhai's location on the far horizon, 'I'll be glad to see Tal again. If not the pile of work Rafi has in store for me.'

Kett chuckled. 'I did tell you that if Tali Bonded to the Koh-Lin family you'd have to quit travelling and get used to a desk job. I'm surprised you could get away for this trip. Two months is a long time. How did you manage it?'

Corin screwed up his nose. 'Tal's a xiao-bear in her first trimester. She practically threw me out. The wire she sent me at Newmec sounded promising, though. I think it's safe to go home.'

Alere kneed Rumi into motion again, heading down the mountain. 'Is Shasa excited about her new sister? Do you have a name picked out for her?'

'Well…' Corin looked sideways at her. 'We were thinking of Radan, actually.'

'Radan!' Alere tightened the reins and Rumi tossed her head in response. 'A boy?'

'Hey.' Corin cocked his head. 'Tal did the gene splicing very carefully. Just as she did for Gav and Ella. There's no chance at all of him being xintou.'

Alere gave him a wan smile. 'I know. It's just going to take me awhile to get used to the idea of a trained, Bonded Xintou having boys.' She stroked her own growing belly, then touched the stones at her throat in absent habit. 'Still, the name Mina was already spoken for and we did, after all, fight for the freedom to break traditions and move ahead.'

After a moment's silence, Kett passed a protesting Gavon across to Saric, who tickled him mercilessly, grinning at his irritated glare.

'You four go on ahead, we'll catch up in a minute,' Kett said. He dismounted and flipped the reins over his horse's head.

Corin, after a swift, assessing glance beneath his lashes, kicked his mare into a fast walk. He raised his voice in a silly children's song that had Ella giggling as she sang along in clear, sweet harmony. Saric's baritone joined in and, with a resigned sigh, Gavon lifted his treble to complete the quartet, until they sounded like an experienced troupe of the purple. Indeed, they'd had a great deal of practice on this trip and Corin was quite enthused about bringing the twins along on future missions, to act as a cover.

Kett watched them in fond amusement then turned to Alere. She swung a leg over and he lifted her down. She leaned into his shoulder, walking with him down the hill. Reya and Lila took to the air again, dancing a loving duet overhead and trilling a complicated song.

Kett broke away after awhile and looked at her, hesitating. She waited.

'There was a message for you,' he finally said, 'in Paradise. From Elmira.'

Knowing him, she waited again.

'I wasn't sure how you'd take it.' He grimaced. 'Jarran's betrothed to Shah Jahil's eldest daughter, Naisha.'

Alere stilled, surprised at how mixed her feelings were at the news. It was ridiculous to feel he'd betrayed Mina's memory when almost six years had passed since her death, and they'd known each other less than a month. Still.

'Was it…' she sought Kett's honesty, needing a truthful answer, '…arranged?'

'No. According to Elmira's message they met last year when Jarran went to Chengdu to celebrate Lan's hunli ceremony. It's a love-match that happens to be politically advantageous.'

'Wasai,' she said, tucking her fingers under her arms and scuffing a foot on the ground. 'I'm glad he's happy. I wondered why he was a little stand-offish when I was in Madina last.'

'Alright?' He murmured, kissing her hair, his arm around her waist.

'Yes.' She touched the yanstones again. 'I just get a little low when I wear these, now. It's been over a year since I last put them on. They're useful on these diplomatic missions, but they remind me…and her presence is fading. I miss her, still.'

'I know. You were right before, though,' he said. 'You both fought for the freedom we now have. Look at the progress we've made in the last six years.' He gestured at the broad valley ahead. 'Wirecoms to every town, wind generators bringing electricity to most homes. And they're even getting better at iron extraction. Xintou house has taken the lesson to heart. With Elmira as Mistress, it's making great strides in using nai-xintou as healers, and breaking down barriers between xintou and common folk. Saric said Wei has even moved to Madina to train in both Xintou and Weishi Houses. Things are improving, for everyone.'

'I suppose.' Alere stroked the warm stones again, listening in vain for Mina's voice. 'I still can't help regretting…thinking I should have acted differently… that I could have saved her. When she showed me her last Seeing that day, I was sure it would be me. I didn't expect her to sacrifice herself...' she sighed. 'The House stone made me feel invincible and I waited too long to kill Rohne.'

'Hey.' Kett stopped. 'We've been through this. This is just the yanstones talking. She chose.'

'But in the end she didn't want to die, Kett,' Alere said, aching. 'But to save her would have bound us to the Xintou stone. *I* chose. I let my own sister die.'

He took her face in his hands. 'No. Stop torturing yourself. She knew what was going to happen. She'd told Jarran about her Seeing and they made the choice together. She was right: no-one should have that much power. Not you, Rohne, Nasra, or the House Mistress. She did it so you and I, Jarran, and all of us could live better lives. Don't waste yours living in the past.'

'No.' Alere kissed him, tasting the chill mountain air on his lips, moulding herself against his warmth. Her spirits rose, lifted by the strength of their connection, the steady constancy of his love, and the memory of Mina's.

Perhaps it was finally time.

She stepped away. Taking off the necklace and bracelets she tucked them into her saddlebags and buckled the leather straps shut. Then, lifting her face to the teal-green sky, she danced a few steps. Rumi shook her head. Reya and Lila swooped low then soared into the sky again. Alere smiled, following their gleaming, gold-winged flight overhead, even as her boots kicked up dust off the packed-earth road. Spreading her arms, she laughed aloud at the joy of being alive, released the self-blame of losing Mina, and embraced her hard-won freedom.

THE END

Other books by Aiki Flinthart

Discover other titles by Aiki Flinthart at: **www.aikiflinthart.com**
Or
The 80AD series (YA Adventure/Fantasy)
80AD Book 1: *The Jewel of Asgard*
80AD Book 2: *The Hammer of Thor*
80AD Book 3: *The Tekhen of Anuket*
80AD Book 4: *The Sudarshana*
80AD Book 5: *The Yu Dragon*

The Kalima Chronicles (YA Adventure/Fantasy)
IRON – Book one in the Kalima Chronicles
FIRE – Book two of the Kalima Chronicles

Sold! (Contemporary Romance/Adventure)

Short Story Anthologies
Return
Like a Woman
Elemental

Connect with me on Facebook
Twitter: @aikiflinthart
Instagram: Aikiflinthart

APPENDIX

Story facts and background

Kalima means 'World' in Arabic. The planet was settled by idealists from Earth seeking a world without conflict. The planet's sun is a K-type orange star in the Gliese 167 system. Rayleigh scattering of light combined with atmospheric dust high in copper oxide, gives Kalima a pale teal-green sky. The sun's orange colour led to dark blue and black-leafed plantlife. Kalima is third planet from this sun. Gliese 167 is a cooler sun than Sol, but Kalima is closer to their sun than Earth is to Sol. Kalima's. 14 month year and its axial tilt and elliptical orbit means the southern hemisphere (the location of the colony cities) has a long spring-summer-autumn cycle and a short, 2-month winter. The northern hemisphere has larger extremes of weather and is, as yet, uninhabited.

Kalima has an active geologic past, which formed continents, volcanoes, oceans and rivers. But, until the terraforming teams arrived, Kalima was bare of life. The rocks created by the presence of life on Earth—such as marble, oils, methane, coal, chalk, limestone, or banded ironstone—do not exist on Kalima. The few iron deposits in existence are iron-sand beaches created by volcanic activity, and meteoric iron. The planet has high levels of copper and a vast desert of copper-rich soil on one of the other continents has contributed to the levels of copper oxide dust in the atmosphere, which causes the green sky.

The colonists chose a lifeless planet and paid to have it Terraformed and seeded with life and complex ecological webs.

Initial terraform teams were sent to Kalima on faster-than-light ships, while colonists took slower, jumplight sleep-ships to allow the teams sufficient time to complete the infrastructure. Five hundred years after departing Earth, the first of three ships arrived, carrying twenty thousand carefully selected colonists.

Mainly of Chinese, Arabic and European descent, colonists were chosen and screened for their desire to live a peaceful, agrarian existence. Kalima's twenty-one Jun families descend from the original twenty-one Funding families who financed the expedition.

Two hundred years after settlement, supply ships from old Earth ceased and colonists were obliged to be self-sufficient. Lack of iron prevented the colonists from creating a high-tech society, forcing them to live in semi-medieval conditions, although many old ideas and skills have been retained. Electricity generation through wind or water power exists in limited form. The ability to make telescopes, lenses and microscopes has not been lost and, although medical understanding of surgery, physiology and healing exists, it is limited by the lack of modern technology. Many books on old technologies have been preserved and, some colonists retained information regarding warfare and weaponry—the basis of knowledge in the Weishi House.

Kalima society is substantially feudal, the Jundom of Mamlakah being ruled by 21 Juns, under the leadership of the Jun First and two Jun Seconds. Melcor, to the north, and Jadid, to the south, are also feudal societies but Melcor's society and economy is built on slavery. Shemal is a democracy.

Languages are mixed. A version of English, borrowing many words from Arabic and Mandrin, is the dominant language in Mamlakah, the first colony site. Similarly, cultural crossovers are normal. Women and men wear robes or high-collared shirts and trous (loose trousers tied at the waist). Robes are worn indoors or while employed in non-active trades and management positions. Otherwise it is common for trous and shirts with jackets or cloaks to be worn. Women wear their hair long and loose or, if of a higher caste, long and up in elaborate hairstyles. Men in Mamlakah wear their hair long and tied back in a mawei (low ponytail or plait). Although now less fashionable, women may wear a transparent veil that covers the eyes and nose only. The veil is symbolic of mystery and high ranking rather than an indication of women's inferiority.

In Mamlakahn society, women are, basically, equal in standing to men. They may be Juns or Trade Masters in any House and are free to undertake any training and job. In any colony, however, women are more valuable than men. Built into the psyche of the colony is the need to protect women that has continued into today's thinking. Weishi House came into being primarily as protection for women of childbearing age from natural hazards, though its scope expanded as the colony grew. Women are the bearers of the next generation and the survival of a colony depends on how quickly women can give birth and outstrip death rates.

The need for high birth rates, and genetic diversity, led to the practice of kin-children. In the early days of the colony, a couple unable to have children was a wasted pairing. Women needed to have children by several fathers in order to keep the gene-pool as diverse as possible. After seven hundred years, the population is approximately half a million.

People/Places/Things

Adeghal – capital of Shemal

Ahmar – Red (Ahmar Mountains run down the Eastern boundary of the kingdom)

Alzin – an aluminium-zinc alloy.

Asalam – northerly seat of the Zah-Hill family.

Aswad – Black (Aswad ranges run down the centre of the kingdom)

Ceramic Swords are made of zirconium dioxide

Chengdu- capital of Melcor

Days are: Ahad (one), Ithnan (two), Thalatha (three), Arba'a (four), Khamsa (five), Sitta (six)

Ghadeb – 'angry' (Ghadeb sea to the northeast)

Gharb – west (Gharb ranges run down the Western boundary of the jundom)

Gunpowder = saltpetre + sulphur + charcoal

Jiali – 'home' – Capital city of the Ma-Safra family lands

Jadid (New) Jundom – south.

Kabir – big (the Kabir river runs through the middle of the kingdom and empties into Melcor's port 700 gongli away to the east)

Kalima – World. Earth-sized planet. Kalima has a 6-day week and a 5-week month. 30 days per month. 14 months in a year and 422 days in a year – two days at the end of the year are not part of any month and are called yirun and er'run. Axial tilt and slightly elliptical orbit means northern hemisphere has extreme seasons but southern is mild with short winters and long growing seasons.

Kuaisu River – 'fast/rapid' river (wraps around the eastern side of Shanzhai)

Luna-Yi – red moon

Luna-Er – blue-white moon

Madina – capital city of Mamlakah. Palace - The Alkazar.

Magnal – magnesium aluminium alloy – light and strong

Melcor – second kingdom to be settled – to the northeast of Madina and on the Ghadeb sea. Reached by trade on the Kabir river.

Metsa – the river running through the western section of the Ma-Safra Jundom, near Newmec. It eventually joins with the Kabir just north of Madina

Mianshou – end of year 2 day celebration during Yirun & Er-run.

Plants are dark blue-black-leafed (absorbing different, greater range of spectra and reflecting less green)

Seryeh River – 'quick' river (wraps around the western side of Shanzhai). The two rivers join and become the Kabir, just north of Madina

Shanzhai – seat of Jun Second Koh-Lin.

Sulcrete – concrete where the binding agent is sulphur rather than lime (limestone does not exist on a planet without an organic geologic history)

Yan – 'flame' = yanstones

Yirun & Er'run – extra two days at the end of the year. Mianshou = End of year celebrations last for these two days and anything done on these days (apart from violence) is unpunishable.

Zalam – slums within Madina

.....

Trade Houses

Artist House (purple veil/purple hat)

Healer House (white veil/hat, grey robe)

Jiaoji (Courtesan) House (red veil)

Merchant House (green veil/green hat/robe)

Messenger House (orange)

Miner House (grey hat)

Trades House (brown hat/veil)

Weishi House (black veil/black hat)

Xintou (telepath) House (gold veil, gold robe) Mistress Li

…..

Jun Families

Jun First Radan Zah-Hill (deceased) (Wife Hanna; Son Ven (deceased)) – Silver and Black.

Jun second Petar Ma-Safra (wife Leah) - silver and purple. No children.

Jun second Rafi Koh-Lin (wife Yasmin;) - silver and green.

Jun third Kennor Han-Asad (daughter Farima) - gold and black (controls Madina city guards. Vassal to Zah-Hill)

Jun Third Yu-Smith - gold and green (vassal to Koh-Lin)

Jun Third Dal Lee-Hay - gold and purple (vassal to Ma-Safra)

Jun Fourth Hassan Wen-Gates - copper and purple. Kin-brother to Jun First. (vassal to Ma-Safra)

Jun Fourth Bren Gray-Saud - copper and black (vassal to Zah-Hill)

Jun Fourth Qin-Turner - copper and grey (vassal to Zah-Hill)

Jun Fourth Knight-Hun - copper and green (vassal to Koh-Lin)

Jun Fifth Jaber-Lun - red and purple (vassal to Ma-Safra)

Jun Fifth Seif-Li - red and green (vassal to Koh-Lin)

Jun Fifth Zhou-Issa - red and teal (vassal to Koh-Lin)

Jun Fifth Easton-Green - red and black (vassal to Zah-Hill)

Jun Fifth Amoudi-Mann - red and grey (vassal to Zah-Hill)

Jun Sixth Ortega-Miller - blue and black (Zah-Hill)

Jun Sixth Quing-Mai - blue and grey (Zah-Hill)

Jun Sixth Price-Khan - blue and green (Koh-Lin)

Jun Sixth Yasif-Do - blue and teal (Koh-Lin)

Jun Sixth Khoury-Ban - blue and purple (Ma-Safra)

Jun Sixth Blake-Swift - blue and indigo (Ma-Safra)

Johnston house - blue & green tartan

…..

Mandrin

Numbers and distances and times

Yi – one (Luna-Yi = first moon – reddish)

Er – two (Luna-Er = second moon – silver)

San - three

Si - four

wu - five

Liu - six

Qi - seven

Ba - eight

…..

Chi – approx 33.33cm

Zhang – approx 3.33m

Gongli – kilometre

…..

Months:

Yiyue – first month of the lunar year (1st month of spring)

Eryue – second (spring 2)

Sanyue – 3rd (spring 3)

Siyue – 4th (summer 1)

Wuyue – 5th (summer 2)

Liuyue – 6th (summer 3

Qiyue – 7th (summer 4)

Bayue – 8th (summer 5)

Jiuyue – 9th (summer 6)

Shiyue – 10th (autumn)

Shiyiyue – 11th (autumn)

Shi'eryue – 12th (autumn)

Shisanyue – 13th (winter1)

Shisiyue – 14th (winter2)

.....

Words:

ading – antiseptic/disinfectant

Bai - to pay respect / worship / visit / salute

Bei – flower bud

Bi – coin

Che-ma – cart horse

Chuizi – a hammer-strike

Erheyi – two-in-one

Feihua – nonsense, rubbish.

Gangzhi – made of steel

Gongren - worker

Gu – archaic - legendary venomous insect / to poison / to bewitch / to drive to insanity / to harm by witchcraft / intestinal parasite

Hepan – river plains

hunli - wedding

Huoche – wagon/truck/van

Jiali - Home (name of Ma-Safra city)

Nari – double-edged sword

Jiaoji – courtesan

Jin - gold

Jinbi – gold coin

jiu – rice wine/liquor/alcohol

Jun - monarch/lord/gentleman/ruler

Junren – soldier/serviceman/military personnel

Khaan – king/horde leader (Mongolian)

Kuaisu – fast/rapid

Kuai long – fast dragon

Kui - Chief/head/outstanding/stalwart/exceptional

Lanhua - orchid

Lanse – blue (lancha tea)

Lu – deer

Luotuo – camel

Manxing – slow poison

Mawei – ponytail

mayao – anaesthetic

Mianshou - - to avoid suffering / to prevent (sth bad) / to protect against (damage) / immunity (from prosecution) / freedom (from pain, damage etc) / exempt from punishment

Molian – to temper oneself/ to steel oneself/ self-discipline/ endurance

Nai – mother

Quan - dog

Rong – salamander

Runiu – dairy cattle

Shangwei – captain (military rank)

Shanzhai – fortified hill village/mountain stronghold

Shen – deity/soul/spirit/mysterious

Shenshi – my lord

Shi - is / are / am / yes / to be

Shifu – teacher

Shunu – my lady

Si-xing – death penalty / to act recklessly

Song – sponge (cake)

Tiebi – iron coin

Tongbi – copper coin

Watu – poison frog toxin

Weishi - guardian/defender

xiao – similar to/resembling (ie: xiao-cat)

xiang - elephant

Xintou – thoughts/heart/mind

Xiongshou – assassin

Xituo – to cleanse/to purge/ to wash away

Xue – blood

xun – herb

ya-zheng - correct (literary) / upright / (hon.) Please point out my shortcomings. / I await your esteemed corrections.

Yan – flame

Yinbi – silver coin

Yinghan – man of steel/tough guy, unyielding

Yongbing – mercenary/hired gun

Zaohua – good luck/nature (the mother of all things)

Zhi – to stop/prohibit

Zitan – red sandalwood

Zuoce – left side

…..

Insults/swearing

diyu – hell/underworld

Feihua – nonsense / rubbish / superfluous words / You don't say! / No kidding!

gaisi – damn it!

gouri - lit. fucked or spawned by a dog / contemptible / lousy, fucking

hundan – scoundrel/bastard/hoodlum/wretch

huo-zui – living hell/suffering/hardship

jian-gui – curse it/to hell with it

Jiba – penis (vulgar)

Jiche – pain in the ass/damn!/crap!

Jijin – elite/best of the best

qusi – go to hell/drop dead

salai – make a scene/raise hell

shazi – idiot/fool

suilie – disintegrate/shatter into pieces

Wasai – exclamation to express amazement/wow!

zhen-shide - Really! (interj. of annoyance or frustration)

…..

Rabic

…..

Days: Ahad (one), Ithnan (two), Thalatha (three), Arba'a (four), Khamsa (five), Sitta (six)

Ahmar – Red (Ahmar Mountains run down the Eastern boundary of the kingdom)

Al Mamlakah – the kingdom

Alcazar – from Al-qasr – fort, castle, palace

alem'erekh – fight

Aswad – Black (Aswad ranges run down the centre of the kingdom)

Badiya – desert

Dafdae - frog

Gharb – west (Gharb ranges run down the Western boundary of the jundom)

Herq – burn

Heryeq – fire

Hilya – trinket/ ornament/jewel/finery

Iblis - Devil

Istilqa – sleep

Jabal – Mountain

Jadid – New (name for the southern jundom)

Jiyl – generation.

Kabir – big (the Kabir river runs through the middle of the kingdom and empties into Melcor's port 700 gongli away to the northeast)

Kalima – World

Khiba – tent

Madina – City

Malik – King

Mamlakah – the kingdom

Menzel - home

Mhareb – warrior/fighter

Mumit – deadly

Nasir – vulture (nasiri = plural)

Sabat – coma, lethargy, torpor

Sahalia - lizard

Shaytan – demon, fiend, serpent

Selb – Steel, betterment, loin, crucifixion

sery'eh – Quick (Seryeh River to northwest of Shanzhai)

Tabib – doctor

Zalam – Darkness

Zanbur – hornet, wasp

Zibal - scavenger

Zinzana – cell/prison

…..

Insults/swearing

Hamagi (hamag = plural) – uncivilised, barbaric

Haraami – thief

Hmar – jackass

Jahim - hell

Kaddaab – liar

Kalb – dog

Kalet – filthy street bastard
Khara – shit! (frustration)
Saafil – base;loathsome
Waa faqri – damn!
Wisix – dirty/filthy (morally)
Zift – Idiot

www.aikiflinthart.com